WAY OF REVELATION

WILFRID EWART

WAY OF REVELATION

A Novel of Five Years

ALAN SUTTON
1986

Alan Sutton Publishing Limited
30 Brunswick Road
Gloucester GL1 1JJ

First published 1921

Copyright © in this edition 1986
Alan Sutton Publishing Limited

British Library Cataloguing in Publication Data

Ewart, Wilfrid
  Way of revelation.
  I. Title
823'.912[F]   PR6009.W3

  ISBN 0-86299-288-5

Cover picture: detail from Oppey Wood
by John Nash.
Imperial War Museum, London.

Printed in Great Britain
by The Guernsey Press Company Limited,
Guernsey, Channel Islands.

BIOGRAPHICAL NOTE

WILFRID HERBERT GORE EWART was a well-known writer in the years after the First World War until his dramatic death at the end of 1922. He established himself by writing graphic accounts of life in the trenches for *The Times* and the *Spectator* from 1914–17, and after he returned home he produced rural, social and literary articles for various publications. His novel, *Way of Revelation*, was published in 1921, and a travel book about Ireland the following year. His detailed and clear style gives his work a lucidity and freshness which has not lost its appeal, and his writing is also interesting for the picture which it gives us of life and attitudes during and after the Great War.

Wilfrid was born on 19 May 1892, into a family with strong military connections. The Ewarts were an established army family of high-ranking officers, while his mother, a Gore, was descended from the Napiers of India and the Peninsular War. Wilfrid showed no promise of following the family tradition during his childhood. He had inherited the physical delicacy of his mother. He had a 'lazy eye', with limited vision in the other, and was too delicate to attend normal school. He went to St Aubyns, Rottingdean, a private school near Brighton, before being sent to a private tutor at Parkstone, then a salubrious area of Bournemouth. During his vacations he would spend long holidays in the Tyrol with his father.

As a youth, Wilfrid spent some years on a farm in Bottisham, in the Fens. Here he developed a great love of the countryside and a fascination with birds and poultry. He wrote articles for *Feathered World* and other agricultural journals and had his work on poultry published.

At twenty-one he was a slim six foot two, with blond hair and grey imperfect eyes, and was about to take a post as secretary to the Princess Dolgoruki in Berkshire when war was declared. In spite of his health and his poor eyesight he considered that he had no alternative but to become a private soldier. His cousin, Master of Ruthven, and a major in the Scots Guards, arranged a favourable medical, and Wilfrid was soon training with the Guards at Caterham. He was leaving not only his career, but also his social circle, which included his friend since childhood, George Wyndham, and, apparently, a lady who did not reciprocate his love. He was quiet and reserved, with a correct and rather imposing exterior hiding an attractive and sincere personality, which was to be shaken and strengthened by the horrors of the years ahead, when he would lose many relations and friends, including Wyndham and his new brother-in-law, John Earmer.

It was in the trenches in France that Wilfrid was introduced to Stephen Graham, a private in the same regiment, already an acknowledged writer and authority on Russia. Graham was ten years older than Ewart, and was to exercise a considerable influence on his future development. The two became close friends. They discussed contemporary literature, comparing George Moore and Thomas Hardy, and Graham, having seen the quality of the articles Wilfrid was writing under a pseudonym for the English press, recognized his talent and urged him to give up the army as soon as possible, and devote himself to literature. He suggested that the articles Wilfrid had written might be collected into a book, but after the two had criticised Bennett's *Pretty Lady* and Mackenna's *Sonia*, this idea developed into a plan for a novel about the War which, by basing it on first hand experiences, would be more convincing than either Bennett's or Mackenna's. Thus was sown the seed for *Way of Revelation*.

A True Tale of Three Days, written after Wilfrid had been home on sick leave in 1915, because of a leg injury, provided the kernel for the later novel. The following extract from an article written for the *Spectator*, shows how closely Ewart relied on his own experiences and original articles (*cf* p. 304):

Outside the mist crept in, crept out and roundabout. Like a ghost, like a wraith, it stole along the dim streets whose secrets were buried beneath tons of bricks and masonry, beneath heaps and heaps of ruins. At first you could see nothing in the filmy darkness after the brilliance of the dug-out; instinct alone guided your footsteps. In the dug-out all sound was deadened; you could hear nothing from without. But now you discovered that the guns were firing in Ypres itself – fitfully yet frequently their banging and booming awoke a thousand echoes. Every time a gun fired, the reflection of the flash lit up jagged ruins, a naked wall, or the skeletons of houses . . .

During his leaves, like his hero, Adrian, Ewart went to Paris, fascinated by the decadent atmosphere of the threatened capital. *C'est la valse brune* . . . haunted Ewart's mind as it would the pages of his novel.

In 1917 Ewart fell from his horse, suffered concussion (like Adrian), and was sent home. His fighting days were over. Encouraged by Graham, he refused an army posting at the end of the war, thus enabling himself to concentrate on his writing, and an exploration of people and places in post-war London. His experiences had broadened his outlook, and he was drawn towards the liberal left as he visited the slums with Stephen Graham and a new friend, the American poet, Vachel Lindsay. Ewart was attracted by the Bohemian life of Soho, where Graham lived, and of Kensington, home of his artist friend, Lowinsky. He was intrigued by the legal system, and became a regular spectator at the Old Bailey. His descriptive account of a morning's hearings is to be found in Graham's biography (Chap. 5).

Ewart shared his love of the countryside with G.A.B. Dewar, writer and editor, for whom he wrote a series of articles on post-war society, to appear in his magazine, *The Nineteenth Century and Later*. He also contributed articles to *Country Life*, then edited by Graham's father, and wrote literary articles for *The Sunday Times*. The latter included articles on Thomas Hardy, whom Ewart visited twice, and for whom he had the greatest admiration. He never read Shakespeare or Milton, but he knew Hardy's work thoroughly, and had learnt from his example. At the same time he was working on his novel. The first draft of *Way of Revelation* was so long that it daunted the publishers, but after revision it was accepted by Putnams, who were so sure of its success that they paid Ewart one hundred pounds in advance. In November 1921 the novel appeared, to enthusiastic reviews. Critics were impressed by his descriptive powers and his emotional intensity. *The Times Literary Supplement* of 24 November, 1921 sums up:

> In the treatment of an obvious theme he has made use of the obvious characters, the obvious situations, the obvious emotions, and yet, because of his sincerity, because of his faith in his own vision of life, he has reached through the obvious, the universal.

Ewart became the fêted centre of attention in the literary world for the next four months. Then disaster struck: in March 1922 he suffered an incapacitating nervous breakdown, which prevented him physically from writing.

For three months he rested, and then in June he accepted a commission to write the history of the Scots Guards for his former regiment. In the meantime, *A Journey to Ireland* was published. This book was a collection of articles written the previous year, when Ewart had made an exciting and potentially dangerous walking expedition from Cork to Belfast, through a troubled country, learning first hand about the situation and interviewing local leaders.

His literary success lead, naturally, to an increase in income for Ewart, and once again we find him heeding the advice of Stephen Graham, who recommended him to 'capitalize' his life, by travelling and gaining experience, rather than living safely in England on the interest from investments. He accepted Graham's invitation to join him in New Mexico, taking with him his research material for the regimental history.

The witty and perceptive *Four Sketches of Atlantic Travel*, written during the voyage of 1922 for *Harper's Magazine*, were, after his death, separated and published as a memorial in the *Evening Standard* and *Cassell's Weekly*. Ewart found that he was recognized in the States, where *Way of Revelation* was selling well. He enjoyed a holiday in New York, walking regularly in Central Park, before crossing the States with Graham to stay at Santa Fe, New Mexico. He made several expeditions with the Grahams to observe Indian ritual festivals, one of which, the Jemez Dance, provided the material for his last completed article, *The Secret Land*. This final article is typical of Ewart's style at its best, with its fine descriptive passages, and a haunting quality of sadness and fatalism emerging from its imagery and gentle tone.

In December 1922, the Grahams left Santa Fe to travel in Central America. Ewart decided on the spur of the moment to go down to Mexico City, where he met up with the Grahams. They found that he had been captivated by the city, and was planning to spend some time there, working on his history, writing articles on modern Mexico. He had been stimulated by his solitary journey, had thought out his future, and defined his political beliefs. He was, he had decided, a conservative, in spite of having liberal sympathies, and he wanted to become a foreign correspondent, to travel the Canadian frontier, to spend time in New York and Paris.

Full of ideas and energy, he spent New Year's Eve with the Grahams, returning near midnight to his hotel, where he prepared for bed. The next day his dead body was found, near his balcony, by Graham; he had been shot through his left eye. It is presumed that, attracted by the sounds of New Year revelry outside, he had gone to the balcony, and been killed by a stray bullet. As news of his death reached the British public, he was buried at the British Cemetery in Mexico City.

Stephen Graham commemorated his friend by writing his biography, *The Life and Last Words of Wilfrid Ewart*, published in 1924, the only known study of Ewart, and the major source of information for this note.

SHEILA MICHELL

CONTENTS

CONTENTS

PART THE FIRST:

ILLUSION

Behold, I come as a thief. Blessed is he that watcheth, and keepeth his garments, lest he walk naked, and they see his shame.

And he gathered them together into a place called in the Hebrew tongue Armageddon.

REVELATION XVI, 15-16.

WAY OF REVELATION

CHAPTER I

Pageant of a London Night.

§ I

A MIDSUMMER night in the year nineteen hundred and fourteen lay heavy upon London.

The West End of the city offered no suggestion of rest. Its streets were brilliant with electric light, a-whir with motor-cars and taxicabs, crowded with those returning homeward from the theatres, or, by way of restaurants, supper-clubs and ball-rooms, beginning the night life of the town. The roar of the omnibuses and of the lesser motor traffic made a background for the hurrying crowds, for the cries of the newspaper-sellers, for the cab whistles, the insistent hooters, and the scarcely-heard chimes of the clocks. Nor was there lacking a quieter, kinder note, when fitfully from alley-ways and side-streets came faint sounds of piano and violin where street musicians played, or where in some upstairs-room gay people danced. Over all brooded the summer night.

Something of the careless, ephemeral quality of mankind seemed to linger here. Those who passed, chattering and laughing, were possessed by the moment, none knowing whence the other came or whither went. All were alike, in that all were actors in this drama of London : in that it was possible to weave around their figures pulsing, grim, and romantic fantasies of life.

The past too rose up from among these crowds ; and out

of a dim vista of bygone days appeared the countless men and women who had trod these paving-stones, these streets. The tears that had wetted them, the laughter that had rung back from them, seemed at moments to hover still. Time had wrought changes, the unknown future held many more; but no change had ever altered the face of the fluttering crowd. It is true that all had passed out in their turn—with their generation : the newsboys, the *filles de joie*, the commonplace ones, the strange-looking men. Many had passed out before their turn : nobody knew ; nobody cared. Individuality does not count here. It is sufficient that the crowd remains, that the wingéd archer poised above his fountains in the heart of Piccadilly Circus remarks no pause in the ebb and flow, no dimming of his brilliant halo, no foreboding of an impending judgment upon humanity.

Two young men attired for the evening were strolling from the direction of the Empire Music Hall towards Piccadilly. They were due to meet a party of friends at a ball at 11.15 precisely ; and were late. Not that it mattered to be late for a ball ; the friends would probably be late, too. It was altogether fashionable to be late ; it was fatal to be punctual.

At the portals of the great Hotel Astoria, in the heart of Piccadilly, a long line of motor-cars disclosed successive pairs of lamps stretching down that thoroughfare towards Hyde Park Corner. Each, as it drove up, discharged its four, five, or six occupants, and, amid the exhortations of enormous uniformed porters and policemen, passed on. The two young men pushed through a circular moving doorway into a brilliantly lighted *foyer*, mirrored almost the whole way round and leading to a large, less brilliantly lighted winter-garden or palm court, beyond which steps led up to a kind of dais whereon tables and chairs were set. This outer hall was crowded with people—gentlemen taking off their hats and coats, ladies in opera cloaks and gowns of shimmering material.

All the while the doors kept revolving as fresh parties arrived. The two friends having handed their hats and sticks over a counter to a rather ostentatiously grand lacquey—with whom they seemed to cultivate something more than a hat-and-stick acquaintance—proceeded to draw on normally difficult white gloves.

Let us look at them. Both are about the same age, twenty-one, both belong to a class obviously—even to a type. That is to say, you would not single them out as individuals in a crowd but would recognise that they belonged to one category in the crowd. The taller of the two stands rather below six feet in height, is narrowly but proportionately built, and wears his dress-suit with an air of custom. At a first glance his face, a clear-cut oval, appears to signify no more than a conventional amiability. His features are regular and his complexion that almost swarthy brown which so frequently accompanies English youth. The hair is a dark chestnut, the eyes brown; and it is these eyes, liquid and large, rather than a suggestion of weakness about the clean-shaven mouth, which imply to the whole face an expressiveness, a capacity for experience above the ordinary. An Irish strain might have been predicted—and it was so. Such is Adrian Charles Knoyle.

Of his companion, Eric Quentin Sinclair, it may simply be remarked that he is a good deal the shorter of the two, slightly, even delicately made, with blue eyes, a pink-and-white complexion, and the faintest hint of the fairest moustache. A more conventional sort altogether, in whom neatness may be said to amount to fastidiousness and fastidiousness to the verge of effeminacy, the effect being pleasing if somewhat commonplace.

And to what category, to what order of beings do these young gentlemen belong? They may be described as "London young men"; by which description is meant those mortals, favoured or otherwise, who after a laudably undistinguished career at a sufficiently expensive private school, at a sufficiently expensive public school, and afterwards at some *pension* abroad, or at a University, have at length launched themselves upon the " gay world." Adrian Knoyle is the only son of a reputedly impecunious baronet, a retired Army gentleman, possessed of a " town house " and an estate in the West of England which is " always let " ; his mother was a Cullinan of County Down. Eric Sinclair, too, has a mother—vaguely—his male parent having joined the majority ; however, there's money here, and the young fellow is next heir but one to a barony. With regard to the future, neither has the remotest idea what he means to do in life. Knoyle lives at home—which is at least economical—and draws a modest allowance from a prudent father. Sinclair has rooms adjacent to St. James' Street and frequents front rows, first nights, and stage doors. Both euphemistically are " looking round."

One of them at any rate knew—whenever he reflected on the matter at all—that this state of affairs could not last indefinitely, but that at the end of this exciting summer he would have to " do something." " Sufficient unto the day," he would quote upon these occasions, " is the evil thereof. If worst comes to worst one must marry."

So the couple had settled themselves comfortably to " having a good time "—which for young male persons of presentable antecedents, manners and appearance, was not difficult in those days.

§ 2

The party of friends at length arrived. It consisted of Mrs. Rivington (of Rivington) and an elderly gentleman— *not* Mr. Rivington who had long since retired to a quieter world—but a certain suave Mr. Heathcote ; of three young women ; and of what is commonly known as a " tame " young man.

Mrs. Rivington was immense, short and florid—" stout ;"

she was exceptionally ugly, very rich, and full of good nature. She was, indeed, one of those beings perennially useful, who are accepted by the world as a fully-established fact which there is no desire to deny or to decry, but of which, on the contrary, everyone is anxious to take the utmost possible advantage —she was an " act of God," somebody had said. Of two of the young women, Eric Sinclair's opinion may be quoted, for, having surveyed the party, he turned to his friend, saying in a tragic aside : " Oh ! my Gawd, not *both* the Miss Kenelms ! " Knoyle laughed. The ladies named were two nieces of Mrs. Rivington, penniless and motherless, whom she kindly had taken under her wing, ostensibly as a measure of charity, but really on account of her own entertainment. For she was a lady who though often bemoaning her sleepless lot, loved society. The Misses Kenelm were indeed plain, solid, stolid and execrably though most expensively dressed. Like Mrs. Rivington herself they wore quantities of ornaments. The third damsel of the party formed a contrast to the rest, and winked at Knoyle immediately upon arrival. She was tall and slim, with golden hair of a remarkably luminous quality, held back by a narrow royal blue ribbon. Her gown was of white and silver satin. She wore a string of pearls. Her features gave promise of a rare, an even seigneurial beauty when character should ripen in the childish face and maturity assert itself in the slender limbs. There was, at present, piquancy rather than a classic contour, young vitality rather than defined expression—or was it that expression chased itself ? Her complexion was of a delicate carmine tint, the eyes changeable, of no certain colour—wilful as a kitten's.

Having discarded their cloaks, the four ladies reappeared by way of one of the numerous mirrored doors, and the whole party proceeded to descend a red-carpeted winding staircase that promised to lead nowhere in particular. At the first turn, however, strains of ragtime music greeted their ears ; and at the foot they perceived the giver of the entertainment attended by an obvious daughter and conversing very ably with a large number of people at the same time, while shaking hands with a number of others whose names were being successively announced. At this stage, as though by a common impulse, Mrs. Rivington might have been observed to adjust her manner, two of the three young ladies to stiffen slightly as between self-consciousness and anticipation, and each of the three young men to put both hands to his white tie, his features taking on a bland if somewhat strained expression. They then went forward, the names being bawled out in turn by a patronising varlet in silk stockings, white breeches, blue dress-coat and powdered head.

"Mrs. Rivington (of Rivington)."

"How d'you do! *So* glad you've been able to come and have brought your nieces."

"Yes, here we all are—just come on from the play."

The ball-giver is a mass of smiles and gushes ; the daughter well-meaning but horribly shy, inadequate quite to the splendour of the scene and her own magnificence.

"Miss Kenelm."

"How d'you do ? "

"Miss Lettice Kenelm."

"How d'you do ? "

"Lady Rosemary Meynell."

"How d'you do ? "

"Mr. Eric Sinclair."

"Mr. Adrian Knoyle."

"Mr. Pemberton."

All pass, as it were, the jumping-off place, Adrian Knoyle remembering with curiosity, but without alarm, that he has no idea of his entertainer's name or of her daughter's. From his friend he learns that that most ambitious and most efficient-looking lady (with the most reluctant and most inadequate-looking daughter) is the whilom wife of a somewhat mysterious South American—but all South Americans are

mysterious !—of whom she rid herself at the expense of a small
though rather painful paragraph in the newspapers ; that she
has a large (and vulgar) mansion in Grosvenor Square, and that
a few evening entertainments, at the cost of a thousand pounds
or so a time, are as a dip in the ocean so she can marry the
newly-hatched daughter to the (preferably eldest) son of
a peer.

"How are the mighty fallen !" murmurs Mr. Sinclair,
looking round as they all pass on into a throng of people. "And
why are the rich always so damned uninteresting !"

§ 3

Both young men—as was to be expected of their age and
kind—had a favourable opinion of themselves which did not,
however, necessarily appear except in uncongenial society,
when they were apt to lose patience and even indulge their
sense of humour. Knoyle may have been spoilt, he was
indubitably vain, but he never had lacked a certain critical
intelligence. And he was rather too emphatically aware of
that.

Both held a very definite set of ideas about things and
people—standards which they applied with all the rigour and
self-confidence of their twenty-one years. These ideas were
the innate or imbued traditions of the Victorian hierarchy,
of an English public school, and of a small world which they
imagined to be a big one. To the onlooker such standards
might appear ridiculous ; they did not to those who were
steeped in them. Narrow, arbitrary, and on the whole meaningless, they nevertheless represented the full force of the class
tradition in England. The Ten Commandments had long
since given place to a more rigorous code. "Thou shalt
not say this." "Thou shalt not say that." "Such-and-such
a word shall be pronounced in such-and-such a way and none
other" or—excommunication. To steal is bad and so is to

dishonour one's father and mother, but to abbreviate one's bicycle, one's photographs, or one's telephone means a black mark at the Day of Judgment—or worse. Sir Charles Knoyle preached minor vulgarity as original sin ; Lady Knoyle hardly got a look-in with the tenets of her Christianity.

So it was that Adrian Knoyle had grown up. Those were the standards—those and certain sartorial distinctions, certain facts about tie-pins, hats, and the stuff a man's clothes were made of, certain excommunications of fish-knives, cake-stands, and other aspects of gentility—by which he was brought up to value, to discriminate between his fellow-creatures.

And with such ideas at the back of their minds, the two young fellows went forward, gibing together, in train of the four ladies. It seemed almost certain that the hospitable woman with whom they had just shaken hands said the " wrong " things ; she was so obviously " not quite " or even " very nearly." Somebody else—Mrs. Rivington, for one—had kindly asked all the people to her dance. Mr. Pemberton followed slightly in rear. " Uncouth " was the mental note the two friends made of him. He had untidy hair and a " good plain " face—a quiet, amiable creature who looked rather out of place in a ball-room. And he wore black-striped kid gloves. That was enough to finish Pemberton.

They now passed through a kind of lobby which opened upon the ball-room. The lobby was full of grand-looking people who sat about in couples on brocade chairs and sofas, by their united chatter making a continuous murmuring as of starlings. A dance was just over and a crowd of gay folk came swarming out of the ball-room. Gowns, jewels, colours, white arms and necks ! The whole effect was un-doubtedly attractive—the blue carpet of the *salon*, the pale blue chairs and French tables, the great round white ball-room supported by pillars and panelled with mirrors, garlanded with festoons of flowers, the facets of electric light gleaming here from huge crystal chandeliers, there from clusters cunningly concealed in cornices, and at the far end a wide flower-banked daïs upon which was grouped the Blue Hungarian band.

After chairs had been found for the four ladies, and each of the younger ones had been invited to dance, the three gentlemen were left standing surveying the scene. They quickly espied acquaintances.

" Well, Adrian, how are you to-night ? "

" Oh ! Going strong. Shall we have a dance ? "

" The next ? "

" No, I'm dancing it and the two after. What about missing three ? "

" Wretch ! But anything to keep the boy amused. All right—three from now."

That sort of thing went on in all directions. Knoyle with undeniable cynicism felt that he must do his duty by the Misses Kenelm and had better get it over quickly. Then he would dance with Rosemary Meynell, for whose sake alone— the fact must be recognised—he had come. She was young —only just " out " indeed—but she had scored a palpable hit in the best market ; and she possessed a combination of qualities deeply attractive to Adrian. Her father, an Earl of Cranford, had not " appeared " for many years—there was a " queer " streak in the family—and since his retirement (nobody quite knew whither), her mother, an admired and intelligent woman, had managed the Yorkshire estates almost single-handed and with uncommon skill.

To the best of his ability and amiability, Adrian Knoyle polished off the Misses Kenelm in turn. All three comported themselves strictly according to the rules, A repeating to C the same profound amenities as he or she had already perpetrated to B, B and C replying in a corresponding strain.

Knoyle : " My goodness, it's hot to-night, isn't it ? There's going to be an awful squash, too."

Miss Kenelm (or Miss Lettice Kenelm) : " Yes, it's

frightfully hot, isn't it ? And there's going to be lots more
people. Whose band is it ? "

Well, the thing was obvious ! From their chairs within
the lobby, both could perceive the one and only Hirsch with
his pale conceited face, his mincing mannerisms and vapid
sensual mouth, conducting the orchestra—he who had been
made such a fuss of that, it was commonly reported, he'd once
asked a duchess for a dance ! But it *was* something to say.
Ten minutes' conversation are allotted on these occasions.

Miss Kenelm (or Miss Lettice Kenelm) : " I always like
this place to dance at. The roof garden's lovely."

Knoyle : " Yes, it's cool out there. And one gets such a
nice breeze."

Miss Kenelm (or Miss Lettice Kenelm) : " The pillars are
rather in the way though when you're dancing."

" *Rot !* " shrieked Adrian inwardly. " Confound it ! Can't
she or won't she say anything sensible ? "

And Miss Kenelm (whichever it happened to be) was communing with herself : " How am I to amuse gentlemen ?
He seems a nice young man. I'd better agree with everything he says. There's nobody else here who is likely to ask
me for a dance. I shall have to sit out the whole evening."

That was the trouble—she always agreed ; whether it was
dances, whether it was races, whether it was people's clothes
or their faces—she echoed, she agreed.

An old-fashioned valse had been succeeded by a *maxixe*, the
eccentric gyrations of which caused some food for comment,
as did the varying expressions of self-consciousness of the new
arrivals. The crowd swept round and around—some in a frenzy
of enjoyment, leaping, darting forward or backward, doing
the oddest things, others ambling through the various movements as though performing one of life's more solemn duties.
Along the sides of the ball-room on golden chairs and brocaded
settees, were established, like faded goddesses, the mammas,
aunts, and grandmothers, together with a sprinkling of elderly

male persons, the majority of whom, to judge by their appearance, were retired colonels, or country gentlemen bi-annually galvanised into life.

Near the doorway, standing in one large group, was a bevy of fairs—a dozen or twenty perhaps—who had so far failed to find partners for the dance or for any dance. Not far off some young gallants, too *blasé* or too lazy to take part, lounged against pillars, chatting and laughing. Eric Sinclair was to be seen talking to a thin, dark, good-looking man—a soldier obviously. Adrian Knoyle had engaged young Mr. Pemberton in conversation, who smiled continually, but whose shyness only permitted him to announce that he didn't often come to dances. He was studying for the Bar and liked to go to bed early. The chief fear in the minds of most of the gilded youths was that one of the unpartnered should be introduced to them; they simply dreaded being "landed with a stumer." The thing of course was not "done," and yet well-meaning people—people's relations, and other people's relations —persistently did it.

They were a study in themselves, these debonair fellows— chaffing, joking, merry. They were full of jokes of a daring nature appertaining to mutual friends or enemies, or extracted from the sayings of comedians or from the sporting papers. They had their own code of ethics, their own particular code of ideas—for them life portended a huge pretence. Those who felt the keenest emotions or the keenest curiosities, religiously overlaid the fact with a coverlet of half-ingenuous, half-cynical wit. For such, existence contained two main interests—feminine and sporting. And their business in the world? Had they any? They were subalterns in regiments, they were in the Foreign Office, about to enter the Diplomatic Service, or commercially engaged, or like Knoyle and Sinclair just "looking round." Nor could there be denied to them a certain *flair*, even though the curious might be disappointed by their cut-to-pattern notions bred of a

common upbringing, and future, and by their unvarying
similarity in outlook and appearance born of your Englishman's
terror of differing from his neighbour.

Their foibles were amazing, but by creating fashion they
appeared illogically correct. . . .

A young man had turned up one night in a delicately tinted
evening waistcoat. The offence was heinous and talked about
for weeks as if the unfortunate youth had committed a public
act of impropriety. People's moral sense was indescribably
shocked. A young officer was seen somewhere in a short
evening coat and white waistcoat. Next morning he appeared
before his Adjutant and received condign punishment, everybody joining in pointing out the enormity of the crime—
which was, however, mercifully ascribed to the extremest youth.
If the same young gentleman had met his Colonel while
spending the week-end companionably at Brighton the affair
would have been chuckled over for days—his enterprise univers-
ally applauded.

One night a provincial lady with more ambition than knowledge of the world she aspired to enter, gave an extremely
expensive party and invited a large number of people (very
few of whom she knew by sight). Thoughtfully but still pro-
vincially she introduced programmes for the convenience of
the guests. What is more, they were convenient. However,
the thing was a perfect scandal and the ball a failure from
start to finish. Everybody said "Programmes! How perfectly awful! Who are these people? Did you ever see such
a show? Let's flee!"

And they did.

§ 4

The young ladies who stood together in a group near
the doorway were the very antithesis of light-heartedness.
Most of them were plain, some proud, some frankly depressed

On this face, thoughtful, full of character but not of beauty, was written the look of one who says to herself " Oh ! to be out of this—to fall through the floor—to hide in an empty room— to be in the dark—to escape somehow from the noise, the people, and this pitiless isolation. I've only danced once the whole evening. And there's Angela and Phyllis, and Betty— they've never missed a dance. Everybody's looking at me too." A beaming damsel—probably her particular friend— passing hand-in-hand with a partner as they step out of the dance, remarks brightly, " Well, Edith, how are you enjoying yourself ? Isn't it fun ? Why aren't you dancing, my dear ? " Now and again a good-natured female brings up to her one of the gilded youths, who eyes the young creature rather as an expert eyes a heifer in the cattle market. " He didn't even ask me for a dance ! What's the matter with me ? What's wrong ? My clothes ? . . . No. Young men don't like me."

At this moment a gallant, who has lately been introduced to her, slowly and deliberately walks along the row of " wall- flowers " obviously thinking to himself : " Is there anything here one could possibly dance with ? There's that little Winsom girl, but she's hopeless. Oh ! my Lor', what a collection ! "

Meanwhile little Miss Winsom is feverishly trying to con- ceal her agitation, thus communing within herself : " Will he see me, will he—will he—ask me ? I mustn't catch his eye, I mustn't look his way. He sees me—this is too awful ! " Never- theless, hope rises for a moment to be succeeded by a sort of quivering despair. " He's passed on ! Another dance to stand through. I feel famished and almost faint. I'd give worlds for some supper. But who's going to take me in except mother, and that would be *too* degrading. Oh ! We must get away soon ; but Marjorie's enjoying herself, and of course she'll want to stay till any hour. I shall absolutely break down in a minute, and if anybody asks me to dance I shall look as if I'm going to cry. How proud and beastly they all are! Oh! for my little bed at home and never to come near this awful, noisy, sordid world again."

A voice whispers, "As if it mattered. . . ." But it *does* matter!

Rosemary Meynell, on the other hand, is having her usual success. Three or four admirers are asking for dances at the same moment, and she may be heard saying four, five, or even six from now. Only the "particular friends" are so favoured, and these may be numbered on the fingers of one hand. Knoyle secures his second dance with the promise of another and longer one later on. Rosemary dances well; she does most things well. Adrian has great fun for a quarter-of-an-hour, and begins to think he is falling in love. They have plenty of things in common, these two; they criticise their acquaintance from the same standpoint—than which there is no readier bond of human sympathy—and generally make each other happy. With a sense of keen anticipation they agree to meet again later in the night.

Knoyle makes up his mind that there is nobody else worth dancing with, and decides to go on for an hour or two to the Doncasters'—if that's boring, somewhere else. For the fellow has no fewer than five invitations, generally in the shape of large, oblong printed cards, for the evening. Blithely accepting all, he intends to partake of those which are likely to amuse him only.

"Come along, Eric!" he calls to his friend whom he finds at the buffet; "let's sample Doncaster House."

CHAPTER II

Humoreske.

§ 1

HAVING reinforced their spirits with champagne, Adrian Knoyle and Eric Sinclair called for a taxicab and were whirled to Bryanston Square, which they found lively with lighted vehicles, and with the brilliant windows of the noble House of Doncaster thrown open to the night.

Couples in evening dress, betraying a faint glimmer of jewels in the lamplight, promenaded the pavement, seeking any cool breeze that might be abroad ; there were people, too, on the awninged balcony, while through the windows came the fitful cadences of a valse, which floated out on the heavy air and lost themselves in the night murmur of London.

"What is that thing ? " asked Adrian of his friend as he paid off the cabman.

" Never heard it before."

The two young men dashed into the somewhat bleak hall, where several couples were sitting out like stray worshippers in a temple, and sought Lady Doncaster—a shrivelled-up little old woman who shot out a claw at you, and snatched it back as though afraid you might want to keep it for good. Altogether the atmosphere, even on so hot a night, was chilly. What Eric Sinclair called the " cold shade of aristocracy " pervaded the stately mansion, which could so easily have accommodated twice the number of people present. All were on their best behaviour, the very servants were mournful. A toy royalty was present, not to mention an upstart Balkan prince and a downtrodden Grand Duke, supported by members of the diplomatic corps in ornaments and ribbons : those who possessed them wore miniature medals and orders on their dress-coats. Supper was just beginning, the royal personages leading the way downstairs. Lord Doncaster—who is known to have been mistaken for his butler more frequently than any other living nobleman—followed, talking in a loud staccato to a stagey duchess.

A Court party of some kind that evening gave to a limited number of elderly gentlemen the prescriptive right to air their handsome legs in knee-breeches and silk-stockings, and to tell their acquaintances what a bore it had been.

Mounting the staircase the two arrivals came face to face with a stooping, middle-aged man whose iron-grey hair and moustache set off the half-wistful expression of his un-laughing eyes. His shirt-front was slashed with a black-and-gold ribbon, while upon his arm descended a tall woman with a magnificent tiara sparkling from reddish-golden hair. The figure was familiar to them both. It was that of Lichknowsky, the German Ambassador. . . .

From the ball-room came quivering fragments of the elusive valse accompanied by a thin patter of dancing feet. Victorian *grandes dames*, loaded with tiaras and other ammunition of their sex, occupied the settees and chairs, staring at everyone who appeared in the doorway, audibly and shamelessly inquiring of one another his or her name. The younger people seemed stiffly conscious of the formality of the affair; the mode of dancing was sedate in the extreme.

" Is there anybody here one could pick the leg of a chicken with ? " demanded Sinclair, eyeing the somewhat sparse couples with a cold eye of appraisal; " or must we depart in peace without even tasting the champagne ? "

" Come along ! " said Knoyle, pulling at his friend's sleeve. " It's the sort of show where you're expected to ask the mother's permission before you speak to the daughter."

Sinclair always followed his friend's lead in such matters.

But just then they espied Lady Arden and *her* daughter, and proceeding to pay their respects, all four agreed to go down to supper together.

Lady Arden, a scion of the house of Doncaster—for she had been a Wardour—was a youngish middle-aged woman with a vague dignity and prettiness of her own. Faith Daventry had inherited her mother's charm with an additional freshness that bespoke something pleasant—an English spring perhaps or a Constable landscape. Hers was a beauty that belongs peculiarly to England—not original or uncommon, but perennially charming—a beauty of fair hair, regular features, and a country-bred complexion : of large blue eyes that looked out upon the world with a serenity unusual in her then surroundings ; a face memorable, Knoyle thought, for a certain courage and honesty. It was not the first time he had met Lady Arden, but it was the first time he had met Miss Daventry. She was Eric's friend.

The conversation began as usual with a recital of forthcoming events, of balls lately given, of balls about to be given—more especially of the Ascot Races that were due the week following.

"How glad I shall be when it's all over ! " sighed Lady Arden. "And how tired this child will be ! I shall send her to bed for a week. *How* delightful to look forward to a quiet life for another year——"

Unlike Mrs. Rivington, she meant it.

"Mother ! " protested Miss Daventry, "you don't expect me to look after the vegetables for a year on end without a soul to talk to except the garden boy ? Or perhaps you do ! "

The gentlemen laughed—lightly, suitably.

"And you young men ? " inquired her mother. "What do you do when the summer's over ? Go to bed, I suppose. . . . By the way, Faith, didn't we say we wanted somebody to come and stay with us for that dreadful Bank Holiday ? "

"Yes," said Faith, promptly; "ask them! . . . Both."

Lady Arden turned to the couple with her comprehensive smile.

"I'd like to come very much," was Sinclair's unhesitating reply.

"I know it's ages off," said Lady Arden, addressing Knoyle. "But isn't there something on then?" ("Cowes!" interjected Faith.) "Ah, Cowes! I can't tell you who's coming except Lady Cranford and Rosemary Meynell. I think we've asked them, haven't we, my dear?"

"Of course, mother. You wrote the note this morning."

For some reason the three young people looked at each other and laughed.

Knoyle had hesitated a moment; it was against his principles to stay with people he didn't know well. Perhaps the name last-mentioned decided him. At any rate, Knoyle, too, accepted.

Faith said:

"Splendid! You can take it in turns to punt me and Rosie on our majestic river. Do you understand rivers?"

"Only the Thames, ma'm," Eric bowed.

"*Except* the Thames," said Adrian.

"I quite agree," pursued Miss Daventry. "Boulter's Lock on Ascot Sunday . . . !" She made a face.

"What's the name of your river, Miss Daventry?"

"The Rushwater. Isn't it a pretty name? And it's a pretty little river flowing out of a pretty little lake. And there are all sorts of queer birds nesting beside it. And you can go on and on to where it's very deep and quiet and you get lost. Isn't that the sort of river you like, Mr. Knoyle?"

"I do," the young man replied. "I've a queer hankering sometimes for getting lost."

"Oh, really! . . ." laughed Eric. "Sounds like Earl's Court."

They rose from the supper table and Knoyle took his leave. Faith Daventry and Eric Sinclair went up to dance.

Of his friend's friend, trivial as the exchanges had been, Adrian Knoyle felt that he had made a friend—with a certainty that one rarely feels on meeting a person for the first time.

§ 2

It was to a small party given by an uncommon young woman called Gina Maryon that he now repaired, directing his cab-driver to one of those miniature houses which, unknown to the majority, lurk in the corners of Berkeley and other great squares. This Gina Maryon occupied a conspicuous position. She had pretensions to advanced literary and artistic tastes, " adored " the Vorticists, " worshipped " at the altar of Matisse ; a little later no doubt she became a devotee of Mr. Wyndham Lewis. Poetry—and people—were her particular obsessions (or possessions). Of the former she wrote quantities in a hectic, exotic and not insignificant strain, though people complained that it was overloaded with impropriety ; most of her friends wrote poetry, too. She had also a *penchant* for *extravaganza* in clothes and in house decoration.

Knoyle walked straight into the Berkeley Square " maisonette," for the door stood open. There was nowhere to put one's hat so he hid his behind the front door. The narrow staircase, painted green and without a carpet, was so choc-a-bloc with people that he had the greatest difficulty in reaching the first floor. Miss Maryon at the top of the stairs was engaged in having her hand kissed by a young man who was evidently on the point of departing. This young man was perhaps typical of the breed affected by this young woman, which collectively had come to be known as the " Clan Maryon." He had a pale, rather unwhole-some face, large dark eyes of the sort called " soulful," heavily-oiled hair brushed straight back from the forehead and an elaborate manner. As he bent down he said :

" Ah, my Gina ! What an evening—what an evening ! One of your best. The *maisonette* reborn and your exquisite liqueurs and your still more exquisite self—my Gina, I see life through the perfumed haze of your personality."

(Knoyle had noticed a queer musky scent on entering the house.)

" And after all that you leave my house at the preposterous hour of two," was Miss Maryon's reply. " What ingratitude, what *mauvais ton !* But, ah ! out of the way, Harry—out of my sight, monster ! A guest ! . . . Do you know this silly fellow, Mr. Knoyle—Harry Upton ? "

The two men nodded.

Adrian had met Miss Maryon only two or three times before, and had been surprised at receiving an invitation —scribbled in pencil on the back of an advertisement of hats—to her " teeny party, very mixed." For these were essentially Clan Maryon affairs and he was in no sense of the sacred hierarchy. Why had he come ? Impelled by curiosity, stimulated by the unexpectedness of the thing, intrigued by what he had heard of the Maryon orgies—intrigued and on the whole flattered.

And Miss Maryon herself ? There was something bird-like about her. Like a bird, she seemed to live and move on springs. She never walked, she hopped or darted. She chattered away like a willow-wren in a high-pitched treble. She often sang. . . . She was very small too. Her features were small and sharp, extraordinarily animated and mobile, half-a-dozen quick expressions flitting across them in as many seconds. Easily-pleased people called her " fascinating "— and really she was. Her violet eyes were fascinating when they flashed sideways up at you : she fascinated deliberately, especially when she thought her victim resented the effect. And there was the unusual offset of her wavy auburn hair. Her

quick bird-like intelligence was attractive too—her versatility
—her sympathy, simulated or otherwise, her retaliatory wit—
all these people found magnetic.

" Sit down and talk to me ! " she said. But Miss Maryon
did all the talking—mainly about nothing. Adrian, for his
part, was too much interested in the doings around him to
take particular heed of what she said. All the same, he became
subtly aware that she was out to dazzle, that sex-consciously
she was sizing him up, that all the while she was asking him
questions out of the side-glance of her violet eyes.

The room was an extraordinary one. It had—as Miss
Maryon assured him in requesting his opinion of it—been
newly " done up." (This happened on an average once a
year according to fashion.) The walls were of peacock green,
the ceiling yellow and in one corner stood a sort of shrine
half-hidden by black and gold striped hangings. The furniture was of ebony inlaid with triangular ivory patterns and
looked as if it might have come from Munich via Paris ; the
enormous sofa upon which they sat and which occupied the
whole of one end of the smallish drawing-room was black,
littered with rainbow cushions. Instead of pictures on the
walls, one found white marble bas-reliefs of archaic men
and women, while upon the mantelpiece reposed curious dis-
proportioned wooden figures, egg-shaped heads cast in bronze,
and white china bowls filled with fruit carved in cream-
coloured stone.

In this curious apartment with its waxed floor—and on
the landing outside and on the stairs—the whole of the Clan
Maryon was congregated. At either end of it was set a green
baize table around which were gathered groups of men and
women. Laughter, but also a certain intensity of expression
was written on their faces, and such remarks as " Banquo ! "
or " I pass," or " Your ante, "came out of silences ; while from
the other table came the perpetual whir of a spinning-top, and
there " little horses " could be seen careering very fast round a

squared and coloured board. Money gleamed in the electric-light, momentary pauses were broken by the " chink " of it. The peculiar scent of the room may well have derived from the cigarette-smoke which hung about like a heavy perfume until Knoyle began to feel queer in his head. It appeared to surprise nobody that a couple had dropped off to sleep on a divan. At the piano, a trio sang to the accompaniment of drum and banjoline. Now and then another couple would rise from the floor, on which a fair proportion of the company disposed itself, dance a few steps, then squat down again. From below-stairs came the " pop " of champagne corks. Laughter came from the upstairs direction. . . .

Gina Maryon though by birth a " perfect lady " (as she was wont to describe herself)—and even a Mrs. Maryon was hidden away somewhere, invalidish—Gina Maryon made a speciality of, apart from her own little mutual admiration society, gathering together the oddest people, or, as she said, " anybody with talent, anybody with character." The men were certainly unusual-looking : one, with hair as long as a girl's, was attired in a suit of green velvet, another affected a D'Orsay bow with a soft-fronted evening shirt ; the majority, to Knoyle's critical gaze, appeared none too well shaved. As to the women, they included musical comedy actresses and " real " actresses, professional singers, and clever little comics who killed you outright on the variety stage. There was " Chips " who plays " any old part you like to name " and Trixie of the peroxide hair. There were the daughters of peers and the sisters and first cousins of peers. There were no *chaperons*. Downstairs in the passage was to be found an amazing array of cocktails and liqueurs of rainbow hue and a man in a white coat mixing them—but not much to eat.

Although Society (with a big S) smiled or frowned, said the Clan Maryon was " extraordinary," " impossible " or " not nice," while its avowed enemies called Gina " second-rate "—

its doings were the source of the most enjoyable scandal. And Society respected, feared, and even rather adored the Mary-onites; for Society loves to be despised. They were clever after all, you couldn't get away from that—they were clever. And—original! . . . And what did young Mr. Knoyle think as he descended the stairs (for there was no particular reason to stay, he didn't know anybody except Gina)? He couldn't forget that dusky, musky cloud. There it was hanging over you, hanging over the house and all the people in it. He knew these people—or thought he did. At the last—they were sensualists. They hungered for a full and changing life. Their life was a cinematograph. They were actors and actresses, every one of them. All the same, he did feel flattered—it wasn't everybody who could float into the *maisonette* Maryon or be encouraged thereto by the genie herself. No. . . . Yet a more imperious magnet drew him back to the Astoria.

§ 3

Everything was still going full swing in the mirrored pillared ball-room. Here Knoyle felt himself back in an atmosphere of normality. The Blue Hungarians were sawing away at their violins, the multi-coloured frocks were whirling round and round, the gallant young men, each of whom had by now drunk his bottle of champagne, were uplifted on a pinnacle of gaiety; only the " wallflowers " with their mammas and *chaperons* had faded away.

The first person Adrian's glance discovered on his entrance was Rosemary Meynell. He stood for some time watching her: he was held by the grace of her movements, the facility of her steps—by elderly sporting gentlemen such as she had been compared to a thoroughbred filly. A warmer flush had risen in her cheeks now, a spark of devilry had come into her eyes, and these corresponded to his own heightened impressionability. She was graceful and she was naive. . . . And then unaccountably his mind went back to Gina Maryon. But it was not until he had been watching Rosemary for some minutes that he realised with whom she was dancing. Her partner was the young man to whom he had so lately been introduced. His name ?—he could not remember.

The music stopped and the various couples passed out of the ball-room. Rosemary and her partner sat down at a table in the outer *salon,* and during the brief interval Knoyle found himself studying them in the opposite mirror—the man's declamatory conversation accompanied by smiles and a play of hands like a foreigner, the girl's animated response. Mr. What's-his-name evidently chose to make himself agreeable outside his own circle! But what was he doing her~—this palpable Maryonite ?

The violins quavered. He went to claim his dance with Rosemary, saluting her partner with a brief nod. Then they were gliding together over the comparatively empty floor. It was not until they had made a full circuit of the room that the rhythm of the music impressed itself upon him, and he recognised the air whose fitful cadences had floated out through the open windows of Doncaster House.

" What a queer, lovely thing ! " said Rosemary. Their eyes met.

" Yes, it's haunting—and gay and sad," he replied, lightly " all in one. Hirsch always gives you value for your money." Somehow his little finger twined round hers. " By the bye, I simply must go somewhere and have a lesson in reversing."

" What's it called ? " she asked, ignoring his last remark.

" We'll ask."

He had caught Hirsch's fishy eye, and when they passed close to the great man he called out :

" What's this thing, Hirsch ? "

" ' Humoreske,' Meester Knoyle . . . of Dvorak."

" Ah, thanks."

She bent her head to catch the word and he was suddenly

aware of the graceful curve of her neck and of her ear with its little pearl, which reminded him of some transparently delicate sea-shell.

"'Humoreske!'" she repeated. "I must remember it."

§ 4

Neither he nor she perhaps ever forgot that dance: how it stopped; how they applauded; how it stopped again, and how they—and the other remaining couples—insisted that it should go on yet again. And it went on. Lost as he was in the pleasure of steering his partner, their joint movement seemed to synchronise without effort; in the first moment of dancing they felt drawn to each other by an impalpable sympathy. An electric thrill sent them turning, turning in long sweeps round and across the room, talking the while, and laughing. Their hands gripped and pressed. At last they fell silent. They seemed to dance as one person. Their thoughts:

Hers: "A nice boy. He dances well. He's interesting—and quite good-looking. I wonder . . . what's he like really?"

His: "Something must come of this. She's not a girl, she's a dream. I wish this would go on—and on. . . . No, I don't. I want to talk to her, to be alone with her, to *know* her."

The dance over, they climbed up to the famous roof-garden and sat down on a seat in the darkest corner. They were alone. This roof-garden looks out over the Green Park and down Piccadilly westward. The London night was already paling towards dawn. Except for the occasional whir of a taxicab, rumble of a market cart or swish of the hose-driven water sousing Piccadilly, no sound came up to the ears of the two, seated close together.

They were intensely aware of each other.

Adrian said:

"How wonderfully you dance, Lady Rosemary!"

" Do I? Well—it rather depends on whom I'm dancing with."

A glow of pleasure suffused him. He became sensible, powerfully sensible, of the gentle, musical, almost caressing timbre of her voice.

" I find that, too," he said. " With some people one can dance—endlessly without an effort. And with some people —the Miss Kenelms for instance—it's the very devil to get round the room once."

" Yes—it depends."

" Don't you think it's like people one meets for the first time—sometimes you've got to make conversation for half-an-hour before you say anything, and sometimes you get on with them like a house-on-fire straightaway."

" Are you still thinking of the Miss Kenelms ? " she laughed.

" No—of life in general."

" I really know so little of life in general. So I can't say."

" You don't expect me to believe that ? "

" I know nothing of life at all."   He had an idea she was laughing at him : all the same her hand lay very temptingly near to his. " Mamma's always been so strict, you see. I've only been outside the front door about twice without a maid or somebody. It's frightfully annoying when lots of emancipated young females have such a good time."

" I think you ought to take the law into your own hands."

His fingers touched hers. " There's nothing like being a law unto oneself in this world."

" What—how do you mean ? "

" Why—having a good time."

" You—you'll have to lead the way, then."

" I will—Rosemary."   He held all of her hand now and she made no attempt to withdraw it.

" By the by . . . who told you you could call me by my Christian name ? "

" Not your mamma, my dear."

Both laughed. She said:

" What a very go-ahead young man ! . . . Please ! "

She attempted to withdraw her hand.

" Oh, no ! No, my child. Not so easy. I *don't* think "— and he squeezed her hand as tight as he could.

In the gloom, he could just discern the outline of a shapely head on a slender neck.

" Are you in the habit of—of doing this sort of thing, Mr.——? "

" Adrian," he put in. " Yes—no."

" Which do you mean ? "

" No—you're the first."

" I'm flattered."

His arm was around her.

" Don't Mr.—Whatever-your-name-is—*please !* Leave me —leave me, alone ! "

" Mamma wouldn't like it—eh ? "

" *I* don't like it. It's—silly."

" Is it ? I'm teaching you . . . . a thing or two—see ? "

" Behave yourself then ! "

" Not a gentleman, am I ? "

" No, by Jove ! " she laughed. " You're a — ass."

" ' By Jove ! ' Who taught you that expression ? How in the name of girlhood——! "

She looked up at him. She deliberately provoked.

Their lips were near.

" I want—to know you better."

" I daresay you do, but you won't ever know me better unless you let go of my hand *at once*, and take your arm away from—where it's no business to be."

Instead, he drew her quite firmly towards him.

" No, really—be good ! I ask you . . . *Adrian !* " she protested—yielding.

Gently he kissed her on the lips.

They remained enclasped for several moments, the dawn breaking opaquely above them.

" Hark ! " A chord of familiar music came faintly to their ears through the glass doors and up the iron stairway. It was the first bar of " God save the King."

The ball was over. . . .

" Great Scott ! " she exclaimed. " We must run for our lives."

" Yes, but we shall often meet again ? " He said this pleadingly as they hurried down the stairway to the ball-room ; " at Ascot next week and—at dances ? "

" Not after Ascot." She was suddenly and irritatingly demure. " We go away after Ascot. Mamma wants to pay visits."

" You're coming to the Ardens' later on though, for the week-end ? "

She did not answer at once. She laughed—unexpectedly. They had reached the outer hall.

" That depends." Her glance challenged his. " We may go to Cowes. . . . Good night ! "

§ 5

Adrian Knoyle walked home. The many clocks of London were striking four, and a clear pearly-blue light reigned in the streets, deserted now except for twittering sparrows and scavenging cats. Once or twice a taxicab or market-lorry rattled down Piccadilly. But of the city's myriad human population the only visible signs were an occasional policeman and the haggard uncivilised-looking waifs who nightly take such rest as they can get on the bare wooden seats of Piccadilly, or against its inhospitable railings.

Something fresh, clean, and even beautiful, nevertheless, seemed to come to the familiar thoroughfares in this, their unfamiliar, guise. And it was difficult to believe that half-a-dozen hours earlier they had pulsed beneath the moving mystery of the London night ; that six hours hence they would again be the vortex of the everyday whirl.

The pavement forsook the young gentleman. He trod on air. It had been a memorable night—perhaps the most memorable of his life so far. Was he " in love ? " Had he that very night set foot on the unknown road ? . . . The fact is he wasn't quite sure. How could he be sure ? There had of course been mild experiments in different notes and keys—indifferent experiments. These, it is true, he had not sought ; they had been made for him. Lily, for instance —Miss Truss. How at last he had come to detest this young woman who threw a leg at the Hippodrome, an eye at the stalls, and her womanly virtue at the highest bidder ! How he had come to detest her, with her " Haven't you got a present for me, dear ? "—her " boys in the Guards," her ubiquitous " girl friend," her censorious allusions to " commonness " in all who were less common than she. Eric and he had quarrelled about Lily. For it was Eric who insisted on Lily—as a sort of diet— Eric who insisted that Miss Truss must be " made up to "— that he, Adrian, was " slow off the mark "—and " unenter-prising "—that Miss Truss regarded him as " one of the sweetest boys she had ever known," and that in return for this unearned compliment Miss Truss must be regaled with supper and champagne. At length, after a little enterprise and much expense, his inveterate repulsion to Miss Truss had got the better of him : he had struck, not indeed Miss Truss, but his friend—very nearly.

And there was Miss Pearl Stucley. Pearl, it is true, came into a different category, but she likewise had been introduced by Eric under the label " hellish hot-stuff." Not that he disliked Miss Stucley : she was *provocative* and she was amusing. She was a lady. But he disliked making love to Miss Stucley—still more he disliked Miss Stucley making love to him. To the one or the other there seemed no alternative—in gallantry (and yet unaccountably) he became an accessory after the fact. What a relief it was when Miss Stucley came to the decision that he was " hopeless,"—and so informed her friends ! With what pleasure he turned to less exacting pursuits after Eric had affably called him a " bloody fool " !

As to " love " then—a word he detested—it was an un-imagined—and in any conscious sense, an undesired—thing. Its only concrete expression for him were Eric's bi-weekly occupa-tions with chorus-girls. And of these he grew weary ; the details were always the same. If, therefore, he had ever thought about the matter at all, it was to look up at the sky and see a child's vision of Heaven—some ultimate vision of perfection, but one without any sort of comprehensible reality. . . . Then Rosemary sprang into the picture. " A girl-and-a-half," he muttered to himself : he wasn't a poet—yet. There she was with her saucy way, her beauty and her dashing grace. No wonder London raved about her. . . . There she was, beckoning to him, laughing at him, then eluding him, then being a darling again. The night had been a rapture. What would come of it ? More nights like this before the summer ended, nights when one saw all people and all things—even Mrs. Rivington having supper—in a pearly, rainbow-tinted mist ; a series of nights culminating in—a week-end. Was that " love ? " The vulgarity of the interpretation struck him —it sounded like a joke at a music-hall ; he didn't laugh. She dominated him—there was no doubt about that. She possessed him altogether. Life without her—unthinkable. But—life at that moment sparkled like the dew on the Green Park.

CHAPTER III

At the Races

§ 1

THE fashionable and famous Ascot Races duly took place in the week following the Rodriguez ball. Glorious weather combined with first-class racing. "'Everybody' in London," as the halfpenny newspapers paradoxically said, "was to be seen in the Royal Enclosure."

The first and second days of the meeting, Rosemary Meynell and Adrian Knoyle spent together—Faith Daventry and Eric Sinclair also pairing off—running up and down stands, Adrian struggling to the railings of Tattersall's and offering Rosemary's shillings to unwilling bookmakers, darting to the telegraph office, rushing back again, walking about in the Paddock, and having long-drawn-out teas and luncheons *à quatre*. It was a merry time. . . . Perhaps my lady of Cranford came to the discreet conclusion that her admired daughter —as to whose future she soared a good deal higher than Mr. Adrian Knoyle—had been seeing enough of this young gentleman. Anyhow on the third day, that of the Gold Cup, the ladies were nowhere to be seen when the bell rang for the first race. This was a heavy blow to their respective admirers, who spent some time wandering disconsolately between the luncheon-tent and the stands. Adrian, for his part, was surprised at the force of his inward disturbance and apprehension : would Rosemary finally turn up ? Then he lost Eric (who went off to make a bet) and found himself high up in the stand awaiting, like everybody else, the Royal Procession, which presently appeared at the Golden Gates and came bowling up the lawn-like sward of the Straight Mile, its scarlet outriders bobbing up and down against the dark green of the pine-woods. Its approach was heralded by the faint cheers of the crowds in the further rings which floated up the course, swelling to a roar as the procession passed, and all the hats went off.

The polite crowd then began moving towards the paddock. Adrian's attention was held by the varied movement, though he searched for one figure only and for one face. What a conundrum it was, he reflected, this world of fashion, what a conundrum and what an illusion ! He saw, upon the one hand, those who, standing upon the verge of the Court and par-taking of its Conservatism, represented that which was best in the old order of England : the la .downers, the feudal title-holders, the aristocracy of sport and of tradition, men of prin-ciple, men who lived by a strict code of ethics for the established order, their class, and their dependents. He saw, upon the other hand—and they were unmistakable—those who, freely endowed with this world's goods, recked neither of yesterday nor of to-morrow, but lived for to-day, remaining themselves insensible to the democratic trend of the hour, because they ignored it.

Of the women, England seemed to him to produce a class which no Continental country has produced, and of which the United States has served up only an imitation (unless by absorption) ; this class lacking the *chic* of the Frenchwoman or any parade of up-to-dateness, yet excelling in an elegance of manner and of disposition, in a kind of personality not to be engrafted, but by its very unself consciousness instinct with the dignity of a Romney portrait. Not that vulgarity was absent. It everywhere jostled with good breeding and correctness, in the mere unimaginativeness of conventionalised people, in the flaunting class-consciousness of the occasion. It everywhere presented itself. Even at times a touch of crudity crept in, of the music-hall, something bizarre, a rather blatant sex-vanity.

The unreality of the scene and its composite glamour were not lost upon Knoyle any more than the stirring movement of the midnight crowd in Piccadilly Circus had been. But did he reflect upon its potentialities, upon the substantial quality beneath these masks of men and women who had pursued the same round as their forefathers for a century or more—and would continue so to do ? The bubble pricked, the bubble of manners and ancestry and fine clothes—— ? But was it a bubble ? . . . What then would the catastrophic act reveal ? A bubble burst, a conscience and a character behind, a mask torn from the face of mere pretence, a fine and noble human spirit, emptiness only—or what ?

Knoyle did not in fact debate these abstruse questions—why should he ? In the brilliance of the June afternoon, in the strong whitish glare, in the crowd and colour and movement, he looked only for one face. In the brilliance of the June afternoon the parasols made a variegated screen, and there was needed no other to hide the thunder-clouds gathering slowly above the Swinley Woods.

§ 2

It was not until after the race for the Gold Cup that he ran into Rosemary Meynell. He had previously met Gina Maryon, marvellously attired in black and gold, tortuously embroidered, and crested with Bird of Paradise feathers. She flashed upon him a " brilliant " glance—which annoyed him—and, not having been previously acquainted with her daylight aspect, he was struck by the bright auburn of her hair in contrast with the violet eyes and the vivid scarlet lips.

" Mr. Knoyle, assist a woman in distress ! My friends avoid me. Even my Harry has left me in the lurch. He went to back a horse . . ."

" I hope you had a good race over the Cup."

" Me—a good race ? Aleppo ! My dear man, I *never* win.

I bet to make money. But the only people who make money are the people who don't try to—and don't need to. Come! Let us find our friends, let us find these base people who have deserted us."

They walked round the paddock, and every other minute Gina stopped to talk to somebody she knew, her tinkling laugh sounding high above the general hum. She talked in a curiously random manner, darting from one subject to another with disconcerting freedom.

"My God, isn't it hot? Don't you long to take *all* your clothes off? Why are the most energetic days of the year *always* the hottest? And why isn't it fashionable to wear bathing dresses at Ascot?"

"Some people wouldn't be much cooler if they did," he answered. A diaphanous frock had just passed. He was wondering why Gina had selected *him* to accompany her on her quest.

Then—it was singular—they came upon Rosemary, talking to a pale-faced young man who wore a bow-tie, a hat with a curly brim, and was altogether rather untidy. Gina cried out:

"The guilty couple! Harry—where have you been? I waited for you—and no you. If there is anything more inconstant than a modern husband, it's a young man at a race meeting."

"My apologies, dear friend." He bowed and turned deprecatingly to Rosemary. "I found Lady Rosemary—in distress. We made a little bet together. We returned to the stand. We looked for you. You were gone—like a beau-ti-ful butterfly."

Rosemary and Adrian had exchanged no greeting, but a new thing had crept into their faces, into their whole demeanour. Gina's violet eyes watched them from under half-closed lids, though they did not know it.

Adrian thereupon introduced Rosemary to Gina, the two

girls looking at each other with frank interest—the one already a fixed star in the social firmament, the other as yet a planet of uncertain magnitude. In her grey muslin frock and hat, Rosemary (thought Adrian) looked like a fragile piece of Dresden china. The contrast between the two couples was indeed unmistakable, the one representing something actual and mature, the other, Youth on the threshold of Experience.

Then the saddling-bell rang and Gina announced that she wanted to go and see the race for the St. James's Palace Stakes. Adrian, turning to Rosemary, said:

" What about tea—and strawberries ? "

So together they strolled across the course, through the gipsies, through the scrambling children who begged for pennies, the " outside " bookmakers, the ice-cream and sherbet vendors, the cocoanut-shy men, until they found refuge in a club marquee comparatively cool and yet not too full of people.

Their world had become interesting again.

§ 3

" Who's that friend of Gina Maryon's you were talking to ? " he inquired, after he had called for strawberries-and-cream and iced coffee. " I met him at that dance of hers the other night, and for the life of me I can't remember the blighter's name."

" That ? Oh, that's a man called Upton. He's private secretary to somebody in the Home Office—or some sort of office. He's quite too appallingly clever, and also rich, and also—oh ! well, funny."

" Where did you meet him ? "

" In the street, I think—no, I mean Mrs. Clinton's tea-party, or somewhere. He's a poet."

" I should think so. He's very much ot a Maryonite, isn't he ? And what did you think of the inimitable Gina ? "

"Oh, attractive, Adrian—very! Different from what I expected, too. I thought all the women had dead-white faces, large liquid eyes, and looked at you for five minutes before they spoke. But, Gina—I should like to meet her again."

"She's like that sometimes, too. It just depends. It depends on the people she's with, the sort of frock she's got on, how she's feeling, and perhaps the kind of light she's standing in."

Rosemary laughed.

"I'd like to meet her again, though. I like meeting funny sorts of people—different sorts."

"Do you call me a funny sort of person—or a different sort?"

"Oh! you? You're neither. You're just—you."

"A fixture?"

"Just so, sir."

"A bit of furniture."

"That's it."

"A chiffonier—or a bedstead?"

"I dunno . . . something pretty substantial, I should think."

"Not a brand-new thing from Maple's, all rawness and shine, but a good, solid, handsome, worthy bit of mahogany— eh? Something you'd like to have about the home and keep by you—to last?"

"Yes, I like something that'll last—that won't break if you sit on it or knock up against it or kick it—something that'll go on for ever. And I'm rather violent sometimes, you know."

They watched each other's eyes, forgetting all about the strawberries.

"You get tired of things and want to scrap 'em, eh?"

"Perhaps," she answered briefly. "Not old friends, though."

"But you like constantly meeting new people—odd people? I wonder where you get that from."

" I like being amused. . . . And then I like having—one—or two—pals I can come back to. That's me. That's Rosemary."

Under the table her small foot was held prisoner between his big ones. And in the subdued light of the tent she appeared puzzling, evasive, childlike, and in a sense unreal. But he was perfectly clear now as to what she meant to him.

They did not speak for several moments.

" We must make up our minds," he said suddenly.

" *Apropos* of what ? "

" That week-end . . ."

" But you've made up your mind—you've accepted."

" I shall get out of it then—unless you go."

" I don't think we shall go. Mamma's let us in for the Doncasters' yacht—practically."

She said this teasingly.

" You leave London next week ? "

" Alas ! yes."

" Then we shan't see each other again till—God knows when ? " There was an injured note in his voice.

" I suppose not," she answered with the politest show of regret.

" You've definitely decided against going to Arden ? "

She detected chagrin—she smiled.

" Well, I couldn't possibly decide without consulting mamma, you know . . ."

" Oh—mamma ! " he groaned.

A cool, quiet voice intervened behind them.

" What are you two being so earnest about ? " It was Faith Daventry.

" Oh ! the racing—the heat—the pretty people—never you mind ! " Rosemary answered flippantly. " Come and sit down, both of you. Make yourselves at home."

" Well, there's a storm coming," said Faith ; " we'd better——"

"They don't seem to care about strawberries-and-cream, do they?" remarked Eric. "Shall we eat theirs for them, Faith?"

"Come on, Rosemary—eat!" urged Adrian. "Let 'em order their own."

The four spent a merry half-hour, dallying with their strawberries and with each other. And Eric, who was an adept at such performances, showed them a new trick whereby you dip a strawberry in cream and drop it neatly into your mouth minus the stalk. Rosemary declared it was rude and Faith told him to behave himself.

When they rose to go Faith said:

"By the way, Rosemary, *are* you and Lady Cranford coming down to Arden for August Bank Holiday, or are you not? Mother—at least mother's me—simply *demands* an answer. Eric's coming, Mr. Knoyle's coming, we're all coming, so chuck windy old Cowes and come too."

There was a momentary silence, broken by Eric.

"Give the poor gal a minute to think. She wants to say no and doesn't know how to!"

"Don't be a fool, Eric!"

Rosemary's eyes challenged Adrian's, and he read mockery in them.

"Thank you very much, Faith." The words almost slid from her lips. "I think . . . yes."

Adrian desired to embrace her.

At this moment the thunderstorm broke. Great drops of rain fell on the roof of the marquee, making a queer drumming sound, while sheets of blue and green lightning were succeeded by peal after peal of thunder that sounded like batteries of guns.

The storm had an oddly depressing effect upon their spirits, and when, a quarter of an hour later, they emerged from the tent, it was a somewhat subdued party that travelled back to London.

CHAPTER IV

Alarms and Excursions

§ 1

THE London summer as recognised by civilised society had
drawn to a glorious close when Friday, July 31st, found Adrian
packing a suit-case and kit-bag for his visit to Arden. As
usual he found the greatest difficulty in compressing within
the prescribed space articles of equipment and attire appropriate
to every conceivable situation. He was very particular. He
was particular about taking two, if not three, of everything.
In fact he could hardly imagine a disaster more appalling than
to arrive at a house-party minus any essential, be it a lawn
tennis-racquet or a pearl stud.

Lady Knoyle attempted to assist in these proceedings,
knocking tentatively at his bedroom door and calling out in
gentle tones :

" Can I help, darling ? Is there anything I can do ? Don't
forget your white silk handkerchiefs again ! "

To which her son would reply :

" No, mother, it's all right. *Please* don't bother."

Once Lady Knoyle did penetrate into the sacred chamber
with a bottle of eau-de-Cologne. " I just brought this, darling."
She had a passion for making her son small gifts whenever he
went away and for however short a time.

Every few minutes Sir Charles' voice would be heard from
below :

" Now then, my boy, hurry up ! Your cab's at the door.
What the devil are you doing ? "

Sir Charles always prowled in the hall when his son went

away. He enjoyed girding at the servants, keeping his boy "up to the mark" and "waking things up" generally. He was a white-haired, spirited old gentleman.

"Silly young ass! What do you want to run it so fine for? Come! Bustle along! Put the suit-case in first, Albert! I suppose you've left half-a-dozen things behind as it is."

"Oh! it's all right, father. There's plenty of time." His fond parents never could remember that he was'nt a boy going back to school.

"Darling!" crooned Lady Knoyle, embracing him. "Take care of yourself and have a good time! You'll be passing through again on Tuesday, won't you? Give my love to dear Mary Arden, and Edward too, if he remembers me; and *many* messages to Helena Cranford!"

At last he was off, thrilled at the prospect that lay before him. Nobody shared his secret. Rosemary really was going to be there—was already there, in fact, for she and Lady Cranford had come on from another visit—and he had not seen her for a month. What an endless month, and how bereft of—vitality! They had only exchanged letters—long ones. In the interval he had got to know Faith Daventry, Rosemary's particular friend, so well that she had become a common possession almost between himself and Eric. Everything, in fact, promised a glorious week-end.

At the Waterloo bookstall (by assignation) he met Sinclair, who had already secured opposite corners in a crowded carriage, and who in a straw hat and flannel suit looked almost indecently cool, exhaling a scent of eau-de-Cologne and fresh soap.

"I got her," said the latter.

Adrian, whose mind at the moment was adjusted to one individual only, thought he meant Rosemary.

"What! You've seen her——?"

"Yes. Last night. The one with the long legs."

When he realised that these cryptic remarks referred merely to one of his friend's "amusements," he felt—well, injured.

" In God's name, who——? "

" Why, Joyce! Little Joyce."

" Not that awful wench in the second row ? . . . Great heavens ! "

" Of course. Haven't I waited long enough ? I took her to the Savoy Grill——"

" Oh, dry up ! I know all about it. Who's going to be at this party besides Rosemary and Mamma Cranford ? Have you seen anybody ? "

Eric laughed.

" Only a certain Orde whom I know slightly. That's the chap. He's going."

A tall, dark, finely-built man in a grey suit and straw hat passed them and nodded. He was followed by a servant carrying various articles of luggage. Adrian recognised him as the individual to whom he had seen Eric talking at the Rodriguez' ball and whose face had attracted him. It was a good-looking and a strong face.

They took their seats. Whistles blew. Guards and porters began to shout. Ladies embraced. The engine gave a shrill scream. Newsboys yelled their loudest. At this exciting moment—inseparable even from the briefest journey—a whirl-wind apparition projected itself into their vision, to the amazement of the onlookers and the amusement of the friends.

The apparition consisted of Gina Maryon in a red, green, and black striped garment that scintillated like an insect's body, without a hat but with green gauze streaming from her brilliant hair—a jewel-box in one hand, a Pekinese dog on the other arm—Gina Maryon, laughing, panting and crying out, " Come on ! Come on ! Run, run ! We'll miss it ! Here you are—no you aren't, it's full up. Hold the dog ; give me the coat. Run for your life, Mathilde ! Oh, Harry, I shall die ! " A French maid in a hobble-skirt cannot as a rule run—even for her life. Mathilde was no exception.

Harry, the pale-faced young man, pursued resentfully. The rear was brought up by three porters loaded with queer little cases, hampers, satchels, baskets, cardboard-boxes—running their very hardest. Eric whistled. Adrian muttered " She would ! " and thought to himself, " Can *she* be bound for Arden ? "

As the train moved off, it seemed that the whole party, porters and all, precipitated itself into a carriage.

§ 2

Adrian rarely read a newspaper. But in the train there is seldom anything better to do. And before they reached Woking, this sunny 31st of July, he had begun to realise that something (rather odd) was happening in the world.

He drew his friend's attention to the matter.

Something about a war. . . .

In fact, the *Daily Mail* was full of the new idea. " Oh ! Ireland, I suppose," growled Sinclair. Sinclair was sick of Ireland. Old men in arm-chairs had been mumbling of nothing else for months. Moreover, he was tired, and in the suffocating heat simply wanted to go to sleep.

" No, not Ireland. WAR—a real one."

" Yes, the blasted civil war we've been hearing about for years. I wish all politicians would go and drown themselves. They're more unreliable than women, and not half so amusing."

" Wake up, you fool. I tell you it's *not* Ireland. It's a *real war*. My dear chap, do you never take any interest in anything except chorus-girls and cocktails ? Oh ! sit up, do, and show a bit of intelligence about the thing ! We're going to fight the Germans, I tell you."

But his friend had already fallen asleep.

Adrian for his part was now very much awake. Why, the

newspapers were full of it! *The Times* had staring headlines on its main news page:

> "FATE OF EUROPE IN THE BALANCE.
> "CAN WAR BE AVERTED?"

And *The Times* at least could not lie!

But why did the newspapers spring this sort of thing upon one? How was it he hadn't heard of this business before? Then he remembered Sir Charles reading an extract from some leading article two or three weeks earlier—something about the consequences of an Austrian Archduke being murdered (though how in heaven's name they could affect his papa passed the young man's comprehension); something, too, about the Balkans being in a ferment, and the possibility of another Balkan war. But what did that signify? It had happened at breakfast, and Sir Charles was always reading extracts from the newspaper at breakfast, uttering false predictions on the strength of them—had done so for years. And it wasn't the extract that had impressed itself upon Adrian's memory, but the fact that he had been down to breakfast on the occasion. What the "old man" might be driving at he didn't know or care at the time—probably some hare that had been started at the Travellers'.

A much more serious war had intervened when the "old man" found his coffee cold. "Ring the bell, Adrian! Shout for that damned Albert!" The Balkans were soon forgotten.

But now (rather impudently) the Balkans had reappeared. They even drove a face, a voice, a dream, a personality from his mind for nearly five minutes!

And Russia, Germany, Austria, France—England were involved. Well, it was a change from Ireland, anyway. But what was at the bottom of it? That was the sort of safe general question you asked your neighbour. There must be something afoot—in spite of the *Daily Mail*. He lit a cigarette. That was a non-committal act. He read a few lines of the leader . . . looked up and thought of waking his friend, but the friend was sleeping off a dissipated summer—and Adrian knew better.

Two men in the carriage began to talk, bearded, prosperous-looking men who would no doubt be well up in this thing. "City men," to use the vulgar phrase. . . . Anyway, it was less trouble to listen to their conversation than to try and puzzle out the contents of a leading article.

"I'm hanged if I can see how we're to keep out of it," one was saying. "Germany seems bent on war. Austria's the tool of Germany. I fail to see how a rupture with Russia can be prevented if this mobilisation report is true. Then France is bound to come in. And if France comes in, even Asquith can't keep us out of it for long. To put it on the lowest ground, we can't *afford* to let France or Belgium be smashed. If either is involved we ought to declare war at once."

"There's just about one chance in a thousand," agreed the other. "The Conference proposal seems to have failed. Grey may put somebody up in the House on Monday to rattle the sabre and trumpet the Big Fleet. It worked at Agadir. There's a chance in a thousand "—he leaned forward, speaking slowly and beating out his words on the other man's knee—" there's a chance in a thousand that it might work this time. But only about one chance. That's my opinion. Personally, I think the fat's in the fire. It seems to me too late for any of them to draw back now."

§ 3

The express drew up at Basingstoke. They changed and, feeling unequal to Miss Maryon (who took some time to extricate herself, dog, and packages), hastened to seat themselves in the forefront of a local train that stood waiting at the opposite platform.

Eric Sinclair glanced at the *Tatler* and *Sketch*, mumbled something, and fell asleep again. Adrian, impressed by the conversation he had just heard, felt no longer in a mood to talk. His thoughts of Rosemary and of all that this week-end implied to them both were momentarily obscured by the apparition of an Event.

As the train rattled along the branch line he gazed out of window at the pleasantly undulating Hampshire country-side. He saw a land of tossing woodland and hedgerow, of long winding valleys, leaf-tufted copses and nestling villages, of wide distances fading towards hill and sea. The harvest was being carried, the deep gold of the fields was tinted by the deeper gold of the setting sun. . . . Above the jolt and rattle of the train there rose a shrill laugh and a snatch of some song. It was Gina Maryon's laugh and Gina Maryon's song. At that moment he hated the girl. She embodied his very enemy at that moment. He hated her aggressive modernity, her pose, her complete incapacity for repose, her violet eyes, her everlasting fluttering about the fringes of life, her sex-dallying, her " poetry," her " art," her " originality," her—" wonderfulness."

That laugh—how it jarred against the reflective landscape, these immemorial, elemental things—the garnering of fruit of sun and earth !

Abruptly, inconsequently he thought of his home. He thought of his home that lay fifty miles away at the foot of the Plain, with a sharp, inexplicable longing, a curious, half-melancholy yearning which used often to take him unawares, but which he had not known for months now or even years. Perhaps he, too, was caught up already in this high-power dynamo of existence ! . . . Stane Deverill ! It was his birth-place. There in the shadow of the Three Hills he had spent his earliest and many of his happiest days. He thought of it as he remembered it—its walled gardens, its courtyard wherein sunlight lingered upon mossy damp, through hours of which an archaic sun-dial and chiming stable clock alone took count ; of the westward-looking terrace where reigned a changeless order of flowers and scents and birds ; of the swelling downs behind where lay in barrows-deep mysteries of his boyhood's recollection.

Strangers dwelt there now. . . .

The train pulled up with a jerk, and the mood was gone— a mere shade across his reflections. Eric awoke and swore. They tumbled out upon the wayside platform. They fell into the arms of Miss Maryon.

" You unsociable couple ! You don't mean to say you've travelled all the way from London in the same train ? " She threw a brilliant glance at each of them. " Make good your lack of manners by holding the dog and the book. I'll stand over Mathilde and the baggage. "

Upton joined them and made a sort of bow. He and Eric were introduced. A footman appeared and led the way to a car which stood purring in the station-yard. Nobody had noticed the tall, good-looking individual who now appeared smoking a cigarette, attended by his servant bearing the suit-case and the tennis-racquet. He flourished his hat and inquired whether they were going by chance to Arden Park. Eric introduced him as " Captain Orde."

In the car Gina insisted on having a young man on each side of her ; and this privilege fell to Adrian and Upton. Every time they turned a corner she leant against one or the other, and once, when the car pulled up short behind a harvest wagon, her hand pressed Adrian's—he thought— unnecessarily.

She talked. She talked every moment of the way to Arden, interrupted only by polite monosyllables and by Upton's occasional repartee.

" What sort of welcome shall I get ? You see, I've not been invited ; I've invited myself. And, what's more, I've invited this young man, who doesn't know a soul.

But he always travels with me—don't you, Harry ?—he carries the dog and the book. (And mind you don't let that animal commit suicide out of window, Harry !) . . . Well, the fact is we were going to the Gerard Romanes for the week-end, Harry and me (*sic*)—it was all arranged weeks ago—and then that preposterous old woman, Mrs. Christopher Romane, Venetia's mother-in-law, thought fit to expire suddenly, thereby annihilating what would have been an amusing party. Not that one can regret it in the present charming company, of course ! But it was tactless, to say the least. Well, I immediately wired to Edward Arden—who, by the way, is the only hospitable cousin I've ever had—and announced my arrival (Harry in hand) for this very hour."

The implication of these remarks, addressed mainly to Adrian, was that Miss Maryon was patronising a society to which she did not profess to belong. " Harry " was presumably included on her side of the implication. The stranger, Orde, said nothing, but his dark face, with its crisp little moustache—he looked about thirty-five—wore a faintly sardonic smile.

§ 4

They flashed through iron gates, and some distance further on came in sight of a long, low, grey stone house representing an eighteenth-century style of architecture very frequently met with in this part of England. It stood on a slight rise amid flower gardens and shrubberies, on the reverse side of which shady lawns sloped down to a large lake, wooded to the edge, which wound away, narrowing into the distances of the Park. As they drew near and passed through secondary iron gates into the drive leading up to the house they perceived that a cricket match was in progress. White figures could be seen against the green grass, and beneath a group of shady chestnuts was gathered a group of people watching the game. Eric exclaimed "Help! We're not expected to play cricket, are we?" Adrian's eyes were only concerned to single out one figure in the group; and though they failed in this, he became keenly aware of the serene and spacious beauty of the scene, of the soft greens and greying brackens in the distance, of the placid lake and a few browsing deer, and of the light of the westering sun that gilded the tops of elms, beeches, and oaks.

Immediately the car stopped he heard shrill cries of water-fowl coming from the direction of the lake.

The butler proposed to lead them forthwith to the cricket-field where, he said, the company was assembled at tea. Lord Arden, in grey flannels and a panama hat, met them half-way across the lawn. He was a short, square, middle-aged man with a heavy fair moustache, merry blue eyes—his daughter's—and a countenance of mulberry hue. His manner was cordial to the point of heartiness.

"Delighted to see you all!" He led them across to the tea-table. "And have any of you brought an evening paper? We were almost afraid these tremendous events might have upset the trains."

Adrian wondered what he meant.

"It's an age since we met, Edward," cried Gina, taking his arm. "You're grey-haired and respectable, otherwise not changed."

At this moment Adrian espied Rosemary, who was sitting at an angle to their approach. There was a general uprising. She gave him the faintest of smiles, the carmine warmed in her cheeks—it was enough.

Gina Maryon embraced Lady Arden, exclaiming, "My dear!" in a peculiar, emphatic tone of voice as if she was announcing some mysterious but conclusive fact. Faith she addressed as "darling" in the manner of an actress uttering the last word of a melodrama. Lady Arden with an indefinite gesture said , " You all know each other, don't you ? " But they didn't, so Faith repeated their names.

" Sir Walter and Lady Freeman—Miss Ingleby—Mr. Heathcote."

Adrian heard them vaguely and without interest. For him there was only one person present.

Lady Cranford greeted him with studied affability and asked after his mother as though bestowing a minor honour upon the family. She was a tall, handsome woman with white hair and very brilliant dark eyes, the combination making her conspicuous in any gathering. Her reputation as *confidante* of various powerful constellations lent her personality a distinction which her unbending manner had made up its mind to support. Her period was Victorian, but now and then she made the mistake of being up-to-date.

Mr. Ralph Heathcote had bows and smiles for everybody. He was dressy and elderly, with a beautifully-brushed moustache. The paragraphists called him a " society man "—a description which he did not in the least resent when his friends said it meant oiling the wheels of tea-parties. However, he knew—more or less—everybody worth knowing ; ladies (above the age of forty-five) were very partial to his company. For the rest he was an authority on Crown Derby, never revoked at bridge, and knew Debrett better than his own soul.

Miss Ingleby, a robin-like person, hovered in the background, coping with the Arden children, who shrieked with laughter and wept bitterly with versatility.

And what were the Freemans doing there ? They seemed a trifle incongruous. But no, Sir Walter was a rising Unionist, bound to rise, people said, because you couldn't sit on him ; and Arden dabbled in politics. Sir Walter was a successful business man from the Midlands, and he was large and corpulent, with big, strong features and a bald head. Financially he was useful to the leaders of his party, but they liked to feel he was some distance behind them. And Lady Freeman ? She was the kind of woman every self-made man takes to his bosom. Adrian thought her vulgarly handsome with her bold, straight features, her large pearl ear-rings, and her down-to-date clothes, which might have come from Paris or New York, but were more appropriate to either than to Arden Park. Where Sir Walter went Lady Freeman went as a matter of course. As a joke she was so carefully cultivated that she never knew it.

Arden plunged hot-headedly with Orde and Sir Walter into the question of war—to be or not to be. The former was evidently an old friend. The latter had an echo of the House of Commons in his voice and the same institution stamped alike on his manner and his clothes. The ladies sat round in a suitably awed suspense, except Lady Cranford, who occasionally interjected remarks in the form of questions.

Meanwhile the cricket match went on merrily, and the strong man with the one pad—the village grocer, Miss Daventry informed the company—was bowled out by the policeman from the next village in blue serge trousers and white boots. The "young people" (as Mr. Heathcote liked to call them), sitting in a small circle apart, took no interest in the war talk, having heard the same sort of thing from their elders times out of number before—and it never came to anything. Ireland, for instance. . . .

"Did any of you creatures go to the Warringtons' ? " demanded Faith.

"No," replied Rosemary, "we were away. Mamma thought sea-air would improve her *coiffure*."

"I went," said Eric. "It was brilliant, but dreadfully dull."

"Look at Heathcote ! " whispered Rosemary maliciously. "He's been telling Miss What's-her-name that mamma was a friend of the late king and a daughter of dear old Lord Laverstock—who died. He loves mamma—especially when she treats

him like a footman. Why the devil doesn't he call her ' m'lady '
and have done with it ! "

They all laughed.

" Poor old boy," said Faith. " It doesn't matter. They
get like that sometimes. . . ."

" ' Poor ! '—not a bit. He likes it," her friend retorted.
" Whenever she's particularly rude to him he turns round
and tells somebody what a regular *grande dame* she is."

" Old-fashioned manners ! " murmured Eric.

They laughed again, except Adrian, who was lost in the
complete suitability of his friend's saffron-coloured frock and
coarse-straw hat of cunning shape. He was watching the
constantly changing expressions on her face while she talked
—by turns naive and childish, sparkling and *insouciante*,
puzzling, with a kitten's playful uncertainty. Once or twice,
glancing up, he found Faith's eyes bent upon him ; she had
so looked at him before in the course of their acquaintance,
always averting her gaze without self-consciousness and without
haste.

His serious mood was quite a thing of the past. It
had been shattered by Gina in the motor. It had vanished
completely the moment he caught sight of Rosemary.

Eric was doing something elaborate — nobody quite
knew what—with Faith's necklace of green jade which she
had been induced to part with. Harold Upton, a little aloof,
was awaiting his opportunity to edge across and talk to Gina
about Life.

It was a pleasant hour. A cock-pheasant crowed from
surrounding woods ; they could hear the shrill whistle of a
gamekeeper as he called up his young birds for the evening
feed ; they could hear a man's voice calling cows.

Play ended. The match was won and lost. Stumps were
drawn. The players walked in amid hand-clapping.

Lady Arden, breaking in upon the political discussion, said,
" Well, I suppose it's time to dress."

Lady Cranford said, "What a divine evening!"

Miss Ingleby said, "Yes, it's dreadful to think they'll soon be shortening, though."

Gina Maryon said, "Everything looks like Wilson Steer."

But already the shadows were closing round.

CHAPTER V

The House of Arden

§ 1

" Post-impressionism," remarked Gina Maryon at dinner, " is the truest form of art because it depicts you or me at the moment of tensest expression—at a crisis. I mean at the moment when ' all is discovered,' or war is declared, or something's gone wrong in the kitchen. . . . It brings into a person's face a person's soul. What do you think, Edward ? "

" My dear cousin "—Lord Arden looked round apprehensively, trusting that the servants were out of the room— " your art, like your conversation, is always beyond me. You not only speak of things I don't understand, but, what is more ill-bred, you speak of them in parables. What do I think about post-impressionism ? What do I know of it ? . . . Only that *le bon Dieu* has given me a countenance of normal dimensions, and that I'm content with it, and that you want to re-fashion it as a cube or a lozenge or a dot or a dash—or something it isn't. You want to depict it at a ' moment of crisis '—take me at a disadvantage—seize upon my suffering physiognomy when Mary and I are going over the house-books, for instance, and make it a thing out of the Chamber of Horrors. Can you expect an elderly nobleman to submit to a modern idiosyncracy.? "

" But people are so much more *interesting* in a crisis, my dear Eddie ! "

" That's an idea for an artist, eh ? " put in Upton, who was sitting next to Gina. " The man who specialised in painting every circumstance and kind and form of domestic crisis——"

"From 'The Fall'——" interrupted Gina.

"To 'The Confession,'" continued Upton, "would make his fortune. The middle-classes love 'scenes.' There is nothing the British middle-class enjoys so much as seeing its loftiest passions depicted in bad paint."

Arden leant back and laughed with his head on one side.

The four young people in the centre were keeping up a lively flow across the table, mainly around the substantial figures of Mrs. Rivington and the Misses Kenelm.

"They always remind me of a hen and two chickens," said Rosemary.

"Why not ducklings ? " suggested Eric.

"They're very nice in their way, though," protested Faith, "only a bit on the heavy side, like many 'nice' people."

"Say 'good-natured,' Faith," contributed Adrian.

"Or 'worthy,'" from Eric.

"It's the prerogative of all 'nice people' to be one or the other you know," said Adrian. "It lets 'em down lightly—and doesn't mean anything."

"Don't be clever, young man.!"

"Not clever, only young," corrected Rosemary.

Adrian smiled.

"Mrs. Rivington and Co. will be at Sheringham in full force," said Faith. "That I know for certain."

"Oh, joy ! " commented Eric. "I hope you'll run straight into the bosom of them. When do you go ? "

"We've got the house from the fifteenth. Rosie, when are you coming ? "

"As soon as I can drag mamma away from Aunt Kitty's, I suppose. What fun it will be, won't it ? I shan't wear clothes, only bits of things. I hope our lodging is close to your mansion."

"Our public-house overlooks the golf-links. Eric—Adrian

—can't you join the merry party ? We can't put you up because there won't be room—unless you sleep with the children."

"Mixed bathing, golf, tennis, and Us," said Rosemary.
"What more do you want ? "

The young men thrilled at the prospect.

"It shall be managed," they said jointly.

"Even if we have to sleep with Mrs. R.," added Eric.

"Or toss for beds with the Miss——"

"Tush ! " said Faith.

It was an animated scene in the Arden dining-room, with
its panelled white walls and shaded electric lights gently
illuminating portraits of bygone Daventrys by Lawrence,
Raeburn, and Sir Joshua Reynolds. The table, lighted by
candles in silver candelabra, appeared as an illuminated ellipse
in the centre of the room, the rest of it being in shadow.
The menservants flitted silently to and fro across the thick
carpet. All the windows were open, and the scent of flowers,
of dew, of the country sleeping after a day of great heat crept
into the room. . . .

Lady Freeman was discussing with Mr. Heathcote the
subject of a Royal marriage. In view of the fact that the
eldest scion of the blood royal had barely reached the age
of twenty, the matter might not have appeared pressing—
but it did to Lady Freeman. And they discussed—with an
avidity which Eric at the other end described as indecent—
first one party, then another, first this Princess of the Blood,
then that. They damned Italy on religious grounds ; they
barely skimmed the house of Karageorgevitch of Serbia (in their
anxiety to please), they even went so far as to discuss the chances
of certain humble British subjects. A German lady they did not
want (but feared). A Scandinavian princess was in the running,
could a suitable one be found. Finally they decided (con-
ditionally) on the House of Romanoff.

Hardly anybody noticed Miss Ingleby, who had been carrying
on a mouse-like conversation with Captain Orde.

"I am a shamefully idle and useless person," she was saying fiercely. "I have a tiny house at Windsor, and beyond a little local organisation work for the Girls' Friendly I do *nothing* that is useful. I have, of course, my garden and my sketching—but what are these ? What *can* a woman do —that is, of use—nowadays ? The position of women like myself in England is deplorable, Captain Orde. We have no vocation. We are useless."

Orde politely murmured a flat denial.

"The world could not get along for half-an-hour without you," he contended. "Men are really very helpless creatures, you know, Miss Ingleby—at any rate, the moment they become helpless women have to run the show, soothe the fevered brow, and make things comfortable. That's the one thing of all others every man is a hopeless duffer at—making himself comfortable."

"But how often do women—in our class of life—get this opportunity ? " Miss Ingleby pursued. "What is our sphere —our *raison d'être ?* " She responded readily to Orde's quiet and attentive manner, though here, indeed, he was somewhat out of his depth. With Miss Ingleby it was a sort of obsession that she was of no use to anyone, never had been, and never would be. All her life—she was about forty—she had never done a single thing—that mattered. Yet it was curious that if any one of her innumerable friends—Lady Arden, for instance—had been consulted, it would have transpired that the little lady spent her life playing nurse to their children, playing doctor to their parrots or their dogs, playing mentor to their cooks—that in the houses where she stayed she could never stay quite long enough.

Still she persisted in her mania—women such as she had no vocation.

At the far end of the table Lady Cranford sat in full-dress debate with Sir Walter Freeman on the Irish question. She was a woman with a firm grasp of politics and affairs ; and she had a forceful sympathy and attraction for intelligent men. Lady Arden, as it were, browsed on the discussion, interjecting a large phrase or two here and there. After surveying the chances of war and after Lady Cranford—who had once stayed at Ischl—had related one or two stock stories of Francis Ferdinand's *amour propre*, the talk had drifted back to the subject of the Buckingham Palace Conference.

"Ireland," Sir Walter laid down, "is one of the tragedies of the human race. Her past is a tragedy, her present is a tragedy, her future can be but the culmination of a tragedy. Even her leaders, you see, her potential kings and presidents, are tragic figures, makers of tragedy. Parnell, O'Donovan Rossa, Devoy! She has attained the anti-climax of a nation or of a human being—she has no future, only a past. I say 'no future.' She is a dwindling race, a played-out race, a member of the sisterhood of nations who never acquired the art of government, and has even lost the gift of common-sense. She is an unbalanced aristocrat with a bee in her bonnet."

"What a pessimist!" sighed Lady Cranford. "Possibly I know the Irish better than you do, Sir Walter. I spent much of my early life in Ireland. George Wyndham's Land Act gave them hope. Sir Horace Plunket's co-operative agricultural scheme has given them opportunity, method. Now they want a stimulus, a *raison d'être*. They want to feel that the future of their own country lies in their own hands—and that it's a future of their own shaping. They want to feel that they are working for themselves and the generations of Irishmen to come—not for Englishmen with Irish names or Irishmen with Scotch names, who merely calculate how much they can get out of the peasantry and how little they can live amongst them. You say they haven't a future. I say, *give* them a future."

"Forgive me, Lady Cranford—but you're confusing the local and the national issue—the Land Question and the National Question——"

§ 2

At this point Lady Arden rose, and all the ladies with her. Mr. Heathcote insisted on running to the telephone to try and obtain the latest London news from his club. He had been very tiresome in this respect all the evening, repeatedly fussing off, saying he had told a friend—who was, or was the friend of, such and such an important person, et cetera and so forth —that he would ring up for news at such and such a time. He presently came back and announced, with a poor attempt at nonchalance, that, according to London, war had already been declared between Germany and Russia and that a French ultimatum was only a question of hours.

There was no doubt about the sensation produced. All drew their chairs together, Arden, very flushed, began talking rapidly. Freeman poured himself out another glass of port with a shaking hand. Heathcote himself could not sit still for excitement. Upton's face lost some of its pallid cynicism. Even Adrian and Eric paused in a conversation of their own and looked along the table. Only Orde continued puffing immovably at a cigarette.

"By Jove, you know!" exclaimed Arden. "I've been expecting this for years, but now it's come one can't realise it . . . one can't realise it. If all this is true we're bound to be drawn into the damned thing, and then—oh! well, one can't think of it. . . . Cyril—send the port round. Do you think we're prepared, my dear chap—or what ?"

Orde took time to consider.

"We-ell," he said very deliberately, "I suppose we could put across half-a-dozen divisions pretty quickly—within a fortnight, say. They're good troops, of course, but whether they can make much difference where millions are concerned I shouldn't like to say. Personally I've always thought that with our little army we should only begin to make ourselves felt on land when the whole thing was practically over."

My dear Cyril, I entirely agree with you. That's what I've always said. I always said Roberts was the only man in the country who knew what he was talking about. If we'd had the sense to adopt national service, as we ought to have done years ago, we should now be able to throw a large Territorial force across to France as well as the whole of the regular army, and hold the fort with half-trained troops. Instead we're—impotent. What do you say, Freeman ? "

" If Heathcote's news is true, and in any case war seems practically inevitable, I think we shall have to rely almost entirely on the Navy as our fighting arm. Of course, we shall be dragged in sooner or later if France is, but, mark my words, it won't last long. Modern war will be terrible—too terrible to endure. Don't you agree, Orde ? "

" I give it six months."

" And who do you think will win ? "

" It'll be a draw. They'll fight themselves to a standstill."

Upton, who was in the Home Office, observed that if the situation were developed as far as announced, he was surprised general mobilisation had not been ordered and that he himself had been allowed to leave London.

" It may be going out now."

So the talk went on, the news completely preoccupying the minds of the older men.

Not so the two youngest of the party, who, after listening for a while as in duty bound had resumed their own conversation. This was concerned with the prospect lately dangled before them by Faith. How could it be realised ? Could they " cadge " an invitation to stay with some of their numerous friends who repaired to Sheringham in August and September ? The name of the worthy, good-natured (and useful) Mrs. Rivington had suggested itself. She gave large parties every year. Of course, the Misses Kenelm would be a trial, but one had to put up with something. The conspirators began to deliberate upon a plan for bringing themselves and their desire before the good lady's notice.

§ 3

The gentlemen sat on late. Ten o'clock had struck when they rose and went out into the hall where, rugs having been removed, Gina Maryon and Rosemary were practising the steps of the *maxixe* to the strains of a gramophone. Miss Ingleby, Orde, and Sir Walter and Lady Freeman immediately went off to the drawing-room to play bridge, Lady Arden consented to play the piano, while Lady Cranford and Mr. Heathcote established themselves on a sofa and gossiped. Arden led Gina off to another sofa, where, to judge by frequent exclamations and shouts of laughter, they were " telling stories "—a pastime Arden delighted in. The indefatigable creature, however, presently relieved Lady Arden at the piano and treated the company to a selection of her favourite ditties, including " 'Arry and 'Arriet," " She hasn't done her hair up yet," and " Who were you with last night ? " Gina prided herself on these rare specimens and rendered them with an accent not unworthy of their titles. Adrian turned over the music ; a sheet fluttered to the floor. Both stooped to pick it up, their fingers meeting and touching —a fraction of a second longer than (to him) seemed necessary.

Lady Cranford enjoyed this form of entertainment as much as anybody, laughed heartily, and broke in unsparingly on Mr. Heathcote's discourse upon whether the first husband of old Lady B. was a Jekyll or a Hyde, also whether the noted affairs of Lord and Lady K. were likely to come into court at last, together with a further true history of the alleged disgraceful connection between young Lord Charlie and Mrs. Fitz.

Then Gina insisted that everybody should sing—everybody,

that is, except Lady Cranford (who declared her singing days were over) and the bridge players. Lady Arden, who had a pleasant, untrained voice, sang the " Requiem," with words by Robert Louis Stevenson, Eric followed with " Snooky Ookums." Faith gave " Songs of Araby," and Mr. Heathcote, in a high, thin tenor " rendered " " Home, Sweet Home " to the accompaniment of suppressed laughter and loud applause. Then it was Rosemary's turn. Both she and Adrian declared that they had never sung a line or a note, but, put to shame or inspired by the Arden champagne, the latter made rough weather with something out of " Our Miss Gibbs." Rosemary was at length persuaded to sing a verse of an Apache song she had picked up in Paris. She stood beside Faith at the piano, the candlelight casting vague shadows upon her face and gown.

> " C'est la valse brune
> Des chevaliers de la lune,
> Que la lumière importune,
> Et qui recherchent un coin noir."

The minor key of the little air suited the slender timbre of her voice. Everybody said the thing was charming ; Adrian for his part was so haunted by its wistful quality that it came back to him in after-years with the power of a presentiment.

Arden brought the concert to a close with " D'ye ken John Peel," which he roared out with great heartiness and his head on one side, insisting upon everyone joining in the chorus.

And so, laughing, they all trooped off to bed.

CHAPTER VI

Incidents

§ 1

THE building at Arden Park was not architecturally remarkable. The exterior was plain, but the interior expressed a degree of elegance and comfort—falling short of luxury—that is seldom found outside your English country house. The hall, with its blackened oak-panelling, great fireplace, comfortable arm-chairs, and red-carpeted staircase mounting broadly from it; the saloon and drawing-room with their red and yellow brocades and flowered chintzes; a few quite fine pictures here, and in the dining-room; a smoking-room peopled with Morlands; a library sombre with shelvesful of books and diamond-paned windows admitting mellowed rays of ecclesiastical light—all these bespoke a cultivated, if not a cultured taste. And Lord and Lady Arden were certainly "cultivated." And Lord and Lady Arden might have been selected from their native county of Hampshire as fairly representative of the dutiful order to which they belonged— Arden, with his rather erratic interests in sport, agriculture, and politics, his disposition towards an uneventful and leisurely existence; Lady Arden, who, amiable and a little aloof, never shirked the duties of her position, opening impartially bazaars, sales of work, and guild entertainments, patronising everything that asked to be patronised, looking at her garden with a correctly amateurish enthusiasm, reading a little, thinking a little, looking out upon the world with a quiet, fastidious and secluded mind. Their daughter, Faith, followed in these footsteps. That it was an ambitionless, aimless, and indolent existence must perhaps be admitted. Arden had to his credit, it is true, nine years' service in the Foot Guards and had been acquitted as co-respondent in a *cause célèbre* before espousing the hand of Lady Mary Wardour and becoming domesticated. But he was not lacking in a sense of duty. He was not lacking in a proper sense of responsibility in the approved sequence of democracy. Once a week (on an average) he went up to the House of Lords when Parliament was sitting; he never spoke. He was subject to manias about things.

§ 2

Adrian Knoyle awoke early on the morning following his arrival and saw from his window the Arden lawns and gardens bathed in dew, the sun peeping through walls of blue-grey mist. Pheasants and peacocks were pecking about the grass and gravel walks, the cries of the foreign water-fowl came from the mist-enshrouded lake. That sound, indeed, had already come to be associated in Adrian's mind with Arden.

But it was to Rosemary that his waking thoughts turned. Was she awake and was she, too, gazing out upon this enchanting prospect? To that she belonged; something of her fragrance, of her beauty and personality, seemed to exhale from it. He frankly resented the fact that he had as yet obtained no private word with her: they had, after all, been in the house only a dozen hours. Would their opportunity come to-day—to-morrow? Lady Cranford was watchful; that she was on the look-out to prevent just such a meeting he felt certain. If the opportunity did not present itself—well, it would have to be created.

Interspersed with these thoughts of Rosemary were side-glances at Gina Maryon. Her active eyes followed him, but with an interest indifferently reciprocated. Faith's eyes, too, followed him: here were clarity, steadfastness—

something maternal almost. Well, she was Eric's friend, and so was he. . . .

He descended to breakfast in a cheerful frame of mind. Of the feminine members of the party only Lady Arden and Miss Ingleby had so far appeared ; of the men, only Sir Walter Freeman, who announced with urbane apologies that a telephone message from London had summoned him to a meeting of his Party in connection with the crisis, but that with Lady Arden's permission he would motor down again the same evening, bringing the latest news.

"Women at breakfast," Eric had once laid down, " are a contradiction in terms. They're out of place—like colours at a funeral. Their bedroom doors ought to be locked till 10 a.m." Rosemary and Faith were, of course, exceptions— and they appeared last ; except Gina, who had her breakfast in bed and might be heard singing in her bath. A little later she shrieked observations from her bedroom window to whomsoever happened to be beneath. Lady Freeman was unforgivably punctual and talked about the weather.

After breakfast there was a rush for the newspapers which lay in the smoking-room ; and it was not until the middle of the morning that the younger members of the party foregathered on the terrace. Faith proposed that they should walk round the garden ; Gina appeared just as they were setting off. Eric was walking with Faith, and Upton had appropriated Rosemary. It fell to Adrian, therefore, to wait for Gina, who, attired in a brief, transparent frock, literally sparkled in the sunlight. This brilliance of sunshine emphasised the peculiar pearly hue of her complexion with its vivid heightenings of colour which, one suspected, were hardly of Nature's doing. She wore no hat. She exhaled scent.

Standing on the threshold of the French window, she made a gesture of admiration.

"How it reminds me of mornings in Florence ! Venetia and I—Venetia Romane has a villa there, you know—used to sit every morning in the Boboli gardens, read poetry, and analyse each other. The dark greens, the formal ilexes and acacias—seraphic, my dear—amazing! But—Mary has taste. Don't you *adore* the place, Mr.—Adrian, I shall call you?"

He assented. They had fallen some distance behind the others. They came presently to a shrubbery in the midst of which a stone pergola supported clustering late roses. Here Gina stopped, saying that, come what might, she would have a creamy tea-rose which depended high overhead—she adored them also. He picked it for her and, as she stood breathing the scent, became aware that her curious violet eyes were watching him, inviting or questioning, above its petals. They were alone, the formal shrubs enclosing them entirely.

Then she held out the rose to him.

"For you—Adrian!" His eyes rose—unwillingly, and as though impelled by some force that was too strong for him— to the level of hers. For a second they stood facing each other, her smiling face upturned in the sunlight. It was a moment of expectation on her part, of diffidence and difficulty on his. . . .

He took the rose and put it in his button-hole.

"Thank you, Gina. Now I must give you one."

He picked another big creamy tea-rose and offered it to her with the most matter-of-fact air he could summon. A look of pique crossed her face—then she smiled. She took the flower without a word and led the way out of the garden singing.

§ 3

There was little at Arden of that polite yet rather futile hanging around, that admiring of pictures which are not admired, that lounging about the hall or the terrace or the billiard-room, making desultory conversation—" waiting for the house-party to begin," as some wit has described it—which characterises gatherings where people do not begin to know each other until they are going away. Everybody did as they liked —literally. Arden himself did not appear till luncheon, having been busy with his agent. Near to the luncheon-hour Adrian and Eric joined Orde under the trees where, with an iced whisky-and-soda at his elbow and his feet cocked up, he was studying the newspapers.

"Well, boys," he said in his deep voice, "looks as if there's goin' to be a war, doesn't it ? "

In point of fact, it was the first time either of them had thought of the war since dinner the previous evening.

Eric said :

"Do you think it's really coming off, though, Orde ? The papers talk an awful lot of rot."

"I do."

"Well, if it does, we shan't necessarily be dragged into it ? " suggested Adrian.

"Shan't we ? I think we shall be. . . . And what's more "—Orde sipped his whisky-and-soda, thoughtfully contemplating the tops of some cedars as though they held the key to the matter—"and what's more, if we *are* dragged in, I think it'll be a question of every able-bodied chap in the country takin' a gun and shootin'—or tryin' to. . . . Let the damned politicians say what they like, in the long run we shall have to back up France and Belgium if they're invaded. Why ? To save our skins, to save our own bloomin' selves from bein' invaded."

Adrian and Eric—who hadn't read the papers—were more respectful than impressed. Captain Orde had a reputation as a big-game hunter ; he was said to be a wonderful shot. Still, they felt they really could not take this war-talk too seriously.

After finishing his whisky-and-soda and further contemplating the tops of the cedars, Orde inquired abruptly :

"Either of you lads ever think of joinin' the Army ? "

"Not this one ! " replied Adrian promptly.

"Yes, I've *thought* about it," said Eric.

"Well, you may want to think about it again, young feller. In fact, if war does break out, you will. And while you're about it you may as well join a good regiment as a rotten one— eh? So "—he produced a cigarette and deliberately lit it— "if the worst—or best—happens, just you write or wire me. I'll see what can be done."

The afternoon was spent lazily and agreeably. The four "young people" went off in a punt; Lady Cranford and Mr. Heathcote continued to propound their own version of "Who's Who" on the lawn; Lady Arden and Miss Ingleby amused themselves by amusing the children, and Gina and Upton announced that they proposed to read each other's poems in the Italian garden—they were producing a book together. Orde went to sleep over *Horse and Hound* in the library. Arden, too, slept.

After tea a tennis four was formed consisting of Faith and Eric on the one side and Rosemary and Adrian on the other. The remainder of the party were content to sit under a shady cedar and look on. Gina said she didn't play and Upton that he couldn't.

"How lovely it all is!" observed Lady Freeman to Arden, who was sitting beside her. "Adrian Knoyle is *such* a nice-looking boy, and Lady Rosemary a *sweet* girl, don't you think? As for your daughter, I think she's a dear. We're already the *greatest* friends."

"Yes. They play well, don't they?" Arden agreed rather drily.

A close struggle was going forward. Rosemary and Adrian won the first two games without much difficulty, but by taking the next two Faith and Eric brought the scores level. The fifth game was prolonged by repeated "deuce" and "vantage," but went in the end to Adrian and Rosemary. It was agreed to play the best out of three; fortune swayed first to this side then that. Adrian and Faith were the steady players on either side, and the lobbing rallies between them provoked applause. Rosemary played with a certain nonchalant and effortless grace, by turns placing the ball unplayably in the far corner of the court and driving it a few inches below the top of the net.

" That girl's got a beautiful style," Orde remarked to Arden. " If she took more trouble, she'd win tournaments."

Eric was the best player of the four, his agility at the net and smart returns eventually winning the set. After a brief pause a men's double was proposed, Adrian and Eric opposing Arden and Orde. Two hard games followed, Orde revealing a powerful service and volleying-power, but owing to his elderly partner's comparative weakness, the younger pair succeeded in bringing the score to two games all. Orde was about to serve for the second time, and stood poised with his racquet raised, when a footman appeared bearing a salver.

Lady Arden called out his name.

He lowered his racquet and dropped the balls he held in his hand.

" A telegram for you."

He met the footman half-way across the court. A hush fell upon the little group while he tore open the orange-tinted envelope and glanced at its contents.

He thought a moment.

" What time is the next train to London ? "

" Seven-fifteen, sir."

No one spoke. Those under the cedar, as by a common impulse, rose from their seats.

" Sorry I shan't be able to finish the set," Orde said.   " This means mobilisation.   If you'll forgive me, I'll go in and change."

" My dear chap——! " protested Arden, suppressed excitement in his voice.   " Surely—you can stay to dinner ? "

" Thanks. I'm afraid not."

A sort of dismay followed Captain Orde's exit from the tennis-court. But it was soon relieved by Lady Freeman :

"Dear nice Captain Orde! What a shame he has to go I do *hope* we shall see something of him in London."

§ 4

Half-an-hour later the whole party was bidding Captain Orde "good-bye." Everybody seemed sensible of the prescience of the occasion—everybody, that is to say, except Orde himself, who appeared in his grey flannel suit, smoking a cigarette and followed by his servant carrying the suit-case and tennis-racquet. A car purred at the foot of the steps.

At this moment Sir Walter Freeman's Rolls-Royce was seen approaching round the bend in the drive.

"What news?" several voices cried as he drove up.

Sir Walter, with evening newspapers bulging out of his pockets, looked important.

"Bad, I'm afraid; the situation could hardly be worse. The German Ambassador is leaving Paris. General mobilisation is ordered in France and Germany. Our own Army and Navy are mobilising. The whole of London is yelling for war. Only the Government wavers."

"Well—I must be off," said Orde.

All stood grouped upon the steps while, hat in hand, he made his farewells.

"Don't forget what I said this morning," were his parting words to Adrian and Eric.

There were hand-wavings, and cries of "Good luck!" Little Miss Ingleby made no secret of a moist eye. Then Captain Orde was borne swiftly away into the lengthening shadows of the park.

*   *   *   *   *

The rest of that evening was spent quietly by the house-party. The conversation at dinner was all of the great events now indisputably developing. Even the younger members appeared serious, even Miss Maryon curbed her tongue. Arden, Sir Walter, and Mr. Heathcote embarked on a long discussion which hinged upon whether Mr. Asquith would be equal to backing up France. Arden said it was a point of honour; Mr. Heathcote gravely doubted (from rather special information received); Sir Walter opined that pressure of events would decide the matter for us, if not at once, at any rate very soon. Sir Edward Grey would make our position clear in the House of Commons on Monday. If Germany invaded France through Belgium—and it appeared likely— we *must* come in. To put it at the lowest, it was our interest to support France (and Belgium) with every man and with every gun we could command; and the sooner Grey made it unequivocally clear that we should do so if France were attacked or Belgium invaded, in his (Sir Walter's) opinion the better. Germany was slowly but surely revealing her hand—she had done so unmistakably in refusing the Foreign Secretary's proposal of a Conference—and it was seen to be the hand of a *provocateur*. He, for his part, considered that the affair was now practically beyond the control of the statesmen—certainly beyond the control of the diplomats.

The only dissenting voice was Upton's, who contended that England's rôle was to wait and see how the opening exchanges developed before involving herself in a European War; that this course would place her in a position of arbitrary power. His view was so virulently combated by the other men, however, that he soon retired into silence.

Lady Cranford, or Lady Arden, or Gina Maryon occasionally put in a remark, the remainder listening or appearing to. Really, perhaps, everybody's thoughts were with Captain Orde travelling Londonwards. . . .

After dinner card-games were played in an atmosphere of subdued gaiety. Adrian's hopes of a *tête-à-tête* with Rosemary had been, of course, completely dashed. There seemed something unreal about the party that night, and it was barely eleven o'clock when Lady Arden rose and suggested bed.

" The best place," said Gina with a yawn. " The only place where there isn't a war." And the ladies swept off up the stairs.

Adrian was in no mood for sleep. At a discreet interval he followed them, with the intention of fetching a book from his bedroom. The corridors were very dark, and he presently found himself stumbling through a baize door into quarters that were unfamiliar. A light gleamed at the end of a passage as of somebody's bedroom-door standing ajar. At the same moment he heard voices.

" Good night, Harry ! "

" Good night, Rosemary. *Dormez-bien !* "

A door slammed, footsteps passed away along the corridor, which he now realised was the main one, leading to the staircase. Upton must have been passing Rosemary's room on some such errand as his own. That was natural enough.

Yet in that moment something stabbed the heart of him. . . .

He found the way to his room, turned on the light, and sat down on the bed.

" Good night, Harry."

" Good night, Rosemary. *Dormez-bien !* "

A perfectly ordinary good night spoken in perfectly ordinary tones of voice.

Yet—who the devil had given this Upton permission to call her by her christian name ? Who was the fellow, anyway ? So far as he was aware the two hardly knew each other, had danced together once or twice, had met at Ascot. Rosemary — Upton—what could they possibly have in common ? Yet here they were calling each other by christian names at her bedroom door !

He realised quite definitely that he disliked the un-wholesome-looking young man with the " soulful " eyes, the faintly affected manner and speech—had, in fact, disliked him from the moment he set eyes on him at the Maryon party. This " Harry "—he was Gina's friend, not Rosemary's.

Was he jealous ? . . . Could he be jealous of this—person ? And Rosemary ? What earthly right had he to act the part of censor on her friends ? . . . And, perhaps, it was all very simple. He would ask her about it in the morning. That she liked the man she had declared openly at Ascot. " He was quite too appallingly clever, and in the Home Office—or some kind of office." And he was—" funny," she had added. He wrote poetry ; he was that type of man whom women like and other men never understand why. But the christian names ? Very young ladies were fond of calling young gentlemen by their christian names—it was rather " done " in their current idiotic phrase. Yet that was not Rosemary's kind of affectation, he reflected : rather the other way. . . . Still, there was doubtless some simple explanation.

He did not return downstairs that night, however ; he went to bed.

CHAPTER VII

Adrian and Rosemary

§ 1

It was not until the afternoon of the following day, Sunday, that Adrian's *raison d'être* at Arden was fulfilled.

At breakfast news came that France had declared war on Germany and that German troops had actually occupied the capital of Luxembourg. Mr. Heathcote found that he could no longer importune his club by telephone, owing to the telephone wires being engaged; instead, stories began to arrive via the servants' hall of the train service being disorganised and of lively movements on the main line.

At ten-thirty they all trooped off to church in the customary manner of week-end parties. It was cool and pleasant in the church, though six rubicund little boys sang like a choir of magpies. Sunlight dimmed by coloured glass fell in pools and patterns upon the flags; the whispering of ivy-leaves made a sibilant accompaniment to the voice of an archaic vicar who prayed with consuming earnestness that in God's wisdom peace might be preserved. Memorials to the Daventry family, scattered about the walls on marble slabs, couched in quaint phrases and diversely embellished, occupied Adrian's attention, while in robust tones, and with something of the smack with which he was wont to tell doubtful stories, Edward Arden read the lessons.

Adrian for his part took little interest in the service. He and Eric were acutely distressed by what they considered Sir Walter Freeman's unnecessarily hearty accompaniments and responses.

During the sermon a queer fancy came to him.

Close at hand upon a stone pedestal lay a vizored knight and his lady side by side, as they had probably lain through five centuries. Their hands were clasped, the knight's legs crossed, the expression upon their stony faces was of Time incarnate. Nor could it be said so much as who they were, for the same inscrutable philosopher had chipped and blotted out the Latin inscription upon this, their last earthly bed.

Rosemary sat in the seat in front of him. He could see her half-turned profile—a study in tense and quickening life. Gaiety, innocence were written there—yet something else ; something, indeed that he had seen before and did not understand but that added to the attractiveness of the face. Waywardness, was it ? Something disingenuous ? Fickleness ? Temper ? Not these altogether. . . . Or was it a suggestion of sadness about the mouth and eyes ?

It was then his strange fancy came to him. He saw this girl and himself centuries hence, lying side by side as this knight and lady lay, their faces carved in stone, their hearts withered to dust, and from their last earthly bed the very names blotted out.

§ 2

When they returned from church Upton found a telephone message summoning him to report to his Ministry at once.

"Sorrow !" he exclaimed. "Oh ! ye sons of Israel, of Isaac, and of Jacob ! What have I done to deserve this ? Gina, *ma chère*, this is indeed cru-el ! And all the afternoon we were going to dream ' Dreams ' ! And what do they want me for ? I can't stop the war. There is no poetry, I tell you, in Government departments."

"My Harry !" declaimed Gina. "Consider yourself a martyr ! Since you desert me—for your country's cause—I give you leave to kiss my hand."

"A smart young man. A clever chap—take my word for it," said Sir Walter Freeman, when Upton had departed.

" He'll do well when we want the best of them. He'll make a name for himself. In the Office they think the world of that young chap."

Early in the afternoon Lady Cranford was unexpectedly removed. She went with Lady Arden, Mr. Heathcote, and Lady Freeman in a motor to visit some neighbours who inhabited an Elizabethan house. There remained Miss Ingleby, who, as usual, engaged herself with the children, and Gina, who, bereft now of her particular young man, was led away between Arden and Sir Walter Freeman to see the home-farm and the young pheasants. Left to themselves, and after an insincere suggestion of tennis, the younger members of the party took to the lake, Faith and Eric disappearing in a row-boat in one direction, Rosemary and Adrian in another, paddling a punt.

Thus it came about that in the sultry heat of the August afternoon the couple last-named found themselves gliding along a little river which, branching off from the extreme end of the lake, wound, narrowing, to the heart of the Arden woods. On either hand great coverts of oak and beech made labyrinths of shade. Overhung by weeping willow and ash, low banks bounded the water's edge. Clumps of alder pressed down almost into the stream. Along its borders the purple loosestrife, the willow herb, the marigold—and pools of sunlight. Tall bulrushes rose out of the stream itself, vast lily-pads lay placidly upon its surface. Here a little peninsula, there a miniature isthmus or island, farther on a deep, cool recess where the bank curved inward.

At such a place Rosemary and Adrian tied up their punt; and on cushions piled and spread, half-sat, half-reclined, one beside the other. The stream eddied past. It was that hot hour when deer and all the lesser elves of copse and chase lie deep-concealed in fern and bracken. Silence curtained the woodland, that sultry August silence under the spell of which the birds rest, and only the purr of the stock-dove is heard as the timepiece of summer. This and a humming of wild bees between lime and river bank made their murmurous background.

Nor were the boy and girl themselves oblivious of the magic of the hour. Strange it had been if they, so full of the dawning glamour and curiosity of Youth, were not drawn to one another now. They seemed, indeed, to belong naturally and inevitably to each other accepting their fortune with simplicity. They were simply, immeasurably drawn to one another, immeasurably of one spirit. Side by side they lay for a very long time, and, dappled by sunbeams piercing the canopy of leaves and boughs, must have looked like children sleeping, so quietly and solemnly happy they.

Afterwards, when for the one

> " Wind and winter hardened
> In all the loveless land,"

when for the other life assumed a different shape, Adrian thought of this hour with steadfast gratitude and faith. After all, while it lasted it was the perfect thing without which no human story can be complete. What might it have been ? What might it not have been ! A love-making on a backstairs, a momentary clasping on a terrace or a roof-garden of some London hotel, a hurried embrace in a cab, a snatched instant in a drawing-room, a glimpse, a ghost of romance, an outstanding moment in a multitude of trivial incident—and that memory to carry them through Time ! To him—to them —it had been granted otherwise. Around them the whispering leaves, the trembling sunlight, the washing of the living water, the benediction, the tenderness and cleanliness of Nature's breath.

§ 3

Thus did Adrian Knoyle and Rosemary Meynell plight their troth. And thus through the hazing afternoon they rested side by side, but little speaking. Once Rosemary said :

" It's a queer thing, this thing they call love ; it's like being part of someone else or someone else being part of oneself. You know what they're thinking before they speak."

" Yes," he answered, " that's just how I feel about it. I don't believe there's a thought you could think or a word you could utter that I shouldn't know it before it came."

" Do you think it will always be like this, Adrian ? Do— dreams last ? "

" For us—yes. But, you see, there is another, a different thing. That's Gina, I think. That only lasts as long as the superficial part of it does. But our love will go on —and on—because we understand each other as—as we said just now."

" Gina attracts me though—I don't know why. You don't like her ? "

" I don't say I don't like her. But we—well, we must be different."

A long silence followed, during which they lay quite still.

" I can't imagine how we existed before we met each other," she whispered presently. " It seems so funny—to think of us growing up and living and feeling—and yet knowing nothing about one another ! "

" I believe in—what is it ?—predestination. We were bound to meet. We were bound to fall in love. Perhaps Faith and Eric were too. Love like ours—I think—goes beyond Death and Time."

" How is it so many people fall out of it then and make a mess of their lives, wise boy ? "

" When Fate or circumstance cuts in, I suppose, and obscures their vision or distorts instinct or when mere human laws cut across natural ones. Then people suffer, Rosemary. Nature exacts appalling penalties. Nature survives and—wins in the end. At least—that's my idea.

"How deep you are, and what a lot you've thought! I hope we shall never have a quarrel—ever."

"We shall. But we shall make it up again."

"Why?"

"Because we can't—well, get across one another—you and I. We can only pretend to,"

"I hope we never, never do have a quarrel, little fellow," she whispered, nestling close to him. "I hope you are always my darling, loving Adrian and I am your perfect little Rosemary. Because . . . I am perfect, aren't I?"

§ 4

It grew late. A fresh coolness crept into the air—very pleasant after the fierce heat. A deeper tint of gold glinted on the tops of the oaks—glinted back from her hair. A little breeze sprang up and stirred the spruce-firs, the lovers unconscious still: a new evening life softly began to move around them. Followed by their late broods, moorhens crept silently out from the shelter of the rushes and fed contentedly. Out of holes and rough sedge along the bank water-voles peeped—and sprang and splashed. Above their heads a willow-wren began his song-race, perched on a shoot of alder, and, trilling, twittering, clattering in an undertone, whirled up and down the scale of his incalculable notes. Everywhere burst forth the choir of blackbird and thrush; from among the oaks and chestnuts of the deep coverts came the throbbing notes of a wood-pigeon and the murmur of life-pairing doves.

Now the light began to fail and now the shadows stealing out of the corners of the park grew and lingered—deepened. Still the couple dreamed on, living their swift-flowing lives to the full. . . .

Once or twice the foreign waterfowl called from the direction of the lake. It had seemed to Adrian that there was something dissonant, ill-omened almost in their cries, but now they merged not harshly in the general harmony of the evening. A great cawing and ca-ing of rooks began as the noisy birds settled to roost in a clump of elms not far away. There were sounds of cows lowing and of a keeper's whistle from the woods.

Suddenly a bell tolled briskly from the great house.

Rosemary stirred.

" What's that ? "

" I don't know and I don't care. Let's spend the night here."

" But, my dear, what's the time ? My wrist-watch has stopped. It's getting dark. Good heavens, we've missed tea and everything. Mamma will slap me ! "

" Your mamma will ask where you've been. You will look her in the face. You will tell her you are engaged to marry the best of boys. You will then thank her sweetly for her consent. No, you'd better not, though—yet. . . . All the same, my angelic Rosie, nothing can alter the fact that it's been the most wonderful evening of our lives."

" No, Adrian."

They embraced.

Adrian punted and Rosemary paddled.

" We shall be late for dinner, and my hair's like hay. What *will* they think we've been doing ? Pray Heaven, I don't run straight into the infuriated woman ! "

" You certainly will," he laughed. " Why worry ? She's got to know later, if not sooner."

" But you don't know what she can be like. And I'm— disgraceful ! "

She certainly was untidy—she who (he had long since dis- covered) was so particular about her hair. But she had forgotten about her hair this evening. That was, after all, the supreme distinction between this and every other evening !

Adrian suddenly recollected Upton, and smiled to himself

as he thought of his over-night perturbation, and the fact that he had intended solemnly to tax Rosemary on the subject !

They raced across the lawn, forgetting to tie up the punt, and fled to their respective rooms.

As he turned the corner of the corridor Adrian could hear Lady Cranford's voice as her daughter entered the room, which opened out of the maternal one :

" My dear child, where *have* you been . . . ? "

CHAPTER VIII

Gina Maryon's Bedroom

§ 1

ADRIAN felt self-conscious—and looked it—when they gathered in the drawing-room, a somewhat reduced party. But Rosemary carried off the situation, declaring, in response to Lady Arden's gentle inquiry, " And what have you two been doing ? " that they had got lost up a backwater and that that ass Adrian had led her astray. At which there was laughter.

Gina remarked *en passant* how easy it was to get lost when the evenings began to draw in. Arden announced, as they went in to dinner, that he would have sign-posts put up on the lake pointing the way home.

Lady Cranford showed no visible signs of displeasure. As for Eric and Faith, they appeared somewhat *piano*.

At dinner he found himself sitting next Lady Freeman, with Miss Ingleby on the other side and Faith opposite. Rosemary was sitting near Gina down at Arden's end.

For some reason or other—perhaps it was a reaction from the previous night—everybody was in high spirits, Gina talking sixty to the dozen, Arden telling facetious stories, and all freely partaking of champagne. Sir Walter Freeman even dropped his House of Commons manner, laughed loudly, and betrayed a lively flush on his bald brow and expansive face. He was doing himself well, too, feeling perhaps that it was the last excuse for hilarity any of them would have for a long time.

Lady Freeman, Adrian found chatty. Some remarks from Gina on the subject of current literature set her off.

" Are you fond of reading, Mr. Knoyle ? I'm sure you are.

I love a nice bright tale with plenty of incident. But modern authors are so unsatisfying, aren't they?"

"Oh! any old thing does," the young man answered flippantly. "The *Winning Post Annual*, or Dostoievsky—as long as you haven't read it before."

"Oh, dear! You young men——"

She wasn't sure whether he had said something smart or something shocking.

"Ah! You prefer a variety," she rallied, steering a middle course. "Most young people do. And no doubt you're right. It broadens the mind."

"I find mine gets broadened without much reading, Lady Freeman."

"Yes? The life of a young man about town! I know." She was intolerably arch. "Well, Society, in my opinion, is the best education a young man can have. It broadens the mind. And I like to think myself a little broad-minded, you know, Mr. Knoyle. It's my little weakness. I believe—I may be wrong—in young men sowing their wild oats, not being molly-coddled. Nothing unpleasant, of course. But now I'm talking like a grandmother, and it's not so long——"

As a matter of fact, he wasn't listening. He had become aware of a pair of violet eyes watching him. They met his return look with a challenge—then turned away.

Gina Maryon had been "chaffing" Arden and Sir Walter Freeman (to the latter's considerable gratification) vigorously. She now transferred her attention to Adrian.

"A penny for yer thoughts! What's he dreaming about? A young man—do you know this, Sir Walter?—never looks so interesting as when he's in love." Adrian played with a dessert-spoon and turned his ear to Lady Freeman. "Which is not being personal, because I don't think Adrian's capable of being in love. He's cynical—which means he's young. What do you think, Lady Freeman? I've noticed young men always grow cynical about the time they come of age. It's just then, you know, they begin to have a ' past '—you can't have a ' past ' before you're twenty-one ; you can't with your utmost endeavours accomplish anything more than an ' indiscretion.' But what I really meant to ask was, Can a cynic fall in love ? I say not—genuinely. What do you say, Sir Walter ? "

" Oh ! Miss Maryon, really, you must not ask me these questions ! " protested the elderly gentleman, flushing with pleasure. " I am not a man of the world, you know—a mere politician ! "

" You mean a person who rolls other people's logs and gets four hundred a year for doing it ! Even politicians, though, are men of *affaires !* "

There were groans at this, and Gina herself deprecated it as the worst thing she had ever said.

" I've never heard of a politician falling in love," said Arden. " They're all cynics."

" Parnell, Edward ! " suggested Lady Cranford unexpectedly. She had not appeared to be aware of the discussion.

" Ah, Parnell was a genius, Lady Cranford ! " Gina rapped out. " To genius anything is possible—and permissible. Genius has a soul. Politicians have no souls. Sir Walter, I can see, has a soul."

Sir Walter bowed, smiling all over his crimson countenance.

" That's true," Lady Freeman reflected aloud, " what Miss Maryon was saying about genius being able to do anything. I remember hearing Mr. Hall Caine once. . . ."

Gina rose precipitately.

After dinner games were proposed. Dancing on Sunday, Faith said, was not considered good for the servants' hall. Card games, too, were prohibited. Gina proposed hide-and-seek. Was it possible to do anything more harmless ? For this everybody was pressed into service except Lady Arden, who went to say " good night " to the children, and Arden, who was left conversing with Lady Cranford on the subject of London society in the 'eighties. Miss Maryon deliberately chose Sir Walter Freeman to "hide" with, and they were absent so long that the only possible presumption was that they were repeating the adventure of the afternoon, until it was found that she had locked the worthy gentleman and herself in a summer-house, of which they had jointly lost the key. When it came to Rosemary's and Adrian's turn Lady Cranford intervened unexpectedly.

"No, Rosemary, I think you'd better not," she said. "I don't want you to catch a chill. Mr. Knoyle won't mind finding somebody else to hide with."

A glint of anger so fiercely petulant that it surprised Mr. Knoyle himself leapt into her eyes. She said nothing.

Adrian hid Miss Ingleby instead.

§ 2

An appreciable time after everybody had retired to rest that night, a somewhat over-excited party of five might have been discovered in Miss Maryon's bedroom, which was at some distance from everybody else's. It was what Gina called a "dressing-gown party." At an hour when Lady Cranford imagined her daughter to be sleeping in the adjoining room —they had parted on a note of admonition—that young lady might have been found in a dressing-gown, her golden hair flowing to the waist and bound together only with a ribbon, lying on Miss Maryon's bed, smoking a cigarette. Faith, similarly attired, sat on a sofa. Gina herself was seated on a gold cane chair in front of the looking-glass, robed in big, coloured flowers, and apparently transferring the contents of a number of small pots to her face.

Adrian and Eric, also smoking cigarettes, lolled on the edge of the bed. Altogether it was such a scene as must have annihilated the goddess of Convention, had the good woman appeared that night.

A scent hung about Gina Maryon's bedchamber, faint but

uncharacteristic of the rest of the house. It was a musky scent. Beside the bed, in addition to an elaborately-bound book, stood a little travelling decanter containing brandy or whisky, a syphon of soda-water, and some glasses.

They had talked of every sort of thing; there had also been pillow-fighting, telling of stories, and such-like entertainment. At length, Faith—in her capacity of daughter of the house—thought it had gone on long enough, and Adrian and Eric, taking a hint, left the room together.

When they stopped at Eric's door Adrian said:

" Congratulate me, old boy, it's fixed ! "

Eric looked at his friend without surprise. He slapped him on the back.

" I do congratulate you. My blessings on you both. Rosemary's a duck, and you're a lucky lad. . . . As for me — well, I'm sent empty away."

Eric laughed, but there was the faintest note of pain in the laugh.

" You too—? "

" This afternoon."

" No luck ? "

" She says try again in six months ! Sounds like an application for something out of stock, doesn't it ? "

" I'm sorry, my dear chap. But it'll be all right. Faith's a slower sort than Rosemary. She takes longer to make up her mind, that's all. You can't—take her by assault."

" Six months ! God alone knows what will have happened by then. I may have—married little Joyce or something ! "

" You'll be a *parti*, instead of a prospective one ! Good night."

§ 3

" You've not been letting the grass grow under your feet then, young Rosemary ! " laughed Gina after the young men had gone.

"I've known him a good long time, you know," the girl protested.

Rosemary and Gina had been on a christian-names footing almost since their first meeting. That was Gina's way when she liked people.

"Well, you're a very beautiful, attractive little puss, aren't you ?" she said, coming across to the bed and looking at her friend attentively. "And I think you'll make Adrian an immaculate wife. I'm sure he's the sort of young man who wants an immaculate wife. He's so very celibate himself—really—isn't he ? Beware of the world, the flesh, and the devil meanwhile ! "

Rosemary laughed.

"Trust me ! "

"By the way, have the Knoyles anything to bless themselves with ? " Miss Maryon inquired casually, returning to her chair at the dressing-table.

"Goodness knows ! " There was a touch of resentment in the younger girl's voice. "I know nothing about the £ s. d. and don't want to."

Gina turned to Faith.

"As to you, my dear," she said, "I think, if you ask my opinion, you're a damned fool. Here's a nice young man, plenty of money, and plenty to come. How much more do you want ? . . . What a double event, though ! Fancy ! Two proposals in an afternoon ! "

She poured herself out a brandy-and-soda.

Faith had been sitting quietly on the sofa. She looked remotely unhappy.

"No, Gina, I don't think so. I'm very fond of Eric. He's nice and gay, and dances well and all that, but one wants something more than that—and he's very young. The money part doesn't count with me one little bit."

She spoke very seriously.

"Well, I ask again—what more *can* you want ? They're

much better when they're taken young "—it was a peculiarity
of Gina's to speak of the male sex collectively, as of a species—
" you can mould them to yourself. Later on they get 'set'
and principled and have their own opinions. That's such a
bore, don't you think ? "

" But that's just it, Gina," Faith interrupted. " Eric lacks
that. He lacks character. He's—finicking. He's a little
playboy, and no more. Very much like a dozen other little
London youths one knows. . . . And he thinks too much of his
clothes. I told him so to-day. He's amusing with his tricks
and jokes and ways, and he's nice in himself. But I'm not in
love with him, and—you can laugh, Gina !—I want something
more than that. Of what use is he ? Will he ever *do* anything ?
Will he ever show what he's made of or that he's got anything
in him ? Has he a profession even ? Frankly, I could only
marry a man who means to make something more of his life
than—just fooling around. And I told him that, too."

" Well, if you ask me, I think you're flying too high, judging
by the majority of 'nice young men' one meets." Gina
studied herself carefully in the glass. " You're looking
for a prospective General Gordon or something."

" I don't think so," Faith replied resolutely.

" Of course, he's very young, he may develop," put in
Rosemary from the bed. " They often do. Adrian's come on
a lot since I've known him."

§ 4

At this same moment, the individual named happened to be
searching for his cigarette-case in his bedroom. He had written
a letter, and he wanted a cigarette before going to bed.

He had looked everywhere—on the dressing-table, in the
drawers, in his pockets.

Gina's room ! He remembered leaving it on the bed after
offering Rosemary one. Could he go and ask for it ? The

other two would probably still be there. Besides—with Gina anything was possible.

He opened the door. Someone came along the passage. It was Faith.

" Not gone to bed yet, naughty boy ? " she whispered. " Don't make a noise ! "

" I was just going along to get my cigarette-case. I left it in Gina's room."

" You'll find her visible—more or less. We've just left her. By the way, old Adrian, *all* my congratulations. Rosie's told me." She pressed his hand.

" Thank you, Faith. I value them from her greatest friend." She looked at him—slowly and thoughtfully.

Her face was in shadow, but he suddenly realised she was crying.

§ 5

He found Gina's bedroom-door wide open. She was sitting at her dressing-table in front of the looking-glass so that her profile confronted him. He was astonished at what he saw.

Instead of the animated expression, they had worn a few minutes earlier, the features were wan, relaxed, disillusioned.

It wasn't Gina—but it *was* Gina. Not the mask but the face. Not the child of the twentieth century but the ghost of that child. When he tapped at the door he had an almost guilty feeling, as though he had suddenly come upon something the eye was not meant to see.

She called to him to come in. Her voice, too, was changed— the life had gone out of it. Having made his apologies and secured his cigarette-case, he would have retired. Gina, however, seemed anxious to talk, anxious for sympathy or for company. Nothing loth, and indeed wishful to penetrate the curious creature's mood, he sat down on the bed and lit a cigarette.

He again became sensible of the scent pervading the room, —a scent which vividly recalled the Berkeley Square "maisonette." Nor could he help noticing the profusion of trinkets and articles of toilet on her dressing-table—gold and silver pots and boxes, gold-backed and ivory brushes, bottles of scent in finely cut glass. He particularly remarked a gold snuff-box of the Louis XIV period, beautifully enamelled. He picked it up to examine it.

" No ! Be careful ! Give me that, Adrian ! " she cried almost snatching it from him. " It's—it's precious. It belonged to my father and my grandfather." Having recovered possession of the article, she added more calmly: " It's a lovely little thing, though, isn't it ? I never go anywhere without that."

She locked the little box away in a drawer.

§ 6

That Gina was sensitive to Adrian's opinion of herself there could be no doubt. Her personality, her versatility, her magnetism, which, one was told, had brought her fifty proposals of marriage, made apparently no impression upon Adrian Knoyle. That struck at the roots of her vanity. She even felt that he despised her, as men despise the vanity of women whom they view sexlessly. She was not even sure— and this genuinely pained her—that Adrian so much as recognised the substance, the accomplishment, the real cleverness and adaptability which she rightly estimated as hers. Actually he did recognise these qualities. But he would under no circumstances concede the fact.

For his part, Adrian took another view of the young woman from that night onward. First knowing her, she had alarmed him ; she then alarmed him at intervals ; she now alarmed him no more. By some curious power of discernment he had always seen through the scintillation of her social self—even when he knew her only by sight and reputation. He had suspected (without interest) that there might be more underneath. He had never genuinely admired her. On the other hand, he had only spasmodically disliked her. Now he frankly pitied her.

For there she sat before him, huddled together on a gold-caned chair—weariness, reaction, self-pity inscribed upon her face. The appeal for sympathy was so obvious, the self-pity so unmistakable.

Yes—he felt sorry for her. He also liked her better than he had ever liked her before.

"What's the matter, Gina ?" he said cheerfully. "Overtired ?"

"The matter ? Nothing. Only that I'm overdone and fed up and desperately sick of everything," she burst out. "I don't know what's the matter with me. . . . Have you ever felt like that ? . . . I'm on the verge of an abyss. And I don't know what's at the bottom of it. . . ." She gave a queer little sound that was more like a sob than a laugh. "One leads the life of a maniac. *Good God*, how hopeless it all is ! How rotten, how empty, how futile ! Just think of what one's been doing all this summer ! One's never been still for a moment, one's never been alone, one's never thought of one damned thing worth thinking of, one's never done a damned thing but amuse oneself. And nothing, *absolutely nothing*, to show for it. The older one grows the more discontented one becomes, and the more one asks of Life the less one gets. . . . Heaven knows, I've had everything I could ever want, and yet I'm never really happy—never, never, never. Why *can't* one sit down and think, or not think ? Why in God's name can't one sit still ?"

She began to do something to her hair—put pins in it or take them out.

"What's to be done, Adrian ? Are *you* happy ? . . . I suppose you think I'm just foully selfish and vain and all the rest of it—a sort of glorified joy-girl, what ? Most people think that. . . . You needn't deny it. I can see you do. . . . I tell you the Leicester Square ladies are happier than I am, a hundred thousand times. . . ." She laughed again hysterically. " Oh, *God*, how fed up I am with it all ! The only thing to do is to marry. And yet I couldn't stick being married. Or could anyone stick me—beyond the honeymoon *?* Do you know I've never been in love in my life ? . . . I seem to be full of contradictions. I wish I could be good and go to church and be charitable. I feel like the ' bad girl of the family ' in the last act but one. And it's getting pretty near the last act with me. Do you think one would be any happier, though, if one was like that ? Adrian, how *is* one to be happy ? "

" Don't ask me, Gina. I'm all right—but then I've hardly begun to live yet. I always thought you got more out of life than anybody I knew."

" Most people think that. . . . And I get nothing out of life, neither pleasure nor peace nor happiness nor love. I don't believe I've even got any friends—not real ones. Look at Harry, for instance ! " Her voice became contemptuous. " I don't tell him so, but I know Harry inside out. I know perfectly well he plays about with every woman who'll let him. And when he's bored with them he comes running back to me. Not that I care that much ! " She crushed a cigarette-end into the carpet. " As long as I keep the colour of my eyes and my hair, my ' friends ' will do that. Useful sort of friends ! And when that dies I shall die too."

" You're suffering from the Age, my dear Gina. You're suffering from having everything you want and nothing to do with it. It's the disease of society just now. The world's been going round too long without anything happening—anything real. One can't get a grip on anything unless one has to. One lives a life of—well, sham, I agree. But there you are, you don't want to take up district visiting ! You don't want to marry. If a war comes it may alter things. . . ."

She offered him a cigarette. It was scented, sickly, but he could not at once think how to get rid of it. Presently he began to feel dizzy.

He knocked the burning end off with his finger and threw the stump under the bed.

She stared at herself in the looking-glass, yet, to judge by her expression, saw nothing.

But he noticed something he had not noticed before. There was no rouge on her cheeks now. They were of a pearly hue, transparent almost. And they were the exact tinge of Upton's unwholesome complexion. . . . And her eyes. They were not brilliant, exciting as half-an-hour before, but glazed, lack-lustre. The only thing left was the auburn hair —and was that her own ? Was there *anything* genuine about the woman

When she spoke again it was in a brighter tone. She began " touching up," smiling at herself mechanically in the glass. He knew what that meant.

" Oh, well ! " she sighed presently, " it can't be helped. We must make the best of life, nasty as it is. I don't know why I've poured all this out on your boyish, curly head—except that I don't feel you're spoilt yet, and what you say is perfectly true. Give me another brandy-and-soda and have one yourself ! "

She suddenly came and sat on the bed beside him. The " colour " was back in her cheeks, she looked amazingly—herself. She sat so close to him that her hand touched his.

He then understood her. She *was* herself again. She was deliberately taking advantage of the impression that the only glimpse of nature she had ever revealed had made upon him. She had detected the effect, and she was exploiting it. That was Gina. With all her egotism, all her self-pity, she had been interesting in her brief mood of self-revelation. Now she was aware of having been interesting.

Nor could he know that she had been discussing with

Rosemary Meynell the subject of their engagement barely half-an-hour before.

" Oh, well, and, in fact, alas ! I suppose I must get into my pathetic little pyjamas. . . . Would you like to see them, all silk and saucy—if you're very good ? "

She watched him, smiling, and was somehow pressing his arm.

He rose abruptly.

" I'm going to bed."

Her face changed. She looked like an old, malicious woman.

CHAPTER IX

A Summer's Day—and After

§ 1

On the morning of that August Bank Holiday Sir Walter and Lady Freeman departed in their car at a quarter-past eleven, Sir Walter desiring to be in his place in the House of Commons for the Foreign Secretary's speech that afternoon, while Lady Freeman no doubt felt her presence also was required in the centre of events. Faith had to walk down to the village to visit her " poor people," in which good office she was accompanied by Eric. Gina disappeared with Arden. Rosemary and Adrian strolled over to the farm, then sat in the garden until luncheon-time. After luncheon the two couples went off in the boat and punt respectively, armed with baskets, kettles, and packages of food, the idea being to picnic in the woods on the opposite shore of the lake.

" How delightful to see them all so happy, Helena, my dear ! " remarked Lady Arden to Lady Cranford as she watched them start from her shady chair on the lawn.

" Yes, but we could not do that sort of thing in our day, Mary. Well, I suppose one must give them their heads or they'll take to their heels——"

" The young people enjoy life more than they did then," observed Mr. Heathcote. " Not so much restraint, not so much formality. I am undecided whether it is an unmixed blessing." He chuckled rather foolishly.

" I love to see them amusing themselves," said Lady Arden.

" You're lucky with Faith, Mary," remarked Lady Cranford. " She's such a sensible young woman. Rosemary one has to be firm with—very. She's so naturally headstrong—like all the Meynells—and she's just reached the age when gals are apt to think they can do what they like. This young Adrian Knoyle she's making such friends with—he seems a nice young man—but of course—there couldn't be anything—really."

" Oh ! let them have fun while they can, my dear Helena ! "

The four returned just as the dinner-bell was ringing and their elders were beginning to be apprehensive. They were hot, flushed, and in a condition of extreme merriment. After dinner they walked arm-in-arm about the gardens until they were summoned in. Then Eric amused the company with card-tricks, and other tricks with handkerchiefs and glasses of water turned upside down, and boxes of matches, and feats of strength which weren't strength at all, until bed-time, when they separated, happy and tired, vowing that it had been such a perfect day as they would never forget.

Nor did any one of them feel that his or her allotted span of careless youth was drawing to a close.

§ 2

Tuesday broke hotter than ever, and at his waking Adrian experienced a sense of reaction. He dreaded the return to used-up, washed-out London, where he would have to spend at least a week. Sir Charles and Lady Knoyle had taken a furnished house at Ascot, which would not be available immediately Then there was the Sheringham business to be squared up with his father. Sir Charles would infallibly resurrect the whole question of a profession. He knew that the last thing Sir Charles would approve of was Sheringham. . . . Was this young man an idle vagabond, or more selfish than idle ? No. He did intend to work (in earnest) somewhere about October, when people begin to come back to London. But until then—well, really he must take leave to amuse himself.

He and Eric breakfasted alone together at ten-thirty. No

one else appeared. Both were depressed at the thought that the cheerful house-party was about to disperse. Both envied Miss Ingleby and Mr. Heathcote who were staying a day or two longer in the placid Arden world. Lady Cranford and Rosemary were motoring across-country after luncheon to the house of relations in Oxfordshire. Gina, Eric, and himself were to go up to London by the two-forty-five train, since the earlier one by which they had intended to travel had been cancelled.

And when the two friends walked round the gardens together in the hot morning it was not of the future they talked, but of that subject which in the world's crises has never been far removed from the thoughts of men. Eric was the less impulsive, the less emotional of the two. And it was evident that his self-confidence had survived the set-back he had received from Faith. Glancing at his blandly-smiling countenance, it might have been suspected that no surcharge of emotional capacity lay behind it. Eric's conduct was ordered by that large measure of conventionality, which in most people takes the place of an original and active mind. So far was his horizon limited. In Adrian, on the other hand, there were always possibilities of revolutionary or of evolutionary change. The nature and quality of their affections revealed the difference in temperament between the two. Eric's blood, it might be felt, would never warm beyond the point when he would be likely to exceed the sharply-defined limits of a public-school tradition. One could not conceive of Eric being "carried away"; nor could one imagine him carrying away anything much more substantial than a good time.

Strolling back towards the house, they met the three girls coming arm-in-arm down the garden path, talking and laughing. They joined them, and while all five wandered slowly round the gardens Adrian found his opportunity to have a few last words with Rosemary. The latter went straight to the point.

"Mamma's furious about Sunday, Adrian."

" Has she been lecturing you ? "

" No, but she kissed me this morning as though she meant it. That's a bad sign."

" She was amiable enough to me—almost cordial. In fact, after breakfast we talked about the war as if there really was one."

" Fatal, my dear. *We're* in for a war, I can see that. If she'd been ordinarily, decently rude, all might have been well. . . . Meanwhile, what's to be done ? Shall we tell her we're engaged ? "

" No, leave it till Sheringham, when we'll spring it on her as a *fait accompli*. That's the way to do these things."

" I wish she wasn't such a difficult sort of woman. Some girls are so inestimably blessed in their mothers ! Faith, for instance. Could anyone be more unpractical or more sensible than Lady Arden ? I don't believe she knows she's got a daughter."

" It's just the same with father—in a different way. He wants to know the whys and wherefores of everything—and hasn't even the decency to tell you the amount of his bank balance. I always thought there should be perfect confidence between father and son, and that the prerogative of gentility was generosity. With him it's just the other way."

" By the by, what *are* your ' prospects,' Adrian ? Not that it matters. But mamma is sure to ask. She always does about every young man who speaks to me under the age of fifty-five."

" None—at present. But in October I'm going to be a diplomat—or something."

" Mamma's idea, you know, is that I am to retrieve the family fortunes. Now that the best pictures at Stavordale are sold I'm the only marketable asset."

" I quite understand. The Knoyles are one of those high-principled old families which show their contempt for the empty lure of meretricious gold by keeping it locked up in the bank."

" Have you anything much of your own ? "

" About five pounds, darling. But the Leger's run in less than a month, and a friend of Eric's has a horse running."

" What are we to do, my dear boy, if we want to be married soon ? "

" Compromise each other hopelessly and blackmail our respective parents into giving their consent. There are advantages, you know, even in respectability. . . . Don't worry, my angel ! I'll have it out with the old boy. He always manages these things in the end—has to."

When they came to the Italian garden where Adrian had stood with Gina and where the shrubs and high surrounding hedge hid them from view, they stopped. Both knew that the moment of farewell had come. Adrian took Rosemary in his arms and held her so for a long time.

Through the hot stillness rasped the cries of the foreign water-fowl on the lake.

§ 3

After luncheon, the three went off. Until the last moment the talk was of the forthcoming *réunion* at Sheringham—not, of course, in Lady Cranford's hearing. The two girls implored Gina to join the party. Gina gave an enthusiastic assent, which Adrian hoped and believed to be insincere. She would assuredly only come if she could be accompanied by a retinue of poets, artistes, and " long-haired, pale-faced young men." That was the safeguard.

Rosemary and he shook hands at parting in a suitably formal manner. No ghost of prescience rose between them—only a sense of regret at a good time ended, and of looking-forward to good times to come. His final impression of Arden Park was of Arden himself standing at his massive front door with his head thrown back and a little on one side, laughing, and shouting after them " not to get mixed up in the war." . . .

The train was a slow one. Gina read a book, Eric went to sleep, and Adrian studied a newspaper upside down. The first-named, entirely her normal self, had betrayed no consciousness, by word or sign, of Sunday night's happenings.

The only incident of the journey was when they passed a noisy trainload of troops and horses—artillery or cavalry—on their way down the line. At Waterloo they noticed a number of soldiers in unfamiliar khaki, carrying little bags and packages.

They left Gina at the miniature green house tucked away in a corner of Berkeley Square. Faded pink geraniums drooped in the window-boxes ; it wore an air of cheerful *déshabille*.

" Good-bye, boys ! " the volatile creature cried. " Be good, and if you can't be good, be careful ! We shan't forget each other, shall we ? "

§ 4

Adrian dropped Eric at his rooms off St. James's Street, drove home, unpacked, had tea, and wrote some letters. The friends had agreed to dine together at a club and go to a music-hall. Eric had suggested taking certain young ladies to dance and supper at Murray's—a project which, however, Adrian firmly negatived.

The house in Eaton Square was empty, Sir Charles and Lady Knoyle having gone down to Ranelagh for the afternoon. Clocks ticked, the glaring sunshine beat into rooms, scarcely mellowed by drawn red blinds. August sounds drifted up from the streets—cries of children, a dusty rumble of traffic, the song of a cage-bird.

Soon after seven o'clock Adrian, in evening clothes, set out to walk to St. James's Street. He had barely reached Hyde Park Corner when he became aware of a peculiar and indefinable atmosphere about the streets which even their post-holiday, dead-season effect would hardly account for. Wherever a house was occupied maidservants or care-takers were standing at the area-gates ; at the corners of mews coachmen and chauffeurs were reading newspapers; groups of two and three people stood at the street-corners.

Hyde Park, it is true, seemed to own its usual population of grimy children, lovers, and tired workers sitting on seats. The usual cross-streams of traffic rattled noisily past Hyde Park Corner. The sense of "aftermath" was strong—but there was a sense of something stronger.

Walking up Piccadilly, he began to look closely at the faces of the passers-by, seeking in each what he could not define. They appeared wan, jaded, dusty—it was not there. He sought for it in the aspect of the clubs and shut-up houses —nor there. In the policemen, the omnibuses, the closed shops, the Hotel Astoria—everything he was familiar with. He could not identify it.

While he was still puzzling a newsboy rushed out of Dover Street, yelling. What he yelled was:

"War with Germany to-night!"

A score or more of Londoners rushed upon the youth like a pack of hounds, jostled him and each other, tore the papers from him; their halfpennies jingled upon the pavement. Men who had never met before shared the same paper, looking over each other's shoulders. People jumped off omnibuses and stopped taxicabs. Groups gathered round individuals who read aloud from the Stop Press news.

Adrian thought of Cyril Orde.

CHAPTER X

The Voice of London

§ 1

Hot darkness covered London like a velvet pall.

Adrian Knoyle and Eric Sinclair stood in a crowd outside Buckingham Palace. A kind of hysteria had seized the populace. Cheering crowds paraded the streets ; cheering crowds had waited for hours outside the house of the King, calling for a speech. The Royal Family had graciously appeared upon the balcony ; nothing further happened. But the crowds went on cheering, and groups of people sang "O God, our help in ages past," or "Rule Britannia," or the National Anthem. The majority, as by a conjuring trick, had produced Union Jacks. If they had not Union Jacks, they waved handkerchiefs.

"Speech ! Speech ! "

"Down with Germany ! "

"Down with the Kaiser ! "

"Three cheers for the British Empire ! "

"Three cheers for King George ! "

As the couple stood there, a strange murmur seemed to rise from all London. It was near midnight, but that low-pitched sound rose from every quarter of the city. It might have proclaimed a mob in revolution, it might have proclaimed the crowning of a monarch. It might have meant the acclamation of a national triumph or the dawn of some great popular reform.

It signalised the death-grip of Europe.

§ 2

The two young men moved out of the crowd and passed, by way of St. James's Park, to Whitehall. Birdcage Walk was quiet and very dark. On their right the barracks loomed as though asleep. No light showed. They thought that strange. . . .

Out of the darkness and quiet they passed into the murmur of a yet larger crowd. They reached Parliament Square, and the giant lighted dial of Big Ben trembled. The giant voice behind struck eleven times. . . . A voice sounded the knell of the world. . . .

Cheers and echoes of cheers rose from the crowds. Processions of men and youths drifting from Whitehall into Bridge Street stopped and wildly cheered, throwing up their hats, waving flags. Now an undistinguished group, now a single voice, broke into fragments of "God Save the King," or the "Marseillaise." It was as though a miracle of good fortune had befallen London. Men and women, boys and girls, policemen, the very street-urchins seemed beside themselves with joy.

The two friends pursued their way to Whitehall. An occasional taxicab whirred past aflutter with Union Jacks, loaded and overloaded with yelling men and girls. Parties of people drifted past—drifted through shadows into glare of electric-light and back into shadows again :—singing, shouting, laughing, like figures in a ballet. Eric Sinclair and Adrian Knoyle turned into Downing Street and crossed the Horse Guards—silent, empty.

Out of the dim bulk of the palaces on Carlton House Terrace, the German Embassy loomed, massive and white. Adrian's mind dwelt on that. His fancy depicted the bowed figure of an ageing man with iron-grey hair and moustache, a clever face, a half-wistful, half-sombre expression of un-laughing eyes. He seemed to see echoing rooms and passages, half-deserted and half-packed-up, and, sitting in a dim-lit study, this man with his tired and now doubly-tired and grave and wistful face. His work done; his mission ended; the future of his country pledged. What passed he wondered, in the secret chambers of that mind through the slow hours of the unsleeping night? Heard he in the privacy of that room, littered with books and papers and things finished with and things torn up, the clamour of the English mob, the execration of his Emperor and his country; or saw he before him standing, the million phantoms of doomed yet living men? Looked he back with triumph and defiance upon the ashes of his embassy—or was there writ upon that face something more sinister and more sad?

§ 3

Now they came to Trafalgar Square. Carnival. How the crowds roared and shouted, how they sang and cheered, how they lived and laughed! They cheered the war, they cheered the King, the British Empire, France, Russia, Belgium, Serbia. They cheered the Navy and the Army. They actually sang soldiers' songs of the jingo period and the South African War, and revived the cry "England for ever." Again and again they roared "God save the King," "Rule Britannia," and the "Marseillaise."

It was the spectacle of a people drunk—drunk with sensationalism, with over-excitement, with lust for war, with the realisation of a menace long-delayed, with—they knew not what. They wanted to glorify, to idolise; they were out to vent the pent-up feelings of half-a-century of European peace—of a generation of Germanophobia. In doing this, Knoyle perceived, they cheered their own peril, cheered the triumph of the anti-Christ, cheered the downfall of the world. . . .

The spaces and declivities of Trafalgar Square were lit up

this night with an unusual brilliance. The powerful electric arc-lamps had been reinforced by flambeaux which, burning high and bright, threw floods of light around the pedestals whereon the lions crouch, and from which daring spirits yelled to the crowd beneath. The people pressed like night-moths toward the glare. In the angles of the granite pedestals the two friends found place to stand.

They watched the throng go surging by. There were parties of young men, arms linked and marching four-by-four singing frantically, carrying Chinese lanterns, waving Union Jacks. There were parties of girls. There were soldiers borne upon the shoulders of civilians. National songs were being shouted incoherently in a dozen places at once. A youth, springing onto the parapet of the pedestal immediately above their heads, began to make a speech:

"Men and women," he screamed, "we are at war with Germany. Germany has plotted this war, Germany is the God-damndest country the world has ever seen. Shall we *ever* give in to Germany? Remember what Lord Roberts said! Down with the politicians, three cheers for the Army——!"

"Hip! hip! hip! hooray!"

"Three cheers for the Navy!"

"Hip! hip! hip! hooray!"

"Down with the Kaiser, the man who plotted this war——!"

Groans, hisses, jeers from all.

The youth grew hoarse; at last, could no longer make himself heard. They could just see his face above them, lit by the glow of a torch, working maniacally. It was a weak, pale face—the face of a shop-assistant or a solicitor's clerk: an ordinary London face; no distinction in it, no nobility, character or power, only an overmastering excitement. There he stood in his threadbare office-suit, his arms making vehement gestures, one hand grasping a soft felt hat, cracking his high-pitched voice—for the British Empire.

" Now then, boys, ' Rule Britannia ' all together———"
He waved time with his hands.

> "Rule Britannia,
> Britannia rules the waves,
> Britons never, never, never
> Shall—be—slaves."

Cheering, cheering—a flickering of the flambeaux, white glare
of the arc-lights—white faces staring up at the puny, gesticulating figure perched beside the British Lion—a myriad flags
waved, discordant voices raised—frantic, fantastic crowds
surging through the summer night. . . .

And behind all that, unseen—throb ! throb !—the steadfast
beat of the nation's heart.

§ 4

Darkness was in a fair way towards dawn when Adrian and
Eric walked homeward along an emptying Piccadilly. As they
passed the Hotel Astoria their thoughts turned instinctively
to the hours played out within its portals, hours which,
if the voice of the crowd spoke true, might never be for
them again.

They turned into their club, which had kept its doors open
long beyond its usual time. A few members were still pressing
round the tape-machine. With difficulty they read the news

" At 11 p.m. no reply to the British ultimatum
had been received.

They bade each other goodnight and, obeying some un-
defined impulse, shook hands.

CHAPTER XI

A Telegram and Two Letters

§ 1

FORTY-EIGHT hours later—at breakfast—Adrian received a bulky letter in a sprawling handwriting :

> "WOODCOTE MANOR,
> "OXON.
> "*Thursday*.

"MY DARLING OLD ADRIAN,

"I hardly know how to write this letter. The news I have is *too* awful, and I am *so* miserable I don't know what to do. Adrian, darling, just as I told you, there's been an awful row, and mamma's been at me ever since we left Arden. She began in the motor almost before we'd got out of the gates. You know—or p'raps you don't—how awful and bitter she can be. Oh ! Adrian, I simply can't tell you what that drive was like. She started by asking me what on earth I meant by going off with you on Sunday afternoon and not appearing at tea. She said everybody noticed it and Lady Arden was very shocked—which I think is ROT, because I don't think you can shock her—and what could I have been thinking of and so forth. This sort of thing went on for about half-an-hour, until she said she had never interfered with or even mentioned any of my friendships with young men (as if I'd had such a lot !), but she really could not have me behave like this, and how long had I been on such terms with you as to stay away for hours at a time in a boat—it was a punt—and had I taken leave of my senses, etc., and so forth.

" Well, Rosemary hadn't said anything much so far, but when she said that I thought the moment had come to make things plain. So I said she needn't wax so roth (how does one spell that word ?) as, if she wanted to know, we were engaged. I can't tell you what mamma's face was like when I said that. Have you ever seen a large, quiet Persian cat in a passion ? Well, that was her. For several minutes she said nothing ; she gets all cold and funny when she's like that. Then she said, well, what, if she might ask, might your prospects be, because to the best of her knowledge you hadn't got a ha'penny to your name or even a profession. Just as I told you, Adrian. And what did *I* propose to marry on ? *Poor little me !* Don't you pity me, Adrian ? I felt absolutely helpless and an awful fool, because I really don't know a thing about it. How many ha'pennies *have* you got, though I don't think it really matters ? Rosemary wants to marry you, even if you haven't got any.

" The end of it all was she said our engagement must be broken off *at once*, and she wouldn't have me see or write to you under any circumstances whatever. You can imagine what I felt, though I thought Rosie thinks otherwise. Hence this letter. She said I must absolutely put out of my head any idea of my ever, *ever* marrying you, and that if you were a really nice young man (which you aren't, of course !) you would never have asked me which, of course, is absolute ROT too, and I told her so. I got in an awful temper too, Adrian, I told the heartless woman the more she went on like that the more determined I was that I *would* marry you ! Brave of me, wasn't it ?

" Well, this went on, with pauses for refreshment, till we got to Aunt Kitty's. Mercifully she had no party staying there, so I said I was frightfully tired, and had dinner in bed and afterwards locked the door. But oh ! my eye, Adrian, it was a miserable evening, and I did long for you so. I simply cried like anything, but, thank goodness, had your photograph

and lace hankies to comfort me a little. I think mamma
must have ralented a bit during the night, or talked it over
with Aunt Kitty, or p'raps she sees (which she ought to
know by this time) that opposing me only makes me more
obstinate. Anyhow, she lured me into the garden after
breakfast, and was, I must say, comparatively polite. She
said that, as a reasonable young woman, as I had always
been so far (sounds like a Salvation Army lassie, doesn't it ?)
I must see how impossible it was to marry a man
without any money or even a profession, and that it
would be very wrong in any case for *her* to encourage
such an idea, as she was in the place of papa. Also nineteen
was much too young to think of marrying or to decide for
myself. Also she did not want to seem harsh—they always
say that—so on *one* condition she might *possibly* think over
the idea, if you could come back with some money (and a
profession, I s'pose) in a year's time. The condition is that
we do not see each other or write for a year, which she
says is all for my own good.

"Adrian, damn ! I've been thinking it over all day, and
I don't see any way out of it. Do you ? Unless you've got
hold of any money and we can be married at once. After all,
a year's not so very long really, and it will give you time to
make some money and get a profession. (Why don't you go
in the Army ?) P'raps we shall be able to meet now and then,
with any luck, and anyway, we can always write. Adrian, can
you see any way out of it ? The worst of it all is, what mamma
says seems so beastly reasonable. *Do*, DO write and tell me
what's to be done. I am so *utterly miserable* and *longing* for
you. How I wish I could get out of this and away somewhere,
though Aunt Kitty is a peach really, and means to be very
kind, and so does Uncle Arthur, but under the circumstances
they fairly shatter the nerves.

"Thank you *ever so much* for your *darling* note. It really
does look as if there's going to be a war, doesn't it ? Don't

get mixed up in it, as old Arden says. But *do*, DO write at once and tell me what's to happen. We shall be here about ten days, then go to the Lynmouths', and then, I s'pose, Sheringam.

"Sheringam! My God! *That* makes me more furious than anything, absolutely tigrish, in fact. But I can see it would be absolutely fatal for you to come. I must write and tell dear old Faith about it all, and *darling* Gina. Gina knows *so much* about *everything*.

"Now good-bye, my darling old Adrian, and *heaps* of kisses! From

"Your loving   ROSEMARY.

"P.S.—*Please* be careful about letters after this. Write as often as you can but put them in an envelope inside another one and address the outside one to my maid Bolton, who is alright.

"P.P.S.—Love to Eric."

§ 2

It took Adrian some minutes to realise just what had happened. He felt out of breath. His first decided mood was one of fury against Lady Cranford. A sort of catechism went on in his mind:

Q. What right had this steely old devil to interfere?

A. She was Rosemary's mother.

Q. Couldn't Rosemary decide for herself whom she wished to marry?

A. She was a minor.

Q. Supposing Rosemary and he chose to marry without Lady C.'s consent? Other people had done so.

A. He had not (as Lady Cranford truly said) one halfpenny in the world except a trifling allowance from his father; he was up to his ears in debt, and he had no prospects of making any income whatsoever.

His mood changed from anger to despair, back to anger
and then stuck at despair. It further alternated with spasms
of pity—pity for Rosemary, alone, at the mercy of a heartless
mother—and, yes, pity for himself.

Having rung up Eric on the telephone and put the matter
to him, certain facts began to assert themselves uncompromis-
ingly. By luncheon-time he was freely blaming himself.

Why in the name of heaven had he not thought out these
little matters of money and Lady Cranford and Lady Cranford's
consent ? How could he have dreamt of marrying under the
circumstances ?—not that that made any difference to their
being engaged as long as they liked. And then, again, if he had
thought it out—however laboriously—what practical difference
could it have made ? He knew well enough in his own mind
that Sir Charles could not, or at any rate would not, give him
the wherewithal to marry. He knew well enough Sir Charles
would tell him to go and earn it.

As to a long engagement, Eric had something to say when
they met at their club in the afternoon. He ordered two
cocktails. Was it fair, did Adrian think it decent, to keep
a girl of Rosemary's age pledged to him indefinitely ?
Oughtn't he to give her the option of breaking off the engagement during the year's separation ? At first Adrian was
dead against the idea—vowed it was unnecessary, that he
was perfectly certain Rosemary wouldn't wish it herself. Eric
persisted, however. Wouldn't it be fairer to give her the
chance ? Finally he came to the conclusion that Eric was right.
Whereon a wave of the noblest sentiment suffused him. He
would do the right thing, yes, he would, whatever happened.
He would take Eric's advice and, cost what it might, do
the right thing. . . .

A deeper sting had touched the quick. His self-esteem was
pierced. He saw himself quite uncomfortably and nakedly,
not as he valued himself, but with the appraising, material eye
of a parent contemplating the marriage of a daughter. Lady

Cranford's words were, "he hasn't got a halfpenny to his name or even a profession." Well—and what sort of a picture did these words conjure up ?

His father had told him to his face more than once that he was an idle, good-for-nothing fellow. He did not care in the least. He didn't particularly care what Lady Cranford thought of him so far as Lady Cranford went. But—would Rosemary, some day, come to view him in this light ? What about Rosemary—— ?

"Without a halfpenny to his name, without even a profession."

Of all this he said nothing to Eric. But this, in fact, was the thought that caused him silently to writhe. It was just a little more than he could stand.

§ 3

His mind made itself up.

The so-moving events of the last few days had not been lost upon him. The night of the Fourth of August had been succeeded by a period of quivering suspense. Already the plain duty of every free and able-bodied young Englishman was becoming clear.

After tea Eric despatched a telegram in their joint behalf.

Returning home at speed, Adrian wrote a letter to Rosemary in which he formally accepted Lady Cranford's contract, while firmly renouncing most of its stipulations. He expressed the hope that they might even meet within a month, and this restored to his after-reflections a measure of optimism.

Early on the following morning the two young men received a reply to their telegram. It was a request to report at once to the lieutenant-colonel commanding Orde's regiment in London. . . .

A fortnight later they were gazetted second lieutenants (on probation).

END OF PART THE FIRST.

PART THE SECOND:
DISILLUSION

. . . and lo, there was a great earthquake ; and the sun became black as sackcloth of hair, and the moon became as blood ;

And the stars of heaven fell unto the earth, even as a fig-tree casteth her untimely figs, when she is shaken of a mighty wind.

And the heaven departed as a scroll when it is rolled together ; and every mountain and island were moved out of their places.

And the kings of the earth, and the great men, and the rich men, and the chief captains, and the mighty men, and every bondman, and every free man, hid themselves in the dens and in the rocks of the mountains ;

For the great day of his wrath is come ; and who shall be able to stand ?

REVELATION VI, 12–17.

CHAPTER I

The Baptism of Fire

§ 1

Near daybreak of a March morning, the battalion to which Adrian Knoyle and Eric Sinclair belonged was forming up in the main street of Estaires, a small manufacturing town in the province of Artois, Northern France.

Six hundred bayonets were mustering, but in the darkness, through which snowflakes lightly fell, little could be seen save the shadowy line into which the column by degrees resolved itself. There could, however, be *felt* an obscure sound of men moving : there were shouts and words of command, a motor-bicycle panted past, there were the grate of wheels, the stamping of horses' feet where a group of chargers stood, and the jingling of their bits.

If a key were required to the character of the scene, it was winter. An icy wind blew down the street. Newly-fallen snow lay upon rooftops and pavements. The troops wore greatcoats. As the light grew and the column with repeated halts began to edge forward, it was possible to discern that the soldiers were khaki-clad and British, that they were men of exceptional physique—burdened with the weight of full marching equipment—that many carried their rifles slung. Limbers loaded with machine-guns, with belts of ammunition, and with big bluish-grey boxes of rifle ammunition followed in train of each battalion ; stretcher-bearers carrying their stretchers on their shoulders followed in train of each company. The cause of the incessant stoppages was a long procession of transport wagons and field artillery which, having been parked in the town *Place* before the old *Hotel de Ville*, were now on the move, and somehow or another had to take their place in the middle of the apparently endless column.

Daylight had far advanced by the time the main body of infantry reached the outskirts of the town. Early as the hour was, the inhabitants stood at the doors of their *débitants* and *estaminets* or peeped from the windows of their dingy tenements. Women with shawls over their heads formed groups at the street-corners; men in blue blouses and peaked caps, the traditional costume of the French industrial worker, watched from the kerbs or passed stolidly to work. For them it was the customary apparition of an army marching out of the night.

For three days, it is true, the town and neighbouring villages had been packed with troops; all night long the rumble of guns and tramping of an easterly-moving soldiery had been heard in the streets. Yet considering the proximity of the front line —no more than four miles distant—everything in that direction seemed curiously calm and silent.

The two friends marched side by side in rear of their company, Captain Cyril Orde at its head. For three miles or more beyond the town they followed with countless stoppages, the main *pavé* road which leads from Merville by way of Estaires and Sailly-sur-Lys to Armentières. As they marched a low muttering began to tremble along the eastern horizon, the effect of the sound on their ears being that of a number of small drums tapping in the distance, with the occasional thump of a big drum obtruding itself above or rather through the rest. Aeroplanes appeared, humming, purring, whirring. And then eastwards, again, an occasional pale flash against the grey, morning sky showed where a hundred guns were firing.

The battle of Neuve Chapelle had begun.

The men turned to each other and pointed. The mist

lifted, the sun came out. A Staff officer rode past on a bicycle, shouting:

"The first three lines of trenches have been taken with slight loss."

Once the whole Brigade halted for half-an-hour in a big field near a red-brick factory. The men had breakfast, the white-haired Brigadier rode round on a grey horse. A roar like an express train followed by an explosion and a cloud of smoke close to the factory-chimney, gave the alarm. The Brigadier shouted an order. Battalion by battalion they moved out and on.

Orchards and ruined cottages full of troops in concealment bordered the road. An unceasing stream of traffic attempted to pass the marching column. To Knoyle, who had so far seen no more of war's paraphernalia than the trench-foreground and the silent approach to the trenches by night, all this was vitally interesting. It was much as he had imagined it would be. Red Cross ambulances and grey Staff-cars pushing past, motor-despatch-riders, cyclist-orderlies, artillery-limbers and ammunition wagons, all impatiently trying to move back or forward. Eric, on the other hand, nothing seemed to interest except the march-discipline of his men.

Progress was slow, but after winding about among a number of lanes, during which all sense of direction was lost, they found themselves in the battery-area, and, once in advance of the firing guns, could no longer hear or speak with comfort. Yet even here, with one exception, actuality was not at variance with anticipation. Knoyle saw the black noses of heavy howitzers peep forth from their canopy of leaves and belch flame and blue gunpowdery smoke—a whole battery simultaneously—followed by a collective detonation that was overpowering. He smelt the cordite. He saw the barrels recoil fiercely on the carriages and the gunners, clad only in shirts and breeches, cleaning, loading, reloading, working like ants or little demons. What he had not anticipated amid the turmoil that would naturally reign within a couple of miles of the fighting-line, was the spectacle of a French peasant ploughing with an old white horse.

They halted in a sunny meadow by the roadside. Winter had begun slowly to merge in spring. The cannon roared, but a spring breeze stirred grass and tree-tops. Aeroplanes hummed and whirred, but a lark sang as on any March morning above English fields.

Thinking of such things, the young man made acquaintance with pain and death. Soldiers came trickling back from the battlefield—men with bloodstained uniforms, and white-bandaged heads and arms and hands : not badly wounded men, but frightened, shaken creatures with sallow faces.

The waiting troops crowded round, asking questions.

" What's it like down there ? How are things going ? How far have they got ? Did you see many Germans ? "

The replies were :

" It's bloody hell down there," or

" We got their front line, but we're all wiped out."

Occasionally one would say :

" Going fine. We've got all three lines, and the boys are shoving right on."

A little later stretcher-cases came along. And these impressed Adrian with their likeness, as he conceived, to corpses—so white, so still, with eyes closed.

Long processions of prisoners began to pass—tall, fair Prussians with mien expressive of a proud stolidity. Morning merged imperceptibly in afternoon, afternoon in evening, and still they sat on their sunny bank—Orde, Eric, and Adrian— smoking, munching sandwiches or chocolate, dozing. German shells burst with mathematical regularity round a haystack half-a-mile away. The thunder of the artillery never ceased.

" What do you think of it ? " The voice was Pemberton's— Pemberton, the hero of black-striped kid gloves. The young man had been Adrian's companion on the journey from

England, and was attached to another company. Khaki suited him better than a dress-suit. His large, simple face expressed an amiable placidity. He had strolled across to ask for news.

" It reminds me of a sham fight at Earl's Court," Adrian replied. " More noisy, though, and——"

" *So* tiring," put in Eric. " Such a beastly row."

" It *will* be fun if it's like this to-morrow, won't it ? " said Pemberton.

" Sufficient unto the day——" quoted Adrian. " Let's hope we ' young officers ' don't make fools of ourselves."

"Yes—have you boys inspected emergency-rations and water-bottles in your platoons ? " demanded Orde, looking up sharply from the field-service pocket-book, in which he was writing. " The order for the attack will be marching-order without greatcoats. Hear ? "

" Mine are all right," said Eric.

" Oh ! lord, I forgot the damned water-bottles," said Adrian.

" Don't forget, then ! Have you both counted your three hundred and sixty rounds per man ? "

" Yes."

" No. Sorry, Cyril. I'll go and do mine now."

" Yes, and get a move on, young feller."

" Well, so long—I must be getting back," said Pemberton, taking Orde's instructions as a hint. " Hullo ! What on earth's that ? "

A curious and increasing sound like an impending whirlwind made itself heard.

Orde looked up, shading his eyes with his hand.

" Gee-whiz ! " ejaculated Eric.

A couple of hundred yards away an aeroplane came spinning, whirling, twisting to the ground.

" Heavens ! " gasped Adrian.

" Like a shot pheasant," said Orde.

Ten minutes later two stretchers were borne down the road. On each lay a limp figure in overalls, the face covered up.

Adrian thought they looked like mummies. He and Pemberton, who had joined the battalion a fortnight later than Eric, did their best to suppress any visible evidence of shock or surprise.

A certain sympathy born of common experiences and new emotions had sprung up between them. Outwardly and visibly it expressed itself in offering each other cigarettes. They said little to each other; they had little to say. But, for his own part, Adrian saw and freely recognised in the other a new man born out of the harmless individual who was "all wrong." For one thing, he could not forget that in the crowded railway-carriage coming "up the line," Pemberton had insisted on lying under the seat while he lay on it.

In Eric, Adrian had already noticed new and surprising things. Eric did not appear to take his soldiering any more seriously than might have been expected; in fact, in England he had earned the reputation of being "idle"—the "could-if-he-would" sort of officer. But on active service he had disclosed a curious faculty for getting things done. With him they happened—and he smiled. He never noticeably exerted himself—never. He retained his old foppish neatness of personal appearance. He was still partial to small tricks —but they were enlisted in the service of the commonwealth. It was Eric who got the fire going; it was Eric who kept it going and boiled the mess-tin; it was Eric who made the tea —and Eric who did odd things with twigs and boughs and waterproof sheets. It was Eric who "contrived;" he revealed a genius for these things. Orde was too busy: Adrian at a loss. Eric smiled frequently if fastidiously.

When dark fell the order came to move.

"We're going to billet in a farmhouse about a mile from here for the night," Orde announced. "We shall probably attack to-morrow morning, so hurry along, boys, and bag some sleep while you can."

They did their best to hurry along with their platoons. But they crept. They crawled. Troops moving in both directions, and wounded and transport, made progress well-nigh impossible. There were collisions, stumbles, and much hard swearing in the pitch-darkness on the rutty road. Cavalry coming up the side-roads with jingle of bits, clatter of hoofs, and neigh of horses, blocked the way. Artillery ammunition-limbers nearly ran over them. All this, however, was considered of good augury for the battle.

§ 2

It was midnight before Captain Orde had found sleeping-quarters for the whole of his company. With oaths he turned a number of Hussar troopers out of an *estaminet* and barn. Eric meanwhile, having discovered a heap of fairly clean straw, had made a large pallet which he proceeded to spread on the floor of the farmhouse kitchen ; on it there was just room for all three to lie. Adrian lost his way in the dark, and finding it again, felt ashamed. Orde looked—and said nothing. The three of them then lay down under their greatcoats, too tired to talk. A peasant-woman, wooden-featured and incredibly ugly, brought hot coffee, and, with a maternal air, tucked up each of them in turn.

"Good old gal ! " ejaculated Orde. "Damned good coffee, too."

"Oh ! charming woman ! " murmured Eric.

These two fell asleep.

Not so Adrian ; he could not sleep. The heavy, old-fashioned oil-lamp burnt itself out, casting queer shadows about the beamed kitchen that had been the home, no doubt, of many generations of peasants. The old woman went into the next room and for some time her sabots could be heard clanking about the brick floor. At length these, too, became silent. Only the rats scuffled. The men snored in the outhouses and passages. On the shelf an ancient wooden clock ticked. Orde's and Eric's regular breathing told of a dreamless rest. Adrian, weary though he was, lay on his side staring into the embers of the fire, going over and over in his mind the last six momentous months of his life. Out of a medley of memories three events stood in relief. First the August day upon which he and Eric had introduced themselves to the novel perplexity of wooden huts, parade-grounds, mess-rooms, and ante-rooms represented by Aldershot. There followed a dead-level monotony marked by signposts, labelled with such terms as " Squad-drill," " Company-drill," " Musketry, Course A and Course B "—all pointing in the same lurid direction. Then Eric had left for the front. A fortnight later his own turn had come, and he recalled a dour evening when—after days of unimaginable rush—he found himself sitting opposite his father and mother in a little restaurant somewhere near the King's Road, Chelsea. He recalled the atmosphere of false jocularity that pervaded the occasion, his parents' pathetic solicitude, the sharp twinges of conscience and of regret that smote him then. What had he ever done for them (he remembered reflecting) except take them for granted in the brief intervals of his restless search for pleasure ? . . . There came the bright cold January noonday at Waterloo, with Pemberton bidding farewell to a frankly sobbing mother, and his own fiery father crumpled up, inexplicably humbled, and yet parentally proud, waving farewell with a bamboo-handled umbrella as the train glided out of the station. And they had passed through Basingstoke.

Next followed an impression of going up to the front— a two days' train journey in biting frost, a rat-ridden night in a tobacco factory at Merville, a twelve-mile march through a misty morning, and a greeting from Orde and Eric outside a farmhouse. Yes—Orde, oddly rough and unfamiliar, was at the end of it. By a stroke of luck (and special application) he had been posted to Orde's company, to which Eric already belonged. There had then come his first night fatigue and his rst four-day tour in the trenches, during which nothing more exciting had happened than an introduction to the uttermost degradation human existence seemed capable of amid mud and slime. Finally they had moved back in preparation for the attack.

It was a source of the utmost satisfaction to him that he had not been frightened at first. The trenches were ghostly and hideous and mysterious—but not frightening. A shell had burst within a hundred yards of him and he had not " ducked " ; he had " ducked " on subsequent occasions, but only when he wasn't thinking. It is true nothing much had happened—one machine-gunner killed by a bullet, but it was in Eric's bit of line. Yet how abominable it had been ! Frost and food mixed with mud—above all, mud !

Ever in the background of these later impressions was the Grand Illusion of the bygone summer and of that—now—puny world which sank daily further and further behind them all. And there was Arden : that strange interval which so sharply divided the one set of memories from the other.

Rosemary. She had been in his thoughts in all places, at all hours, but especially in the loneliness of nights—and this night above others. For what would the morrow bring forth ? That he could not even visualise. . . .

The firelight flickered on in the beamed kitchen. Again and again his mind went back to the intense moments of his great experience ; again and again he dwelt on every little incident with her. His brain worked in a groove, round and round it went like a bicycle-chain. Trying to immerse himself in the past, forgetting the present, he found only insubstantiality.

With sleep at last, came a knock at the door, and an orderly's voice :

" Is the Captain there, please ? "

He woke Orde, who rubbed his eyes, cursed, and locked at his watch.

The orderly handed him a slip of paper.

* * * * *

Dawn broke across the Flanders plain in streaks of black and ashen-grey, shedding upon the countryside a cheerless light. They soon left the road along which they had been marching, and in single file followed a light ammunition railway across fields. No word was spoken. It was all a man could do to pick his way along the narrow track on either side of which lay liquid mud. Now and again they met parties of weary Highlanders trudging back from the firing-line. In the distance a gun boomed. Close at hand another answered. One by one that sullen booming was taken up along the line behind.

As the light grew, bullets began to whiz and hum above their heads, making every variety of odd sound. First occasionally, then increasingly until the air sang with them. Quite close in front there was a sudden little burst of rifle-fire like the crackling of dry sticks. They came to a road swarming with troops. It was the front line.

All were ordered to press close together behind a high, thick sandbag breastwork. Shells were bursting on and behind the road with an accuracy that was evidenced by the loud, child-like whimperings of men who had fallen or were crawling along it. Bullets, too, pattered against the breastwork's outer face.

They formed a sort of line. Orde looked at his watch. The advance was timed for seven o'clock. There were ten minutes to go. The two friends crouched close together. Eric was asking questions of his men, making suggestions to his platoon-sergeant, and giving orders in sharp, business-like tones. He seemed to know exactly what was expected of him; Adrian looked on, anxious to do whatever the situation demanded, but chiefly conscious of his own inadequacy.

Glancing along the line, he could just see Pemberton's smiling face. Pemberton was all there; Pemberton was equal to the occasion; was he not directing and inspiring his men? All that was most likeable in the fellow seemed to radiate from him at this moment : his simplicity, his solidity, his stolidity. Adrian studied the faces of individual soldiers ; some of them wore a smile, some were unnaturally composed, some sickly-white. He was very frightened, nevertheless tried to compose his own to an unemotional rigidity. The word to " fix bayonets " was passed down. A long-drawn rasping sound followed. His platoon-sergeant—a hulking fellow, already the hero of battles—said to a friend, " Don't stick me, Jimmy ! " and laughed.

The colonel of the battalion came along, with his adjutant, shouting bloodthirsty expletives in a sort of fox-hunting vernacular.

Orde had his whistle between his lips ; every man's head turned that way. In that moment, Adrian saw Orde in flannels on a tennis-court.

Every man was poised in a crouching attitude, with one foot on the side of the breastwork and one on the ground. It was like waiting for the start of a race. Above the crash of the bursting shells and the gradually increasing crackle of musketry he could hear his Colonel bawling :

" One—two—three ! . . . Now, boys ! "

Orde's whistle blew. Adrian caught sight of his lean figure on the skyline—and himself and everybody else clambered onto the parapet. But he found he could not run. He could only flounder and stumble forward through the mud. He had to leap trenches. He had to extricate himself from loose strands of barbed wire which snared him by the puttees. He barely apprehended a landscape that consisted of yellowish-brown mud, watery shell-holes, piles and rows of whitish sandbags, crooked iron stakes with bits of barbed wire hanging from them, one or two splintered stumps of trees. A hundred yards of this, and he saw low, irregular heaps of battered sandbags immediately in front—beyond these a shallow ditch. He saw the man on his right throw himself flat. They all threw themselves flat. One or two grey heaps of clothes and some pieces of revetting material lay about. He conjectured that they were in the German front line, and not a German to be seen—except those muddy grey heaps.

The men crowded into the ditch and behind the sandbags, but there was not room for everybody—or shelter from the bullets. The big sergeant who had said " Don't stick me, Jimmy ! " suddenly jumped up with a shout. Adrian thought he had seen a German, and shouted, " where ? " But the man began groaning and sobbing, his hands clasping his forehead, from which blood poured down his face. Once, when a boy, Adrian had seen a man bleeding after an accident, and it had turned him faint. This sight only filled him with a grave wonder and disgust.

Every other moment somebody was hit. It was like shooting down animals. Every other moment he heard the half-strangled shout or whimpering cry which told of a man killed or wounded. Two or three soldiers lay propped, half-conscious, against sandbags, looking like stuffed figures. One, near him, lay stretched motionless. Then the line jumped up again. Now he lost sight of Orde, but he could see Eric away to the right loping across an open stretch of plough. An old grey-haired soldier in his platoon, with whom he had made friends in the trenches, tumbled down, shot through the stomach. His instinct was to stop and give succour, until he recollected that it was not a street accident but a battle. They dived under a strand of barbed wire and streamed diagonally in batches across an enclosure. He felt he must do all he could to keep his men together. No regular formation was possible in such ground—the men followed their officers in groups, or singly, as best they could. How the bullets hummed, sizzled, and zipped ! . . . They came to another breastwork which afforded better protection than the last. It was the second line of German trenches—and still no sign of a living German. In front of them the ground had been blown into a mound some forty feet high by the action of heavy high-explosive shells. The soil had been hollowed and scarred and rent into a great cavity which provided a last shelter for many—a pit of horror indescribable. Here all the refuse, all the material of the neighbouring trenches, seemed to have fallen. Many German dead lay here, grey and bloody amid the upturned earth. By itself lay the body of a British soldier, the face covered with a piece of white tarpaulin. Adrian vaguely wondered how anyone had found time to perform that act. All the trivial things of life lay here—biscuit-tins, scraps of food, hand-mirrors, ration-tins, boots, books even. And everywhere litter of equipment —black shiny German helmets with the golden eagle emblazoned on the front, German caps and accoutrements, rifles, clips of bullets, pistols, weapons of all kinds. . . . The tradition of blood and iron seemed to have found its consummation in that one place.

Out of the pit they clambered, and up the mound beyond ; and then along a kind of ridge. A small river or large ditch of stagnant water had been bridged at one place by a plank which had broken down. As he approached this a high-explosive shell burst with a staggering concussion and reek of gunpowder on the farther bank. Adrian's inclination was to throw himself flat, but it was not a time to hesitate. He waded through the greenish, sulphur-streaked water, which rose to the level of his chest ; his rifle, clogged with mud, was already useless. Then he came upon Orde. Orde was lying back in the arms of his orderly, his face yellow and so twisted as to be hardly recognisable. Adrian threw himself on his knees beside his company-commander.

" Cyril ! " he shouted. " Cyril ! "—the guns were deafening—" where are you hit ? "

" The shell got him full," the orderly said. " I fell flat ; he went right on."

Adrian could just hear Orde's whisper :

" It's got me—all over the place. Go on. . . . and good luck! "

He made a feeble gesture as though to urge his subaltern forward.

The latter obeyed though to do so seemed an outrage on friendship and the humanities. He stumbled across a ploughed field heavy with recent rains. Men were falling right and left. Khaki heaps dotted the open ground like milestones. Some of his men had got slightly ahead in the race; others unwilling to face the stream of bullets, were crawling forward on knees and elbows. Eric he could just see drop down into a slight depression in front. Here the thin line began to re-form itself, everybody wanting breath.

He made for Eric. A number of men of various regiments and battalions formed an increasingly thick firing-line on either side of them. Through the mist he could see skeletons of trees and the tall red-brick chimney of the Moulin de Piêtre—their objective.

When he had flung himself down, it took several moments to recover breath. Then :

" Cyril's done for."

" Good lord ! Killed ? "

" Knocked over by a shell a couple of hundred yards back. What's to be done ? "

Eric thought a moment.

" I suppose I'd better take charge, as I was second-in-command. We'll have to rush that damned mill. Come on ! Tell your chaps to get ready."

Adrian afterwards recalled how naturally, how inevitably, how unconsciously indeed in that moment of peril he had accepted the leadership of his friend—reversal of their old relationship though it was. He crawled along to where some of his own platoon were lying.

Bullets were humming overhead like flocks of hurricane-driven birds ; a machine-gun was enfilading from some vantage-point. The Moulin de Piêtre was evidently a formidable nest of Germans.

Both realised that it was the critical moment.

Eric's voice snapped out the cautionary words. His whistle blew. . . .

With what was left of his platoon Adrian started forward. He leapt a ditch. Two strands of barbed wire lay in his path— all the world seemed concentrated in those two obstinate strands. Interminable, intolerable moments passed. Men fell against the wire, groaning, lopsided, and were riddled with bullets. . . . Himself was violently struck. He staggered. He shouted out, thinking that some concealed enemy had hit him with the butt-end of a rifle. He felt a thudding pain in his right thigh, and fell backwards into the green, brackish water of the ditch.

Someone dragged him out. A voice said :

" Are you hurt, sir ? "

He realised that he was wounded.

§ 3

For a long time he lay on his face. His leg ached and was limp and helpless. Presently it lost all feeling. He heard them pass down word that he was wounded ; he wondered what had happened to Eric. He took his little phial of iodine from his haversack and tried to reach the bullet-wound. That was painful and too difficult.

Most of those lying around were wounded. Two or three dead lay near. It seemed that the line of advancing men, mown down here, would get no further.

Then he saw Eric coming to him. He came over the top of the ground without haste, and knelt on one knee as Adrian himself had done beside Orde.

" Where is it ? Thigh ? Keep still and let's have a look."

" Lie down, Eric, for God's sake, or you'll get a bullet through the head ! "

" Lie down, sir! Lie down!" voices shouted from all sides. " They can see you!"

"All right! All right! I know what I'm doing. Now then——"

He slit the coarse khaki material with his clasp-knife, examined the tiny punctured wound and applied a phial of iodine. He then began carefully to bind up the wound.

Shrapnel burst low with a shattering crash. Eric's hands gradually ceased in their task: he sank very slowly backward. As he did so, he clasped the back of his head with fingers through which blood trickled. In his own helpless state Adrian could not raise himself sufficiently to reach his friend.

Eric rolled gently over on his face and lay still. A spasm of fear amounting almost to certainty, shot through Adrian's mind. Eric was dead! He shouted for help. The groans of the wounded answered. Through the other's clasped fingers blood continued to ooze.

§ 4

A kind of ghastly stagnation descended upon the battle-field. Through the smoke and the mist and the noise the tall, red-brick chimney continued to stare down at them with maddening serenity. An unceasing stream of bullets came from it, but bullets also came from their right flank and even from their right rear. A machine-gun enfiladed them with a monotonous "clack-clack-clack" at regular intervals. Regular as a heart's beat, minute by minute, came the wail of high-explosive shells. These skimmed their heads, bursting every time a few yards behind. Bits of iron hummed through the air and hit the ground on either side, hissing hot. Showers of earth and stones fell upon the back and neck. The earth around was soon tainted a yellowish-green. Hands and uniforms assumed the same colour. Adrian silently prayed for the end.

Then to his unspeakable relief, Eric raised his head and looked round. His face, papery-white and smeared with earth and blood, was indescribably shocking. Adrian had never conceived of his friend so. The first thing the company-commander did was to drink from his flask. He then took out his handkerchief and proceeded to roll it into a bandage.

"Gurr-r-r," he sputtered. "Are you there, Adrian?"

"Yes. . . . Thank the Lord! I thought you were done in."

"I've got a bit of shrapnel in the back of the head. How difficult it all is! I must have fainted or something."

"Keep still, or you'll faint again!"

"I shall be all right in a minute—if only—I can—blast it!—get this bandage fixed."

"What's to be done?"

"Oh! hang on here and dig in. You and the other cripples had better make your way back. Wait till the shelling slacks off a bit, though."

"What about you?"

"I've only got a scratch. You've got a leg. If you can crawl—crawl."

"Plenty of time when you go."

"Don't be an ass! If you can crawl—crawl."

"Why?"

"Because I tell you to."

"I can still shoot."

"Yes, but you can't run. Frankly, you'll be quite dreadfully in the way. Go—quit—hop it, there's a good boy!"

But the moment had not yet come. There had been a brief pause in the racket of shelling. Now it began again with redoubled fury—the whistle and roar, the ear-splitting crash, the sulphur reek, the showers of earth and stones. Behind, in front, the clamour of the guns never paused. Boom—boom—boom—boom! A German field battery was firing salvoes at short range, and Adrian thought the four clockwork piercing reports at intervals would drive him crazy.

Bang—bang—bang—bang. Away to the right lyddite was bursting in clouds of sulphuric smoke amid the ruins of Neuve Chapelle. An aeroplane sailed overhead. He longed to be in it, to be at least *above* all this, with one turn of a lever to sail back and in a few moments leave behind the fumes and the flames and the noise. Shrapnel cracked low, enormous high-explosive shells burst a short distance away, throwing up fountains of earth amid billowing black smoke. Rifles spat at intervals, more often a machine-gun swept round. The boom—boom—boom—boom of the German field-battery went on. Once or twice only in those weary hours was there a minute's complete silence—like the pause that now and then falls upon an animated conversation—and then they could hear a lark sing.

Late in the afternoon the opportunity for reorganisation came. Guns and men seemed to have grown weary of killing; at least to have grown weary of shooting at that which they could not see. Eric gave the word to dig in, and those who could began working feverishly with their entrenching-tools. A medical officer and two stretcher-bearers came up over the open and set to tending the more desperately wounded. Eric passed the word:

" All wounded to the rear ! "

He turned to his subordinate.

" Now be off—and good luck ! "

That tone of admonition admitted no dispute; and with a heart heavy for his friend, Adrian started to crawl back aided by both elbows and one foot. Half-way across the ploughed field the shelling began again. He now found himself in the centre of the shell-area, of which the firing-line was slightly in advance. 5.9 inch shells, that tore through the air with a mild whistle, finishing up with a roar like high-power machinery, seemed to burst on top of him. Shrapnel exploded above his head in a series of ear-splitting crashes. A high velocity shell arrived like a bullet simultaneously with the report of the gun. He crept into a shell-hole and lay flat. It reeked of lyddite and contained a German pistol of curious shape, bearing a Birmingham trade mark. He could see the blue sky above flecked with fleecy white puffs of aerial shrapnel. At intervals between the booming and banging of the guns, the detonation of the bursting shells, and the incessant metallic clatter of machine-guns behind, he could hear the droning hum of aeroplanes. Death from above, from before, from behind, death, shapeless and repulsive, in every shell-hole; death usurping, beckoning, tyrannical. Terror seized him, such terror as he had never known in his life before. Hitherto he had been conscious only of the profound unpleasantness of the whole business; now it was all he could to do to prevent himself from yelling hysterically.

A head appeared above the rim of a shell-hole.

" Ye'd better give me yer-r pack, zur-r. Ye'll never be able to get on with it as y'are."

He blessed the sound of a human voice. And there was something familiar about this voice—something inexplicably friendly :—not the voice but the accent. He recognised it as a West Country accent. And with that came a second's vision of the hills behind his home as they would look in the bright March sunlight, the white chalk horse on Stane's steep side, the silent spaces of the down-land beyond.
He yielded his pack gladly to those large, willing hands.

Slow as his progress was, and often as he stopped for breath in shell-holes, he came at last within sight of the white, irregular sandbags which marked the old German second-line The stream through which he had waded during the advance lay between, with one visible means of crossing—a single greasy plank, across which lay a dead soldier. He poised himself on the plank straddlewise, bullets hitting the sandbags on either side. Several times he came near to falling off sideways, but recovered. Reaching the boots of the dead man, with extraordinary repulsion he dragged himself across the stiff, unnatural figure, whose dark blood was dripping slowly from a bullet-wound in the neck. He felt the cold blood moist on his hands, and brushed over the soft, clammy face, so unlifelike—a mere heap of flesh. He saw a head looking over the breastwork.

"Come on, sir! Pull yourself up! Here's a hand!"

With the assistance of the arm extended he dragged himself over the heap of sandbags and found—his own stretcher-bearers.

Near to fainting now, he knew little more until he felt the swaying, jogging motion of a stretcher as they carried him along a road which he did not recognise. But he saw the battlefield receding, the setting sun, dead horses and dead men, a tableau of khaki—and one German—in an orchard, as though all had there lain down to sleep. Then he heard the purring of a motor, and was hoisted out of daylight into the gloom of an ambulance's interior. Almost before he realised where he was the vehicle had started, with a jarring of brakes—full-speed ahead. The journey seemed a long one. At first he thought he heard shells bursting; then the sound of traffic. His companions were noisy. One groaned loudly and ceaselessly. Another, with a pronounced Irish accent, poured forth volleys of blasphemy, proclaiming that he had "done in" at least half-a-dozen Fritzes. A third whistled "Tipperary."

Beside him lay an officer without sound or movement.

With no noticeable transition he found himself lying on a bed in a large whitewashed room which looked out upon a courtyard. Something about the place told him that it was either a convent or a school. Once a young doctor came in, looked at his wound, gave him an anti-tetanus injection, and tied a white label on his chest. Once an orderly brought him a bowl of soup. Lying very still, he watched evening steal into the courtyard and saw the sunlight fade on a red-brick wall. He heard the twittering of sparrows without, ivy leaves rustling against the window-ledge, and at infrequent intervals a moan from the next bed.

In the failing light the door opened, and there slipped in a gaunt figure in a cassock, who, after glancing at him and doubtless thinking him asleep, turned to his neighbour. It gazed long and earnestly, made the sign of the cross, then went out silently as it had come.

Adrian peered at the adjacent bed. It was growing dark, but a last sunbeam lit up the pillow, illuminating features that were familiar and yet strange. Blood had gone from them, their fulness being drawn into thin, ugly lines by pain. It was only at the second or third look that he realised Pemberton lay there.

CHAPTER II

Adrian and Eric

§ 1

WITH the coming of night and the lighting of the oil lamps. Adrian noticed figures, diagrams, and queer elemental series of pictures of birds and animals on the walls. He must have slept; it was not the room he had been in before. Beds were set at ordered intervals round the room, each covered with a blue-and-red Army blanket, and every one occupied. In the centre a number of stretchers lay side by side upon the floor, and every one occupied. Red Cross orderlies, doctors, and a nurse in army uniform, grey faced with red, hurried in and out; stretchers were constantly being carried in with much trampling of hob-nailed boots. A sound of motors came through the open door.

"Oh-oh! Yah-ah-ah! Oh-h-h-h!"

Groans, cries, and moans accompanied him through the night. Now and then, from the neighbouring bed, came a half-moan, half-sigh which voiced something that expressed itself also in the spasmodic contortions of Pemberton's face. For the rest, there were loud cries, cries more pathetic in their helplessness than those of children in pain, petulant queries, calls for water or attention, deep, full groans, heavy, effortful breathing of men trying to stifle their suffering; then again the clatter of nailed boots and the subdued conversation of those who could converse.

Amid the shattered limbs, the mutilated heads and faces, the patient, weary eyes, the low moaning, hard breathing and sighing, the unearthly quiet of approaching death, the white, bloodstained bandages, the ragged uniforms and almost unrecognisable figures of men who looked like bundles of old clothes—beneath the yellow, sickly light of the oil-lamps— the army surgeon made his way. He was a dark-haired young man, wearing pince-nez, and was followed by a sergeant, who, ledger and stylographic pen in hand, wrote down diagnoses of the wounds with businesslike precision.

The surgeon came to Pemberton first, looked long at his face, felt his pulse, and with a shake of the head murmured, " Touch and go, touch and go."

Then it was Adrian's turn. His inspection was of the briefest.

" Nothing serious. Slight fracture, laceration of the tissues. You'll be laid up for two or three months. Next convoy for England ! "

He passed on.

Adrian could hear the name and diagnosis of each case called out in turn. After two or three such he began to doze. But he soon awoke.

" Lieutenant Sinclair ! "

" Well, what's the matter with you ? Bit of shrapnel in the head. Any concussion ? "

" No."

" Sickness or dizziness ? "

" No."

" Take care of it in England. . . . Next one ! "

Adrian looked.

" Eric ! "

" Hullo ! " The reply came from a stretcher on the floor.

" I'm here ! "

" Who's you ? "

" Adrian ! "

" Cheers ! I'll get them to carry me over to you."

" And how the devil did you get here ? " Adrian demanded when carrying was accomplished.

" God knows ! I suppose I must have ' gone off ' again. I just woke up and found myself here."

Owing to the bandages about his head, Eric had some difficulty in articulating.

" So we're on our way back to England." Adrian suggested. " I don't mind telling you I feel all chawed up. I expected something pretty bad, but—it was worse." There was some emotion in his voice. " I feel as if I'd been turned inside-out —and left exposed to view. The war's no joke, you know."

A sigh, followed by a deep groan, came from the next bed.

" That's Pemberton."

" Ah ! "

" I think he's going west, Eric."

" Poor chap ! But you'll soon get over feeling queer about it. Going through a battle's like having an operation without an anæsthetic."

" I wonder——"

Eric yawned.

" What I don't like is leaving the sheep without a shepherd. But it can't be helped."

" The company, you mean ? "

" Yes."

" What's that you've got there ? "

Eric, after much fumbling, produced a black-and-gold emblazoned object from the pile of equipment which lay beside him on the stretcher.

" A Prussian helmet. The fact is—well—Faith and I had a bet whether I should get one or not. Give it her, will you— with my love ? "

" Give it her yourself."

" Shan't see her, my dear chap."

" You'll see her as soon as I shall."

" No, I'm not for home."

" But the doctor's just tied an ' A ' label on you ! "

" Well—he'll have to untie it. I shall be all right in a fortnight. England, home, and beauty don't appeal to me just yet. War is the poor man's pastime, you know—and the despair of his creditors."

Adrian suspected this reasoning. But he only said:

"I'll take the thing, of course, if you like. But—we shall probably all be at Arden again in a few weeks."

"I doubt it. And on the whole you needn't say anything about me at all. Just—give it her."

Adrian took charge of the helmet. The events of the past twenty-four hours had revealed new and unexpected lights in Eric; still, he felt no doubt that they soon would meet on the "other side."

Then his friend was carried away, waving a hand. The evacuation had begun, and the stretcher-cases on the floor were taken first.

§ 2

It was a calm spring-like morning when Adrian's turn came to be carried out across a courtyard, under an archway to a waiting motor-ambulance, which drove rapidly to the station. The sun shone upon Pemberton, who was borne out next—his features a little paler, a little more of the quality of marble than they had been the night before. Pemberton had ceased to make any sound.

The flap of the ambulance was not lowered, but Adrian had a strong sense of active life going on around. He knew without seeing that a number of people were standing at the entrance to the clearing-station, watching the wounded being carried out; and as they dashed through the crooked streets, with their cobbled paving-stones and red and blue and white houses, he glimpsed Staff cars rushing past, officers riding, soldiers in English khaki and French blue swarming on the footpaths, parties of German prisoners marching by under escort. When, crossing a square, they passed the Hotel

Normandie and turned down a narrow street, he recognised the place as Merville. The hospital train stood at the very platform upon which he had detrained one bitter night barely a couple of months before.

And as he lay in the long car on a well-hung, comfortable bed which swayed with the motion of the train, he contrasted his present feelings with those of the earlier journey. Then the unknown lay before him. Now it stood revealed: the ordeal to which he had so long looked forward was past, and he was going back to England, to orderliness, to the old atmosphere, the old distractions and interests, to—Rosemary?

That afternoon was a thing of joy. The train rolled slowly and lazily on its journey after the manner of such trains. He cared nothing for its dilatoriness, but watched, with a sort of overful happiness, the flat fields, poplar-plumed spinneys, and drab farmsteads flit past. How different they looked, basking in the first grateful warmth of spring, from their earlier greyness under the frost of a winter's evening! The countryside smiled at him, the future smiled at him, and in the primrose beauty of the budding year he read a smile more cheerful than any of these. Physical pain he had none. He could not move his right leg; on the other hand it caused him no active discomfort.

And as the atmosphere of the battlefield receded, his old optimism was reborn in him. He refused to be daunted by the war—refused to surrender his youth, his hopes, his aspirations, his ideals, his dreams to this first disillusioning. He refused to treat it as other than a disagreeable incident in an, on the whole, well-ordered world.

And he asked himself—it had never occurred to him to do so before—how he and Eric really had come to be mixed up in the business? It was considered suitable at this period of the war—at any rate, public policy—to regard the young volunteers as in some sense heroic. But in respect of two fairly representative young Englishmen, he asked himself whether their motives in joining the Army had been either altruistic or patriotic, or whether they were not in point of actual fact purely interested and personal? For his own part he had no violent antipathy to Germany nor any violent enthusiasm for Belgium, nor any peculiar affection for the British Empire because he didn't know much about it. Adventure, the prospect of experience, the first glamour of the thing, the natural reaction from a futile existence had in a measure attracted them both. Both were in a sense disappointed, or disappointments who had somehow to justify themselves. And in his own case there were yet more personal reasons.

Always in the end his mind went back to Rosemary. True, she had passed out of the region of contact, for he had received only half-a-dozen notes and letters from her since leaving England; yet that was natural. She could not have had his address for some time. Yorkshire was a good deal further away than London—posts were bad, they had been constantly on the move, and in any case she must have been preoccupied by the hospital that had been established at Stavordale. Lady Cranford would see to that. But now his face turned once more towards England.

There was that in the young man which demanded, or failingly, created an abstraction. He idealised this girl, and, so far, experience of the war had had the effect of sharpening this idealising or idolising faculty. She was the antithesis to all that; she breathed about him a perfume of romance in a world of crudest reality.

The spring entered his blood. Everywhere signs of it—primroses and crocuses on the banks of the cuttings, aconites sprinkling little woods, green shoots of wheat pushing up in the fields, a quickening life in the hedgerows, and among the tree-tops. Spring, too, in the swift breeze that rushed past the train. He longed to be out in it, remembering how quietly, delicately, as it were on tip-toe, it came to his West Country home—the grassy dell aflame with daffodils, blackthorn snowing the hedgerows, the cawing rooks rebuilding their nests in the parkside elms.   These were the old familiar signs.

And when summer came . . . ?

Hope surged roughly in his heart.

§ 3

A slight rustle at his left hand caused him to turn over.

A nurse was looking down at Pemberton with an odd, solemn expression on her face.

Through the window, tossed-up sand-dunes, pines, and the blue dimpling waters of the Channel. . . .

He stared for a full second into Pemberton's eyes before the nurse drew the sheet over them.

Something went out of him then : his whole theory, perhaps—of black-striped kid gloves.   His Grand Illusion crumbled ; for the first time in his life he saw—face to face.

CHAPTER III

Fortune's Wheel

§ 1

EARLY in April Sir Charles Knoyle died. He died of double pneumonia following upon the chronic bronchitis which had troubled him regularly for many winters. At the age of sixty-five it finished him off.

Adrian heard the news from Mrs. Ralph Clinton in whose hospital he was near Bury St. Edmunds. Mrs. Clinton was one of Lady Knoyle's particular friends. A tall, handsome woman, with an efficient manner, she came to him one morning as he lay in bed looking out upon the cedar-shaded lawns—it was nearly a week after an operation had been performed upon his thigh—and handed him a telegram.

" Father died this morning—Mother."

In this moment he realised that the often crotchety and increasingly decrepit and of late rather pathetic figure of his father—that figure which, unknowing, he had seen for the last time on the departure platform at Waterloo Station three months before—had vanished for ever. The real pathos of it for him was that he felt inadequate before the death of this father, whom he had never loved so much as respected, whom he had never intimately known, and who had never intimately known him.

The personal shock he experienced was in no sense comparable to that which he had experienced when Pemberton had died beside him. That impression, that first familiar *rencontre* with death, remained vividly. It obliterated every other. Pemberton in life had meant little to him, but they had undergone the same trials, had passed through the same series of emotions and the same initiation—had shared in fact a great common experience.

And so he thought more often of Pemberton than of his father.

The real though impalpable change, the central fact, was that through Pemberton death had become familiar, instead of remote, incredible—a thing that might concern the old but had nothing in common with the young. His mind reacted quickly to experience ; could it be staggered by anything of this sort any more ?

By the second post upon that same day came a letter from Eric. The moment Adrian saw the envelope he knew Eric had had his way. The envelope was franked and bore the battalion stamp. How the devil had the fellow managed it ? The letter explained itself :

"I was sent to R——, where I got round the Medical Officer after being X-rayed and found to be unconcussed. To make sure, I tipped the R.A.M.C. sergeant 20 francs. My 'wound' was nothing, and healed practically after three weeks, but they insisted on keeping me an extra week. So here I am, and you were wrong! . . . I've got the company. This will seem to you extraordinary, and I can't altogether make it out myself, as there are plenty of people senior, but there it is ! It certainly makes life more interesting, but also a jolly sight more strenuous. . . . I suppose you've heard about poor old Cyril. He's in hospital in Park Lane. I'm afraid he's a goner. Better perhaps if they had done him in. . . ."

The letter contained information about the company and the men and the line they were about to take over. It even hinted at an impending attack. It was an ordinary letter, but, reading and re-reading it, Adrian apprehended suddenly the man's enthusiasm—and his courage.

A day or two later Lady Knoyle came down, escorted by her brother, Sir Patrick Cullinan.

Before Adrian was permitted to see his mother he had a talk with Sir Patrick, who, had he not lately come of age, would have been his guardian. He was a red-faced, ginger-haired Irishman with a hearty manner which he tried creditably to subdue in deference to the occasion.

"You must have had a bad time, old chap. Very glad to see you safe home again. And then this—sad affair. A terrible loss for you! Poor Charles! Poor old Charles!"

He stared, with the ill-worn melancholy of a robustly cheerful person, down at the carpet.

"Your poor dear mother, too. What a terrible time! The long illness and the incessant anxiety about yourself. . . . But it's really about the business side of things I came to talk to you." His features brightened in spite of themselves, his voice became more naturally loud. "Of course, you succeed to everything. As trustee, under your father's will, I went into it all with old Payne, the family man of business, and I'm happy to say we found matters in a better way—a much better way—than either he or I expected."

Sir Patrick paused to let these words soak in; he lit a cigar.

"You'll be comfortably off. Your mother, of course, has the jointure from her own estate. Your father was always, as you know—at any rate, in his later years—a careful man. You know, too, the ambition of his life—to pay off the mortgages on Stane. My dear boy, I'm glad to tell you that, so far as Payne and I can see and unless you make an ass of yourself, there's every chance of that ambition being realised."

"At the termination of the present lease?"

"The lease comes to an end, as you know, on December 31st, 1918."

"I always thought we hadn't a bob."

"Your father saved. He—er—invested modestly—and on the whole successfully. He doubled, or rather nearly trebled, his capital. He reinvested. Payne and I knew nothing of that. Even your mother knew nothing of it. He kept you short, I know—on principle. He thought young men ought to learn to economise—perhaps he was afraid of your following the example of your great-uncle Algernon. Ha! ha! ha!"— here Sir Patrick laughed frankly and loudly, as though at some insupportably entertaining reminiscence—"anyway, we reckon, as far as we can judge at present, you should have an income of rather less than five thousand after paying off death duties, and providing you live with reasonable care meanwhile. Stane, of course, brings in a couple of thousand a year and is kept up."

Therewith and thereunto the uncle went into a number of particulars—about farms, cottages, legacies, old servants, Lady Knoyle's jointure, duties and taxation. Adrian murmured "Yes," "Exactly," and "Oh! quite," without any very clear idea of what it all amounted to. Towards the end of the conversation the worthy gentleman, abandoning quite his avuncular rôle, became jovial and even facetious. He wound up by saying:

"The next thing is to get you through this damned war. Then you must find a wife and settle down." He shot a smart glance at his nephew. "Meanwhile nurse that thigh, and as soon as you're fit enough come over to us in Ireland for as long as you can—we can give you a bit of fishing, at any rate."

The invitation was accepted. Sir Patrick departed impetuously, enjoining upon his nephew the advisability of visiting the firm of Payne, Payne & Payne, Solicitors, Lincoln's Inn Fields, at the first convenient opportunity, and leaving as a legacy a large box of Corona cigars.

As soon as Adrian saw his mother it became evident to him that she was crushed beneath a weight of grief which she fought, and in part subdued, for her son's sake. Though she and Sir Charles had married late in life, their devotion had been none the less complete.

"He spoke of you towards the end. He asked after you repeatedly, and said how happy he was to know you were safe. That was almost the last time he spoke. He said his greatest wish was that after the war you should settle down at Stane."

Lady Knoyle completed her little speech without faltering though tears coursed down her cheeks as she spoke.

That first talk (to Adrian's relief) was cut short by evening dressings, and Lady Knoyle rarely referred to the subject again. She could not do so without emotion, and that, as she well knew, embarrassed her son. And she was there to superintend his convalescence; she was there to enliven, to hearten him. Day after day she would flit in like a September leaf and sit by his bedside—or by his wheeled-chair out in the garden —a bent and fragile figure, her head covered with a black lace mantilla, her white hair strained back from a forehead and face that bespoke character, some sensitive or artistic perception, and was still not devoid of the beauty which had once notably been hers. She had a gentle, sympathetic way; she was so obviously anxious to make everybody about her happy, even if she could not be happy herself. Thus she would sit and read aloud to her son or knit, or say nothing, or suggest and fetch things that he might want. Mrs. Clinton and the nurses left them together.

Since his uncle's visit with its momentous intelligence, Adrian's thoughts had centred more and more upon Rosemary. And, try as he would, stifle the thought as he might—and honestly did—he could not remain oblivious to one fact: Fate had worked amazingly in his behalf. . . . Fate? But after all this much could be said for him, that on receiving Lady Cranford's *coup de grâce* via Rosemary he had taken destiny firmly in his hands—and had been rewarded. Fortune had then so far played up to him, had so far completed his task, that he stood before the world no longer without a profession, no longer without some positive achievement—the achievement, at all events, of having done what was expected of him—no longer without—prospects.

And yet the nearer he approached fulfilment in these respects, the farther away Rosemary seemed to drift. There was the elusive baffling quality in her ; he could not—reach out to her. Assure and reassure himself as he did that everything was all right, he realised that hers would not be as plain-sailing an argosy as, (for instance), Faith's.

Both the young ladies were hotly engaged at their respective hospitals. He had received a sympathetic letter from each on being wounded, another on his father's death. Shortly before leaving Mrs. Clinton's establishment he heard from Rosemary —after a fortnight's silence—that Lady Cranford had decided to give up the hospital at Stavordale finding it too great a worry and expense—had formed the intention of taking a flat or small house in London " early in the autumn." In London, they felt, they would be more in the middle of things. And that seemed necessary.

The young man was well satisfied with the news. Rightly or wrongly, he interpreted it as a hint from Rosemary herself that she realised the looked-for moment was at hand. This straightforward piece of information, in fact, not only clarified his immediate plans, but stilled absolutely qualms or doubts as to the future.

CHAPTER IV

The Baptism of Pain

§ 1

By the beginning of June Adrian Knoyle was sufficiently recovered to leave hospital, his Medical Board having awarded him ten weeks' sick leave without violent exercise. And from hospital he proceeded to London, en route for Ireland, where at the Cullinans' he purposed indulging in a couple of months' fishing amid peaceful surroundings.

London he found rank, dusty, full of khaki and clamour. Everywhere—the war. In the streets, in the parks, in the clubs, in the theatres and the restaurants (which were almost too crowded to enter), in the shops and the railway stations, at dinner as at breakfast, in the day and the dark—always the war. A sense of stale depression, of recrimination and misgiving, of morbid foreboding, indeed, seemed to harass all. It was not the London, at once hopeful and vehemently patriotic, he had left in January. That had been a London still savouring the victories of the Marne and of the First Battle of Ypres. This was a London still digesting the defeats of Neuve Chapelle and Festubert, the nightmare of the Second Ypres battle. Men shook their heads about the Dardanelles. The "shells scandal," bringing about the fall of the Liberal Cabinet, had shaken their faith in Government. Adrian, while taking little interest in politics, reacted instantly to this depression. Did he not *know?* Had he not *seen* the British dead lie thick at Neuve Chapelle? And had he not read the newspaper accounts thereafter in which it was said the German fallen lay as five to one? . . . Well, he at least

knew the fantastic falsity of that statement; and he could read
the same story between the lines of Eric's carefully-worded
letters after Festubert. He at least recognised how far the
newspaper public was being misled, how far the newspapers
themselves were being gagged, if not hoodwinked.

One thing above all depressed him. He began to realise
what type of men they were who were "getting on with
the war."

§ 2

The very first thing he did on reaching London (after
changing into plain clothes) was to visit Cyril Orde's hospital
in Park Lane.

He found his late company-commander huddled in a
wheeled-chair out on the balcony; it was a sunny afternoon.

Yes, that stalwart figure had shrunk—into a mere bundle
of clothes. And Orde, staring out over the greenish-blue
tree-tops of the Park, did not see Adrian until the latter
uttered his name. Then he turned abruptly, as though glad
of the distraction, and a smile lit up his face.

"Ah! My dear Adrian—delighted to see you! Very good
of you to come! I heard you were leaving hospital. Sit
down and tell me all about yourself."

Adrian took a chair beside him and was shocked by the
changed expression of his face, so much thinner, sadder. It
was the eyes that more than anything altered the face. No
longer keen and alert as of old, they looked tired—and
hopeless.

Adrian, indeed, had difficulty in keeping emotion out of
his voice and face—he who a few days before had reflected
that the war could spring no more or greater surprises
upon him. Orde spoke, however, in his old curt, incisive
tones.

" I heard you were hit in the leg—or thigh, was it ? But I'm glad to see you've only got a limp. I'm, as you observe, a crock. No good to anybody and never will be again. Better out of the way altogether."

" Don't say that, Cyril. Modern surgery works wonders."

" But not miracles. . . . I'm paralysed, you know, paralysed from the waist downwards. . . . Oh, well ! One'll get through the days somehow, I suppose—and the nights. No more tennis, though ! "

He laughed.

Adrian murmured " Rotten luck," and tried to change the subject. He found Orde's laughter rather painful.

" I heard from Eric the other day," he said. " You know, of course, he got a bit of shrapnel in that show. He's back with the battalion now."

" Ah ! Eric. Back with the battalion, is he ? " Orde repeated the remark slowly, as though wishful of assimilating the information by degrees. " I hope he'll take care of himself. A good boy, that."

Orde bit a toothpick meditatively. Adrian said :

" Lovely view you've got from here."

" Yes, it's nice lookin' over the Park. "

Then after a pause :

" Reminds me sometimes of—do you remember ?—that week-end at Arden just at the outbreak of war . . . where we all met."

Adrian assented, racking his brain to think of some means of keeping the conversation off that topic so natural, so living with recollections alike for Orde and himself.

But it seemed as though the other was determined to go back to it.

" Yes—and that was the last time I played tennis, wasn't it——? "

" Let's see," Orde went on after a pause, " who was

there ? Yourself and Eric and all the Daventrys and—oh,
yes ! that old buffer Freeman—and that appallin' wife of
his. By the way, though, have you heard Freeman is to be
one of our war-winners ? Freeman is to be a Cabinet
Minister ! "

"God forbid ! "

"My dear chap, I assure you. . . . this is the kind of
man who gets on—the kind of man who has all the stock
phrases on the tip of his tongue—the beetle-browed, double-
chinned bureaucrat who rolls out 'so far as present information indicates' and 'our future course must be guided by
circumstances'—and fights the bloody war with words while
we're cannon-fodder for lack of shells. Seems to me their
chief qualification for winnin' it is that they spend half their
lives makin' themselves 'useful' to whoever's in power, and
the other half makin' money."

He spoke with an emphasis surprising in one usually so
self-contained, adding presently :

"If one even felt they were out to win the blessed thing,
but they're not, my dear chap. They're out to save their
faces, to stick to office or get office, to please their wives,
to bamboozle the country. . . . They're politicians first,
last, and all the time. The war's a secondary thing ; the
political game is the one consideration for the Freemans and
all the Freeman kind. They spin webs of words while the
country's spinnin' on the edge of an abyss."

And after a further pause :

"Why can't they leave the executive side to the soldiers and
sailors ? Why can't they organise shell production and man-
power at home instead of interferin' with the generals and the
admirals at the front ? But no—it's words, words, words—
and officemen and ex-lawyers and adventurers dodgin' and
schemin' for power and place and kudos, while our pals get
killed. . . . And they'll whitewash 'emselves. You see,
they'll come out on top in the end—and Festubert and Neuve

Chapelle and all these hellish casualties that might have been halved—they'll be forgotten."

There was bitterness in these words. Orde however, soon recovered his normal dry tones.

"Talkin' of Arden, though, a friend of yours came to see me the other day—that pretty gal of Lady Cranford's. I must say I thought it devilish nice of her—she's so like her mother who was no end of a beauty in her time—and she brought those gorgeous roses. Lady C. is apparently still up at Stavordale closin' or openin' a hospital or somethin'. She's an intelligent sort of woman, but it's a pity she lets that extremely good-lookin' daughter run about entirely on the loose. She brought along a chap I don't care for—that black-eyed cove who was at Arden—what's his name?— Topham, or Upham, or something?"

Adrian sat up straight in his chair.

Orde went quietly on:

"Who do you think is nursin' here—nursin' *me*, in fact? Another of the Arden contingent—that extremely amiable Miss Ingleby—do you remember?"

As though in response to his remark the door opened and Sister Ingleby entered. She was the same as at Arden in every important particular—red-faced and rather plump, with kind, cheerful eyes and a suggestion of bygone good looks brought out of a cupboard. She shook hands warmly with Adrian, putting the conventional questions that the war inspired. Then she turned to her patient.

"Captain Orde, there's a visitor for you—a surprise! Another beautiful young lady—and more roses! Aren't you a lucky fellow? Will you see her?"

"Rather! Show her up, please—whoever she is."

Sister Ingleby trotted out.

"Do you know, Adrian," Orde said solemnly, "that woman's an angel. She looks after me like a wife and a mother and a sister, all rolled into one. Upon my soul, if I wasn't a crock for life I—I'd like to marry her ! "

Adrian had risen to go, though his curiosity was aroused as to the identity of Orde's visitor. He was making for the door when Faith Daventry entered.

She looked efficient in a blue serge V.A.D. uniform; it suited her.

" *Adrian !* " she exclaimed. " Well—what luck ! I *am* glad to see you. Ought you to be about like this, though ? I thought you were still on a bed of sickness."

They went over to Orde and she shook hands, depositing a sheaf of roses on the table by his wheeled-chair.

" From Arden," she said, " with mother's love and mine."

Orde thanked her.

" And now tell me all about yourselves, poor things." She turned to Adrian. " How is the limb—*really* I mean ? Well, you mustn't think you can run about on it yet, you know. Why didn't you come and be nursed by me ? ' Some ' nurse, let me tell you. But firm—oh ! very firm. I stand no nonsense. I slap the ones in bed if they're tiresome, and the others quake before my tongue. You see, ι m Assistant Commandant ! "

" I didn't know you took in officers," said Orde.

" Well, we don't, as a matter of fact. Father and mother have firmly made up their minds that ' officers ' are not ' nice.' One might think they were a sort of savage alien race, what ? However, you see, we've not done with the Victorian Era. But of course, with old friends it's different. It would have been like old times, too, having you both there ! "

" It does seem the devil of a time since that week-end," Orde ruminated. " I can hardly believe it ever happened—not sure it did, in fact. Weren't we just startin' a second set when . . . or am I dreamin' ? "

He had stopped, as though forcibly recalling himself to the

present. Sister Ingleby glanced at him, and from him meaningly to Faith.

" How long are you up for ? " she asked.

" Alas ! only till this evening. This evening I go back to ' the daily round, the common task '—not that it is really so very common. I love it. I never could have believed I ever could have liked nursing and housekeeping and things—before the war. I did them, but they bored me stiff. Do you know, they really are extraordinarily fascinating ! There's a sort of mysterious attraction about dressings and disinfectants and blanket-baths. I couldn't analyse it, but there it is. "

" And how are Lady Arden and ' his lordship ' ? " inquired Adrian.

" Oh, mother is very well. She wanders about—she's Commandant—I do the work. Can't you see I'm worn to a skeleton of my former self ? Look at my hands ! Look at my complexion ! Wouldn't they do credit to a kitchen-maid ? We're all so terrifically and tremendously efficient, you see ! . . . As for father, he's at Clacton with his Yeomanry, playing at being a soldier and damning and cursing every-body because they won't let him go to the front. Of course, they won't ! But we've got an uncanny feeling he'll manage it somehow. He's so determined, so absolutely mulish about some things, you know. He never comes near the hospital. He says the whole thing terrifies him and he can't stand seeing his drawing-rooms and library turned into dormitories. So one of us has to go off to ' classy Clacton ' every week-end."

Adrian became aware of a duty unfulfilled while Faith was speaking. He thought of Eric's Prussian helmet. How should he broach the subject of Eric, in fact ? Or should he ? Or would she ? It struck him as a little strange that she had not done so already, but he decided that it would be tactless to mention the matter in public. He would wait till Faith departed and **leave** with her. This she did very soon, but not before she had confirmed Orde's news about the Freemans.

"Who do you think I met just now—our friend, Lady Freeman! Gertie! She was arrayed in broad black-and-white stripes and a hat that looked like a badly-folded envelope —a simple creation from Paris! She was perspiring profusely, and fell on my neck. And what do you think? Sir Walter's in the new Government—'got his portfolio,' she called it. . . . He's Minister for Something or to Somebody—I don't know what. She was radiant—she was triumphant—and made me a present of three Cabinet secrets straight off (under promise of perfect discretion)—but I've forgotten them."

Orde gave a groan.

Faith rose.

"Good-bye, children," she said. "I must be going. I've to catch the 4.30 train, and a hundred thousand little fussy things to do before then. *Au revoir!*"

Adrian joined Faith on the stairs. They were shown out with smiles by "nice, kind Miss Ingleby"—who wanted a vocation.

§ 3

As they walked down Park Lane, Faith said:

"And how did you leave dear old Eric?" The question came casually enough.

"Slightly damaged but cheerful. He had a bit of shrapnel in the head and was stoutly refusing to be sent home. But that was three months ago. He went back to the battalion within a month."

"Yes, I heard from him the other day." There was a pause and a note of concern in her voice when she spoke again. "But why—*why* didn't he come home?"

How should he answer the question? Why *had* Eric refused to be sent home? He simply didn't know. He said he supposed the doctors thought it was not a bad enough case.

"Faith, you know," he went on, taking her arm as they walked, "you may not have realised it—I confess I never did before Neuve Chapelle—but Eric is what they call a 'stout fellow.' It's a compliment. He is the youngest company-commander in our regiment—if that conveys anything to you. He's quite distressingly brave, and that sort of thing. . . . War is a funny business. It's always springing surprises on you. Eric's one of them."

Silence followed. They turned into the Park at Stanhope Gate.

"And, by the way," he said presently, "I've got something for you—a Prussian helmet."

She did not mistake that. She coloured. A look of understanding came into her eyes and—more than understanding.

"I see, Adrian," she said quietly.

He knew then that he had done a good thing—and was glad. Yet something remained unsatisfied. Of one person Faith had not spoken. He wanted her to speak. But she had offered no remark, public or private, upon a subject which she well knew meant everything to him. Should he speak? He hesitated. The right word would not come.

They strolled as far as the bandstand, then turned back to Hyde Park Corner and stopped under the clock. Faith seemed preoccupied; a dead cold constraint settled upon Adrian. What had Orde meant about—Rosemary and Upton? As Faith was in the very act of taking her leave he blurted out:

"By the way, what about Rosie? Have you seen anything of her?"

It was a poor attempt at off-handedness. Faith replied with an embarrassment she was far too ingenuous to conceal:

"I saw her some time in March, dining at the Astoria with Gina Maryon and—some people. They were just going on to Ciro's to dance."

"Anybody I know?"

"Oh!—two young men."

He did not put the question that was on the tip of his tongue.

"How was she?"

"She seemed—lively. . . . but I must run."

They shook hands and went their ways.

§ 4

Adrian's took him across St. James's Park—he avoided Piccadilly—*en route* for the offices of Payne, Payne & Payne, solicitors, Lincoln's Inn Fields. He wanted to be alone. He felt confused and wanted a respite in which to pull himself together.

He strode on, noticing neither the dirty children, the bits of newspaper blown about by the wind, the orange-peel and banana-skins, the squalid couples on seats, nor the dreary men and women lying about on the grass—all that sordid aspect of summer London which usually depressed him beyond words.

He thought only of Rosemary and the information which Orde had imparted and which Faith's reticence had corroborated—in fact magnified—to his suddenly inflamed mind.

One thing was certain. There had been deception. And that was a wound in itself.

And then this—yes—this reappearing, disquieting figure of Upton. . . . His mind travelled back to the Rodriguez' ball when he had first seen the two together, beyond that to the afternoon at Ascot, and so to the evening at Arden when by chance he had overheard their "Goodnight, Harry," "Goodnight, Rosemary. *Dormez bien!*"

In a letter from Rosemary written about the middle of March which he remembered receiving much later at Mrs. Clinton's hospital, she had said nothing about Upton, nothing about a dinner-party at the Astoria, nothing about stopping in London or seeing Gina. At the most she gave the impression of having rushed down to London to do some shopping and rushed back to Stavordale because of the strenuous demands made upon her by the hospital. She had not exactly given the lie to what he now heard; merely the impression left on his mind was entirely different.

And one other fact pierced him. Rosemary must have received his letter written a few days before Neuve Chapelle, conveying clearly that he was about to go into action —she must have read the accounts of the battle—she may well have known (for it was early published in the newspapers) that he had been wounded. At that very moment she was dining in gay company at the Astoria, going on to dance. . . Egotistical it was of him perhaps, and unreasonable—but he cared.

Was he jealous? He did not excuse the fact or deny it or attempt to call it by any other name. There it was. He felt a dislike of Upton transcending any dislike he had felt of anybody or anything before. . . . For the rest—he did not know. Whether he had the right to resent Rosemary's apparent callousness, whether Rosemary really owed him anything of consideration or anxiety or interest, whether he had the right to expect her to deny herself the most trifling pleasure or amusement on his account—he did not, in his then condition, could not, judge. He only knew the fact as a fact; that it hurt him more than anything had ever hurt him before—that his belief in Rosemary simply could not be the same again. . . .

As he neared the Lake, mocking cries came to his ears, reminding him of that Arden, where he had first so greatly loved.

CHAPTER V

A Duel à Trois

§ 1

ADRIAN KNOYLE returned from Ireland in the first week of August. His first care was to visit his father's grave in Kensal Green Cemetery. And he was almost immediately summoned to attend his second Medical Board. A benevolent looking old gentleman wearing *pince-nez* and a white moustache decreed him two months' light duty, whereupon he rejoined the reserve battalion of his regiment at Aldershot. He was granted a further fortnight's leave and spent this in London ; he was glad to be back in the centre of life. The mountains of Mourne had been peaceful, beautiful, but dull. Physically and mentally the complete change of life and environment had done him a world of good. He felt once more aglow with zest and confidence.

He even began to think again in general terms of the war which, swaying to this side and the other, rising in high tide and beating against the cliffs of victory and then falling back into the trough of disappointment and defeat, always impended and always darkened the horizon.

He had heard from Eric, who had been home on leave. Eric had written once from Scotland, and once from London.

" . . . I spent most of yesterday with old Faith. We went to a matinèe and afterwards sat a long time in the Park watching the ducks go by. (Such ducks !) She behaved very nicely—so very nicely that I as nearly as possible committed myself to the second time of asking. But would this have been *comme il faut* as they say in Streatham. It's different for you. You fixed up your affairs *before* this infernal war. But when one is only home on ten days' leave I suppose one ought to ask oneself whether it's treating one's guardian angel respectably. You see the dear creature is so confoundedly high-principled about that hospital and me and all. In fact I feel inadequate. What do you think ? Anyway, I didn't. . . ."

Adrian believed he had held the key to Eric's romance ever since his conversation with Faith. He was disappointed. And yet—was not Eric right ; Eric who had gone uncomplainingly back to France ? And he, for his part, re-reading the letter, experienced the first conscious intimation of a duty to return—and that at the earliest possible moment—to the acute physical experiences which, he now frankly admitted to himself, he loathed. Debating these matters, he had moments of almost sinister misgiving. They were succeeded by periods of detached philosophical calm. He felt his own life to be in flux, he experienced the same sensation of loss of control that he had known in the small hours of the Fifth of August, 1914. Nothing was certain, nothing static except the fact that nothing could be static. The world was changing, the nations were changing, and—he was changing.

§ 2

Upon his return, the first person he ran into—in Harrods' Stores—was Gina Maryon.

She was darting from one department to another, armed with parcels, and amazingly attired in a pronounced sort of déshabille which resolved itself presently into gauzy black bespangled with golden fleur-de-lys, a gold girdle at the waist. On her head—flowing—was that which could have been mistaken for a widow's veil, only it was gold too. It streamed away behind so that mean people turned round and sniggered, while the merely virtuous said, " Good gracious ! "

" *Adrian !* " she exclaimed emphatically, seizing him by both hands. " *How* rather wonderful to meet—to-day—now—just here ! "

Still holding his hands, she gazed at him long and earnestly —as if trying to tell his future (he thought) by the colour of his eyes. It was evidently the latest thing.

" And how is the poor lad ? Haven't they shot you or shelled you or something ? What a life ! . . . That hot week-end—do you remember ?—just this time last year. . . . By the way, are you in love ? You've got that far-away look still—or is it the war ? . . . Come along ! I'm absolutely up to my *eyes* in things. Come and buy flowers with me ! I *must* have flowers. Can one *live* without flowers ? I'm selling socks for orphan babies this afternoon at Princes'. . . . Pinks, pansies, geraniums, buttercups, anything. But flowers ! " She rushed off in the wrong direction, and on his pointing out this, said suddenly, glancing sharply at him :

" My dear, she's looking so pretty. I tell you, she's looking lovely. Properly dressed that girl would be a dream. Harry's infatuated. We've all lost our hearts. She has personality. She has charm. She's come on a lot. She only wants time. But she does *not* understand clothes. Helena Cranford's ideas are no use to her. I saw the ravishing creature on Tuesday night at Ciro's. We made up a party—Venetia Romane and Harry Upton—you remember him at Arden ?—and Venetia's *cher ami*—and a young Cornwallis in your regiment and Casavecchia from the Italian Embassy—*such* an amusing little person !—and one or two others. We had the greatest fun. If only they wouldn't close the damned place at 12.30 ! . . . All the same London's a dreary amusement. I'm just about fed up with it. But you see I'm in love with Casavecchia and the Rosebud and all of them, so I can't possibly get away yet ! . . .

Will you *really* give me the gardenias? How really truly sweet of
you! . . . I've been away. I'm only just back, and on Saturday
we're all going down in a herd to Stratford-on-Avon to get
atmosphere for the Shakespeare *tableaux* Venetia's doing.
Characters from Shakespeare, you know; will you be one?
You'd make a good Iago. It's coming off for rickety
Belgians next month. You really must see my Juliet and bring
everybody you can—don't you think it will suit me? . . . Do
you really mean to say you haven't seen your Rosemary yet?
Well, you're a poor sort of admirer. My dear, she's *pining* to
see you. She was talking about you the other night. Ring her
up at—let me see, I've got the number somewhere,"—her
hand dived into a black-and-gold be-tasselled bag—" Gerard
11330—that's it! They've taken a flat till they can get a
house. You'll find ' the Countess' more ' the Countess'
than ever." She laughed trebly. "Hi! A taxi! Thank
you, my dear. Now I must rush, simply tear for my life.
I'm having luncheon at Claridge's at one. It's a quarter
to and I've got to go to a dressmaker and try on Lord knows
how many beautiful garments, though they'll never be paid
for. But it's in the cause of charity—which covers a multitude
of sins, doesn't it? We shall run into each other again though
—sure to. And remember Juliet at His Majesty's on the
23rd. *Au revoir, au revoir!* "

She screamed the address to the driver and was gone.

§ 3

Adrian walked to his club. He walked quickly, oblivious
of all but one fact and one thought. Rosemary was in
London, breathing the same air, living, moving, just round
the corner, liable to be met at any moment, accessible, close!

Their correspondence during his stay in Ireland had been
confined to two very ordinary letters. In addition to these
he had written three very long ones—and torn them up.

Well—Gina had said Rosemary was "pining" for him! On reaching his club, he went to the telephone-box.

His hand trembled as he took off the receiver. Would SHE answer ?

" Gerrard 11330 ! "

The waiting moments were trying. Twice he was given the wrong number. His heart thumped furiously, irrationally. Would SHE answer ?

" Are you Gerrard 11330 ? "

" No, we're the Gas and Coke Company."

He could have laughed—had he been less angry.

Interminable moments of waiting. Would Lady Cranford answer ? God forbid ! He hoped she might be out. If so, what next ? . . . He pulled himself together, schooled himself to speak in normal tones.

At last there was a faint tick-tick at the other end and a maidservant's voice—obviously a maidservant's—said :

" Who is it, please ? "

" Is Lady Rosemary Meynell in ? "

" No, her lad'ship's out. She's not expected back till this evening."

" Will you give her a message, please ? But no—er—just say Sir Adrian Knoyle rang up ! "

A flash of intuition had indicated the safer course. He might have left a message. He might have said he would ring up later —perhaps he would ring up later. She knew his club would find him. The next move lay with her. . . .

It was not by the first, but by the last post next day that he received a note in Rosemary's handwriting. The note ran :

> " 37, Grosvenor Mansions,
> " Thursday.   " Mount Street, W.
> " MY DEAR ADRIAN,
> " So glad to hear you're back. Do come to tea on

Saturday. I'm looking forward ever so much to seeing you.

> "In wild haste,
> "ROSEMARY."

What, he asked himself, did this brief communication imply ? That they were to be on a new footing ? That he had fallen in her estimation ? It was at once a challenge, a disappointment, and a puzzle. Really it told him nothing. The few scribbled lines might mean anything. There was the evasive quality in her.

§ 4

He knew no feelings of trepidation or anxiety, but only of overwhelming eagerness when two days later he ascended in the lift of the Mount Street flat. Somehow or another he had bluffed himself into a condition of high confidence. He had anticipated in much detail the forthcoming *tête-à-tête*, only hoping that Lady Cranford would not appear on the scene to interrupt it. He had in fact rehearsed the conversation in advance, held half-a-dozen ready-made sentences in hand, enumerated half-a-dozen points of view to lay before her, a dozen or so memories to recall—or to revive. He wished, he intended, to straighten things out. Tact would be necessary, indulgence, restraint. He would not charge her with anything or refer in any way to Upton. He would ignore the whole subject of Upton. He would show her that he on his part after a year's absence was in no way changed, and that as a matter of course he assumed she was not.

How rudely were these anticipations shattered !

The flat was not a large one, and when the housemaid opened the door the first thing he heard was a man's voice. He caught a glimpse of Lady Cranford at the tea-table, then— of Rosemary. Then he saw Upton.

Lady Cranford greeted him with a carefully adjusted smile, held out her hand as if she had been doing nothing else all her life and was tired of it, and said :

" So glad to see you back. You know Mr. Upton, don't you ? "

Adrian flickered an eyelid, Upton nodded. Rosemary held out her hand cordially.

" Hullo, Adrian ! How nice to see you again ! How's the damaged limb ? Sit you down if you can in this teeny room and have some tea and be comfortable." Her naturalness was—impenetrable.

It was as if there had never been anything more—than that.

His first glance had told him that something new, some new beauty of grace and height and contour had come to her in his absence. She was dressed in summery grey, she wore her string of pearls. Something firmer, more mature, more expressive had come into her face. A new colour, surpassing delicate, had crept into her cheeks. He noticed these things, though after the first greeting he averted his eyes. And he noticed the rather commonplace little rose-pink and sky-blue drawing-room automatically, just as he remarked the challenging smile on Upton's unwholesome face.

Upton wore a blue serge suit and a black bow tie. Adrian thought he looked like a professional musician or a Socialist Member of Parliament. He was almost blatantly " intellectual." The martial spirit had evidently not yet claimed him.

So this was to be their *tête-à-tête !*

Adrian's chagrin was complete. He was dumbfounded at the girl's audacity. His blood boiled now against the one, now against the other. He felt that somehow he must cope with the situation, but his mind was in a turmoil. What did it all mean ? . . . He knew what it meant. It meant that Rosemary was asserting the independence he had freely given back to her, that she was deliberately issuing defiance.

" Here I am ! " she seemed to say, " Rosemary still—but not so easily captured ! If you want me, you'll have to win me all over again — see ? "

The girl herself then had cold-bloodedly contrived this situation ! And she was quite shamelessly enjoying it. She delighted in confronting these two who, she knew, detested each other. Well, she should enjoy it as little as he could contrive ! If only he had at his command the loud self-confidence of a Sir Walter Freeman, the imperturbability of an Eric or an Orde, the blandness, however odious, of Upton himself ! He had not. He was as ingenuous as a child. Emotions flickered across his face with the infallibility of an index. He felt the tensity of the situation overmuch.

§ 5

The conversation at first consisted of commonplaces. How had he fared at Mrs. Clinton's hospital ? What had he been doing in Ireland and how was his uncle, Sir Patrick ? Where was he quartered, and when was he going to rejoin his regiment ? Poor Captain Orde—had he seen him ? Had he heard of So-and-So's engagement and wasn't it dreadful about such-and-such an one being killed ? The hospital at Stavordale Castle ? Yes, it had been closed down—the methods or rather lack of methods of the War Office were more than she, Lady Cranford, could cope with.

For he found himself drawn into exclusive conversation with her ladyship, who wanted to know the truth of the shell-shortage scare and our alleged gigantic losses on the Western Front. Would the Germans march on Petrograd after the fall of Warsaw, were the Russians completely done for ? And so forth. He found difficulty in concentrating his attention on matters, the interest of which was for him at the moment nil ; he kept catching snatches of Rosemary's and Upton's small talk. He could not but feel, however, Lady Cranford's attraction as a listener, nor could he remain entirely oblivious to the compliment implied in her questioning.

At length, tea being over, she rose, saying that she was going to lie down, as her custom was, before dressing for dinner.

Thus the three were left alone.

Adrian sat facing Upton. Upton sat at right angles to Rosemary. Rosemary occupied the sofa. The tea-table was between the three. From the first the two men stared across at each other with unconcealed hostility. Upton would not meet Adrian's rather aggressive stare, but wore a half-defiant, half-triumphant smile as who should say :

" I know all about you. Now then, a fair field and no favour ! You're no more to her than I am. Don't think I'm going to hand over the reins ! "

How he detested the fellow !

And Rosemary—was judge and jury. Instinctively he knew that all the time she was watching them, watching them out of her quick little eyes and alert brain, comparing them, weighing them up, judging between them, probably, nay, certainly laughing at them both. It was the rôle she had set herself to play.

" When's the war going to end ? " she demanded.

" A good many—— "

" Personally, I don't think . . . beg pardon, Knoyle ! "

Both men had begun to speak at once. Upton smiled ; so did Rosemary.

" A good many soldiers say it will be a draw," pursued Adrian in a constrained voice. " Some have thought so all along. Of course, we've got enormous resources which I suppose are increasing every day, but the Boches are fighting on internal lines and the defence has a huge advantage nowadays. I don't see myself how we're ever to break through."

He happened to have been reading an article by *The Times* Military Correspondent that morning.

" Good heavens ! Is that the effect Ireland has had on you ? " laughed Rosemary. " You're not fit yet—that's quite clear. You want sea-air and champagne ! What can we do for him, Harry ? "

" My chief gives it a year," said Upton, without noticing her remarks. " The blockade will finish them by this time next year apart from anything else. They are getting short even of the bare necessities. They've absolutely no rubber, very little metal, and very little raw spirit, so I don't see where their equipment and ammunition are to come from. Then of course there's the food question——"

" As long as we aren't starved first," put in Rosemary. " You don't think that, do you, Harry ? I'm so greedy, you know."

Upton with a flourish offered jam sandwiches.

Adrian, not to be outdone, handed the bread-and-butter. The competing plates collided.

" Ah ! " she laughed. " Be careful ! Which shall I have ? Well—I can't resist jam sandwiches."

She shot a smiling glance at Adrian, who winced.

Everything about the fellow exasperated him. The large liquid eyes—that women found attractive. His faintly patronising, slightly affected, didactic way of talking. The sort of expressions he used such as "My chief." The undeniable precision of his point of view.

" Look at the creatures we've got filling Government offices ! It's all very well talking about what *may* happen. As Cyril Orde says. . . ."

He checked himself. He realised that he was verging on downright rudeness and appreciated the foolishness of it. Upton grinned malicious defiance, with a hint of impending triumph. Adrian changed his tone.

" Oh ! well," he ended rather lamely, shrugging his shoulders, " I suppose nobody knows much about it either way. I only hope you're right. We haven't heard what you think yet, Rosemary."

Rosemary laughed.

"My dear, my opinions are at present discoloured by the atmosphere of the Countess of Cranford's hospital—a concatenation (is that the word ?) of chloroform, bismuth, disinfectant, steriliser and red tape from which I never expected to emerge alive ! We never had any time to think of how the war was going, we only saw the effects of it, which I thought disagreeable in the extreme. And mamma was terrible grim ! Mamma, you see, *is* efficient. She's the sort of person who enjoys the worst cases. Oh ! no more hospitals for me. Not this child ! I'm going to adopt a general—like Gina."

"Or sell programmes for war-babies or ' walk-on ' at charity matinées for rickety Belgians—what ? "

Adrian could not forego this chance cut at her whom he now regarded as his enemy.

"Both of which Gina does ! "

"Who is Gina's general, by the way ?   I met her the other day but she never mentioned him."

"Haven't you heard ? Oh ! But it was absurd. By dint of the sort of wire-pulling " (" or leg-pulling," Upton interposed) " at which she excels she got attached to this important personage in the capacity of *chauffeuse*. You know what she is. Well, she turned up an hour late the first morning and went to the wrong address the second. After that she was told she needn't appear again. In fact, a red-capped and gold-laced gentleman politely suggested she should try an aeroplane instead, which gets there quicker, he said, and can't take a wrong turning. Since when . . . as you say ! "

Rosemary and Upton laughed.

Adrian murmured, "Typical ! "

The story irritated him as Gina's laugh did. It was typical of her. It was tiresome—and time-wasting. He suspected Rosemary had told it on purpose to annoy him.

And it only needed this to explain the change in Rosemary
—that change which he had been trying to fathom ever since
he entered the room. She was a Maryonite. In his absence,
she had become a Modern Bohemian. Where were the old
candour and simplicity, the ingenuous if sometimes mischievous
look of earlier days ? Now her face showed—well, self-
consciousness. She was conscious of her charm as a woman
—and a beautiful one—where he remembered her only a
child of Nature. She was conscious of power.

And she offered him a scented cigarette.

§ 6

" I believe Adrian disapproves of Gina," she said, turning
to Upton. " He's shocked at her behaviour, aren't you? "

" Oh, no ! Not a bit——"

" You forget Knoyle has been fighting for his country ! "
sneered Upton. " He takes life seriously."

" I meant to cast no reflections on the lady," Adrian protested. " Everybody says she's clever, which is irritating
certainly. I've read the first edition of ' Rays.' Frankly, I
think it's rot. I'm going to see her as Juliet. But she's born
out of due time, don't you think ? To me, she's an anachronism
at this time of day."

" A what ? Great Scott ! "

" Well, I wondered how the war would take her. I mean,"
he finished up, falteringly, " the war—takes people different
ways."

" Well, if you ask me," laughed Upton, " I think it takes her
to Ciro's most nights of the week, don't you, Rosemary ? "

Adrian stiffened. The other two exchanged glances. The
girl said :

" Well, don't *look* as if you disapproved, young man ! We
don't mean any harm, do we, Harry ? What's the use of

sitting down and crying over the beastly war? As Gina says, 'It's a short life, so live it.' Come with us to Ciro's on Sunday night and try one of Harry's new concoctions—what do you call the things, Harry?—a 'horse's face,' or something very odd. I thought it horrible personally, but I'm sure it's just the thing to pull you together, m'lad."

He felt fit to kill her—with his hate or his love, he could not have said which.

They were in league, these two. They were laughing at him. He was outside their understanding—*she* made him feel that. He glanced at the little enamelled clock on the mantelpiece and saw that he had already been there over an hour. But he was determined not to give way. Upton showed no signs of going. He would not go till Upton did. He would not yield a minute or an inch.

Quivering with anger as he was, he set his teeth, determined to see it through. An icy self-possession came to his rescue and he answered with apparent good-humour:

"Can't—thanks awfully. It's the night I rejoin at Aldershot. But we must go there some other time—it's ages since we danced."

They began talking plays. Had Adrian seen "Betty"? Yes—and what an amusing show it was! Upton remarked that he hadn't been to a musical comedy for five years.

"No?" murmured Rosemary. "Have you seen 'The Man who Stayed at Home'?"

Upton met that thrust with a thin smile. Adrian's heart melted like an icicle in sunlight. Upton wasn't having it all his own way, anyhow.

"Anything to get away from the war," she went on. "I'm *sick* of it. It interrupts everything—you can't escape. The papers are full of it and so are the theatres. Everybody you meet is a soldier. It's so much more distinguished, I think, to be a conscientious objector. . . . But, oh! lor', what fun one might have had in respectable times!"

" Be charitable, my dear Rosemary ! " said Upton, with an expostulatory gesture. " Remember you're addressing one whose heart is in such a bad way, he may die of palpitations at any moment. Personally, I have no intention of joining the Army."

Again Adrian thought amused glances passed between them. He was again hotly furious. Whoever or whatever the fellow referred to, it was an equally poor joke.

Really the situation was becoming impossible. Everything seemed a blow aimed directly or indirectly at himself. The two of them were in league against him—the one he loved and the one he hated most. His subtlety in words was not equal to that of Rosemary and Upton singly, let alone combined. He felt at a hopeless disadvantage against them. *Against* her—so it had come to that ! He sat fast in his chair, nevertheless, facing them with set face and steady though mirthless eyes. He would sit on thus and let it come to an open rupture sooner than leave the field to his rival.

At this moment the door opened and Lady Cranford entered, handsome in a black evening gown.

" I don't want to interrupt the conversation," she said, " but do you realise, Rosemary, that you're dining at half-past seven and it's already a quarter-past ? "

" Goodness gracious, yes ! We're going to the play. I clean forgot. We've had *such* an amusing conversation. Now I'm afraid I must turn you both out. Good-bye, Harry ! Sunday night, 8.30 at Ciro's—don't forget ! "

She turned to Adrian and it flashed oddly through his mind that this was the last time he would see her. But he was determined to betray no emotion.

Upton was taking farewell of Lady Cranford with his back to them.

Rosemary was smiling.

He held out his hand.

" Good-bye, Rosemary."

For a long second her fingers touched his. Through those baffling eyes flickered—the merest flicker—the simple expression, at once friendly and affectionate and charming, of the Rosemary he had known at Arden.

She only said :

" Good-bye. Come again."

But it was enough to make him feel that he had found after all what he had been groping for through twelve eventful months.

As he walked down Park Lane (having curtly discarded Upton) he arrived at that reflection which comes to every lover sooner or later—regarding the contrariness of woman, the evasive quality in woman, the psychological apartness of woman, by man never reckonably to be understood.

CHAPTER VI

The Triumph

§ 1

A WEEK later the young man again found himself ascending in the lift of the Grosvenor Mansions flats.

His features were pale, he looked tired. During the week he had slept little, eaten little, seen nobody, and spent most of his time wandering about the streets and parks. Two notes, one of which still lay in his pocket, helped to explain this condition. The first ran :

"Sunday.   " 175, Eaton Square, S.W.
   "DEAR ROSEMARY,

     "When I came to tea yesterday, I thought it was understood we were going to talk over the agreement we came to this time last year.

     "Instead I found you with that chap Upton, whom, as you know, I dislike. If you want to forget everything that happened a year ago, for goodness' sake say so and there's an end of it. But be frank and let's understand each other as we always used to.   ADRIAN."

The answer came three days later :

"Wednesday.   " 37, Grosvenor Mansions,
                             "Mount Street, W.
   "MY DEAR ADRIAN,

     "Of course I don't want to forget anything. But don't be silly about Harry, who's a dear. Come in and cheer me up at tea-time on Friday as I shall be all alone. Love.

                     "ROSEMARY."

Thus it came about that Adrian's state of mind eddied like a cork upon successive waves of hope, disappointment, exasperation, love, jealousy, and profound bewilderment. He could no more form a conclusion in relation to Rosemary than a year ago he could have been persuaded that she would ever be the cause to him of such mental torture and confusion. He repeatedly recalled the night of the Rodriguez ball when it had all begun. He remembered the halo of self-satisfaction, elation, and bland optimism with which he had surrounded himself as he walked homeward in the summer dawn. He would have laughed then at the very suggestion that any woman—least of all, Rosemary—could have so disordered his life! How confidently, how smoothly, and with what un-restrained enthusiasm he had looked to the future then! And now—doubt, disillusion, if not *débâcle*. In the background of it all—the war. Moreover, the philosophy, the composure that had carried him through his first war experiences seemed to forsake him in face of this merely emotional situation.

§ 2

As he entered the little drawing-room, he caught sight of Rosemary's profile against the window and was amazed, in spite of himself, by its beauty : the small head on the slender neck, the hair drawn back by the blue ribbon that made a band across the forehead, the features matchless in delicacy of outline. When she spoke he was conscious afresh of the charm of her voice and of her laugh, of her careless graceful manner that so perfectly expressed her attitude to life.

He resolved to go straight to the point. She perceived the strained unhappy look in his face and smiled amiably, though in the smile was a touch of—defiance ?

" Rosemary," he began abruptly after they had exchanged a few words as to their respective doings since the last meeting,

" what's the matter ? Something's happened. We've got off the rails."

" Really ! " she laughed. " Have we ? Where do you get your low expressions, may I ask ? Off the rails ! What does he mean ? Explain yourself ! "

" Well, it's no good fooling. You know perfectly well what I mean. Things aren't the same as—as when we last saw each other. You're—somehow—changed. I'm not, you see, and . . . it's difficult."

" My dear, worthy goose, don't look so tragic ! Of course, I've changed. You've changed. Mamma's changed (for the worse !) We've all changed. Everybody changes in a year—especially with the war and the price of everything. Our tempers get short. But you can't say I've changed to you because I haven't. . . . And now tell me all about the battles."

" Oh ! damn the battles ! " Adrian saw clearly that he would have to make the whole of the running. " I didn't come to talk about them. You have changed to me and I want to know why."

" It's the other way about, I think," she replied. " *You've* changed. You seem to have become a very serious young man all sudden-like. You never had that far-away look when I knew you—not even on Sunday in a punt ! Laugh ! Smile ! Don't look so glum ! Why this tragi-comedy Hamlet-and-Romeo air ? Will tea do you any good, or would you prefer some of the ancestral cherry-brandy, or shall I produce the remains of a bottle of champagne ? What on earth's the matter ? "

He stared at the carpet.

" Are you in love, by chance ? " she inquired demurely.

" Oh ! hang it, my dear Rosemary ! You get more like Gina Maryon every day ! "

" Well ? "

" Well," he broke out angrily. " It's a confounded pity.

It's a great mistake! Why can't you be yourself? I can *feel* the change in you. Good God, how different you were a year ago! Don't think I'm losing my temper—but what a pity it is! Do you ever see anything of Faith now, do you ever write a line to Eric? Look at this "—he picked up a book, whose cover rayed orange and silver from a gold centre. "'Rays' by Gina Maryon, Venetia Romane, Harold Upton, etc. Now, who would have seen that on a table of yours a year ago? Why, you'd have laughed the thing out of existence! I don't want to be disagreeable, but can't you see it's the most hectic tommy-rot ever printed and paid for? I can just imagine Gina 'educating you up to it!' . . . Why do you run about with all that Maryon crowd, why not stick to old friends like Eric and Faith and people of your own sort?"

"Like yourself, you mean?" she put in—sarcastically.

"Yes, and me, if you like. You were born to a different side of life, a different world altogether. You'll finish up by living with professional comedians and amateur poets, coming down to dinner in a green dressing-gown with gold splodges on it, soaking yourself in cocktails and brandies-and-sodas, discussing your emotions as if—they were somebody else's, and . . . all that sort of thing. Well, I only hope I shan't live to see it!"

A sort of desperation seized him.

"What's the matter with the boy! Why this sudden outburst of—what do they call it?—vit-up-er-ation? What have I done to provoke such a sermon—poor little me!" But she, too, had a temper. A hard minxish look had come into her eyes. "I must say you're extraordinarily polite to Gina who happens to be my very greatest friend—*not* excepting Faith. Of course I'm very fond of old Faith, too—we all know she's a good sort and all that—but I can't see so much of her now because she's buried in the hospital and you know as well as I do she has nothing like the brilliance and charm and talents of Gina. Everybody loves Gina—you can't help it. If some people would try and understand 'Rays' instead of abusing it, they might become quite intelligent in time."

"I don't mean Gina only. I mean the whole crew of them—poets and comedians and Jews and foreigners and all. They may be amusing, but they're not your lot—they're not the people you were born to. You're infatuated with them, I can see, and they're spoiling you as they've spoilt lots of other people. Nobody comes to any good who's taken up by Gina Maryon. It's notorious. And as for your friend Upton——" Adrian paused; he had spoken very fast as if afraid of forgetting what he had to say.

"Ah! I thought that was at the bottom of it," she exclaimed vindictively. "So that's what you've been driving at all this time and never succeeded in getting out! 'My friend Upton'—as you call him. Well I may as well tell you, Adrian, Harry *is* a friend of mine and a jolly good one. I know you're prejudiced against him—lots of people are. . . . Why? Just tell me one sound, sensible reason. Why?"

"It isn't only Upton, it's — all of them. I don't want to begin personalities, but they're a rotten lot—especially the men. They're decadent and superficial and artificial. Compare Upton with Eric or Gina with Faith! They're—unwholesome. And they aren't even happy. I've seen Gina in the undressing-room with the paint sluiced off and the joy-rags torn to ribbons; you've only seen her on the stage with the limelight and the footlights on. She's what novelists and newspapers call 'ultra-modern.' She's the precocious child of the next century. Why not stick to the present one?"

"What you really want is that I should give up being friends with Harry."

Silence fell between them. Each felt that the turning-point

had been reached. After all they understood each other so well. . . .

Adrian's face had grown firm and set. Rosemary's, by turns angry and mischievous, now wore the expression of a kitten playing with its first mouse."

Presently he said :

"Very well, put it that way if you like. But I can be frank, too. I come to you humbly enough to ask whether you mean to stick to the understanding we agreed upon a year ago, or—whether you want it washed out. You remember the two conditions ? I needn't mention them. Your mother made them. I can only say I'm equal to them now. I don't come to claim you. I agreed to our egagement being broken off. I only ask you to look the thing fair and square in the face. You stand up for Upton and ask me what I've got against him ! I've told you already I dislike him personally. You can't marry both of us. It's got to be one or the other. And you've got to choose. If it's to be him, I go—here and now. If me, he's got to fade away—for keeps. . . . That's the case in a nutshell."

A flush had risen in Rosemary's cheeks and her eyes were very bright.

"Things have changed," she said.

"Things ! " he exclaimed bitterly. "Yes—and people. But I haven't. I'm just the same. I tell you straight you've been in my mind every hour of every day for over a year. You've been a part of myself. You've been the mainspring of my life. I've never been without you ; till the last few weeks I've never doubted you. You're as much to me now as you were on that Sunday evening at Arden—under the willows in the punt. It's just because you mean so much to me—everything in fact worth living for—that I say we've got to come to a decision here and now. Time won't wait. Things can't go on like this. Uncertainty's impossible to anyone who feels as I feel.

She saw that he was in earnest, that he was suffering—

and liked him for it. A queer little smile played about her lips.

Adrian did not observe this, but gazed unhappily out of the window, away over the chimney-pots into the blue sky. Only a convulsive gripping of the hands that clasped his crossed knee betrayed him.

When Rosemary spoke, it was in a hard level voice :

" I can't give up Harry. That's too much. . . . Besides, why should I ? He's a great friend of mine—nothing more than a friend. He's never been what you've been to me, Adrian. But—I can't give him up. It's selfish of you to ask me to. He's never said a word against you. Why can't we go on without quarrelling about each other's friends ? I'm very, very fond of you, but—no, I can't simply wash out Harry."

Adrian rose.

" Very well," he said quietly and firmly, though blank misery spoke in his eyes. " Good-bye, Rosemary. It's time I was off."

He went towards the door. She looked up.

" Sit down ! " she commanded. " Don't be so impulsive ! Let's think the matter over calmly and decide in a few weeks' time. Nothing could be more foolish than to rush into things of this sort—or out of them. I may have changed in the last year. I've gained experience, you see." She spoke with a childish sagacity that would have struck him as amusing had the situation been other than it was. " There's plenty of time——"

" There's *not* plenty of time," he broke in, taking one or two turns up and down the little drawing-room. A photograph of Arden in the full-dress uniform of his old regiment stared him in the face and recalled memories that he would sooner have forgotten. All the will in him was concentrated on controlling and crushing the weakness that surged up in him—the longing, the passionate longing to take her in his arms ; to preserve her from a world that would seize her and soil her and make her suffer ; to take her to him for loving, for cherishing, for protecting—from herself.

But he only said :

" There's *not* plenty of time—any more than there's room for—anyone else. I may be selfish. I don't know. I know that I care for you more than anybody or anything I have ever cared for, can ever care for on this earth. I know that I can't and won't share you with any mortal soul. I know that every moment of uncertainty is an agony and that a year's waiting is more than long enough. You've not been frank with me. You neither tell me nor even hint to me of your—friendship with this person until I come to ask you to carry out your part of our agreement—then you fling him in my face. . . . No, Rosemary, you've not been straight with me."

" Well, then, I'll be straight with you now ! " she cried in anger. " I'll be straight with you now ! I can't give up Harry as a friend. What's more, I won't. You're asking too much. You're utterly unreasonable ! I'll make no conditions whatever ! "

In that moment he feared for her as never before.

Without a word he held out his hand. She took no notice, but gazed obstinately out of the window. Sounds of the evening streets came up to them—cries of children at play in the nearby mews, hoots of motor-cars, a distant rumble of motor omnibuses in Park Lane.

Adrian went to the door.

" Good-bye, Rosemary."

Her face was bent away from him and he could not see the sudden look of fear that flitted through the resentful expression of her eyes.

But as he turned she moved her head and looked up over her shoulder at him with an expression that he well knew. She walked deliberately to the sofa and sat down.

" Silly—old—thing," she murmured, her voice suddenly quiet.

His face was still stern and utterly unhappy; he paused, fingers on the door-handle.

" Come here ! " she said softly. " Come here ! "

He hesitated, fumbled with the door-handle, looked at her —moved back into the middle of the room.

She half-sat, half-reclined in a corner of the sofa.

" Silly—old—fool," she murmured almost inaudibly.

Her impudent chin, her eyes dancing up at him, her lips roundly pressed together, her gossamer hair, her damnable charm—drew him. . . . drew him.

*　　*　　*　　*　　*

Very late that night Rosemary Meynell sat at her writing-table in the little pink and blue drawing-room that so exactly resembled a score of other little drawing-rooms in the West End of London.

She was all alone in the flat. Lady Cranford had not yet returned from the play. A shaded electric lamp cast a rose-pink glow on her features. Seen thus, it was a face so full of possibility and charm that it could neither be ignored nor forgotten, but seemed bound to play a more than ordinarily active part in the fortunes of men and women. It wore at this moment a troubled expression.

With long pauses, with much and deep reflection—and an occasional sigh—she was writing a letter.

" It's no good," she wrote, " it's no good a woman thinking she can equally care for two people at the same time. Until to-day I thought " love " and friendship could travel side by side. They can't. Sooner or later one or the other's got to go. It's a question either of a big loss or a big smash. I don't understand myself, Harry, as I've often told you. I seem to be two different people rolled into one—since I got to know Gina and you. I've thought the whole thing over calmly to-night and I realise that I must go back to my true self—the original one. The other, though it's part of me, seems to be only kind of grafted on. I've loved my time with you all—too much. If I had cared for *you* less, it could have gone on with the other thing. But—it's meant too much.

" And so I said—quite voluntrarly (*sic*) because I see it's for the best, in fact the only possible thing, seeing what we've been to each other the last few months—I said we'd each go our own way and that except by acident (*sic*) we wouldn't meet for a very long time. I tell you frankly I hesitated, but to-night I seem to see plainly which way my future lies and that apart from obligations I ought to be true to what I believe is my real self.

" I have given my word, Harry, that we won't meet again."

She paused, fell into reverie, and murmured to herself :

" Yes—Adrian was right. They're not my people. They're amusing, exciting, attractive—p'raps I could have become one of them in time. Perhaps. . . . They're like fireflies, dragonflies, butterflies, shooting-stars—different every time you see them. So am I in a way ! That's where we're on common ground. . . . At times they're wonderful—the maddening. . . . Harry's a wonderful lover—Adrian's clumsy. Harry can—express things. Adrian's always an Englishman—and always the same. . . . How funny they were together ! Why *will* Harry wear black bow-ties, stick-up collars, and say ' Excuse me ' when he gets up to go ? That's when he's maddening. . . . Sometimes wonderful with his big dreaming eyes and way of saying things and—sometimes just a clever little clerk. Adrian's—himself, with something thrown in since Arden. I think I like him better than then. We were a boy and a girl then. Now he's a man and I . . . feel very much a woman."

§ 3

The Yale lock on the outer door clicked and Lady Cranford entered, handsome and young-looking in a dark gown and a diamond.

"Well, child, writing letters at this hour? You look tired! Go to bed. . . . We went to 'Peg o' my Heart.' It's Irish and attractive and——"

"Mamma!" Rosemary interrupted.

"Yes, darling?"

"I'm engaged."

Lady Cranford said nothing while she took off her cloak, nor did she betray the slightest sign of having heard. Then:

"Who to, darling?"

"Adrian Knoyle."

Another pause during which in front of a mirror the majestic lady appeared to be much occupied with the small ornament in her hair.

"Oh, well, he's an old friend, isn't he? Let's talk it over in the morning. Come and kiss me."

Cold and imperturbable as marble, Lady Cranford allowed herself to be kissed. It was her way.

Rosemary sent out her maid to post a letter. Mother and daughter went to bed.

CHAPTER VII

The Dream

§ 1

UPON the expiration of his leave, Knoyle rejoined the reserve battalion of his regiment at Aldershot and found himself back in an atmosphere that had ceased to be familiar—an atmosphere four-square consisting of corrugated iron and wooden huts, dusty parade-grounds worn bare of grass, "orders," "duties," and "shop." War, women, work, and whisky were the staple topics of conversation in that "C" Mess whose atmosphere was as prosaic and hide-bound as the standard corrugated iron erection which housed it. During the morning, and an hour in the afternoon, everybody was on parade. Everybody went to sleep over the newspaper in the ante-room after luncheon; it was a tradition to read the *Winning Post* after tea. After tea, too, most of the young officers played lawn tennis, or by some means, equally mysterious to the licensing authorities as to the ordinary foot passenger, dashed about in small motor-cars.

Every Friday and Saturday afternoon, there was a general exodus in the direction of London, while during the small hours of every Monday morning a really surprising number of arrivals might be noted at the gate of the camp. Lieutenant Knoyle was invariably one of these. A certain proportion of the officers were confined to camp by routine duties each week-end; he was never one of these. For to Adrian's surprise and great convenience he found himself a person of some consequence on rejoining. Many had joined subsequent to himself and were still joining; most of the younger regular officers had been killed, incapacitated, or were " on the Staff " ; his own contemporaries were mainly in France or in hospital. And so he found himself a senior subaltern. The incidence of which was that he also found himself in a position to " arrange " a large proportion of camp duties. Never one minute more than he could help did he spend in the unromantic atmosphere of Aldershot.

The fact was he hardly noticed Aldershot. It passed him by as things pass by a man dreaming ; and the latter part of that August and the whole of that September were for him a dream. At Aldershot, he was an automaton ; it was in London that his pulse throbbed and his heart beat. Practical considerations he could not deal with ; he thrust them aside or just left them alone. And the time-honoured firm of Payne, Payne and Payne, solicitors had bitter cause for complaint, their name triply expressing their feelings.

Adrian was engaged to Rosemary, firmly, boldly engaged ; this was all that mattered. Rosemary was the world and the world was Rosemary. He knew nothing of the war (except when Eric Sinclair wrote), and until these matters were forced upon his attention had not the remotest idea that Warsaw had fallen, that there had been an " affair " in the Baltic, and that the guns were thundering with ever greater intensity along the Western Front. All he was conscious of were the long London week-ends frequently extended to Monday evening, the occasional evenings snatched (on the French system), the thirst and ardour of his renewed approaches to the drawing-room in Grosvenor Mansions.

Lady Cranford was tactful and rarely appeared, or was busy and, safeguarding the proprieties, glad to have her self-willed daughter off her hands. So the couple led a hectic life. They were never still. The love that had sprung up again between them, like an uncertain flame, fanned itself and seemed now to all but consume them. Their movements were erratic— but always movements. They enjoyed no peace as at Arden and knew nothing of Arden's spaciousness or calm entrancement. Something new and turgid—something integral to the war and to the time—had entered their love-making, as indeed it had entered into the lives of all.

Adrian would have been for sitting still. His content was to spend happy hours *à deux* in the little drawing-room between tea and dinner. But no! Rosemary would allow this only after all other experiences had been exhausted. Thus a great deal of their time was spent in taxicabs, in rushing from one place of amusement to another, in frequenting the gardens of Ranelagh and Hurlingham. They played a great deal of lawn tennis. On Sundays they often went on the river at Maidenhead or Shiplake. They went to the play and danced—Lady Cranford unvocally disapproving. Twice a week Rosemary worked at a canteen.

By force of circumstances, the dictum had come to prevail in high circles that "nothing matters in war-time." The old conventions had (almost without exception) fallen into desuetude—not, it is true, with the formal sanction of such confirmed Victorians as Ladies Cranford and Doncaster who entirely disapproved of young people going about in couples; but because these ladies could no longer practically resist the new customs that the new set of circumstances had ordained. Nor were the lovers always together. They were often accompanied by one or other of the Miss Kenelms, who gave no trouble, but on the other hand a *cachet* of respectability, and who carried on a mild spangle with a young brother-officer of Adrian's, Arthur Cornwallis by name—a dreamy youth lately from Oxford.

Once, and once only, they ran into Harold Upton. It was at the Dover Street tube station. He had blossomed into the uniform of the Royal Naval Volunteer Reserve and if they had not run straight into him, would have passed unrecognised. He shook hands with Rosemary who said:

"Whence this vision in blue-and-gold?"

Adrian thought he detected a momentary self-consciousness

" I operate searchlights on the roof of the Admiralty. You must come and see them working, Rosemary."

His voice and manner bespoke a certain defiance. He ignored Adrian after one swift glance in the latter's direction.

" Are you still at the Home Office ? "

" Yes, but I'm a half-timer. I've a weak heart, you know. At present we're busy bringing out a second edition of ' Rays.' In fact, I'm just off to see Gina about it now. By-bye ! "

The couple walked home silently.

§ 2

Lady Cranford showed complaisance about the projected marriage since she was assured by the majority of her acquaintance that Adrian Knoyle was a " possible " young man and that, considering the dark circumstances of the time and its still darker prospects, Rosemary might have done worse for herself. Lady Cranford's common sense affirmed the same view and she put no impediment in the young people's way. Her peculiar pride spoke differently.

She had more than one conversation with Lady Doncaster on the subject :

" Of course, he's quite a nice sort of boy, Carrie, and all that—I've nothing against him. There's five thousand a year and a place, but—I don't know—when one thinks of the chances that gal's had——! One has to think of practical considerations, especially in these times—nobody knows that better than you and Doncaster !—and what money he's got is in land. That young Upton in the Home Office, who wanted to marry her, though one doesn't know much about him, is extremely well off, clever, I think, and very agreeable, but there seems to have been some previous understanding over my head with the Knoyle boy. As you know, I put a stop to it once."

"The gal might have done better for herself," Lady Doncaster declared, pouring out tea. "On the other hand she might have done worse. She's just as pretty as she can be and, of course—though Margaret Knoyle is a dear, I've known her all my life—the Knoyle side is really not very interesting and five thousand with a place to keep up is nothing in these days. However, if they're fond of each other——"

"Oh! there's nothing more to be said. It would be useless for me to say anything. I should like them at any rate to wait. But you know what Rosemary is, you know what all the gals of the present day are—one can't say a word to 'em. . . . Yes—I do feel she's wasted. There she was all last summer, as pretty and well-dressed as any gal in London, with every chance in the world and crowds of very presentable young men hanging about. . . . She could have married Fotheringay —*so* nice, though a bit wild—but no! she insisted on going her own way and choosing her own friends. . . . All these children—I don't know, we're old-fashioned I'm always being told, but——"

"It's no use worrying, my dear. They *will* know better— until a couple of years after and then . . . weeping and gnashing of teeth, followed by the Divorce Court. Edward and Mary Arden are exceptionally lucky, of course. Faith, I think, is thoroughly sensible, not at all your 'gal of the period,' and will soon make up her mind to marry that nice young Sinclair who comes into all the Craigcleuch property. There's plenty of money, and I believe he's done so well in France."

§ 3

Lady Cranford's consent having been won and there being no obvious impediment, the wedding was arranged for the middle of October. Owing to the war and Sir Charles

Knoyle's recent death, it was to take place as quietly as possible in Yorkshire, with no public announcement until a week or so before the event. Lady Cranford described it to her friends as " a hole-and-corner affair."

Meanwhile time was passing, and that month of September, 1915, was not as other Septembers in London. Such an autumn had never been known. London was full of people instead of being, as in happier days, utterly deserted. Whence and why they came none could say. The fashionable streets and more especially the resorts of pleasure were full to overflowing, and if superficially life seemed to be more careless, more intense, more abandoned even than in peace-time, there might yet be found a very short distance below the surface, consuming anxiety, suspense, and mental torture. Upon the public conscience still, in the public mind lay the tragedies of Neuve Chapelle, of the Second Battle of Ypres, of Festubert, and the opening phases of the Dardanelles campaign. In the East, the Russians were everywhere retreating. The grey tide of the German armies seemed to be surging forward East and West.

And it was as though Doom daily, nightly, hourly and invisibly crept nearer to London itself.

Adrian and Rosemary sitting at the open window of the Grosvenor Mansions flat. could sometimes hear the sound of the guns in Northern France. It was usually after dinner when that quarter of the city is comparatively quiet, only an occasional motor omnibus lumbering past at the street's end.

" Listen ! " he would whisper.

And she would bend her head. The low muttering seemed to come from the south-west.

" Funny, isn't it ? "

She would squeeze his hand.

" Oh, Adrian ! " she murmured, " I don't know—there's something awful and warning in it. . . . Please, *please*—you must never go back there ! "

And he would laugh if in the mood, or—kiss her gravely and tenderly; or, again, leading her to the piano, would insist upon her singing that snatch of the Apache ditty which she had sung at Arden:

> " C'est la valse brune
> Des chevaliers de la lune,
> Que la lumière importune,
> Et qui recherchent un coin noir."

"It's a queer little thing, that," he would say. "It will always remind me of Arden and our love."

§ 4

There was a night when, coming out of a theatre in Shaftesbury Avenue, they found hurrying crowds, people gazing upwards, and a saffron glow in the eastern sky.

There were detonations.

A man's voice said: "Can you hear it?"

And another: "No, I think it's passed away."

All around people were calling out:

"Look at the sky! Look at the sky!"—but remained at gaze regardless of danger. Was it lack of imagination or a sort of dumb surprise, he wondered? For Adrian, that night was a revelation of mob-psychology.

And the lurid eastward glow, throwing into relief the chimney stacks and church steeples, the bold stone pinnacles and lofty projections above the city; the dim, hurrying or watching crowds beneath, whose faces were pallid, some with fear and some with excitement; the clangour of the racing fire-engines, the occasional violent explosions near and far, the unearthly droning of aeroplanes in darkness overhead, the mysterious frenzy and confusion of it all—these presented to the young man's imagination a spectacle more tremendous and more awe-inspiring than anything he had seen before.

It seemed to him then as though some Judgment, great and terrible—for all its sins and shames, for all that city's wrongs and self-inflicted woes—impended above himself, above her beside him, above the generality of mankind.

Rosemary clung to his arm in these moments, thrilled and wondering not less than he. And in these moments they *lived*.

He pushed her into a taxicab before half-a-dozen other struggling people and ordered the driver to Grosvenor Mansions. As they slowed down to cross Piccadilly Circus, an hysterical woman tried to climb in. Only then was Rosemary frightened. When they reached home she insisted on changing into a tweed coat and skirt and going off to the City where the fire was raging. . . . When they reached home again, dawn had come.

During all those September days while the artillery duel grew fiercer and fiercer on the Western Front, and from one club to another, from one little forum to another the knowalls ran with their ill-founded tidings—these two lived on in their dream.

CHAPTER VIII

The Awakening

§ 1

THE Battle of Loos broke upon the world on Sunday, September 25th, 1915. Four days later Adrian's Commanding Officer sent for all officers to the Orderly Room.

" I've brought you here to tell you that during the present fighting, I'm sorry to say, our battalions have lost very heavily, especially in officers. It will be necessary to send out a big draft at once with another to follow, and I want every officer who is fit, to get ready to proceed overseas at once, and those who are not passed fit to go before Medical Boards as soon as possible with a view to being so. Please give your medical histories and categories to the Adjutant. There will be no leave of any kind until further orders. Company-commanders, get to work on your drafts at once."

That was a rude awakening for Adrian.

He realised with a jolt that he had not finished with the war, that, on the contrary, the war lay in wait to claim him and use him and engulf him. He fell heavily out of his trance into an unthinkable dilemma.

Yet as a fact the moment his Commanding Officer had spoken he had seen his duty outlined before him straight as a broad white road—clear-cut and perfectly plain. In that same moment something clutched desperately at him. It was not the voice of Rosemary, though that he heard, too ; it was not the mortal fear of losing her at the last that gripped him, it was not the other prime emotion of his life, his love for Eric Sinclair, who might now be lying wounded—or might be dead ;

It was not the sudden shattering of his dream though, God knew, that hurt; nor was it the smaller though none the less bitter thing that his cherished week-end was lost —perhaps his last. It was a fear greater than these. He felt like a man who has given his word not to escape and who sees his prison door ajar. It could be done. It was so easy. It could be done without an effort. He had not to pretend, he had not to act, he need only remain passive. . . . He knew Medical Boards. They did everything by routine. He had had a couple of months' light duty; they would give him a month's home service—probably more. He had only to produce his medical history sheet, answer one or two questions, and—sit still.

Yet it could not be done. He knew it could not be done the moment he thought of Eric, of Eric's attitude, scornful of home and resolute after Neuve Chapelle, of Eric at Festubert unscathed, undaunted, and still determined, of Eric serving long months in the trenches at Bois Grenier, and La Bassée, of Eric leaving Faith—a free woman; of Eric in this mighty battle now. He simply could not shut his eyes to these things.

There were forty-eight hours in which to decide, forty-eight hours in which to decide whether he should state his case and remain true to Eric, true to himself, or, clinging to Rosemary—remain silent. After he had sent a telegram and written a letter to this little tyrant of his, there was no more to be done. He saw that he must fight the thing out alone. He threw himself into the work of inspecting kits, emergency rations, boots and what-not, but all he did was mechanical. He could not concentrate. It was as though suddenly in the midst of an idle meandering he stood confronted by a fateful parting of ways.

His instinct, of course, was to evade decision. He longed to turn his back on the alternative, to let somebody or something or circumstances decide for him. Yet he could not do that

either; the alternatives were too clear-cut. And ever and
again came the little voice whispering in his ear of the wedding
that would have to be put off—till when? But no! why
should he visualise that? The voice whispered, too, of
the futility and unreason of the course he proposed, of
the course that was reasonable and sensible, straightforward
quite, and demanding neither evasion nor pretence. It
whispered of the fantastic character of his sentiment towards
Eric—what would Eric expect him to do? To come out as
soon as he was sent out, of course! If there was anybody
who loathed sentiment, conventional sentiment especially,
it was Eric. He could imagine the very words of Eric's
counsel. . . . And Rosemary—what would she expect of
him, what had she the right to expect of him? Surely that
he should marry her as had been arranged, on the day that
had been arranged. Was it proper, was it commonly decent
to leave her with the profoundly uncertain prospect of a
further long engagement?

The same small voice whispered insidiously, insistently
over and over again the name, Upton.

§ 2

The morning of the Medical Board came and with it a
letter from Rosemary imploring him not to be a fool, imploring him to take no risks of being sent to the Front until
after they were married. She knew, she said, what an ass
he could make of himself; she trusted him to think a little
of her.

But he had made up his mind now. And nothing would
change it. Through the whole of one day and the greater
part of a night he had wrestled with himself, cajoling, conjuring,
reasoning; and at last the still small voice had nearly won. . . .
In the morning came the news which finally decided him.
And so far as this struggle went his mind was at peace.

The news was that almost alone among the officers of the first battalion, Eric Sinclair had been neither killed nor wounded; that, on the contrary, he had achieved conspicuously in the bloody assaults on Hill 70; and that he had been awarded the Military Cross.

Hearing this, Adrian debated no more, was unmoved by Rosemary's entreaty, and when the senior officer of the Medical Board asked him how he felt, replied that he was fit, had been fit for some time, and wished to be passed immediately for active service in the field.

On the following morning he was informed by the Adjutant that with eleven others he had been detailed for the next draft and would be given three days' leave in which to obtain the necessary kit.

§ 3

Lady Knoyle had taken a small house at Ascot, and to her Adrian devoted the whole of one of his three precious days.

This day was harrowing. It was miserable. And yet it was comforting, too. Try as she might, Lady Knoyle could not cloak nor dissemble the emotions she felt at this parting from an only son while yet in the shadow of her earlier grief. All about the windy Heath they strolled, pink and purple heather smiling, pines and birches waving in the breeze that sighed through yellow-prinked gorse of another season gone. Sun and shadow wheeled and wove against the deep green and black of the landscape, light-hearted golfers passed them intent upon their round—to all appearance care-free from the war. The world seemed gay in the bright October weather—it was impossible not to inhale the scent of the pines! They talked of the parent who was gone. Nor could Lady Knoyle forbear to speak of his example of principle and independence, of his great pride in, of his mastering love for, his only son. And of the father's hopes in that son's behalf.

And after they had walked a while without saying much, they began to talk of the wedding that must be postponed, and of the postponed happiness that must go with it. Adrian had hitherto made no mention to his mother of those events which had changed, or at any rate seemed to be changing, the whole aspect and tenor of his life. They had seemed dissonant from her state of mind ; he had feared, too, to hurt her feelings so soon after his father's death. But he had intended in any case to tell her now. He thus made known to her without hesitation the outline of his story, confiding his intention that the marriage should take place as soon as he could get leave, and reserving only those details which touched upon the part Upton had played in his affairs.

He did not regret it. All her patience, all her sagacity, all her sympathy were from that moment his. He had her blessing. She reinforced, she encouraged, she counselled. She asked no questions but by her insight gave him a new courage, a new confidence, a new hope, in the course he had elected to pursue.

" Perhaps it is for the best," she gently said. " It seems hard now, I know—but I think in the long run you may not regret it. You're young, you're both of you young, with, we'll hope, all your lives before you and little, thank goodness, but happiness behind. I have often felt deeply thankful that you have always been so happy. You were as a child. You were at school—and afterwards. But don't think you always can be ! That's the mistake too many people make. So now remember this isn't the *end* of anything, it's only— life. . . . You see, I know you so well that I'm sometimes afraid for you. I'm afraid of the imaginative thing you get from us, Cullinans—the Irish temperament—and then, our, how shall I say, *hardness* in suffering. . . . Never let life knock you down. Meet it fair and square, and if it hits you hard, give to it like a tense spring—and spring back.

"I think you have already begun to feel. I could see a change in you when you first came back. I can see something still different now. This war *happened* for you and men like you."

They walked on in silence. They came to that part of Ascot Heath which is opposite the stands, and Adrian looked across to the enclosure with its white palings, reddish-pink tiers, and thick second crop of hay, all empty and forlorn —that arena where with no thoughts but of gaiety, love, and hope he had watched the social pageant of England moving and changing beneath him. And the ground on which he stood—it must be the very place where in the hot glow of the club-tent Rosemary and he had sat together, dallying with strawberries and cream as they had so far dallied with life. There, too, it was that he had come by his certainty and his decision. Then Faith and Eric had come in. . . . He was lost in reflection while Lady Knoyle rested on a sandy bank. It was only at such moments, when brought face to face with one or other of the events of that far-off summer, that he apprehended the change which had already begun to move within him. He still did not know the quality or the extent of it nor indeed to what direction it tended.

Lady Knoyle was speaking again. Her rather sad Irish eyes gazed at and beyond the waving crests of the Swinley Woods.

". . . And believe me," she was saying, "believe your old mother when she says that in the end it will be worth while. One cannot live, one cannot die, one cannot love or hope or *know* or achieve anything worth having without pain, without experience. Remember that, whether it's the horror and the dreadfulness of the time are breaking your heart, or whether—whether it's anything else. Suffering is the crucifixion of each one of us—the very embodiment of the life-story of Our Lord Who was crucified and rose again . . . the anvil upon which is beaten out the slow-wrought progress of our world and of humanity."

And although her eyes had filled with tears, she presently continued :

"To believe in God, *a* God, to look up to—*something*—to believe in a divine purpose and a hereafter—this is not science or religion or metaphysics or philosophy ; it is instinct—truth."

They were turning in at the garden gate of the little villa when Lady Knoyle added :

"You may die, and if you do, you will have done a good thing. And if you live—you will be the greater and the better and in the end, perhaps, the happier man."

During tea and dinner they talked of his childhood, of his school days, and of Stane Deverill ; of the wide landscape viewed from the Three Hills at sunset when woods and farms and meadows sleep in peace ; of the white chalk horse on the side of the downs, of shadowy cattleways, old encampments, and the grassy barrows of a long-vanished race ; and of the space and silence of the Great Plain beyond.

Only at the last Lady Knoyle broke down. Her son walked through darkness to the station, his heart heavy with the atmosphere—and prescience—of farewell.

The following day Adrian spent in buying and packing. At night Lady Cranford, Rosemary Meynell, himself and Mr. Heathcote—who arrived, triumphantly flourishing a preliminary list of officers in the Foot Guards reported killed in the fighting at the Hohenzollern Redoubt—went to see "Watch your Step."

CHAPTER IX

Last Day

§ 1

THEIR last day together, Rosemary and Adrian decided to spend in a long country walk. Announcing that nobody was to wait up for them, they set off early and took train from Marylebone.

It was a still, misty October morning. London behind them lay, grey and sombrely veiled; as they reached the outer suburbs, sunlight began to pierce through the fog. They passed rapidly through Pinner, Rickmansworth, and Amersham and, descending at a wayside station, set off along a lane past fields and woods and parks where copper-gold sunbeams made broad level paths through hanging mists, while overhead, instead of the grey pall of the London atmosphere, they caught glimpses of an enshrouded blue. On this, his last day in England, Adrian ached for a breath— that he might carry across the sea and beyond—of the English autumn, of that so perfect Michaelmas summer. He found what he sought when they came to the yellow stubble, the ploughman at work on the steep sides of the Chilterns, the black rooks following the newly-turned earth, and heard their clamour on the dry air.

He wanted to make Rosemary, too, feel something of this. He hoped she might share with him that side of nature and life which finds expression in the silence and solitude, the beauty and peace of an autumnal countryside. It was a quality he had found in the writings of Jefferies and Hudson and Hardy; and he spoke to her of them.

She looked puzzled, then smiled.

"Who are all these funny men? It's certainly a divine morning."

It was plain that she did not understand. And the words that trembled on his lips were never uttered.

If he felt a twinge of failure or of disappointment, he corrected it at once. He had only to look at her face—and the landscape became filled for him with a beauty transcending its own. It was so far, this, so infinitely, mercifully far from the social vortex in which they had lived, from—the Gina Maryon thing! So he assured himself: "Some day when we have lived a good while at Stane and she knows it, every inch of it, and loves it as I do—then she'll understand."

They had luncheon in the stuffy dining-room of the principal inn of a small town upon which they happened by chance. Neither had remembered to bring sandwiches, whereat each accused the other. Outside was the market square, grey, red and white, with narrow streets branching from it. They could just see the rounded, burnished tops of the beeches high up on the slopes of the hills beyond. The square was empty save for a foxhound puppy. Once a raw youth in corduroy breeches and leather leggings came out of the inn-yard, rolled the puppy over, looked round and went back through a side door to the inn-yard. That was the only sign of human activity.

After luncheon, they nearly had a quarrel. Rosemary was for calling at the mansion known as Ash-hanger which lies beneath a flank of the Chilterns northward, and which had lately been bought from its owner of centuries by none others than Sir Walter and Lady Freeman. They discovered this through the loquacity of the young woman who waited upon them. Rosemary declared that she would give anything to see the place and that the Freemans might provide them with much entertainment, Adrian that he would give a good deal to see the place, but did not feel in the mood for Freemans on this their last day.

" Let's climb those hills," he pleaded, " and plunge into the beechwoods—and get lost in them if you like—only let's spend the whole of this one day together."

Rosemary became petulant.

" You selfish old duffer," she said. " You never do a thing I ask. Why this sudden passion for solitude and beech-woods ? It won't take us long to go to Ash-hangar, look round, pull their respective legs—and *then* there'll be time for solitude and beechwoods. ' The day is yet young ' as Gina says—of the night ! "

" It's our last day," he pleaded.

" All the more reason why you should do one little thing to please poor little me."

" Very well, then," he reluctantly agreed.

Rosemary said " *Poor* darling ! " and kissed him. But in the way she said it, there was something that reminded him of Gina.

§ 2

Ash-hangar was, in fact, only a mile outside the town. Round the sweep of a broad carriage-way they came into full view of the great Tudor house. Everything seemed buried in unfathomable silence. Not a dog barked. Not a bird twittered. Not a sound of any kind came from the interior.

So calm, so quiet, so self-contained, so devoid of and far removed from life ! It was as though the very spirit of the older, half-forgotten England had fled from a world in which it found no place—and hidden here.

The door was opened by an almost indecently up-to-date butler who announced that both Sir Walter and " her ladyship " were at home. They were conducted through a

panelled echoing hall to an inner walled garden.   Sir Walter
was reading newspapers, Lady Freeman and another lady were
knitting.

" Well," said the stout, large, bald-headed gentleman,
rising heavily, " this is a pleasure !   An unexpected pleasure !
You know my wife ?   You know my sister-in-law, Mrs. Granville-Brown ? "

Mrs. Granville-Brown in a pink tam-o'-shanter, yellow
golf jersey and light tweed skirt, made a formal inclination
of the head and said, " Pleased to meet you."

Lady Freeman exclaimed :

" Oh, how lovely to see you both ! Let me think ! Not
since Arden—fancy ! Have you had lunch ? Reelly ? Oh,
well ! then, you'll stay and have an early cup of tea. We'll
have a little chat and then take you round the sweet old
place."

She threw a sparkling, an almost confidential glance from
Adrian to Rosemary.

The Freemans had been established at Ash-hangar only a
very short time. It was so " old-world," Lady Freeman
explained—and convenient for week-ends. " My husband
has to be at the House or his Ministry all the week,"
she added.

" Yes," Sir Walter echoed, " these are busy times."

They sat in a circle. Under the Freeman influence, Adrian
felt that for all the charm and beauty of the place, the much-
talked-of invasion of England had really begun.

" Everything going splendidly," Sir Walter announced in
response to Adrian's conversational inquiry. " Most of the
confidential telegrams pass through my department and you
can take it from me, young man, the Huns are on their beam-
ends. They're starving, the blockade is wearing them out,
their losses have been terrific, their munition supply is failing,
they're using up their reserves in the East, and in the West
we are in overwhelming strength. In the spring—well, you'll

see. It is not a break-through this time but, take it from me, the C.-in-C. never expected one—that I happen to know. We've got Hill 70, we've got all our objectives, it only remains to finish off the war. That ought to be good enough, eh ? " he finished up jocularly.

" And what about our losses ? "

" A lot of good fellows gone, of course ; a lot of good fellows gone. But there it is—what can you expect ? ' Sailor gare,' don't they say over there ? Our losses ! A mere flea-bite, my dear boy, a mere flea-bite compared with what we shall put across this winter—a mere flea-bite compared with the losses of the other side. So go back with a stout heart ! Hang on till the spring ! Business as usual at home. That's the message you can take back to your comrades—and good luck go with you ! "

He had caught a catch-phrase, probably from a newspaper, and clung to it like a man with a hobby. He was obsessed with it. Meanwhile the rest of the company had been listening to the oracle with awe—except Rosemary, who sat on the grass and played with the cat. Adrian's mind occupied itself with Orde, Eric, and—the sleepers in the orchard at Neuve Chapelle.

Now, however, Lady Freeman began to discourse upon her situation to Rosemary in a high voice. Mrs. Granville-Brown, for her part, announced (not very appositely) that her husband was an Army doctor at the Front.

" Life for us wives of public men in these days is, you can be sure, one long rush. We only just managed to snatch this week-end at a moment's notice. Snatched ! Well—I insisted on it ! Sir Walter was getting run down. Anybody can see he wants rest and change. ' It's no use,' I kept telling him—she glanced fondly at her spouse, who made a protesting gesture—' it's no use trying to burn the candle at both ends, turning yourself into a bit of the office furniture with never a moment to sit down and enjoy yourself.' (He

wasn't taking his food.) ' I *know* they can't spare you,' I said,
' but it don't pay. That's the way to lose the war, not win it,'
I said. I used to sing ' Your King and Country need you'
every morning while he was taking his bath —just to remind
him. Well—it's a wife's duty, isn't it ; it's up to us
women to look after the men in these times—they won't
look after themselves, poor dears. . . . At last he gave
way."

"No, really," said Rosemary with innocence.

"Yes. Woman's part is not an easy one in war time whether
she's the wife of a public man or only of one who's doing his
little bit over there," put in Mrs. Granville-Brown rather
tartly. "What do they say—' the woman waits.' It's very
true. One long anxiety. My husband is at a stationary
hospital. But they have to put up with damp blankets and
Nestlé's milk—and you never know, you know."

"I'm not exactly idle m'self," continued Lady Freeman,
regardless. "I'm on the ladies' sub-committee of the Central
Canteen Board, I'm honorary president of the Bazaar Fund for
Disabled Officers. I'm busy running the Shakespeare Revival
Charity Matinée with the Gina Maryon-Romane set y'know.
It'll be a smart function. Then there's my political work
to help Sir Walter. Oh, dear ! "

Rosemary glancing down saw on the grass beside her a
copy of the " Prattler " lying open at a page which displayed
the photographs of four ladies in natty uniforms. She immediately espied the bold, vulgarly handsome features of
Lady Freeman, who was described in print above the usual
size as " An Enthusiastic War-worker," with the addition of
a few of those personal details which the good lady herself
had just supplied. Rosemary giggled, and found salvation
in a cough and her handkerchief. Adrian saw and smiled.
"Everything going splendidly." The worthy baronet and
his wife were " in it " all right ; their purgatory would be
to be in any way out of it.

§ 3

How glad the couple were to be alone again! With what pleasure they turned to each other after this! On the whole, Adrian was not sorry they had visited Ash-hangar, if only because the encounter with the Freemans—and what the Freemans were and what the Freemans stood for—was the one thing they needed to set off the perfection of their own solitary communion.

And in a moment they were lovers. The slight dissonance of the morning was obliterated. Rosemary put her arm through his, and when he stooped to kiss her looked up with that in her eyes which he had rarely sought in vain during these last weeks. The Freemans were as though they had not been. The mood of prevarication, the mood of laughter, the mood of petulance, the mood of mischief had given place in a moment to their all-absorbing interest in and for each other. They held hands and walked slowly.

They took the road which climbs that wooded range of hills known as the Bledlow Ridge. Gradually the woods began to encroach upon and encircle them. At last they were lost in the woods—those beechwoods so deep and dark that even the westering sunbeams scarcely entered in. They branched off the by-road and took a path that led into uttermost labyrinths. It was strange there and very quiet. They seemed to recover something of the Arden spirit. Yet was it not quite that, for, after all, the wheel of Fate was turning, turning. Something inexorable waited—some Unseen Presence that stood behind them watching from the shadows.

And they were happy as most wanderers in lonely places. They were utterly at one. No need to try and explain himself now. They felt rather than spoke. They looked what they felt and knew all without uttering.

After walking some distance they heard a sound as of a wood-cutter's axe and, coming to a clearing, found two men and a boy, cutting, shaping, and turning wood on a lathe. All around were logs cut into even lengths and the giant unhewn trunks of beech-trees. In the centre of the clearing was a rough wooden shanty covered with tarpaulin which contained piles of white neatly-shaped pegs or sticks. Outside the shanty a fire crackled, giving out the delicious scent of green wood burning. From this rose a thin wisp of blue smoke which somehow suggested the coming of winter to that still leafy place.

Sitting on a heap of logs, they watched the three at work for some minutes. The woodmen evidently represented three generations—an old bearded man of great height and breadth, a middle-aged swarthy man with blue eyes and reddish-brown cheeks, a raw-boned sturdy youth.

The old man announced that they were making chair-legs, as they had always done, as their forefathers had done for generations, as these three would always do. They lived, he said, at a place called Flowers' Folly in the woods two miles away.

After a while, having asked Adrian the hour, he turned to his companions :

" Come along ! Give over ! Time we went home to tea." And bidding the strange couple good night and picking up their baskets they passed out of sight among the beech-trunks.

When their footfalls on the crinkling leaf-carpet had died away, Rosemary said :

" I wish I could be just like those men, Adrian—calm and quiet and very simple and happy. And make chair-legs all my life. And never leave these woods, but watch the colours fade out of the tree-tops as they are fading now and watch for the leaves to come back again in the spring. And I would like to live where those men live—at Flowers' Folly. And I would like to have just you with me—nobody else. And I would like never to know anything of the world outside or about the horrid things in it, but only about the nice and beautiful things—the squirrels and birds and the open sky. . . . Adrian, is that possible ? "

" One cannot turn one's back on life, dear heart. One's got to stand up to it and face it—or it will find one out in the end."

" The terrible thing is I'm not sure, I'm not *sure* of myself. I wish, oh ! I wish I *knew* myself. . . . While I'm with you I'm all right, I'm safe. . . . Then—I don't know. I'm like the weather. In some ways I'm like Gina. I want to be like Faith."

" Silly little thing ! "

" Yes, I know, Adrian, but still—I'm afraid."

" Afraid ! Afraid of what ? "

" I dunno. I think—of waking up different in the morning."

" My foolish one ! We mustn't let ourselves get depressed —now above all."

" Is it very weak of me, Adrian ? What do you think ? "

She spoke with a seriousness such as he had not known in her before. He looked at her, wondering and vaguely disturbed.

Then his arm stole around her.

§ 4

They presently resumed their wandering along the woodland path. They would not hurry, feeling their hour too brief. Shadows gathered round them, lay across their path, followed them, crept after them, dogged them like wolves that follow travellers in the Russian wilderness. A jay mocked them, chattering, from the depths of a thicket of birch and hazel. A green woodpecker flew laughing away. Cloudy blue of wood-pigeons glanced against the bronzing yellow of the turning leaf. Eyes watched them from the shadows—eyes of squirrels from the tree-boles, eyes of wood-mice and brown owls, and those of other darting, rustling things.

Oblivious of time and space though they were, wrapt in their dream, dimly apprehensive perhaps of the fleeting quality of dreams—it was as though they clung desperately to one another.

It was only when they reached the outskirts of the woodland through which they had just passed, and were dazzled by the transverse beams of the setting sun, that they realised night was at hand.

They rested—at her suggestion—on the trunk of a blasted pine, a deep-tinted sunbeam warming it to a rich red, kindling to splendour the pale gold of her hair. A plantation of larch and young pine grew near and a faint, fragrant scent came from it.

" What a quiet, beautiful place ! " she murmured.

He, indicating the log upon which they sat, said :

" Yes, but they evidently get storms. What a sad thing a fallen tree is, Rosie ! "

Each was thinking of the morrow. Years after he recalled her expression. It was that of a tired child.

§ 5

For all their weariness they walked at a rapid pace along the lane whose whiteness shone thinly through the dusk. They were lost, yet knew that the lane must bring them to some farm or village. At last they came to a green where an inn light shone among a group of cottages. Under the light Adrian looked at his watch and perceived that it was already past the hour when the last train left the wayside station towards which they had hitherto bent their steps. They did not even know where they were.

Entering the inn, he found a number of men drinking. There appeared, however, a woman with a broad plain country face who, in consultation with her husband, informed them that their only course was to walk to a junction and market-town five miles distant, where a train to London might certainly be obtained. Gig or carriage was not to be had in that remote place, which was but a hamlet, far even from a main road. Supper, however, she could provide—ham and eggs, cheese, and butter, if that would suffice.

They had not long to wait for their meal in the inn-parlour, which smelt cleanly of beer, its faded yellow-papered walls covered with immense photographs of members of the family and wedding-groups. A piano stood in the corner. In the fireplace was a little coloured Japanese umbrella. The landlady removed this, lit a fire, placed an oil-lamp in the centre of the white cloth, ran in and out with implements for the supper, and every now and again glanced at the couple seated on the horsehair sofa, curiously and not unkindly.

They sat, hand in hand, like two waifs—insufferably happy, gloriously alone.

During the meal they spoke of ordinary things—of how they would write to one another every single day, of what Rosemary would send Adrian for Christmas—in case he did not come home before—of the knitting lessons she was going to have so that she might make him a comforter, of when he would get leave, of the arrangements for having the wedding during that leave, and of what chance he stood of obtaining a month for the honeymoon.

They then found themselves out in the darkness again—a darkness that, relieved by starlight, speedily became familiar. Refreshed by their meal, exhilarated by the frosty stillness of the October night, they travelled at good speed. Rosemary declared she was not tired now—was enjoying the walk more than she would have liked driving.

"We shall have longer together."

"If only we had all the nights and days before us! . . ."

They passed through woods again. Owls hissed, whistled, and from solitary trees out in the fields uttered their mellow and despondent three-syllable cry. They heard the tremulous wailings of plover and once, they thought—though it was early yet for that sound—the bark of a dog-fox. They passed cottages whose lighted windows were fretted with the trailing limbs of plants, suggesting a warm and snug interior. They passed distant farms from which the same warm light came. They were barked at by dogs. The trees, the great wayside elms and oaks, overlooked them. The ashes almost touched them—and the silver birches seemed to smile.

They came presently to a wide main road and from thence the way lay straight. Long vistas of it stretched ahead. A broad heath they came to where a light breeze sang in the telegraph wires which gave them a sense of infinite loneliness and infinite space. Cross-roads they came to, with a white sign-post pointing four different ways, and there rested.

Strange songs the breeze must have sung to them as they sat in the long grass by the wayside, his arms about her, her head resting upon his shoulder. Strange things they must have whispered one to another, and strange those things that wind and grass and fields and the watching night have whispered to hearts of lovers since the world began !

Rosemary confessed herself weary now, and when they plodded on once more she took Adrian's arm, leaning her full weight upon it. They came at last to the summit of a high hill, and saw beneath them stray, half-veiled lights, and many miles to the eastward, an uncertain reflection that they knew to be London.

§ 6

It was long after midnight when the train rumbled into the vast emptiness of Paddington Station.

They were too tired to talk as they drove to Grosvenor Mansions. They had been too tired to talk in the train. After all they were very near the end now—and there was no more to be said.

Like burglars they crept up the steps of the flats, though their careful footfalls resounded hollowly from the stone. It

was very dark. Adrian lit a match and Rosemary put a finger
to her lips. When they came to the fourth floor, they paused,
the heart of each thumping furiously as they pressed together.

Adrian whispered :

" This is good-bye ! "

" Not yet ? "

" Yes, Rosie—I must leave you here."

" Come in ! " she whispered.

" I can't ! I mustn't ! It wouldn't do."

" Why not ? Mamma's asleep ages ago. She knew we
weren't coming back till any hour ; she won't worry about us.
She'll never wake. . . . Besides—it's all right. Come on
—only be quiet ! "

They crept into the flat. Adrian had to light a match
before he could find the switch, and Rosemary gave a subdued
laugh.

In the pink-and-blue drawing-room, she took off her
hat and coat. There were lemonade and sandwiches on a
table. Turning out the electric light, they sat side by side
upon that sofa where two months before they had become
lovers once more.

§ 7

How the night passed neither of them could have said. Both
were utterly weary. Adrian remembered the light of a street-
lamp casting a faint reflected glimmer on the opposite wall.
They heard the wailing of cats in the mews outside and all
those other sounds that in the small hours arise from sleeping
London. He felt her warm body close to his. Their last
common thought was of something impending, something that
overpowered their consciousness and disturbed their dreams,
some vague, dominating, tyrannical threat.

Then they must have slept. But it was the same waking,
sleeping thought that after some time caused Adrian to start

up. He looked at his watch by the faint light of the street-lamp. It was five o'clock. He had no time to spare if he was to report at Aldershot by nine. He must first go home, change, and collect his things.

At his ear, he heard Rosemary's light regular breathing, that told him she still slept.

Should he wake her or leave her as she was . . . and spare them both ?

But as though in her very sleeping she had divined his thought, she started up, with an uneasy dissatisfied sigh.

" What is it ? " she murmured.

" Darling. . . . I must go."

She shivered.

" What ? "   She was still but half awake.

" It's time for me to go."

" *Going?* . . . Where ? "

" Aldershot."

" You don't mean to say—you're leaving me ? "   There was sudden apprehension in her voice.

" I've to catch the 7.30 train.   It's past five already. . . . Besides, the house will soon be waking."

" Oh, but you can't ! . . .   Stay !   Stay ! . . . *Adrian !* "

She was fully awake now and terribly frightened.

For several minutes they clung to each other.

Then he heard her stifled, tumultuous weeping and felt the tears falling one by one upon his hands.

" You're going . . . and it will never be the same again . . . and you will never come back."

" I must go," he whispered.   " But I shall come back."

" You will be killed. . . ."

" No."

Sob after sob broke from her and was crushed against the sleeve of his coat.   It racked him ; it tore the inmost fibre of him.   He had never known her weep before ; he had never known weeping like that.

" . . . and you will love me—always ? "

" Dear heart—you know that."

" Whatever happens—*always* ? "

" For ever."

She put her arms around his neck, drew his face down to hers, and kissed him frenziedly.

"Oh, Adrian! Adrian! come back to me or . . . I am lost."

Day peered in at the window.

He gently disengaged her arms and crept on tip-toe from the room.

END OF PART THE SECOND.

PART THE THIRD:

TRAVAIL

And in those days shall men seek death, and shall not find it ; and shall desire to die, and death shall flee from them.

REVELATION IX, 6.

CHAPTER I

Winter in Northern France

§ 1

ADRIAN KNOYLE rejoined his old battalion in France during the last week of October, 1915. He found it lying in billets at the small town of Lillers. This rather wretched place comes within the coal and industrial area of Bethune, from which it is distant seven miles, and the character of which it shares, in drabness, squalor, and featureless poverty.

There had been days of rain. Grey, rusty-black, and mud-yellow were the streets through which motor-lorries, horse-waggons, guns, motor-cars, and road-stained bodies of troops ceaselessly passed, while the pavements were crowded with foot-passengers, dejected-looking French civilians and British soldiers. Grey, rusty-black, and mud-yellow were the fields beyond, intersected by dykes and ditches, poplar-edged, or lined with pollarded willows. Poplars stood four-square drearily around water-logged meadows which in summer perhaps contained a pool. The cottages in which the troops billeted were built of lath-and-plaster with thatched or tiled roofs; the infrequent farmhouses of sodden brick were dark, cramped and comfortless.

Everywhere—water. Water lay stagnant in the meadows, water glistened beside the narrow roads, water stank in the farm courtyards, and water filled the ditches which, in lieu of hedges or fences, divided the fields.

Such was the country to which Adrian, with six brother-officers and some two hundred men, came in pouring rain—a rain that for many days continued to pour.

They found the battalion scattered on the outskirts of the little town. It was resting, re-equipping, reorganising as best it might, and licking its wounds after the great Battle of Loos, in which it had borne a glorious part, and the subsequent bitter fighting for the Hohenzollern Redoubt. On handing over his draft, Adrian was posted to his old company—Captain Sinclair's—as also, at his request, was the young officer, Arthur Cornwallis, whose friendship he had made in England. Adrian tired, mud-stained and wet, unlatched the door of a particularly wretched-looking farmhouse and beheld —Eric.

The latter was little changed. He was pink-and-white and spic-and-span, with well-brushed hair, and moustache; he exhaled the scent of eau-de-Cologne and fresh soap. Only in his voice and manner was a new note of authority.

Their joy at seeing one another was expressed in an uncivil epithet and handshake.

After introductions between Cornwallis and Eric on the one hand, and Adrian and a thick-set burly subaltern named George Walker on the other, Eric led the way to the narrow whitewashed room which the two friends were to share together. He lent Adrian some dry things into which to change.

"Well, old boy, and how's everybody and everything in England? How's yourself?"

Adrian briefly related the somewhat precipitate circumstances under which he had come out to France, saying little of the more personal aspects of the case, which he felt should be the subject of a longer and quieter talk. He told his friend all the news he had about Faith and handed him a pulpy mud-bespattered letter.

"Ah! old Faith!" was the latter's only comment.

Eric referred to Adrian's handling of the medical authorities in these terms: "You *were* a mug! You ought to be in London now having tea with Rosemary. Asking for trouble,

I call it, to *apply* to come out to this God-damned country. I ask you—look at it!" He made a gesture of disgust at the prospect, visible through the window. "However, you know what I feel about it, my dear fellow. I'm delighted to have you back again. It's been a bit trying sometimes on one's own."

"How's the company?"

"Oh! The company's just beginning to sit up and take notice again. It's had a coarse time lately. That Hohenzollern place!"

He went on to relate some of the experiences through which they had passed.

"That bit of ribbon looks very becoming," Adrian remarked in reference to Eric's newly-won Military Cross as they went into the kitchen for tea.

"Yes," the other replied, "it adorns the manly breast, doesn't it? They gave it me for not being able to run quite so fast as the rest at Hill 70."

§ 2

His fellow-subalterns, Walker and Cornwallis, Adrian found, presented as great a contrast physically and mentally as could well be imagined. Walker was in every way large, with a red face expressive of good humour, and a sandy moustache. There was no mistaking him, indeed —nothing subtle or diffident here. His physical manner, his loud laugh spoke for him. His conversation was hardly less Rabelaisian than the manner of it; it was freely bespattered with oaths.

Arthur Cornwallis, on the other hand, with his angular figure, his pale, bespectacled face and dreamy look, his thin sensitive lips, and nervous mannerisms, belonged to a type which Oxford produces (or used to produce). At dinner that night Cornwallis hardly uttered a word, but looked shyly down at his plate. Walker, on the other hand, was very noisy, drank copiously and told stories of the front line. (Adrian suspected him of trying to " put the wind up " Cornwallis.)

" I waited for the blighter," he told, " morning after morning at stand-to I waited. But he never showed his ruddy head again. At last I got fed up with waiting, so just before daylight I crawled over with my runner, and there the little swine was a-peepin' over his perishin' trench. Well, I out with my shooter and pipped him right off—and I'm damned if another of the blighters didn't show his ruddy head. Well, I pipped him too. Oh, that *was* a morning— *some* morning! Ye Gods! Ha! ha!"

" Reckless fellow, isn't he ? " murmured Eric, and, " For Christ's sake shut up, George! You bore me."

The conversation turned to a different subject, but Walker again led it.

" If you're expecting to pick up any little bits of fluff out here, Knoyle," he said demonstratively, " you've come to the wrong place—the wrong part of the country, anyhow. I've never seen such a lot of frowsy old hags. You should have seen 'em in Lillers market-place yesterday—well, I never! But I don't mind telling you "—he lowered his voice to a confidential key—" that day I went to Bethune I found an *estaminet* —a filthy little place it was, too—where . . . ," and he proceeded to relate various uninteresting details. " That was a bit of all-right, wasn't it ? "

Everybody except Cornwallis laughed. And in this strain the conversation continued.

That night when the two friends were creeping into their sleeping-bags, Eric expressed the opinion that George Walker was " not such a bad chap as you might think."

" Only he will talk ' shop ' and he can't talk sense. But it isn't all gas with him. He really does like being up in the line. He runs about all day with a gun and at night pots imaginary Germans with a Vérey pistol. He doesn't kill much, I must admit, but it's what they call 'the spirit of the offensive, isn't it? You make yourself a damned nuisance to everybody and then you're given a V.C. . . . That lad Cornwallis, though, doesn't look the sort to stand much knocking about?"

Adrian agreed, adding:

"Persevere with him, Eric. Don't be prejudiced and professional and—er—ultra-English with him. It won't pay. The Colonel can do all that. Let's be human about his sort of people in this company—now you're running it. I don't suppose he'll be a success any more than I shall be. He's hopelessly unpractical, extremely well-meaning, keen in his own way, but I should say, dreading the whole business like the very devil. I know what I should go through, joining again, if you weren't in this battalion. Nothing can make one feel so utterly selfless and alone as the Army if it chooses."

"P'raps you're right. I don't care what he is as long as he tries."

"They gave him a pretty rotten time at Aldershot. He was always losing his name in the orderly room for doing most things wrong, being late for parade, having his buttons undone, giving the word of command on the wrong foot, etc.—playing the *imitation* soldier, in fact, rather worse than most of us. Partly his own fault, chiefly nervousness. But he'll do his best. And, after all, it's not quite the same out here as at Aldershot."

"I won't curse him. Steele and Langley can do that," Eric laughed. "They'll lose no time about it, bet your life."

"If you don't break his heart he may be some use. It's the wrong way, the professional way, in a citizen army. I'm certain of that. All very well in peace time where you've got a lot of people of the same stamp who mean to make it their business in life. But out here . . . different altogether. Nobody's gone into the thing for fun, have they? One takes it for granted that everyone's doing his best. To get a lot of blokes together drawn from every line of life and temperamentally as different as chalk from cheese from the regulation type, and treat them *as* the regulation type seems to me the shortest way of making bad soldiers. What do you think ? "

" I agree with you up to a point, though one must preserve some sort of uniformity in a battalion, especially among the junior officers. I warn you that under Steele you'll find this show's run on *very* professional lines. Of course he's a good soldier."

" I know he is, but that's not everything. He's dealing with individual human beings now—not with a type. It's a different sort of army now from the one we came out to last January, for instance. As to what you say about uniformity in principle and method—agreed. But it seems to me one must do in a volunteer army by tact and reason, what in your peacetime professional army was done mechanically and often stupidly. After all the main object is to make efficient officers. Of course, I don't know Steele, except by reputation as— rather a Prussian. In which case Arthur is in for a bad time."

" Well, the lad will get his chance in this company. . . . I rather want to talk to you about Faith, though. My dear fellow, the solemn fact of the matter is—my future happiness is bound up with that young woman. I assure you that she is exceptional. She's got principles, and all ; she is religious. Am I ? I'm not good enough for her. She has an uncomfortable way of making me feel she expects something of me—I don't know on earth what. Of course, I'm a damned fool—not moral or clever or anything. But, tell me, as a friend, do you think she cares a tinker's cuss for Eric Sinclair ? Or—what ? "

" My dear Eric, she's extremely fond of you. That I'll swear to."

" Then, will she ever show it—in any practical way ? . . . Look here ! This is what happens. You remember that time at Arden ? I put the fatal question. She replies affably but firmly : ' I can't make up my mind. Let's talk it over again in a few months.' When I am on leave I only see her once. I go up to Scotland and she cannot get away from the hospital —or says she can't. Now I go on leave again soon after Christmas——"

" Have it out with her again. I lay a fiver to one the answer is in the affirmative, as they say."

" Done. But why do you think so ? "

" Because—I know Faith. I know her in some ways better than you do. Faith is slow and careful and not very emotional, and never does things on impulse—like Rosemary for instance. There's method in everything she does. She thinks. She weighs and judges. . . . You see, that girl's got a head as well as a heart."

" But still—why so positive ? "

" Because I *know*—I'm sure."

They were in that mood so delightful between friends after a long separation when confidence begets confidence and intimate conversation comes as easily to the lips as to the thoughts. And Adrian, for his part, was in a mind to tell Eric of his earlier disillusionments, of his old doubts and fears regarding Rosemary that were now finally set at rest ; of the *affaire* Upton. Yet something restrained him. Was it not after all better left unsaid ? Would it be loyal—even to tell Eric ? He disliked, too, mentioning the very name of Upton. So the matter remained unbroached when, turning over in their sleeping-bags—each with the fragrance of a certain memory as his last waking thought—they fell asleep.

§ 3

Everybody felt confident of a long rest after the recent heavy fighting, but very soon rumours began to circulate of a move northward into winter trenches. And it was not long before these rumours materialised. Some forecasted Ypres, others Armentières, but the matter was resolved when definite orders came that on a certain morning early in November the whole Division would move into the Merville district. On the whole everyone was pleased. It was a water-logged country, of course, but that description applied to the whole of Flanders in winter; Laventie was reputed to be still a quiet part of the line; the rearward billets were known to be good; and—well, anything was better than the Ypres Salient.

All were, in any case, glad to leave Lillers with its associations of interminable rain, damp billets, and liquid mud. The march tended away from the colliery region, passing through a country remarkable for a peculiar featureless ugliness. Swinging along side by side at the head of the company, Adrian and Eric agreed that they knew nothing comparable to it in England —not even in the Midlands or the industrial North. Drab field succeeded drab field, each consisting of greyish upturned loam that looked like the refuse of many factories. The roads themselves, poplar-lined and dead straight, were of rough *pavé*, very tiring to the feet. Rows of sodden-looking cottages with occasional brightly-coloured unsubstantial-looking villas comprised the villages, new-looking farmsteads flaunting scarlet roofs appeared among sparse orchards. The dull November landscape seemed to reflect the dull and windy November sky.

It was shortly after the second halt that Arthur Cornwallis " lost his name " for the first time. Up and down the column rode Lieut.-Colonel Steele accompanied by his adjutant, Captain Langley. The former was a square thickset man with a heavy dark moustache and coarse features, that bore the unmistakable stamp of ill-temper. Allied with these characteristics was a certain joviality, and a loud voice. His adjutant was tall and slim, with a vapid and rather dissipated face, who sat his horse well.

" Mr. Cornwallis ! "

The young officer raised his eyes from the direction of his boots.

" Sir ! "

" Please look after the rear of your platoon. It's all over the place. You're not put there to dream, you know."

" Sir."

Mr. Cornwallis dashed half the length of the company, urging the men to " keep closed up " and " march by the right," whereupon all the platoon-sergeants and all the junior sergeants and even many of the corporals set up a loud chorus of adjuration—a regular shouting-match. *Their* keenness, at any rate, should not be impugned.

" Close up there ! Keep together ! Can't you hear ? By your right, man—no ! your other right. Wandering along like a lot of old women . . ."

Thus the Company Sergeant-Major with his fiery complexion and yellow waxed moustache.

" You can't march ! You can't march—not one of you ! You want a month on the square, some o' you, that's what you want ! Now, then—pick up the step ! It's not a goose-step— it's a man's step. And take that smile off your face—number three from the left in the last section of fours, or you'll find yerself in the guard-room when we get there. . . . I want to see you men march. You walk along, you tumble along— anyhow ! What d'you think you look like, I wonder ? Soldiers, did somebody say ? A lot of skivvies out of a job, *I* should say."

Cornwallis, with humiliation depicted on his face, fell to the rear again. The men smiled.

And he had the pleasure of hearing Colonel Steele remark to Captain Sinclair :

" You must look after that new subaltern of yours, Eric ; he's idle."

Then they were marching up the long, narrow Merville

street, across the railway line, over the canal-bridge, and so
with band playing through the market-square, soon after
midday. Billets were found in farm buildings north of the
town, Eric Sinclair and his officers being assigned to a comparatively up-to-date farmhouse with a small though comfortable living-room opening hopefully on a midden, and two
bedrooms. Here the company mess was established. Walker
and Cornwallis were to sleep at neighbouring farms. Coming
and going, it was to be the home of all of them for some
time.

But they were not left undisturbed long. No sooner were
all comfortably settled than company-commanders received
orders to go up and inspect the new line of trenches which, it
was announced, would be taken over in a week's time. Every
morning there was a parade for drill, gas-drill, musketry and
so forth. Sometimes they had a route march and sometimes
the officers gave or attended lectures. Merville itself provided
little entertainment, there being but a sprinkling of shops in
which could be obtained only such things as nobody required.
Adrian one afternoon tried to renew associations with the
tobacco factory where Pemberton and he had passed their
first night at the front. But that somewhat distracting
episode in pitch darkness had left little impression of locality
upon him and he had to be content with re-discovering the
ex-schoolhouse clearing-station to which he had been carried
after being wounded.

The place was indisputably depressing, and the young man
himself felt depressed. A misty greyness seemed permanently
to overhang the ill-fated land, over Merville itself, when
of afternoons Adrian and Eric or Cornwallis—sometimes all
three—strolled through its narrow streets, thickly thronged
with soldiery. The whole country and everybody and everything in it seemed to merge in a single drab monotone.
The drinking-saloons or *estaminets*, where a few found
solace, were unutterably squalid. Football matches in

which the officers took part were better fun. And at night there were lively dinner-parties supported by whisky and wine.

After all there was no lack of " good fellows " in the battalion. Of the other company-commanders, one only was a regular soldier. This was Vivian, who commanded the Right Flank company—a suave and lively personality, a man of the world. The two other leaders had won their companies by merit as had Eric. These were Alston and Darell—the former a barrister who had joined the Army at the outbreak of war and had something of the legal profession's dry efficiency. Darell had been a gentleman farmer and was an oddly naive and simple character, a natural leader of men—not a good soldier, some said, but brave and liked by his company.

§ 4

They were in a sense unreal to Adrian, these days of early winter. On the first morning but one after their arrival came a letter from Rosemary, full of love, longing, speculation —adjuring him to write, to write at once, to write frequently.

" That day on the Chilterns," she wrote, " shall I ever forget it ? And the night ! Oh ! my dear, what wonderful things happen in life ! How wonderful this thing they call ' love '—a word I always despised—and what a great huge gap it fills in one's existence ! I feel quieter and happier now though it was too awful for words after you'd gone. . . . But do you remember the silly things I said in that wood ? Well, I want you to forget all about them—I did not really mean them. But seriously, I think of becoming a good steady little thing—a sort of Miss Kenelm ! I shall never forget that day and night we had together though, because I have never so had the feeling of belonging utterly and completely to somebody, of being cared for and looked after and being absolutely a part of somebody as I had then. . . .

But why, oh! why, do the good things in this world end so quickly ? And why, oh! why, were you such a perfect fool as to leave your little Rosemary for that beastly country ? Now, I'm going to be extremely vulgar (not to say *banal*, not to say 'second-rate' as Mamma calls it) and put as many x's as I can write at the end of this epistle. What a relief it invariably is to be vulgar *and banal and* second-rate ! "

There followed a long string of those cryptic signs which have embodied the sentiments of kitchen-maids and kings since the practice of handwriting began.

CHAPTER II

Christmas, 1915

§ 1

On a sunny though bitterly cold Sunday afternoon they paraded in heavy marching order for the trenches. An open-air service had been held in the morning. The march was a slow one, taking them through country and through towns that were already familiar to Adrian. Through La Gorgue they passed (as in an earlier time), and then through Estaires as dusk was closing in. When night had come, they were tramping in single file along a lonely road—cigarettes out and no talking. And when he saw the coloured lights rising and falling in front with the flat country stretching, vague and mysterious, on either hand, and when he heard a sniper's shot or two, or the far-off chatter of a machine-gun—Adrian began to feel as though he had never left it all. When they came to a ruined village in front of which the trenches lay, he breathed once more the atmosphere, at once ghastly, ghostly, and obscene, of the old trench world. The same smells came to his nostrils. He heard the same sounds. There was the stench of rotting sandbags, of damp tainted earth, of stale tinned food, the stench indefinable. There was the sharp crack of bullets against the brick walls of ruined houses which, as they tramped down what had once been a village street, were limned grotesquely in moonlight. There were moments of breathless silence, a sense of vast desolation. There was the plashing through water, the clambering over heaps of fallen earth, the stumbling and the stopping, the swearing and the stern injunctions to silence, the wet, crumbling sandbags that felt like cold flesh, the creeping, burdened, ghostly figures of the soldiers. In the front line it was the same— old familiar atmosphere. Only instead of the shallow unconnected series of strong points he had known at Fleurbaix, here were sandbag breastworks, thick and high, with well-constructed fire-bays and stout traverses. Of little account were the dug-outs—mere dens beneath parapet or parados, dripping wet, with water oozing through the floor-boards, and everywhere, rats. Nor was there room for all the men, some of whom had to lie out on the fire-steps—though, it was remarked, by those who knew Colonel Steele, it mattered little, as there would be scant rest for anybody during the four days in the front line.

As soon as his sentries had been posted and his men as fairly apportioned as might be, Adrian clambered onto the parapet and surveyed the scene. Glooming before him stretched No Man's Land with its inscrutable shadows and its baffling mystery. A line of dwarfed willows ran at right angles to the trench. A few hundred yards away (he knew) were the Germans. A powerful and peculiar curiosity to penetrate that deathly veil of moonshine returned once more. He jumped back into the trench and found Cornwallis, at a loss to know what to do or where to go.

" I came along to try and find where my platoon ought to be," he stammered nervously. "And now I can't find it—No. 15."

Before Adrian could advise in the matter, a harsh voice was heard.

"What's that—what's that ? Who can't find his platoon? Hullo, Knoyle ! What's this about a lost platoon ? "

Colonel Steele had come round the traverse, stick in hand, followed by the Commanding Officer of the battalion they were relieving and two orderlies.

"We're just going to look for it, sir."

"Who's ' we ' ? Is it your platoon, Knoyle ? "

" No, sir."

" Is it yours then ? " the autocrat demanded, turning on Cornwallis.

" Yes, sir. I—I was with it a moment ago. I—it can't be far."

" Well, look for it, man! Catch it! Find it! You're holding up the whole relief."

" What's his name ? " the Colonel inquired of Adrian in wearily impatient tones after the unfortunate young officer had gone on ahead. " Is he one of the just-joined ? Oh! well, give him a hand for heaven's sake. The boy's a fool."

The two Colonels passed on down the trench.

Adrian and Cornwallis stumbled about for some time in search of the missing platoon. Cornwallis spoke no word. But whenever a bullet thumped into the sandbags near them, he ducked. And whenever a Vérey light went up, falling with hiss and glare anywhere at hand, Cornwallis crouched. These two movements, Adrian perceived, were involuntary and simultaneous with the event. It was the first reaction on an imaginative, highly-strung nature. And he who had not been without his own earlier struggles saw a further world of trouble ahead for Cornwallis.

However, they at length found the missing unit and put it in its place.

Then Eric came along with the Company Sergeant-Major.

" Everything all right ? Found the machine-gun emplacements ? Got the bombs and grenades and tools and things ? Got all your sentries posted and your men detailed to dug-outs ? Good! Now about the wiring——"

Following Eric, they all clambered out of the trench. The company-commander began prodding the wire with his stick, testing its strength and thickness : presently he found a way through and strolled out beyond it, the rest following. They had not gone far when a light went up followed by the shattering " clack-clack-clack " of a machine-gun, the bullets of which whirred like a covey of driven partridges over their heads. All stood still in the quivering white glare that seemed intent on exposing every detail of the landscape—all except the unfortunate Cornwallis who gave a jump and fell flat on his face.

"Hullo!" whistled Eric. "What's up! Not hit, are you? It's generally best to keep still when these things happen. . . . Now here, of course, we shall have to do a lot of strengthening——"

At this moment Walker joined them.

"Oh, the dirty dogs!" he ejaculated. "They've just put one of their infernal machines into my trench and got one of my blokes in the leg. I watched it coming over. It came from the place where the other people (and what a filthy state they've left the whole place in!) said a machine-gun fires. I swear I'll go across to-night and see what's there. And if there is a blighter there, well, I'll do the blighter in. Any objection, Eric?"

"None, my dear chap—none whatever," Eric replied in the voice of a bored host giving *carte blanche* to an importunate guest. "Shoot anything you like—do. We don't preserve any, you know. Now about this cross-wiring for to-morrow night. . . ."

§ 2

One day slowly succeeded another, and it did not take the battalion long to settle down to the ordered routine of trench life. With three subalterns, in addition to the company-commander, who was himself an example of what can only be called "lethargic energy," the trench duties, working fatigues, and patrols did not fall too heavily on anybody. At "stand-to" morning and evening, Eric was always present; but on these occasions he required the attendance of only one of his subalterns. During the day he was constantly out watching his working-parties, while at any hour of the night he was apt to walk round the sentry-posts. He seemed to eschew sleep, yet his movements were casual and easy-going. He was never known to hurry, get excited, or be in the smallest degree demonstrative. His attitude in general was one of rather off-hand boredom—certainly of flippancy and detachment—as it had been to more trivial matters in pre-war days. An affable, smiling neatness characterised him in the trenches as out of them. He laid particular stress on parade "smartness." He inspired some slight affection in his men—with whom, however, he never cultivated a close personal relationship, declaring they much preferred their own society to that of their officers—considerable amusement, and very great confidence.

Eric, in fact, handled war as he had handled the social arts—delicately, fastidiously, and with a certain air of playful amusement. He was never technical, abstruse, or ultra-professional. It was his little pose to boast that he could not remember "the names of all the bombs and things." Durrant, an elderly and ultra-conscientious subaltern, who kept diaries, notebooks innumerable, any official pamphlets and instructions he could lay hands on, marked maps persever-ingly in his spare time, and always used the correct technical phraseology even in every-day conversation—Durrant was the unceasing butt of his wit.

Adrian, for his part, found a strong human, as well as a technical, interest in his platoon. His men, if not strong individualities, had individual characteristics which, embodying good-nature, patience, humour, and courage, reflected in each of their little groups very much the same contrasting traits as were found among their officers. The bar between officer and man was never passed by him—such accomplishment seemed to require the more robust personality of a Walker—but he endeavoured to consider his men as far as possible rather in the light of a society of individuals than as a platoon of soldiers.

Casualties were few in this line of stout high breastworks,

since unless a man chose to thrust his head above the parapet in broad daylight there was no particular reason why anybody should get shot. The enemy rarely shelled the front line— he rarely shelled at all. When the British artillery forced him into action, he would retaliate by throwing a limited number of large shells within a given area around the batteries.

The one exciting event of every day was the morning tour of the Commanding Officer round the lines. Sometimes he came with the Brigadier, sometimes with his adjutant only. In either event it was Colonel Steele who advised, ordered, suggested, and reprimanded. The grey-haired Brigadier responded—and agreed.

It was on one of these visits during the second spell in the trenches that Arthur Cornwallis again came under notice. It was a question of periscopes.

"How many periscopes have you got in your platoon, Cornwallis? I don't seem to see any on your sentry posts. You know the order."

Lieutenant Cornwallis knew neither the order nor a periscope when he saw one. The answer to such a question had never, therefore, occurred to him. He peered helplessly through his spectacles and said nothing.

Captain Sinclair came to the rescue—with a lie.

"They were all lost at Loos, sir. No issue since."

Then there was the drainage question.

Lieutenant Cornwallis had never been interested in drains, except in reference to a certain rustic cottage which his family had purchased in haste and repented at leisure. Yet here he was— ordered to drain a particular place in a particular way. His Commanding Officer told him how to do it in one crisp sentence:

"Dig a channel to a sump-hole."

The unfortunate youth felt rather less wise after receiving this instruction than he had done before.

However, after much argument and more speculation as to the precise meaning of the order, he begged his platoon humbly to dig a channel to a sump-hole and trusted to an all-merciful Providence that the water would flow away. It did nothing of the sort. On the contrary, the sump-hole freely filled from neighbouring rivulets and proceeded swiftly to discharge its contents into the already water-logged trench.

"What the hell's this mess?" inquired Colonel Steele next morning. "Didn't I say the trench was to be drained? Who's responsible for it, Sinclair? Yourself? Good God, no! I remember speaking to one of your subalterns. Oh! you—what's-your-name—Cornwallis? Haven't you ever drained a trench before or weren't you listening to what I said yesterday morning? DRAIN THAT TRENCH! And come and see me in the orderly-room when we get out of the line."

"That boy of yours wants hunting, Eric," remarked Colonel Steele to the company-commander as they passed down the trench.

"Oh! I think he'll do all right, Colonel, he only wants looking after a bit. It was really my fault about the ditch. I told him to do it like that, it looks better—when it comes off."

All of which was strictly untrue, but contrived nevertheless to save Lieutenant Cornwallis from an exceedingly unpleasant few minutes.

The culprit meanwhile had crept away to his watery little den which courtesy called a dug-out, where he endeavoured to bury himself and his troubles in " Idylls of the King."

§ 3

November went by, December came and Christmas approached. All settled down mechanically because inevitably to that mode of life unto which it had pleased God and their country to call them. Life divided itself definitely into two phases—the eight days spent half in the firing-line and half in reserve billets, and the eight days spent in the comparatively comfortable farmhouse nine miles back. Thus every week or so they tramped the long straight road through La Gorgue and Estaires: forward with philosophical resignation, rearward, tired, mud-stained, and optimistic. Then, indeed, the column would be noisy with jokes and comic songs, buoyed by anticipation of enhanced freedom amid semi-civilised surroundings. At Merville, there were formal drill-parades and occasional route marches; there were also football matches, concerts, rides, dinner-parties. But after a while these amusements palled. Concerts became tame when the comic man had sung his customary song and the sentimentalist had delivered his love lyrics, the quartette had done their hearty part, the sketch-man had given his imitation, and the duologue had provoked appropriate laughter, for the eighth or ninth time. Riding horseback was hardly worth while during that muddy winter, on the narrow *pavé* roads and amid the ceaseless traffic; it was not a riding country. And the dinner-parties—well, they were pretty much alike after all, involving much drinking, much cigarette-smoking, a great deal of "shop," and the rather redundant jokes about women. What Adrian Knoyle looked forward to and enjoyed were his long walks with Eric through country however uninteresting, upon afternoons however depressing in their speaking sense of the dead-weight of war, the negation of life, and the circumvention of hope. Then together they would contrive to create out of their never-flagging conversation an atmosphere that lifted them above their surroundings, took them back into the past and even led them towards possibilities of a future. For all his loathing of war and everything connected with it, Adrian was not "up against it." The thing was inevitable, it was an experience, nothing would alter it. On the other hand, he was sensible of his good fortune in having what others lacked—his association with Eric. He saw always before him the rather pathetic figure of Cornwallis who had to plough a lonelier furrow than he, and a bitterer one; Cornwallis in whom Adrian felt many qualities akin; Cornwallis who was indeed "up against it."

So Christmas came—with its formal message of " Peace on earth and goodwill towards men "—to the drab and motley crew in the trenches.

And soon after midnight, as though to herald the birth of the Saviour in the speaking voice of that sinister time, the guns burst forth in a thudding, banging, booming chorus, the sky became livid with gun-flashes, the German trenches glowed with bursting shells and upward-springing sparks. A Corps bombardment had been ordained, and for miles to north and south every gun fired. Adrian Knoyle, passing on his round of the outposts, stood spellbound by this midnight vision of the Inferno, by the grotesqueness of this irony, this voice of Terror incarnate that ushered in the Christmas dawn.

Silence succeeded thunder, a silence in which the iron-shod ground alone responded to the frosty glitter of the stars. Morning broke with a grey sky lowering upon the brown world, with its spectral trees, its leaning crosses, its white husk of a church-tower. Here and there, wisps of moist and vapoury winter mist lingered mournfully, magnifying every feature of the landscape. Smoke of breakfast fires rose above the German breastworks. A black frost still bound the earth. From either side of a belt of ashen grey-green grass, reddened in places by rusting wire and stakes, the two interminable lines of trenches stared at one another grimly.

It was here that British and Germans met. And where Knoyle watched in the bay of the trench, even as the grey and khaki figures stood up and waved to each other, a shot broke the stillness, and a platoon-sergeant who had long been his friend, tumbled back into the trench. There he lay at full length, palpitating and bleeding, yet uncannily natural in the mud until someone brought a sandbag and covered up his face.

To Adrian, that was a curiously shocking and disillusioning experience. After it, the atmosphere of " Christmas," which even war could not entirely disperse, ceased to have any meaning for him. This sudden annihilation of a man with whom a moment before he had spoken, was like the tumbling of a last ideal in a catastrophically falling world. And there was something else. Out on the wire in front hung a queer, grey object. It was only half there; it looked as if a knob of wood, painted blue, had been stuck on a bone. Every time the wind stirred, the grey shreds flapped.

Adrian and Eric watched the scene between the trenches in silence. They had drawn their revolvers, but the effort to hold back even their well-disciplined men was without avail. There was nothing to be done. An insurgent common impulse of the combatants prevailed, and grey and khaki swarmed out to meet each other—one or two Germans in white overalls or smocks among them—at the willow-lined stream. They crossed it and mingled together in a haphazard throng. They talked and gesticulated, they shook hands. They patted each other on the shoulder, laughed like schoolboys, and out of sheer lightheartedness leapt across the trickle of water. An Englishman fell in, and a German helped him out amid laughter that echoed back on the crisp air to the trenches. They exchanged cigars and sausage and *sauerkraut* and concentrated coffee, for cigarettes and bully beef and ration biscuits and tobacco. They exchanged experiences and compliments and comparisons, addresses and good wishes— and even hopes and fears.

So was Christmas Day celebrated upon the battlefield.

There appeared after a quarter-of-an-hour two German officers who wished to take photographs—a request which the men refused. "Our artillery will open on you in exactly five minutes," they retorted. "Get back to your trenches or take the consequences."

And the trench-world was lifeless, unpeopled once more.

The guns thudded again, this time from behind the Aubers Ridge; shells crashed upon all the roads. Fountains of earth and dust and masonry shot skyward around the ruined village;

there were death and wounds for those who lingered in the
open. Only the rifles remained silent. Morning passed.
Silver and still, the afternoon waned into winter's early dusk.
Frost gripped again with night, and along both lines of trenches
torch-like fires burned. Extra rum was issued. There were
sounds of singing.

§ 4

In a low cave or structure roofed with corrugated iron and
lit by four candles stuck in bottles, the floor of which was some
two feet deep in water—Adrian Knoyle and Arthur Cornwallis sat together. Walker was on leave, Eric Sinclair going
his rounds. In front of each was a white enamelled mug
containing port-wine. They were smoking.

" That was a funny show to-day," observed Adrian.

" It was," answered Cornwallis ruminatingly. " I've been
thinking a lot about it."

" What do you make of it ? "

There was a moment's silence.

" It was—astounding."

" But how do you explain it—psychologically ? "

" I think it was some sort of reaction : reaction of character,
of human nature, of fundamental truth and order and, proportion against the disproportion and unreality and super
ficiality overlaying our old conception of civilisation." The
youth spoke very earnestly. He was himself with Adrian—
and with no one else in the battalion. " Reaction of the best
against the worst in human nature. . . . Have you noticed
it—only the *real* things seem to come uppermost in war,
Adrian ? I mean reality seems to reveal one to oneself, drags
one out of oneself, and the fundamental truth in people seems
to show up in face of it and in spite of forms. In peace-time
we were always getting across—I mean misunderstanding—
one another, weren't we ? And we were always misunder-

standing—life. We saw each other through a glass darkly, but now—face to face. Now we know even as also we are known."

Leaning his elbows on the table, Cornwallis peered with great gravity at his friend through his steel-rimmed spectacles. Both were caked in mud, and wore two days' growth of beard.

"Yes, my dear Arthur, but "—Adrian looked puzzled—" I confess I don't get you——"

"The impulse at the back of it, the inspiration of the thing. Could one have imagined it? These chaps pouring out over the parapets into No Man's Land to shake hands, to laugh and joke and exchange presents and—their own dead lying around. One has heard of the French and British drinking at the same stream in the Peninsula but—that was nothing to this. When you come to think of it, it's tremendous—amazing, Of course I'm no soldier, and the disciplinary part of it is of secondary interest to me. What that five minutes' affair this morning brought out, to my mind, was the triumph of fundamental good in the average individual, who in this case is the private soldier, over—the other thing. It was a revelation. It was finer than any church service or any Christmassy sentiment, because it was a spontaneous human thing. To me it's an unforgettable experience."

"Yes—that's interesting," said his companion slowly. "I'm glad to have seen it, too, though war never struck me as anything but utterly damnable, utterly destructive, and utterly meaningless. But—yes, there may be some bigger thing at the back of it."

Neither spoke for several minutes.

"Well—I dunno," Adrian presently muttered, abstractedly lighting a cigarette. "I mean war and death and the hurt of it —and all. I feel as if it isn't sane sometimes—can't be true."

"It isn't, thank God," exclaimed Cornwallis devoutly. (He, had, by the way, evinced a habit that was a source of amusement to some of his brother-officers and of admiration to others, of kneeling down every evening wherever he happened to be and saying his prayers.) " It isn't. The only life that counts is the life one lives in one's own mind."

The sandbag that did duty as a curtain over the entrance was drawn aside, and Eric stumbled in.

" I suppose you're both drunk," he said. " I want a drink, anyway. It's too bloody cold for words. . . . They're singing over in the German lines."

He took off his heavy fleece-lined waterproof, sat down on a plank poised between two boxes, and poured himself out some port-wine. He raised the mug to his lips :

" Here's to each of you and here's to all of us ! "

They drank this somewhat complicated toast, and then the company-commander said :

" Arthur, will you take a walk round now ? One of us ought to be about, or the Boche may play some dirty trick under cover of all that joy-making."

For several minutes after they were left alone together the old friends said no word. Speech to them was at all times superfluous. Then Adrian proposed a toast.

" To those we love best and to those who love us ! "

" Very nice,"murmured Eric.

They drank in silence. . . .

Adrian's thoughts had suddenly taken a bright turn. He realised that three months had imperceptibly passed and that only two more separated him from Rosemary. The rest—lay with Fate.

Crump   Crump ! Thud ! Thud !

Muffled by the earthen walls came the hollow sound of shells bursting. The two officers crawled out, but silence had fallen again except in the direction of the German trenches where a chorus of guttural voices was chanting *Die Wacht am Rhin.*

CHAPTER III

Anticipation

§ 1

A BROKEN road by which men and guns and transport journey to the trenches; a broken village where the inhabitants lurk in ruins or underneath them, where the rats run and the birds flit at ease; a broken church whose tower, landmark for miles around, is spared only because the German gunners find it useful as a range-finder. And a decayed railway station, grass-grown, decorated with melancholy advertisements and a melancholy name-board beckoning the traveller who never comes.

Unlike some ruins, there is nothing beautiful about these. They are degraded and degrading. Even the church is of a piece with the rest, modern, red-brick, ugly. . . . And the road leads on, muddy and greasy, straight on through the village. It is broad and planted on either side with young poplars. There is a footpath between the roadway and, at the entrance to the village, a row of houses. Most of these are occupied by their civilian owners as well as by troops; a few are good houses and comfortable. Each has a cellar, which, being the only salvation in case of bombardment, is sandbagged up outside to keep out splinters. Behind the houses are vegetable gardens tilled by the women and old men who have remained.

In this village, barely a mile from the firing line, the Left Flank company had spent many weeks of their second winter in Northern France.

Late at night they would come back to it, caked in mud, stiff from damp and lack of exercise, for here were quartered the brigade in reserve. And in the wintry twilight four days later, by the same broken road they would set off for the trenches again.

There stood nearly opposite the railway station a dilapidated *estaminet*. Its dark and narrow doorway opened upon two ground-floor rooms leading one into the other, the greenish paint and plaster of which were rapidly peeling from their compartment-like walls. In one room the floor was of brick tiles. It had evidently been a café, for here also was a kind of bar counter. Most of the panes were missing from the windows, one or two were protected by brown paper. The adjoining room had been a kind of parlour; a faded lithograph or two still hung upon the walls; there were a stove, a table, and one or two rickety chairs, but no carpet. Both rooms were thick with dirt.

They were inhabited by certain strange beings: a fat, frowsy, elderly woman, with pale complexion and black hair who might be seen waddling about in heel-less slippers, looking like a Bloomsbury lodging-house keeper; a middle-aged man, lean, distrustful and furtive, sitting vacantly at the table opposite a bottle or occupying himself with some ill-defined menial occupation. Always these two lurking there. And sometimes about the middle of the morning—or in the evening —a group foregathered in the room: a few friends came in, slatternly-looking girls and dwarfed, misshapen youths, or haggard, woe-struck, aged people, not less dirty, frowsy, wretched-looking than the couple themselves.

Next this " parlour " and for ever within sound of chattering French voices was a large square apartment, lighted by candles and two oil-lamps. A big French stove where the hearth should have been, a thick, stuffy atmosphere, reeking of tobacco-smoke and cooking. There was much flimsy furniture in the room—too much—and on every hand a litter of objects—caps, gloves, waterproofs, and coats; newspapers, magazines, books, packs of cards, revolvers also lay about. On a side-table in a corner stood bottles of whisky and port, butter on a saucer, pots of jam and marmalade.

It was late on a February evening, and the room was occupied by three officers of the Left Flank Company. Walker, smoking a cigar, with a whisky-and-soda beside him, was playing some card game. Cornwallis was deep in Wordsworth's "Excursion." Adrian, with a writing-pad balanced on his knee, stared into the pleasant glow of the stove.

"Adrian," ejaculated Walker, "I've got a new female in my room. Would you like to see her?"

"No," replied the other without hesitation.

"What!—don't you want to see her?"

"No. I don't like your females. Show her to Arthur."

"Oh, no!" laughed Walker. "Not Arthur! Our little curate would be shocked."

Cornwallis blinked over his spectacles and smiled amiably:

"A new female—what do you mean? A French girl?"

"Yes—of course. A Parisienne!"

"Oh, you know his beastly collection, don't you?" growled Adrian.

"You mean another Kirschner by your bed?"

"No, no! A live one *in my bed*," retorted Walker. "He believes me! Like to see her? . . . Come! Come and play poker patience, you son of a gun!"

"No, George—please! I want to read my book."

"Not that poetical muck—Tennyson, Wordsworth, or whatever the bloke's name is. Oh, no! No! Really, I can't allow it. I'm sick of the sight of you poring and peering over there. Be a bit unselfish for once. Come on!"

Cornwallis removed his spectacles resignedly. It was with him a sign of giving way. . . . He always did give way.

"Eric ought to be here soon."

Adrian returned to his thoughts, although constantly

interrupted by Walker's loud guffaws or by the entry of non-commissioned officers and orderlies bringing notes or printed forms for signature.

The postponed marriage was now imminent, and the yellow leave-ticket had for days past been the centre of Adrian's dreams. What news would Eric bring on his return from leave ? Time had fled like a shadow through hours and days that separately had seemed endless. He looked back to the chill afternoon of his second arrival in France, and could hardly believe that he stood so near to the end of that long vista of dreariness. Now his great happiness was at hand, within his grasp almost.

Letters from Rosemary had been brief lately, but this was to be expected of a young woman in the last weeks before marriage. The final details of the wedding, it is true, had not been settled. This could not be done until they knew the exact date of the bridegroom's leave. They could, after all, be arranged very quickly ; such things usually had to be in those days. In any case, the wedding was to take place at Stavordale. The honeymoon was to be spent at Mrs. Rivington's Sheringham villa.

Footsteps sounded in the stone passage.

" Hullo, all of you ! "

In the doorway stood Eric, his fur-collared overcoat lightly sprinkled with snow. He carried a haversack.

There were general exclamations of welcome.

" Had a good leave ? "

" The best."

" Come and sit down and get warm, and tell us all the news. There's some dinner being kept for you."

Adrian drew up a second chair in front of the stove and looked his friend up and down, scrutinising his face, as though to read there some information he sought. It was not like Eric to betray information in this way. And Eric was entirely his cool and collected self.

But after divesting himself of his outer garments and un-lacing his boots, he produced a bulky letter from an inner pocket and flung it into Adrian's lap. With the letter was a five-pound note.

§ 2

Impatient as they were for the other two to depart to bed, they discussed general topics while Eric was eating his dinner. Contrary to his established custom, Eric talked " shop." How was the Company—had there been any casualties—any news of a move ? And Adrian—what were things like in England, when did people at home think the war was going to end, what plays had he been to, who was coming out next to the battalion ?

Then, while Eric devoured ham, Adrian devoured the half-dozen sheets covered by Rosemary's sprawling handwriting.

" . . . Time flies," she wrote, " and this time next month I s'pose we'll be duly wedded man and wife. Doesn't it sound funny—and respectable ? Don't be rough and full of odd expressions when you come back, and *don't* talk about the war, or I shall refuse to accompany you to the altar. . . . I'm a very busy child. I'm going to act in ' Lady Winder-mere's Fan ' at the Court next month in aid of blind soldiers or something. I sold programmes twice last week, and every morning I pack parcels for prisoners at Princes'. Then there's the wedding trousseau to prepare and mamma to manage, and sometimes golf. So what do you think of that, my man ? You can never call your beautiful Rosemary an ' idle little skallywag ' again ! "

The phrase referred to an expression used in one of Adrian's letters. He laughed to himself, partly at the expression, chiefly to relieve the burden of his ridiculous happiness.

When at length Walker and Cornwallis departed to bed, the two friends threw coke on the fire, placed their feet close to it, and lit cigarettes.

" Well ? " ejaculated Adrian.

" You won."

" Congratulations are so conventional. Only give me the pleasure of saying ' I told you so ! ' . . . And now we're all joyfully and suitably affianced. If it wasn't for the war we'd have a double wedding in the largest church in London with all the rank and fashion and beauty of the town—what ? "

" Of course, it's not settled down to the last detail yet. But the official sanction is given. Only his lordship wants us to wait till the end of the war. What an obstinate old boy he is ! ' Mary ' is willing for it to be as soon as possible. However— much can happen between now and next leave. Meanwhile, Faith and I agreed it would be best to rest on our laurels and wait—for the present. She'll get round the old chap in time."

They talked far into the night while the sleet pattered against the brown paper in the window-frames. Adrian could not help reflecting upon—while not envying—the cool and collected quality of Eric's and Faith's regard for one another. Yet how different from his own feelings for Rosemary ! But he no longer doubted the durability of their affection. Faith he had never doubted ; it had needed the war to reveal Eric.

The latter showed an inconvenient dilatoriness in respect of Rosemary. He dilated upon the charms of " Bric-a-brac " and " Shell Out," upon a couple of days' shooting he had had at the Rivingtons' (together with a few poignant details of his experiences with the Miss Kenelms, one of whom had become engaged to the local curate), upon a day's racing " over sticks " at Gatwick, and upon a bachelor dinner-party he had given at the Café Royale. But of Rosemary—nothing.

At last Adrian's impatience got the better of him.

" By the bye, did you see anything of Rosemary ? "

"Yes, we dined at the Berkeley and went to the play. She and Faith and old Cyril and myself. She's very fit. She talked a lot about you, of course. I gather the preparations are well on."

"Ah!"

For an instant it crossed Adrian's mind that there was the faintest suggestion of reserve in his friend's manner. Then Eric spoke again.

"Poor Cyril—it did him good. He's looking better, though. We ran into Gina Maryon—I didn't know, by the way, she was such a friend of Rosemary's. I confess personally I can't cope with the woman. She talks sixty to the dozen, says '*a-ma-teur*,' and looks at you as if you were a bit of old French furniture. . . . Hullo! What's this?"

An orderly had entered with an official envelope which he handed to Adrian.

It contained a yellow ticket.

"My leave!"

He leapt up, seized it and sat down. A slow flush rose in his cheeks as he stared at the slip of paper.

"Why, they've given me a month!" he cried, looking at his treasure. "It's marked 'special.' How the devil—— ? I suppose you managed that, you old blackguard?"

"*C'est ça, mon garçon.*"

"Just like you, damn you. But I can't take it, you know. It's not my turn."

"Rot! You weren't fit when you came out. They never ought to have sent you. I'm not going to have my second-in-command crocking up with the 'shooting season' coming on——"

"I'll take a fortnight of it."

"You'll leave to-morrow at midnight and you'll return one month from that hour."

"Well—we shall see. At the moment I can't—I simply cannot—believe it's at last going to happen."

"The natural feelings of a bridegroom!" commented Eric, putting coke on the stove.

"It's pretty bad luck you can't be my bottle-washer, Eric."

"Oh! get Cyril—or somebody. He'll do it equally well, wheeled-chair and all."

"Very nice—but not the same thing!"

"Don't think I want you to be married, my dear Adrian! Not in the least. Say what you like, when a man enters what they call the 'blessed estate of matrimony,' he invariably prefers his own drawing-room to anybody else's smoking-room."

The two inseparables went on philosophising in this vein for some time.

Both agreed that it would be better to say nothing about the forthcoming event in the battalion until it was a *fait accompli* —except, of course, to Colonel Steele, who had generously recommended the granting of "special leave" for "urgent family reasons." His real reason probably was that, prompted by Eric, he saw a chance of conserving the health of his senior subaltern, and one of the few young officers with experience in the battalion. Adrian—if the truth were known—dreaded the unmerciful chaff he knew he would receive at the hands of his brother-officers—especially Walker.

It was near daybreak when the couple finally climbed the rotting staircase to bed. Looking out, they saw snow falling upon a landscape inexpressibly drear. This provided a rapt contrast for Adrian, who for a long while could not sleep, so joyfully his heart leapt and sang.

CHAPTER IV

Nightfall

§ 1

IT was shortly after the midnight next following that Adrian set out upon the happiest journey of his life. A two-mile walk from the billet over a rough shell-torn road brought him to the railway station. He carried nothing save a bulky haversack and a walking-stick. He strode along, engrossed in joyful imaginings, through the frosty starlit night. Searchlights, German and English, occasionally swept pale fingers across the sky; eastwards, a few miles away, the familiar Vérey lights rose and fell in an objective loneliness. Laventie slept.

He had curiously the feeling of leaving behind him, finally, this ghost-haunted and sombre world. It was not so, of course; he would be back in a fortnight—a month at the outside. But to visualise returning to it was at the moment impossible.

At the station there was a long wait. The leave-train was due to start at one o'clock; by two, it had not moved.

He found himself sharing a carriage with three other officers. For some time he walked up and down the platform to keep warm. His spirits brooked no damping; he cared little indeed how long the journey was protracted, so it ended—with Rosemary. Mechanically, almost unconsciously, he carried on half-a-dozen conversations with different people whom he did not know and whose faces he could not see—each, it seemed, exactly like the last.

" Cold, isn't it ? "

" Damnably."

" Going on leave ? "

" Yes."

" I wish the confounded train would start."

" It's an hour overdue already."

" Where's your Division now ? "

" Fauquissart-Laventie."

" Quiet there ? "

" Nothing much doing."

" Heard anything of a ' push ' coming off ? "

" Not immediately."

" In our part of the line——" and so forth and so on.

Adrian's preoccupation rejected these platitudes and, as he paced up and down, his mind roved as far as could be from things of the war, finding its goal in the small parish church of Stavordale, in Yorkshire.

§ 2

At last the train did move—inconsequently, as it were, with a jerk and without warning of any kind.

Thereupon the four officers composed themselves in their carriage after the approved fashion of such farings, one each along the seats, one crossways, and one lying on the floor. Adrian reclined crossways. But he did not sleep. His mind would not contemplate repose. Doze he sometimes did, to awaken sharply with such mastering thrills as set him staring, staring out into darkness, his face lit with a smile which he self-consciously feared might be observed by his companions.

So the night wore away. Rumbling, jolting, stopping, starting again ; the dim, greenish, half-veiled lamp always quivering and shaking ; trees flitting mistily past, and through frosted windows a vague prospect of moonlit country.

They stood for an interminable time in the silent glass-covered station of Hazebroück. Daylight found them no farther than the sidings at St. Omer, sandwiched between two troop-trains. Looking at their occupants, obviously troops

going "up the line" for the first time, Adrian felt a sort
of joyous pity. In the measure that he was sorry for them,
he was glad for himself. Thenceforward the leave-train
speeded up, and by ten o'clock they were through the flat
country, and the snorting engine was taking in water on
the arid outskirts of Calais to the monotonous chant of the
children: "Bisquee, s'il vous plaît, m'sieur! Bisquee!
Bisquee, s'il vous plaît!" And then, through the sand-dunes,
past the great new ranges of hospitals and camps beside the
railway, they came to Boulogne. For two or three hours,
Adrian's three companions had talked remorselessly about the
war. "Minnies" and "whiz-bangs" and "coal-boxes" and
"stunts" played a chief part in the conversation, darting in
and out of it, like ladies and gentlemen in a pantomime.

At Boulogne he found the boat was not due to start till three.
Plenty of time to wash, shave, and eat a comfortable meal
at the big white hotel which fronts the quay. And what an
experience that first breath of civilisation after four months!
The gilt-and-marble hall, the red-and-white dining-room, the
concièrge, the waiters in stiff, shiny shirt-fronts, the white table-
cloths, the gleaming spoons and forks, the glasses, the amazing
cleanliness of everything! All was so surprising, so unspeakably
eloquent and delightful. And what a long step they seemed to
carry him towards—Rosemary!

He met officers whom he knew, but he avoided them after
passing the time of day, in order to be at liberty to sit by himself in a corner and devour and enjoy every moment of this
reunion with life—this divine anticipation.

At two o'clock he went on board. Would his leave-pass
be in order? A frantic, unreasoning spasm of fear nearly
choked him. *If . . . ?* But of course it was in order. And he
stoutly walked aboard. There were already scores of officers and
soldiers on the boat, crowds standing on the quayside, quantities
of military officials; here and there, a Frenchman or two.
Everybody had a merry face, was cracking jokes, and forming

noisy groups on deck. There were gold-laced and red-capped generals ; many Staff officers. There was a red-capped gentleman bawling people's names through a megaphone. That appeared to be very much part of the business of embarking. Now and then the steamer hooted warningly. At the last moment officers of the highest rank rushed from nowhere, throwing themselves on board and their dignity to the winds. How living, how amusing it all was !

Then they moved.

A level, blue winter's afternoon sky smiled overhead ; a level, blue sea waited without. And perhaps this was the gladdest part of all that glad journey :—when the boat glided out into the basin, glided out among the fishing-smacks, and Boulogne, her piled-up houses and hotels, her spires and fort-crowned hill in the background, her crowded quays and hectic Anglo-foreign life, receded into a fast-gathering haze. For with all that went the war. . . . To the prospective bridegroom pacing up and down the encumbered deck and looking now ahead, now backward at the French coast, life reopened amazingly. And in it was no guile.

As the day began to wane, gleams of sunshine made silvery play upon the waves. Seagulls hovered whitely about the masts, uttering, it seemed to Adrian, cries of revelry. Outside the breakwater they picked up a destroyer which acted as flank guard. A wake of snowy foam boiled and eddied behind them About half-way across they passed the returning leave-boat, alive with the khaki of those whose brief respite was over, and who were journeying back to try their luck in the great lottery once more.

From time to time he met his companions of the train journey and exchanged a word with them. In addition to the hundreds of soldiers on board, carrying packs and rifles and greatcoats, and British officers, Staff-capped and otherwise, in all shades of khaki, there were foreign military attachés, Americans, Japanese, Italians, Frenchmen, Belgians, civilian

English, Government officials in spectacles and fur coats—
women, too, Red Cross nurses, V A D.'s, and privileged refugees.

From the forepart of the boat Adrian strained his eyes for
a first glimpse of the English coast. Eventually, however, it
was only by the twinkling of suddenly near lights that he
discovered Folkestone. The sea grew vague and grey in the
evening; far away along the coast solitary revolving light-
houses glimmered, then vanished. He shivered—first intimation of the night's impending frost. Now they glided within
the breakwater, and he knew that nothing but land separated
him from his earthly paradise.

He began counting the half-hours, translating them even
into minutes. . . . Queer little jerks of happiness, hot little
thrills of anticipation, shot through him from time to time.
And for all the sharp bustle that went on around, he was not
in spirit there. Yet how he revelled in it! How he revelled
in the plain, rough faces of the English porters who tumbled
aboard as soon as the boat drew to the landing-stage, in their
coarse, familiar speech, in the physical sensation of stepping
ashore, in the shouts of the newspaper-boys and the inviting
appearance of the train.

He thought of sending a telegram to Rosemary and to his
mother. He did not do so. His arrival should be a complete
surprise to them both!

§ 3

A man was made to feel a hero in those days. Ladies
approached him on the landing-stage, offering their services
for this, that, and the other thing; ladies offered him, free and
gratis, packets of chocolate, cups of tea, cigarettes. For his
part, Adrian made a dash for a seat in a Pullman car, where he
found an arm-chair and tea. Pandemonium reigned in the
station; it seemed as if they would never get off. An officer
who sat opposite made appropriate remarks about the glad

feeling of once more setting foot on native soil. Adrian frankly pitied him. Remarks of that sort seemed ridiculous. Risking rudeness, he protected himself behind a newspaper, finding his own thoughts during this last stage of his journey too absorbing, too precious to waste or lose.

And he travelled through a dream country. Perhaps all did in those strange days on the home-coming leave-train. . . . The whole journey to London was unreal, and ever afterwards remained unreal, in his mind. It was a wonderful, cherished looking-forward, in which he now heard Rosemary rush to the door, saw her fling it open, saw her look as she welcomed him ; now went over in his mind the plans for the wedding five days hence ; and now with all his senses was worshipping at the shrine of Rosemary's re-found beauty. . . . Again, it was the moment of finding themselves alone, supremely unresponsibly, at Stavordale or Sheringham—that moment when they would set out on the Great Adventure splendidly, like ships in full sail.

Before he realised it they were in London. And he was plunged back into London, the all-embracing sense of London swayed him, uplifted him. And *she* was in London ! Already they breathed the same air, were divided by minutes only and by yards—and still were drawing nearer. He experienced a curious sense of imminent realisation after an infinity of looking-forward, of imminent crisis—of crisis how great he could not know. He would, of course, go straight to Grosvenor Mansions—just as he was—as fast as cab could carry him. . . . The train slowed down going over Grosvenor Bridge and outside Victoria Station stopped. That was maddening. He stood ready, waiting, at the door of the corridor, haversack over shoulder, stick in hand. He stood thus a quarter-of-an-hour, occasionally looking out of the window and seeing the foggy, tantalising lights inside the station. Anyone watching closely the young man's face in these moments, with its straight English features, sensitive mouth, and dark, contemplative eyes, might have perceived in it an intensity of expression, a degree of concentration, a dominating thought or idea, that boded ill for him if aught should cross the purpose of his life.

A murky gas-lamp or two burned in the grimy, high-storied brick buildings between which the train stood. The dingy light showed enough to suggest a yet more dingy interior, conveying to his mind one swift negative picture of London life. . . . Then the train moved. The train glided ever so slowly, ever so smoothly into the wide, dim-lit spaces of Victoria station—beside a platform crowded with friends and relations, with soldiers and officials. He glanced at the illuminated station clock. It was exactly seven o'clock. If he went straight to Grosvenor Mansions he would find her.

He ran a race for the nearest taxicab. He won.

" To Grosvenor Mansions, quickly ! "

His voice was already husky with excitement. A long line of motor-cars and cabs was filing out of the station. He was enthralled by London's winter evening, by the variety of sounds that came to his ears—the shouting of newsboys, the whir and buzz of motor-cars, the hootings of motor horns, the high-pitched whistles of railway engines, the shuffling and pattering of many footsteps, the omnipresent roar of traffic. It was all satisfying beyond words.

Then he was being whirled up Grosvenor Place, the gloom of which seemed, if anything, intensified since the previous autumn. In his preoccupation he had forgotten to wash or tidy himself in the train. He now frenziedly tried to improve his appearance, smoothing his hair and arranging his tie in deference to—Lady Cranford !

Would her ladyship be in the drawing-room, or would their first few moments be alone together ? His future mother-in-law might with luck be resting or writing letters in her bedroom. In any case, Rosemary would certainly rush out into the hall. He had only to ring. Intuition would tell her the rest !

The cab flew across Hyde Park Corner, up Park Lane and, turning down Mount Street, drew up at the familiar portals of Grosvenor Mansions. . . . At this penultimate moment he delayed, he hesitated. Should he enter ? Should he prolong the sweet agony awhile—go home and change, then return ? Should he walk up and down for a few minutes and prepare a little speech ?

He did neither. He paid off the driver with a cheerful good-night and a double fare. It was good in itself to pay a taxi-driver again, above all, that god in a car who had driven him from the station to the threshold of his happiness.

He entered. The stone stairs were very dark, as always at Grosvenor Mansions. There was fear of air-raids, of course. The lift-man was absent—as usual. It was all happening so exactly as he had rehearsed it over and over again in his mind, as he had countless times pictured the situation to himself !

He tramped noisily up the oft-counted steps, no sound coming back to him but his own echo. He thought with a smile of the last occasion of his mounting them, when together they had crept up like burglars. Reaching the fourth floor, he expected to see light under the front door. This evening there was none. So the switch had been turned off in the hall —a new measure of economy ! He paused to regain breath before ringing. One—two—three seconds . . . and they would be together.

§ 4

He felt for and pressed the bell. The immediate stir within that he had expected did not come. How often before had his first ring not been heard ! He pressed the button again and waited with nerves aquiver. The flat remained silent. . . .

The truth, however, dawned upon him. But of course ! How had that possibility—nay, *probability*—not occurred to him before ! Rosemary and Lady Cranford had gone out early for the evening—to a theatre or a dinner-party—and the servants, after the manner of their kind, had gone out too ! He would stroll round to his club—the house in Eaton Square had been sold—make sure of his room, wash, have dinner, and return, by which time there would certainly be somebody in the flat.

Yet it was with a half-acknowledged disappointment that he descended the steps.

He had barely reached the second floor when the jar-r-r of a taxicab drawing up at the entrance of the Mansions came to his ears, followed by the hard metallic ring which proclaims that the driver is being paid off.

CHAPTER V

God-forgotten

§ 1

HE knew it was she. And, knowing, heard the rippling laugh that had something of a brook's music in it and something of a bird's.

Then he heard a man's voice. . . .

With that he stopped. He had reached the landing of the second floor. The couple could be heard entering the main outer door of the flats. Were they coming up ? Whoever her companion might be, Adrian had no wish for a formal meeting then.

There were upon every landing two doors, each giving entrance to a flat, together with a deep recess which gave access to the lift. Into one of these recesses he stepped. He was in complete darkness.

That was the doing of a second. The couple now stood in the hall beneath. They were laughing and talking.

The man pleaded.

" My Rosebud !—yes. Now—quickly ! Just—just—this once ! "

He knew that voice. He froze.

He drew back into the recess so that, did they pass within a hand's breadth, he could not be seen.

He heard her laugh.

" *No !* "

In the word was witchery but not denial.

" But who's up there, beautiful child ? Your mother ? The servants ? "

" Nobody. Mamma's away till to-morrow. I told the servants they might go out."

" Then—I can come up for a leetle while . . . just a minute
—or two . . . baby . . . mine ? "

" You're not allowed to call me things like that ! " She
laughed again, her voice vibrant with unmistakable excitement. " Don't ! . . . Don't pinch my arm ! "

" My Virgin Mary—my beautiful, maddening angel—but
—yes—*yes*. . . ."

His voice became insistent—urgent, rapid.

" Perhaps he'll be back to-morrow—you never know—perhaps—this is the last time ? "

" I say NO ! "

There was petulance in the words—but what else ?

" We've had some wonderful times together, Harry ; now
don't spoil it all ! "

" But I—*must* . . . Rose——! "

In the recess the listener trembled as one whose last hour
is come.

He knew Upton had seized her, though he could see nothing.
There came the sound of a kiss. . . .

Then she rushed upstairs, one, two steps at a time—breathless, panting, gurgling out her low laugh.

She brushed past him. Her sleeve touched him, he neither
moving nor making any sound. Upton followed.

Higher and higher they rushed, until he could hear nothing
but their echoing footsteps.

Then there was a pause, followed by the click of a key in a
Yale lock.   A laughing cry.   The bang of a door.

Silence.

*   *   *   *   *

Some time in the course of that night Adrian Knoyle
found himself sitting on a seat in Hyde Park, opposite the
Serpentine.

It was cold. Stars winked, remote and passionless.
There was a distant sound like the faint murmur of the sea.
Close at hand he heard water lapping.

Probably he had been sitting on the seat a long time. His feet and hands were numb; his senses, too. He turned on the iron bench and raised a hand to his head, to his temples. They were throbbing—throbbing.

Too weary or too dazed to think or discriminate, he stared vacantly out across the quiet, mysterious water to the dim trees on the far shore. He murmured to himself again and again, " This is the end—this is the end."

He could neither think nor realise nor care; and when a policeman, stalking past, turned upon him the full glare of a bull's-eye lantern, he did not move. The policeman was probably surprised. Expecting to find some abandoned woman, some drunkard or homeless wanderer, he saw—a British officer.

He hesitated, then passed on.

§ 2

And the night passed on. The murmur as of the sea died away. At last complete silence prevailed—that terrifying silence which encompasses the unsleeping in the midst of a city.

It must have been in the smallest, coldest hours of the morning that this silence was broken by a wild and desolate cry.

It might have been laughter, brazen and cruel. It might have been a woman's scream. It might have been the choking shriek of a drowning man.

The sound came again, wild, piercing, sad. . . .

It came yet a third time and could now be traced to a low, wooded islet some two hundred paces distant out in the water.

It was succeeded presently by what seemed to be the subdued murmuring of a number of waterfowl.

During the whole of the night this was the only separate sound to penetrate his brain. During the whole of the night this was the only sound to whip him into recollection.

Hearing it, he rose and walked violently up and down by the waterside. All came back to him, all rushed back upon him—with this mocking echo of a former life.

" It is the end," he murmured, " it is the end."

In the next moment and for the first time there presented itself to his mind a clear realisation of what had befallen him. No sooner had the moment passed than anger mastered him, shook him to the innermost deeps of his being, set him quivering as one in a convulsion.

That moment, too, passed. The alternative was—misery. What use, what meaning had anything for him now ?

She who had promised herself to him, pledged herself to him—not once only—consecrated herself to him, forsworn herself, demanded all of him in return and received all—his forgiveness, his allegiance, his adoration, his body, soul, and spirit, his life's blood, his life's hopes, his life's dreams, the innermost sanctuary of his trust . . . what signified these things now ?

Mercifully he was alone. Mercifully there were none to see or hear him who like a stricken animal had fled to be alone, far as might be from his kind. None should see or hear him in the abasement of his anger and his grief, even as none but the birds and the trees and the sunshine had been their witnesses in the dayspring of their love.

With that, hotfoot, came anger, mastering, verging upon madness ; not against Upton, indeed—who was no more than some loathsome insect in his sight—but against this other who had been his life's very heart.

Blood flows from the lips which teeth pierce. Nails grind into the palms. False as the kiss in Gethsemane. . . . Blood flowed—did it not ?—and there were scars in the Hands—on Calvary day.

§ 3

Illusive calm succeeded.

And with calm, words of his mother, prophetic, wiser than he !

" Never let life knock you down. Meet it fair and square, and if it hits you hard, give to it like a tense spring—and spring back."

And again :

" One cannot live, one cannot die, one cannot love or hope or *know* or achieve in life without suffering, without experience. Remember that, whether it's the horror and the dreadfulness of the time are breaking your heart or whether—whether— it's anything else. Suffering is the crucifixion of each one of us. . . ."

Her belief sprang—as her whole nature did, her innate goodness, her woman's strength—from some Higher Power. And he—what had he to do with God, or God with him ? Yesterday —the day before—in his boyhood—he might have believed, had believed, in some unformed yet all-seeing, all-pitying, and embracing intelligence. Was not his betrothed, had not Life itself been an expression, a pledge of divinity, of pity or hope, in human turmoil and existence ? But now——! Where was this God—of love ? On the battlefield where men killed and died, were crucified and came to their Supreme Agony with blasphemy, with hatred on their lips ? Within himself ? Murder in the heart where Love reigned. Where was this God ? . . . Nowhere indeed for him—who was God-forgotten.

§ 4

Sense of actuality returned. And with it loneliness. To be physically alone is not loneliness. It is often happiness ; it is often peace. But there descended upon him now a loneliness of the *soul*, a sense of severance that was destroying, annihilating. He became aware of intense individual separateness ; of the individual in the mass, each battling along his solitary road, each road leading to a different goal, parallel roads, but none converging ; of an eternal parting of ways—each striving soul a world unto itself. He who had once believed in

unity and love, in the fusion upon earth of two mortal beings
as an Entity, ideal, indivisible, who had experienced the
perfection of spiritual union, had anticipated the unity of
twin-minds—and upon that had pinned his faith !

Well, it was ended : ended their companionship, their
mutual perfection, the jointure and the completion of their
lives ; ended to-night a hundred secrets, a hundred lifelong
moments and discoveries, a hundred common experiences, that
none other might touch, complete or share ; ended a
chapter which could never be reopened and to which neither
of them could ever turn back. All was shattered, all shattered
in a world that, within a few brief months, had become nightmare, madness, chaos blinder than human eyes could pierce.
His hopes, his illusions, his optimism, his self-certainty—
killed in five minutes ; aye, and the very motive-spark of Life
itself.

There was one thing more terrible than Death—finality in
Life.

§ 5

The Park lay grey and quiet about him. Misty moonlight
filtered in between the trees. Always the Serpentine water
lapped, and was lapping at his feet.

That was the voice he perpetually heard—the lapping water
—whispering, whispering to him like a cool, steadfast under-
note of sympathy in the torment and dissonance of his
mind.

Death !

This the word the voice of the water whispered. . . .

All through his pacings up and down, all through his violence,
his grief, recrimination, anger, and despair, this voice had
whispered to him : gently, understandingly, tenderly, lov-
ingly—but insistently. He paid no attention to it at first.
Hearing, he was hardly conscious of it. But it persisted ;

it insisted. He went over to the waterside and stood, gazing down—thinking . . . thinking.

And even as he listened to the soothing voice, his wretched mind revolved the words that she had uttered in the beech-wood :

" I'm not sure, I'm not sure of myself. I wish, oh ! I wish I *knew* myself."

Like a whirlpool unpent, the flood-tide of his misery burst forth, breaking all dams, seizing him upon its incalculable current, overmastering him, hurling him into vortex. He began to moan and then to croon her name to himself again and again.

" Rosemary ! . . . Rosemary ! . . . Rosemary ! "

And then :

" Rosie ! My darling ! My own, own love ! How could you deceive me ? How could you desert me—forget me ? How could you treat me so ? "

He sank down upon the iron seat and buried his face in his hands.

§ 6

Still the voice of the water whispered—that voice to which so many in this same place had listened and made answer :— of escape, of an alternative, of an ending.

Death !

Becoming calmer, he crossed the path, and gazed once more at the little waves lapping the stony shore.

It was tempting. It was restful and alluring. It was lonely and quiet—and near her—and yet in the midst of life.

But no ! . . . He could not, could not—here. God-forgotten he might be, but drag her name through the mire of such a sequel—he could not. Too fearful, too drab an ending, that, too soiled and ugly a curtain to what, after all, in its little hour, had been a good and a beautiful thing.

Fate held for him a worthier weapon than that.

Across the sea, Death waited—on the battlefield, in the trenches, by the wayside. Arms wide to embrace, sleep strong to enfold, a friend there, faithful and true. Constant and tender lover, she, not to deny him, not to betray him. To her embrace, loving, everlasting, he would go.

•   •   •   •   •

Daylight stalked among the trees, paling such few lamps as were visible.

He still sat on, but by slow processes reason insisted. What should he do as a first step? Soon the park gates would be open—if they were not already. His instinct, still that of a hunted animal or outcast felon, was to escape, hide, creep away, meet nobody—escape at all costs from this city of his sorrows.

He felt in his inner pocket the notebook containing his leave-pass—that so-precious yellow ticket! He scanned it. " Special leave " was written in red ink in the left-hand corner, " Urgent family reasons " was added in brackets. He thought for several moments, staring blankly at the slip of paper. . . . Wherein lay the significance of those reasons now?

He tore a leaf from his pocket-book and covered it with pencilled handwriting very quickly. He read over what he had written :

"When I left you to return to France, your last words were a prayer that I might come back to you. I came back —last night. I heard everything. Good-bye."

He addressed an envelope and put the note in his pocket. Then he rose and walked in the direction of the Marble Arch.

§ 7

Workmen and shop-people were already beginning to stream across the park to their daily avocations. Many looked curiously at the mud-stained, haggard officer who strode past. They made a mental note that this one was really from the trenches ; and that he had had a bad time.

He made his way to a small private hotel in Bayswater, where he booked a room for half a day. He washed and shaved, scraped the mud from his uniform, and had tea and dry toast brought up to his room.

At a quarter before ten he called for a taxicab, and was driven to the War Office by way of South Audley Street, and so past Grosvenor Mansions. The streets seemed oddly empty as the cab whirred up Piccadilly, past the Hotel Astoria. He looked neither to right nor left. Not many had assembled in the waiting-hall of the War Office at this early hour. A messenger led him up two flights of stairs, and by labyrinthine passages to one of many doors. An elderly Staff Officer wearing an eyeglass came out into the passage.

"Good morning ! What can I do for you ? "

Adrian saluted.

"I've a special leave pass for one month issued for urgent family reasons. Those reasons no longer hold good, and I should like to know whether I can return to my regiment at once."

"H'm ! " The officer smiled in an accommodating manner, glanced at the yellow ticket and thought a moment. " Better take the leave and say nothing about the reasons." He nodded, as though the interview might be considered at an end, and turned to go

"But I want——"

"That'll be all right."

"——I think I ought to go back, sir."

The officer looked surprised.

" What ? You want to go back ? You're either a very keen soldier, or an exceptionally honest young man—probably both. You mean you want your leave washed out ? "

The officer looked at the applicant kindly, as one looks at a lunatic.

" Yes, sir."

" All right then. So be it. Give me the pass." He took the leave warrant, altered the date and initialled it. " The return train leaves Victoria at twelve. Good luck ! "

" Thank you, sir."

Adrian returned to his hotel, again passing the Astoria and again passing Grosvenor Mansions. He paid his bill, slung his haversack over his shoulder, and drove to the station, on the way posting a letter.

* * * * *

Eighteen hours later, he was trudging back along the road that led to the trenches. His face was hidden by the upturned collar of his coat, his eyes looked towards an horizon above which white star-lights slowly, silently, rose and fell. For it was night.

Rain fell, too. Rain fell steadily, implacably, blotting out the landscape, making pools of the deep holes and ruts in the road. It is probable he saw nothing of the lights nor felt the rain against his cheeks, nor knew that he was wet through.

He came to the shattered village, Laventie, with its derelict railway station and its broken church. As he entered it, a naval gun began to fire at intervals from the railway, such being its habit at midnight. The ghostly battered street was deserted except for a sentry tramping up and down outside a Brigade Headquarters.

He was challenged.

He inquired of the sentry whether his battalion was in the

village. The reply was that it had gone that evening into the front-line trenches.

Two miles more. The rain plashed mercilessly, but the star-lights seemed nearer.

There was a sandbag breastwork across the road. The mud was ankle-deep. There were shell-holes. Adrian stumbled forward, neither feeling, seeing, nor caring. Weak from emotional stress and lack of food and sleep, he lurched to this side and that ; once or twice he shufflingly fell.

Some distance off a field gun fired with a flash and quick glare out of the gloom of what seemed to be one vast surrounding moorland. Occasionally a stray shell went moaning overhead.

He entered a communication-trench with slimy sides and so slimy underfoot that he could not stand up. The skeleton of a ruined farmhouse grinned down at him, and a bullet flattened itself with a startling " crack " against the solitary standing wall. Rats scurried away from him.

He came to the front line. He could dimly perceive the figures of sentries muffled in waterproof capes silhouetted against the familiar pale glow that never left the night sky above Lille. For the rest, the trench was utterly deserted, nor was there any sound but the steady drip ! drip ! of the rain.

He made for the old Company Headquarters and lifted the split sandbag that curtained the entrance. Eric sat on a ration-box writing by candle-light. The dug-out looked precisely as it had looked on Christmas night except that now the floor was a foot or so deeper under water.

The company-commander looked up, and seeing a haggard face framed in the opening, said sharply :

" What do you want ? "

Then his face changed.

" The devil——! "

Adrian staggered down the steps into the low chamber and reeled against the table.

" What on earth's happened ? Why are you back——? "

" It's—well, it's over. So . . . I've come back."

Eric said :

" All right, old boy. Tell me about it in the morning. Sit down here by the brazier. Get out of these things. . . . Have a drink ! "

He poured out neat whisky, almost forcing it down his friend's throat. He then dragged off the latter's dripping garments, laid him down upon a wire-netting bed which stood in a corner just above the water's level, and tucked him up with a greatcoat as one tucks up a sick person.

Day once more breaking above the rain-soaked Flanders plain, found him still sitting, watching there.

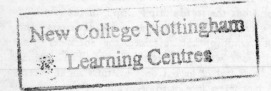

CHAPTER VI

Underworld

§ 1

ADRIAN KNOYLE took the ten days' leave to which he was ordinarily entitled, in the South of France. He at first protested that having had a portion of the leave due, he was very willing to forgo the rest and remain with the battalion. Eric Sinclair merely observed that this was nonsense, and settled the matter out of hand. Nor in reality was Adrian loth to go. He longed for solitude—for quiet—to think things out. In the battalion, this was out of the question, and he found difficulty in facing the inquisitive eyes, the curious comments that he knew were being passed upon his unexpected return. He had given out that the family business which had called him home had been settled unexpectedly. But gossip and inquiry had their way in a life that was monotony itself. Arthur Cornwallis, who held the clue, read much in his friend's demeanour, but held his peace. George Walker, essaying some rallying jest upon the subject of the erratic movements of young men in the spring, was very promptly suppressed by Eric.

And Eric proved right to insist on his friend's leave being taken. The complete change of atmosphere, of climate and surroundings, the solitude in which he wrapped himself at Nice, proved beneficial. Adrian returned in at least a comparatively normal frame of mind.

Already the earliest days of April were beginning to bring warmth, sunshine and illusive hope to a weary and an embittered land. An unforgettable winter had passed. The Battle of

Verdun still racked Europe with its massed slaughter and ferocity. But once more the fighters girded themselves, setting their teeth ironly for—they knew not what. Few among them, perhaps, saw sanely, could think in terms of normality or humanity or, counting the days, could call their lives their own. All felt the irony of an impending doom which, accompanied by bursting buds of trees and flowers, by mating songs of birds, by the lush green of new grass, fresh scents, and gay colouring of fruit blossom in French and Belgian gardens—ushered in the spring.

During Knoyle's absence the whole Division moved to the neighbourhood of Ypres. On his return he found a letter awaiting him. It ran:

> " 37, Grosvenor Mansions,
> " Mount Street, W.
> " *Monday.*

" DEAR ADRIAN,

" Thanks for your note, though I could hardly read it.

" As for what it means I haven't the vaguest idea, except that you seem to have written it in rather a pet—and then rushed back to France like a bear with a sore head. I rang up your club, and they said they knew nothing of your whereabouts and hadn't even seen you.

" One thing I do know, though. I'm not going to marry a man who always wants to be spying on my incomings and outgoings and gets jealous at the slightest excuse. Life's not long enough.

" I may as well tell you I've talked to Gina, who knows the world better than anybody, about it, and she quite agrees. She says you've never taken the trouble to understand Harry, and he wants a lot of understanding—and I don't think you ever will. He's frightfully clever and brilliant, and that's what you don't appreciate. But I do. See ? "

" The fact is you ask too much and don't give enough in return. You're beastly selfish.

"By-the-by, will you please return *all* my letters, as it would be rather a bore their being read, if anything happened to you.

"Good-bye-ee-e-e.

"ROSEMARY.

"P.S.—Have you read 'Stars,' the successer (*sic*) of 'Rays'? We're all going to a party given by Venetia Romane in honour of its *huge* success, to-night!"

Adrian did not reply to this communication. The letters referred to had already been destroyed.

§ 2

He had not so far spoken even to Eric of the disaster that now overshadowed his life. Eric, of course, had at once divined the truth—may even have been prepared for it. But he asked no questions. It was not his way. He knew well enough that in his own time his friend would broach the subject, would open his heart.

In due course Adrian did. But not until after his return from the South; not until after Rosemary's letter put their severance beyond all doubt. The interval had tided him over the first shock, under the influence of which he had felt unable to speak of the matter even to his closest friend. Nor did this reticence imply any loosening of trust between the two. Rather it revealed to them both an instinctive sympathy.

On the evening of the day after Adrian's return they went out riding together. They took the military road which, skirting the town of Poperinghe, led across country to the neighbourhood of Ruisbrugge and Proven. The landscape was uncannily flat. Between the innumerable roads, watched by their sentinel trees, lay wide tracts of minutely-cultivated land, acres of vegetables and hops, little cornfields, root-crops and the like, these being freely dotted with brick cottages, villages, and farmhouses of a nondescript type. Nearer Ypres there were areas of young oakwood broken up by the encampments and cantonments and hut-villages of the troops, but welcome alike for their shade from the growing heat of the sun and for the protection they afforded from the enemy's aerial eyes. For the rest, the whole countryside was alive with men and the doings and the workings of men. Here, new railways being constructed ; there, new roads. Here workshops, great lorry parks and horse lines, there endless rows of wooden huts, tents innumerable, and hideous tin erections. The main highways carried an unceasing stream of traffic. Everywhere men—English soldiers, negroes, Kaffirs, Chinamen, Frenchmen, Belgians, Indians, Egyptians, Canadians, German prisoners, a dozen nationalities intermingling.

Not until they came to the comparatively quiet byways in the neighbourhood of Proven Château (the Headquarters of an Army), with its pleasant gardens, drives, and grassy spaces —reminiscent of an English country house—and its great white building, could they converse at ease. As they walked their horses side by side along a dusty track, Adrian said :

" What news of Faith lately ? "

" She's still working away at Arden. Poor old Cyril has had another operation. His lordship is being desperately efficient down on the East Coast. I suppose it's the privilege of the elderly to be enthusiastic. He's doing all he knows to get a battalion out here, she says. They still live in mortal terror that he'll succeed. That sort of man is apt to. . . . "

" Your future father-in-law ? When's it likely to come off ? "

Eric had always been scrupulously tactful in evading the subject of his own engagement. But now it had been broached he said :

" Oh, goodness knows ! As you're aware the old boy is very obstinate ; he's absolutely got his back up against war marriages. I should like it to have been——"

He checked himself. Adrian completed the sentence.

" Next leave."

" Yes—but it's out of the question. I sometimes wonder whether it ever will come off."

" Oh ! It will."

" You're always so deucedly optimistic. Why ? "

" Because you're fond of her and she's fond of you. And—she's a good sort."

" That's true," Eric agreed.

" Faith's one in a thousand, you know."

" She is."

" All women are not like Faith. They're a queer lot. . . "

" No. She's one of the best."

Eric almost dreaded what was coming.

" Eric—you know about me, and . . . her ? "

When it came to the point he could not bring himself to utter that name. To do so, to utter the *name* was pain. But he found no difficulty in mentioning the subject to Eric now ; only reluctance to go over each little miserable detail.

Eric said : " No, I don't know. Tell me. What the devil's happened ? "

" We've . . . crashed. For good, so far as I'm concerned. She is—well, she likes somebody else."

His tone was level and quiet.

" That—chap ? "

" You saw it going on, then ? "

" I saw—something. I heard—things—vaguely when I was on leave. But I never thought of—anything like that."

" One wouldn't. Well—that's why I came back. I wanted to get away from it all, from London—from England. My only hope is that we may never meet again in this world."

Eric did not respond at once. He was not sure how best to deal with the situation. And he was afraid of touching unnecessarily on some sensitive spot. Presently he said :

"You feel that way now—naturally. . . . But next leave—you'll go and see her. You'll make it up. All women are like that. You needn't get desperate about it. They don't mean it half the time. They can't help it, poor wretches."

"I don't want to see that blasted London again."

"Oh, my dear chap . . . really!"

"Eric—no. She's been all my life, these last two years—since I've lived at all—all my present and future, all my past. Now she's finished it—killed it. I never want to see her again—or England—or London—or Arden—or any of the places we've known and been happy in together."

"Don't be a fool! She'll come round—of course she will. Women always do. Leave her damned well alone—that's my advice."

"My dear old boy, you don't quite understand. It's not a question of 'coming round.'" He laughed. "It's the end—for me as well as for her." His voice sank almost to a whisper. "Eric, she can't—she *can't* go straight. She's all right"—there came a note of old passion now—"she's a good sort, and simple and all that really, and—decent in herself, but—wayward, *mad*. You see, it's not the first time, this. . . . I'm too slow for her. We never could be happy, even if I were utterly devoid of pride. She could never stick to me. I feel sure of that now. She's got caught up in this rotten Maryon crowd—I warned her—I implored. She might—heaven knows!—she might have stuck to me if—if I'd been at home. And—oh! my God, Eric—I'm afraid for her sometimes—I'm terribly, awfully afraid for her!"

Eric made no reply. A German aeroplane—gleaming white in the sunshine and extraordinarily beautiful with its black cross clearly outlined on the silvery breast—passed overhead at a great height, and the two young men—common sight though it was—concerned themselves in the white smoke-puffs of aerial shrapnel that followed in its wake. Besides, an anti-aircraft " pom-pom " on a motor-trolley was firing splenetically close at hand, making speech almost inaudible.

But when the aeroplane had passed and the noise subsided somewhat, Eric said abruptly :

" You must get over this."

" Yes ? . . . And what about her ? "

" She'll come running back to you—one of these days. You see ! "

" Well, it's done with—finished—so far as I'm concerned."

" Oh, yes—but one always thinks that, you know. One gets over these things in time—or else they come right."

" In time—yes. . . . But it's ended, all the same. And she's ended. She'll suffer. And—well, I wish to God I was ended."

" Cheer up ! "

They walked their horses on in silence. They came to the Prisoners' Cage near the cross-roads known as International Corner, where one or two down-at-heel, grey-clad Germans were squatting against the wire-netting, smoking clay pipes in the sun.

The two officers stopped, glanced at them from habit, and rode on. Adrian said :

" I want you to do something for me."

" What's that ? "

" Stand by her, whatever happens—do what you can for her."

" Of course. You'd do the same for old Faith if I got knocked out or anything."

" I would."

They came out on the main Ypres-Poperinghe highway, and the stream of men and traffic setting towards the battlefield with the approach of dusk, precluded further conversation. Nor till many months had passed was the subject mentioned between them again.

§ 3

Adrian had found, in addition to Rosemary's letter, one from Lady Knoyle awaiting him.

He had written to her, stating simply that Rosemary and he had had a disagreement and that the wedding would not take place. He had added, without explanation, that, while disappointed at not seeing his mother, he felt disinclined to return to England at present, and had taken the opportunity offered to go to the Riviera. His mother's intuition would supply the rest.

There was no doubt Lady Knoyle did understand. She expressed an almost formal regret at the abandonment of the arrangements and at his decision not to spend his leave at home, merely adding, in regard to the latter, that he was his own best judge. The burden of her letter was contained in its closing paragraph :

" I feel for you, my dear one, every hour and every minute, every night and every day. Only remember that it is not all blind and negative, purposeless and without end, but that there is a purpose and there will be an end. Some day we shall know—here or perhaps hereafter—and in that revelation we shall attain all that is lasting and true."

As time went on the young man discovered that, in addition to Eric and his mother, there was a third abiding factor in his life. This was Faith. Faith wrote to him about some trifle. He replied, and she continued to write—at first about once a fortnight, latterly more often—affectionate and amiable letters, containing such news as was likely to interest him. The solid character of the woman seemed to breathe through these letters as character curiously does breathe through the written word. He was grateful for them.

And it was strange—or perhaps would not have appeared so to one familiar (but who except Lady Knoyle was familiar ?)

with this divisible personality—how his inborn love of his own countryside came back to him at this time. In the trenches, on the march, out riding, awake at night, on parade, at the most unexpected moments, an almost painful longing for the Three Hills—their shapeliness and wide distances, their solitude, freedom, and indefinite calm—returned repeatedly like the quiet *motif* in a distracting symphony.

For the rest, the old Adrian was dead. He lived no more. He existed, moved, ate, slept, and talked, but without realisation of immediacy or of propinquity. It was as if the *soul* of him had withered. Deep down in his heart he owned allegiance to that new, more constant lover who had appeared to him silently in the hour of life's perishing.

§ 4

Such was his condition at this time. He guarded his thoughts. He watched over them, brooded over them jealously that none might know or guess. And to out-ward appearance the only change in him was a hitherto unnoticed gravity, an absence of light-heartedness that had marked itself on his face, never, perhaps, to leave it again.

His comrades noted this change, putting it down to the effect which prolonged warfare and the environment of war are well known to have on certain temperaments, more especially in that lethal region to which they were now come. For was not this Ypres the very negation of hope, the very atmosphere of the underworld of the spirit, and of despair ? . . . April found them in cantonments and tents amid the young oakwoods which lie to the west of the ruined city ; May in the so-called trenches, better-named ditches which at that time lay a mile or two to the east of it.

And looking back upon this period and upon the four months that succeeded it, survivors were disposed to agree that in all the Five Years they were the most unearthly, the most sinister, the nearest akin within human conception to the last and final state of man. Here it seemed as though the Almighty had passed judgment upon mankind and were levying execution of it inexorably. It was always a crooked and a twisted and a torn and a broken memory in after-years, yet starred with strange intervals of lucid, unexpected peace, during which men saw visions of a wondrous ultimate purity and splendour—else, must surely have perished. It was as though souls had to be tested through denial of the life of the mind, of the realm of the soul, of the celestial human thing. Beauty and Death allied. Nature mocked at suffering. Love gibbered at Despair. . . . Men lived, physically and mentally, in the dim contorted regions of the anti-Christ.

But they saw visions—yes. For if the eves were terrible, the dawns were beautiful. And if there was naked horror in the bright noonday when the sun scorched down upon livid festering corpses, and every grinning feature of the land was laid bare and the buzz of the clustering blue-bottles mingled with a nameless stench—there was sleep sometimes, too, and dreams scented with thyme of Paradise. And if men lived and died in the nether-world, losing sense of individuality and time, they came back every nine, ten, or eleven days to meadows vivid with the lush green of new grass, riotous with wild flowers, instinct with the upward pushing growth of the spring. And if existence itself became a purgatory, there was peace still, and hope, in the faces of the dead.

The process of this thing was slow, selective, partial, and sure. It was not as it had been in the winter trenches, where blind chance might strike a man down but where Providence watched over the majority. Here the scythe-bearer claimed his victims one by one—five, ten, a dozen, or even fifteen together. Men knew that Time was their master. Captain Sinclair watched his company dwindle. Each platoon-commander saw his comrades—those who had borne the rifle, some of them,

since the outset of the campaign, and had played their
humble part always stolidly and always manfully—join one by
one the drab company which, swathed in waterproof sheets,
duly labelled and numbered, morning by morning lay in a row
at the head of the trolley-line. One by one they went—ceased
to be—were no more seen : their laughter, their chatter, the
characteristics of each that distinguished him from the other
—stilled and vanished for ever. It was a strange experience.
But those who remained gave little outward sign. "Bill's
gone," they would say ; "Old Ginger's copped it at last."
And would then go on with their work again.

§ 5

If Captain Sinclair felt these things, he, too, gave no sign.
He was there—always there—never absent from the trenches
for a day or a night as his subalterns were by turns :—"little
Percy," the rank and file called him among themselves, and
sometimes "Strawberries-and-cream." "Little Percy," no
doubt, in respect of his neatness, his fastidiousness, his parade-
ground precision, his detached air of boredom which seemed to
increase as the days went by ; "Strawberries-and-Cream," in
reference to his complexion. Captain Sinclair, it seemed,
carried fortune on his shoulders ; at any rate, he risked his life
so needlessly that the soldiers asked one another—and even
made bets on the subject—how long would his luck stick to
him, and would it stick to him to the end ? They feared
him, too. He had a quiet, terrible way. How he could gaze
at a soldier who betrayed fear ! With what a surprised,
innocent, inquiring glance, as who should say, "My dear chap,
what—what's the matter ? How funny you look ! Anything I
can do ? "—or the glance would say, "My dear chap, would
you rather—er—go down to the dressing-station ? " And
seeing his company-commander's contempt, that soldier would
pull himself together.

It is probable that deep down in his heart (to which even his closest friend never quite penetrated) he felt a respect not less profound than the more emotional among his brother-officers for these rough and faithful ones who, grumble as they might (and perpetually did), never failed ; who, out of the staunchness of their hearts, supported him through these perils ; who by the sweat of their brow and outpouring of their blood made the Ypres Salient possible in those days.

Alone among the officers of the battalion, Eric Sinclair remained unchanged by the ordeal of these four months. If anything he became a little more quizzical, a little more exact and a little more exacting. (It was remarked, not without amusement, that to him from St. James's Street came a special coarse linen cover of fanciful material for the steel helmet, and a special badge worked in the front thereof.) At the same time, new and to Adrian unexpected traits revealed themselves in his friend—not always likeable traits. One was a pitiless strain in the man. It expressed itself on a certain night when two prisoners were brought in from a German patrol captured in No Man's Land. Eric and Adrian met them being prodded along a lonely section of trench by the bayonets of a sergeant and three soldiers, accompanied by kicks and curses. Eric laughed ; Adrian felt an unashamed compassion for the two Germans, fine-looking men who behaved with some dignity under the circumstances and were, he reflected, as much the victims of the holocaust of war as himself or their captors. When the platoon-sergeant inquired what he should do with his prisoners, Eric said :

"They're a couple of the swine who fire the *minenwerfer*, I suppose. Do what you like with 'em ! "

"Oh, send 'em down to Brigade Headquarters, Eric——" protested Adrian.

"Come along ! " said his company-commander, cutting him short. "They're no use to us."

The platoon-sergeant laughed.

Passing back that way half-an-hour later, they found the Germans lying dead in the trench. . . .

As to the rest, all in turn and in varying manner and degree fell beneath the spell of the ghoulish nightmare of the place and of the time. Walker went first—Walker the " thruster," the bloodthirsty, the enterprising, the devil-may-care. But Walker went. In fact, he made a deliberate confession to Adrian one Sunday evening as they strolled together in the fields behind Brielen.

" Adrian," he said, " I've got 'em. I don't know how I shall stick it. I don't believe I can face another show like Wednesday night. It's a hell on earth. It's too—*filthy*. . . . But don't tell Eric."

By " got 'em " he meant that " the shakes " (as the men called it) were upon him. His mention of " Wednesday night " referred to the striking dead by *minenwerfer* of four of his platoon. Hearing for the first time the explosion of one of these great bombs, he had run up and found the four close together in the trench frozen with shock—two crouching, one standing with his head bowed upon the parapet, a fourth scattered in pieces around. He had been sick.

Adrian replied : " We've all got 'em, old boy—more or less. I've got 'em too ; I see things—but I don't worry. I suppose it's all for our sins . . . or other people's." And he laughed.

It was a mirthless laugh, but he had grown callous of late to other people's suffering.

Stick it Lieutenant Walker had to, though he trembled all over, jumped to this side and that, and went white to the lips when shells came plunging into the ditches that lay so immediately beneath the enemy's eye. Cornwallis, on the other hand, though gaining by dint of immense effort more visible control over himself, had nightmares in the back areas. He now rarely spoke. Others became jerky and took to drinking rather large quantities of neat whisky. This was particularly

the case with Darell, who had always been somewhat prone to
the " bottle " and who now contrived to maintain an unnatural
cheerfulness. Vivian, on the other hand, showed a nervous
irritability which at times led to smart exchanges in the mess—
without, however, lasting ill-feeling. Alston, the ex-lawyer,
for all his assumed toughness, began to wear a perpetually
grim and worried, an almost haunted look ; Durrant buried himself more and more in particularity of detail and pedantic
theory. Even Colonel Steele was a different man on his
nightly tours round the trenches from what he had been
back at battalion headquarters—he spoke almost meekly,
and his voice had acquired a stutter as though he held himself under perpetual constraint. As for his elegant adjutant,
Langley, this young gentleman remained firmly at the telephone,
rarely put his nose outside the deepest dug-out available,
and then only to bawl for a whisky-and-soda. Major Brough,
the second-in-command, a portly personage, was subject to
recurring attacks of trench-fever which kept him rather
frequently out of the line.

Adrian was less susceptible than the rest to the purely
physical influences around him, since he lived habitually within
his own mind, and that which *happened* passed by and away from
him. Being intensely conscious of himself, he was seldom taken
unawares, and only once did he give way to the furnace of
suppressed feeling that at times burned within him. This
was during a brief period in reserve when, unable longer
to bear the relentless burden which always lay near to his
heart, and feeling that by his low spirits he was a heavy drag
even upon the rather forced merriment of the rest of the
company, he drank too much, became intoxicated, and had to
be helped to his tent by his company-commander. He awoke
to hear the whir-r-r of aeroplanes overhead and the detonation
of German bombs falling around, whilst from far and near
came the wailing melancholy sound of gas-alarms in a score of
different keys. On the morrow he was mercilessly chaffed by

his brother-officers, and received the only official rebuke from
Eric that the latter thought necessary to inflict during their
long comradeship.

"Getting drunk out here," the company-commander
remarked, "is like a joke that goes too far. It ceases to be
amusing and becomes rather a bore."

The incident was not mentioned again.

The two friends were indeed more than ever inseparable.
Eric did not sympathise vocally; he did so by way of a
score of unobtrusive actions; saw to it that Adrian was
left alone as little as might be, since he feared the effect of
a brooding solitude upon him, and was always ready even at
the busiest times to take a walk or ride. He privily com-
municated the state of affairs to Faith to do as she might think
best in regard to Rosemary. Eric's wisdom was self-contained
but practical.

Two events alone stood out in Adrian's recollection from the
monochrome of that time. These, however, made a lasting
impression where all else was hazy and dark, because they
nearly affected that purpose which had now become a fixture
in his mind. They revealed to him, as nothing else had, the
irony of a Fate against which man seemed too puny to struggle.

The first of these events occurred a couple of nights after
Walker's unsought confession that he had "got 'em." It was
also the occasion of Walker's death.

That had been a curious confidence, Adrian thought—a
curious self-abasement—to come from such a man, one so
normally self-confident, so essentially physical, so purely
"animal."

He had made that confidence, no doubt, perceiving his
brother-officer's sombre state and imagining the cause of it
to be similar to his own. It was as if he had had a foreboding, too.

CHAPTER VII

Love and Death

§ 1

IT was an evening late in June, quiet and peaceful, after the heat of the day, the eternal sniping, and the periodical violent bursts of shelling. It was that hour when the slow dusk not being sufficiently advanced for work to begin, the combatants seemed tacitly to agree to take their ease.

Captain Sinclair had established the custom of gathering around him at sunset his platoon-commanders and sergeants and of discussing with them the forthcoming night's work. At a point close to the company headquarters where a real bit of trench broadened out somewhat, forming a natural little amphitheatre, they were now gathered together. In the centre of this enclosed space, on a petrol-can, sat Eric, notebook and pencil on knee. Adrian, Walker and Cornwallis, also armed with notebooks and pencils, were seated on the fire-step, while the platoon-sergeants—four large, fierce-looking men whose patched and stained uniforms showed the nature of the life they had been leading—stood in attentive attitudes around. Gently, very gently, the evening breeze stirred the long grasses, yellow vetches, trefoil and red poppy that fringed the lip of the trench. A golden haze lay upon the battlefield, kindling its hideousness almost to beauty; a couple of miles away the white husk of a high building amid a mass of greenery showed where the city of Ypres slept its sleep of death.

Captain Sinclair's voice speaking in quiet precise accents very different from the drawl he habitually used, was the only sound heard.

" As soon as it's dark," he was saying, " I want you to lead out by platoons to the point we chose last night—you all know that ? String your men out as quietly as possible at four paces interval—No. 13 platoon on the left, then No. 14, No. 15 platoon on the right—and get to work quickly Adrian, you'll be in charge of that lot. George "—he turned to Walker, " I want you with No. 16 platoon to dig a communication trench back from the centre—choose your own point of starting. Arthur, you'll be with Adrian. Remember you'll be only about seventy yards from the Germans, so go quietly and don't chatter I shall walk round later with the Colonel. . . . Is that clear ? Does everybody know what he's got to do ? If not, ask."

There was a chorus of " Yes, sir ! " followed by a pause that was punctured only by the " crack " of a sniper's rifle. A great bird, dark and sinister, flapped slowly and heavily over the trench on its way to some lair in the wastes of grass. The night crept up quickly.

A sergeant, a shaggy grey-haired old reservist, spoke :

" Beg your pardon, sir—what if they open fire on us ? "

" Lie down in the trench—and wait. Or if you haven't dug your trench—lie down "

" Hadn't we better put some wire out ? " inquired Walker.

" No—no wire. Covering parties. Each platoon will find its own covering party. A corporal and two men."

" How far out ? " asked Cornwallis.

" Use your own judgment, my dear chap. Twenty or thirty yards. You know what a covering party's for ? "

" Yes."

" How deep's the trench got to be, please, sir ? " A smart, fair-haired young sergeant spoke.

" Oh, four feet—about. Until you touch water."

Silence fell again while the velvety evening tip-toed round.

" I'm sorry you've got to do this," Eric went on composedly. " It seems to me a fairly objectless proceeding on the whole and a distinctly dangerous one. However, that's beside the point. It's got to be done. As you know, there's a battle beginning down south any day. The idea of digging these storming trenches is to bluff the Germans into thinking——"

Even as he spoke, and as though in answer to his words, there crashed out a short distance to the right on ground lower than that which they occupied a hurricane-fire of artillery, machine-guns, and rifles. It was like the first resounding chord of an orchestra at the signal of the conductor's bâton. Everybody except Eric jumped up and looked over the parapet. Eric began writing. Battle had leapt to life like a storm at sea. Lights went up, red, white, yellow and green, golden-shower rockets burst against the purpling sky, and the indigo blue of oncoming night was streaked with gun flashes.

Walker muttered " Blast ! " between his teeth. Cornwallis tried not to look uneasy. The red-faced ginger-haired sergeant-major remarked to another sergeant, " What's this bloody turn-up ? "

Eric said : " It's a raid," and went on writing.

It was the overture in the form of a demonstration—they were afterwards to learn—to the battle of the Somme.

Meanwhile the flash and thunder of the artillery, the unbroken roar of machine-guns and musketry, the countless red and white S.O.S. signals sent up by the German infantry in their dire need, formed a picture set in the gilded frame of the summer's evening as terrible, as beautiful, as unearthly as any among those present had seen.

To Adrian's mood it attuned itself completely. It filled him, indeed, with a sort of demoniacal joy, reviving in some way the memory of the night of the Zeppelin raid with Rosemary. It was the embodiment of his permanently haunting conception of the mysterious duality between Love and Death.

§ 2

The storm abated as quickly as it had arisen, but thereafter the night was never still. As soon as the working-party could be marshalled in the crowded trench—no easy matter—they started off, Adrian and Walker leading, Cornwallis in rear. Slowly, with many exclamations, pauses, and much hard swearing, together with fierce injunctions to silence from the non-commissioned officers, they moved in single file along a sap. One by one they climbed out of this into the open. A little winding path, worn by the feet of patrols and working parties, led along a ridge between enormous shell-holes in which water glistened. The men became nervous and silent, realising that they were beyond cover, far out in No Man's Land, and less than a hundred yards from the German line, the exact where-abouts of which no one knew. Walker's face began to twitch like a madman's. Now and then somebody tripped over a loose strand of barbed wire or stumbled into a shell-hole and there was a scramble, followed by a suppressed curse.

Once at their objective, they lined out quickly, the covering parties creeping forward twenty yards or so into the long, dew-soaked grass. Each man worked hard to throw up the few feet of earth in front of him which should afford at any rate an illusory sense of protection. A peculiar, stench clung to the ground, thicker and more fœtid in some places than in others, and as they dug becoming stronger. Mis-shapen, horrible things were dug up or pierced with spades. Drab and muddy, yielding and soft so that it was hardly to be recognised as a human thing—the body of a German. No head, only the trunk. "There's a nice bit o' beef for you," somebody chuckled. "Get out, Fritz!" and he kicked the unsightly object into a shell-hole, having pre-viously cut off two buttons as a memento. Somebody else found a rifle completely rusted and caked with mud. Then a machine-gun was dug up, rusted and mud-caked, too, having evidently at some time been buried by a shell. Originally English, it had been converted by the Germans, and now perhaps might be re-converted.

Early in the night, Colonel Steele came round, accompanied by Eric Sinclair and an orderly. He glanced quickly at the work ; he spoke in whispers, his manner was constrained and jerky. He even said an affable word to Cornwallis, who was himself digging furiously.

Eric explained the situation, also in whispers.

The Colonel desired his company-commander to attend him along the whole battalion frontage. He held the highest opinion of that self-possessed young man's judgment. When they had passed on, the men paused in their digging, wiped the sweat from their brows, and chuckled.

"Old Jack-knife's rattled a bit, ain't he ? Little Percy's got 'im on a leading-string. Why didn't somebody stick a bay'net in the old — ! "

It was on these occasions that they remembered extra fatigues in the back areas and names taken on battalion parades, or at the end of long marches.

Once—about midnight—a German machine-gun opened suddenly and a man resting on his spade, as he contemplated the result of his labours, swore loudly and sat down.

"Oo—oo—oo ! It don't 'arf 'urt. Got me in the ankle, the —— ! Oo—oo—— ! . . . Get me boot off ! Fetch a stretcher-bearer ! Away with it, boys ! This one's a ' blighty.' "

Everybody congratulated him.

§ 3

That slight commotion over, Adrian stood above the half-dug trench watching the line of indistinct figures toiling and moiling below him. The night, like his own mind, was filled with an uneasy silence. His mind, indeed, was full of questionings, of secret promptings and unanswered queries. Premonition stood at his right hand. It was as though *She* watched him as the stars did. . . . Was She waiting upon him, approaching him ? Out of the gloom was She peeping at him now—pining for him—ogling him with Her baffling iris eyes—waiting, as he was, for the moment when he might be taken toHerself ? Profundity, immensity, eternity ! Easy, quiet, sudden ! Yes, he was ready for Her too. . . .

Throughout the interminable sun-scorched day this had been his mood. All through the day it had been in his mind to hasten the end, to seal the compact, to consummate the strongest impulse he had ever known. At times as he lay thinking, thinking, rarely sleeping in his little sandbag den—yet striving not to think—at times the temptation had seemed almost irresistible. Only to go outside, to look over the parapet, to walk once or twice across that gap. Should he tempt Her —tantalize Her—should he not woo Her more strongly, more ardently ? Seize Her ! Capture Her ! . . . Wait—wait ! Wouldn't She come safely, surely, in Her own good time ?

Plunged in these morbid reflections, he had not noticed that a burly figure stood beside him. Nor at first did he recognise the voice that now spoke in a husky whisper.

"Adrian . . . is that you ? I just thought I'd come along —for company. It's a bit funny to-night, isn't it—funny and quiet ? What was that flare-up to-night ? . . . Tell me, old boy, tell me, d'you think anything's going to happen ? "

The speaker was Walker.

"I don't know, I'm sure," the other replied indifferently. "Seems quiet enough now. Anything might happen at any time, I suppose."

It was hardly a comforting reply, and he afterwards regretted that he had not spoken more considerately. After all, he himself had known that sort of fear.

A light went up, Walker fell flat, and rose again with a sickly smile. Two or three bullets whined drearily overhead, and Walker gave a funny little jump forward as though he had St. Vitus's dance in the lower limbs. Both stood thinking.

Presently came again Walker's hoarse uncanny whisper :

" I say—Adrian—I think I see something—look ! what is it ?—don't move, man, don't move for the love of Christ ! My God, it's a man ! I saw it move—look ! Just by that tussock of grass—it's a man's head—there's another, two, three —get your revolver out—get down in the trench. Why, man alive, they're all round us ! " He clutched Adrian's arm, peering forward and shaking from head to foot. " Get down in the trench ! " he shouted, " get down in the trench ! They're right on top of us. Down ! down ! "

These last words he yelled at the top of his voice.

" Fire ! Fire ! "

He let his revolver off—from the hip—and fell back into the trench.

Adrian looked down at him coldly.

" It's the covering party, you fool. Get back to your com- munication-trench."

The fellow went—like a convicted criminal. The Wheels of War grind slowly, but they grind exceeding small.

He had gone very few yards when a low, throbbing hum came to their ears. Looking up, Adrian saw a small spot of light followed by a little tail of sparks very slowly sailing through the air. The light disappeared immediately above his head ; there was a sibilant hissing sound increasing with the volume of an express train. An immense weight seemed to be descending upon them at incredible speed. A voice shouted " Look out ! *Minenwerfer !* " There came a heavy thud close at hand, followed by a profound silence. All threw themselves flat, including Adrian, who obeyed some instinct that was too strong for him or that took him unawares.

Puff !

The ground trembled, all the world went up around them, a red glare lit up the features of those nearest. Another moment's silence followed—then the roar of volumes of earth falling, and of toppling stones.

GROANS and shouts succeeded. Cornwallis's voice could be heard crying "Steady! Steady!" rather helplessly. One or two men bolted down the half-dug communication-trench. A tall corporal staggered past, whimpering like a child and holding his arm, which was hanging from the elbow by a shred of flesh.

Above these sounds Adrian heard one man's shrieks.

"I'm wounded! I'm wounded! I'm choking! I'm dying! Will nobody come? Oh, God! Oh, my——"

It was Walker.

As he rushed forward another bomb came, droning towards them, to fall with the same heavy thud a few yards away. A gentle puff, silence, and the world rose up again. He was knocked down. Earth falling—earth and stones—in his mouth, in his ears—down his neck, on his back—beating, buffeting him.

When he looked up the red glare disclosed nothing but a stricken waste.

* * * * *

This episode of Walker's death, together with that of some half-dozen others who perished with him, disturbed and troubled Knoyle's mind for weeks afterwards. He revolved the circumstances again and again in his thoughts—at night in the back areas and during the long hours of doing nothing in the trenches. He could not comprehend the unreasoning, the apparently senseless processes of Fate. Why Walker? ... Walker, who dreaded, who feared death, who treasured life because he had all in life to live for—and would have lived heartily, happily. Walker gone, vanished, disappeared underground; they had dug for him until daybreak, but there was found no sign and no trace. Walker, his laugh, his jokes, his women, his lavish obscenity—had simply ceased to be; Walker who would have given his last hope of salvation to have been allowed to live—he had been taken. And Adrian Knoyle, remained.

He could have laughed from sheer bitterness of spirit had

he not been so surprised, so—so shocked at the malice—or was it coyness?—of Death whom he courted.

He even felt a kind of jealousy of this Walker who, dreading and repulsing with last vain cries of protest, had been taken to Her arms. . . .

There were times, especially towards the end of the four months' sojourn at Ypres, when unable longer to bear these thoughts, he was driven to tempt, to appeal, and at last to throw himself at Her feet.

When these impulses first came upon him, conscious of the need of some greater than human aid, he tried to pray. " Oh, God ! " he muttered to himself, " help me and save me." But at length even these words died on his lips, which became parched and barren as his heart.

Eric if anything saved him. Eric came to his rescue—a stimulus, a call upon his loyalty. What great, what not less great, burdens had this man to bear ! Not alone the responsibility of the company's welfare and conduct in the line of battle ; not alone the wearing strain of the extra risks he took or of the appalling conditions under which they lived ; not only his own private anxieties—his future with Faith, of which indeed Fate might rob him at any hour of the day or night ; in addition to these, he shouldered more than a share of his comrades' burdens. Yet Eric did not appeal to adventitious aid, did not dwell on his difficulties, did not give way to morbid reflections. He encouraged Cornwallis ; to his men he showed a patience and a forbearance that were not his natural *forte ;* to his friend, a more than merciful consideration. To that friend, indeed, he was at once an abiding example and a putting to shame.

But Adrian failed.

§ 4

The second of the episodes that produced so strong a reaction upon him happened on an evening some four weeks after

Walker's death. It was one of numerous wearisome evenings
spent during the period of reserve in the galleries and " dug-
outs " which honeycombed the ramparts of Ypres between the
Lille and Menin Gates. Here the atmosphere was stifling ;
the heat of July lay heavy upon the land, and within these
chambers air could neither enter nor escape.

On the night in question, the square boarded apartment in
which Eric, Adrian, and Cornwallis sat was a blaze of electric
light. The remains of a late supper lay upon the table ; in
different corners were three wire beds and three sets of
pyjamas ; a book lay upon the table, left open at the page
half-read, as though mutely protesting that the reader
was too weary to finish it. A heap of gramophone records
lay piled untidily beside a gramophone as though the owner
had grown tired of playing that, too. The atmosphere was
thick with tobacco-smoke.

" You'd better not come," Eric was saying. " Unless, of
course, you want to get killed."

He referred to a reconnaissance he had received orders to
make that night of a line of trenches shortly to be taken over
from a Canadian Division.

" Can't you see I *want* to go ? " Adrian replied irritably.
His face was pale and weary. Dark lines hollowing under his
eyes emphasised the look of extreme unhappiness which was
now habitual to it. For an hour or more he had been sitting,
thinking—brooding and thinking while Eric wrote and
Cornwallis read.

" I hate taking over a line and knowing nothing about it.
Besides, the message says ' Company-commanders will take up
a second-in-command or subaltern at their discretion,'
doesn't it ? "

" Yes—well, personally, I consider it would be the height of
indiscretion for you to go. However, if you're so desperately
anxious to commit suicide——"

" I want to go, and there's an end of it," the second-in-

command interrupted. " I'm bored stiff with this—it's like
a rabbit-hutch converted into a saloon-bar."

" Well—have it your own way, you maniac. One must
humour 'em, I suppose." Eric winked at Cornwallis. " So
far as I'm concerned you can take on the whole job with
the greatest of pleasure. Why don't you come too, Arthur,
so as to make sure of a complete *débâcle ?* "

" Oh, no ! thanks," the latter replied promptly.

And so the two started.

No beam of light from the illuminated dug-out strayed
into the roadway, for it was only by devious passages that
access could be obtained to these mysterious internal chambers,
centuries old. Outside, the mist crept in, crept up, and
round about. Like a ghost, like a wraith, it stole along the
dim streets whose secrets were buried beneath tons of bricks
and masonry, beneath heaps and heaps of ruins. At first
nothing could be seen in the filmy darkness after the brilliance
of the dug-out ; instinct alone guided their footsteps. In the
dug-out all sound had been deadened ; they could hear nothing
from without. But now they found that guns were firing
in the city itself—fitfully, yet frequently. Their banging and
booming awoke a thousand echoes. Every time a gun
fired, the flash lit up jagged ruins, a naked wall, or the skeleton
roofs of houses. It was evidently the beginning of a slow
bombardment.

Across a desert open space they picked their way, then
stumbled over blocks of fallen masonry and balks of timber
in the lee of a walled garden. It seemed to Adrian that tom-
cats ought to be yowling and spitting on the top of such a
wall ; but there was no such civilised symptom. Silence, moist
and mysterious, settled down between the reports of the guns.
At the Lille Gate a wakeful sentry and a watchful sergeant said
" Good night ! " In the recesses of a kind of cave which
did duty as a gate-house they could just distinguish the prostrate
forms of the guard, and could hear snores. The sentry opened

a door and the two officers found themselves outside the ramparts, plonk-plonking across a plank bridge. There was water underneath—they could feel rather than see it—water that lay black and stagnant, and seemed to listen.

They spoke little. Every now and then Eric stopped and consulted his compass. Out in the grass a mile and a half from the trenches familiar sounds came to their ears. Machine-guns were chattering. It was like a domestic argument. No sooner did an enemy gun start a steady burst of conversation than a couple of Lewis automatics responded with a whirlwind of vituperation. Further away another German joined in angrily while a sniper's rifle interjected sharp occasional comments. Yes—the night was full of sounds. Strangely, and for a moment, Vèrey lights rose above the mists, silently to vanish. To-night the far-stretching panorama of the Salient, usually outlined by star-shells, was hidden. Only southward the cannon rolled in a dim unceasing chorus, and near at hand the field-batteries in Ypres fired at irregular intervals, the shells, whistling overhead to burst with a quick glare and crash along the German front line. Bombs at times exploded too. Deep, sullen detonations, three or four together, shook earth and darkness.

For Adrian such nights were never without their ghosts. Ghosts crept out with the mists which wreathed and sidled now dense, now lifting thinly ; ghosts and the hideous unknown things which lurk on battlefields. A sinking moon strove feebly with the mist, sometimes momentarily penetrating it ; then all the world became silvery, opaque. Away to the left, etched in a delicate gloom, could be seen the outlines of what had once been a convent. At times, they could discern no more than a yard or two of the ground ahead, which was pock-marked with shell-holes and often caused them to stumble and lurch forward into the long, rank vegetation, the thistles and nettles. Sometimes they would cross a narrow, weed-grown path that once had been a main road ; sometimes they had to leap an old gun-pit or disused grass-fringed communication-trench ; sometimes a landmark was missed ; and sometimes, when the fog grew dense, they seemed to come to a dead end. Then Eric would pause and take his bearings, partly by the star-lights, partly by the bursting shells on the German front line. Those were queer furtive moments when the silence grew tense, when, in the utter absence of any sign of human life, the seething white mists seemed to take on strange shapes—or one shape ; when out of this silence came the cries of some unknown bird—cries that seemed to Adrian weird and unearthly. And they hurried on. . . . There were moments when a formless, nameless presence seemed to follow always, and eyes once familiar watched from the great socket-like holes on either hand, and out of the gloom wraith-like features beckoned gravely. The very earth itself, maimed and scarred, spoke of war's eternal mystery, of God's anger and tribulation, of man's agony and bloody sweat. A mile behind, the broken city slept as one sleeps who can suffer no more.

Clambering over a sandbag breastwork, they entered a trench which was new and clean and handsomely floored with duckboards. Voices could be heard at some distance along it. A snatch of a song came to their ears in a nasal tenor :

> " C'est la valse brune
> Des chevaliers de la lune,
> Que la lumière importune,
> Et qui recherchent un coin noir."

Adrian stopped and listened intently. A queer smile crept into his face, and remained there till the last wistful cadences had died away ; then he hurried after his friend.

Parties of Quebec Canadians were sand-bagging traverses and parapets. Eric spent some time in examining these. He then suggested that they should explore the wire and the ground out in front.

The mist had fallen again, but no sooner were they out in

a waste of shell-holes, half-filled with water and loose strands of barbed wire than it lifted like a curtain and the moon shone out as clear as day. They found themselves alone with desolation, alone in a world where was neither human sight nor sound nor any landmark, save the greyish-white stumps of shell-split trees. The trenches they had just left could not be distinguished from the rest of the dim background. They looked across a vast silvery desert that might have been a weirdity of the imagination or a scene from the Inferno. A German machine-gun sputtered warningly in front of them. Close at hand five rifle-shots sounded in quick succession. A loud clanging ring like the bell of a tram-car followed; Adrian's steel helmet was jolted over his eyes.

Eric sat down in a shell-hole.

"We'd better crawl this bit, we've been spotted," he said quietly.

But—Adrian did not move. He remained standing in the moonlight on the edge of the shell-hole, leaning on his stick.

A cool breeze played about his forehead, the same queer smile about his lips.

"S-zz-z-z-z-z! Zip-zip! Tack-tack-tack-tack!"

Something hit his elbow. It might have been a heavy stone; he was unconscious of the pain. A look of happiness, of long-delayed triumph, smouldered in his eyes, and—he smiled.

"Get down, you madman! Get down! D'you want to get killed?" Eric gave a tug at his friend's puttees.

The latter paid no heed.

"Sz-z-z-z-z-z! Zip-zip! Tack-tack-tack-tack!"

"Get down, I tell you! Are you crazy, man?"

The erect figure neither moved nor made any sign, but continued to gaze at ease towards the whitish spectre of the château of Hooge, while bullets zipped and spat and the German machine-gun knocked up little splays of earth around its feet.

For Adrian was unconscious alike of Eric's upturned face and of the sudden fierce gleam of understanding that sprang into his eyes. He saw beyond, far beyond the German lines, laying bare Mockery, and revealing Despair . . . a wraith.

Love and Death were joined at last . . . ?

Quick as the thought entered the other's mind, Eric leapt up and, putting upon the taller man such a hold as Rugby footballers use, half-threw, half-dragged him down into the shell-hole.

§ 5

Adrian may have been stunned by the bullet which had struck his steel helmet or by his violent precipitation into the shell-hole. At all events, he did not recover consciousness of himself again until they were once more crossing the wooden bridge that spans the moat in front of the Lille Gate. Nor could he afterwards recall the earlier part of the walk back. When actuality did return he found one arm was linked in Eric's ; the other pained him slightly. So they passed through the great gate, and seeing the city dimly opening before them like a scene in some fantastic tale, realised that day was at hand.

They walked without speaking. Sparrows began to twitter in a score of shy gardens that, riotous with greenery, hid like tear-drops amid the ruined houses. Pigeons so often fed by the hands of children in the Grande Place crooned from stony pinnacles, surveying each his fallen world. On a skeleton wall against a purple background, the legend " Chocolat Menier, Dunkerque," confronted them with its message of a bygone civilisation ; when they reached the dark narrow entrance to their inter-mural home, a flush had crept into the sky above the ramparts, the morning star being jewelled in a setting of palest gold and hard turquoise blue.

Without the opening in the wall, Eric stopped and faced his friend.

" Well," he said, " what's the meaning of this ? "

Adrian stared at the ground.

" Give me your word you'll never try that game on again."

The other still made no answer. His eyes would not meet his friend's. He knew he had failed : failed in his duty to Eric, failed in his duty to himself, failed—even of his purpose.

"Give me your word."

Eric spoke sharply.

It was evident a grim struggle was going forward between conflicting natures in the man before him.

"Give me your word or—quit. This is no place for suicides."

A sullen look had come into Adrian's face.

"Damn it ! My life's my own, isn't it ? " he muttered.

"No, my dear chap, that's the point—it isn't. For the time being it's mine. And—well, I happen to want it."

Silence followed except for the crooning of a pigeon on the ramparts above their heads.

"Pull yourself together, for God's sake." Eric spoke more gently now, but very firmly. "Pull yourself together, and face it out. Here we are, all in the same boat—more or less. We've all got to face things. We've all got to go through with it. Look at old Arthur and the rest ! And you don't want to leave me in the lurch, do you ? "

"But Eric——" Adrian stopped, a tremor of weakness in his voice "Honestly. . . . I'm on my beam-ends, I'm standing on my head. I can't promise anything."

"Then you must clear out. You must go down the line. I won't have you with the company."

That threat had its effect. The unhappy man saw what was at stake—knew that in the long run he must give way, knew also that it was the only worthy part left him to play.

"All right . . ." he muttered. "All right. . . ."

The full light of morning streaming over Ypres, seemed to strike at some dark place deep down inside him. He turned hurriedly into the narrow passage, grey to the lips, and as if unable to bear the sight of the new day.

He was in terror of his own soul.

CHAPTER VIII

The Road

§ 1

ANOTHER month went by and autumn approached once more when the long-expected movement order arrived.

The news came one breezy August afternoon and it came direct from the headquarters of the Division. The groups standing and lying about the canal bank got it first; then, lightning-like, it flashed down the Yperlee and reached the innermost recesses of every dug-out, and was even conveyed to the newly brought-in wounded lying in the dressing-station. Near Bridge 4, it collected a crowd; at the point known as Blighty Bridge quite a number were discussing it half-an-hour after the first whisper had got abroad. By nightfall it had crept along the three-quarters of a mile of communication-trench to the front line; it travelled faster than any gas-wave. The only people who knew nothing about it were the three canvas-shrouded figures lying like mummies side by side on stretchers in a *cul-de-sac*. And they would never know.

"We're going South!"

Eric Sinclair brought the news about the middle of the afternoon to the queer little compartment burrowed into the high and steep canal bank, and opening upon the waterside that was called Company-headquarters.

What a magic transformation, what a frank light of joy appeared in the face of young Arthur Cornwallis who lay reading—but now sat up—on his wire-netting bed!

"You don't mean it! . . . Is that official, Eric, or are you pulling our legs?"

" You needn't believe it unless you like. I tell you we're to be relieved to-night."

" Ah ! "

The youth lay back and gazed rapturously at the wire under-part of the bed above.

Adrian who had been staring at the beginnings of a letter to Lady Knoyle, his head between his hands, his elbows leaning on the table, looked up, too.

" Relieved to-night ? Good."

" Don't put on your glad rags just yet, though," Eric added. " Where do you think you're going ? "

" Oh ! Who cares ? Anything to get away." Thus Corn-wallis.

" You're going to the Somme, and over the top. So if you've got anything, make a will. Adrian looks as if he'd made his already."

For all that, everybody congratulated everybody else, every heart leapt for joy that August day. Was not the dead-weight of Doom lifted from their souls ? The Salient was to be left behind with its brown water-logged ditches, its impotence, its festering corpses and familiar stench—its slow unending nightmare by day and by night—its implacable Fate. No more sitting still and waiting. There would be a pause at any rate in the procession of the maimed, the dying, and the dead.

So all rejoiced. And only Adrian Knoyle looked in-differently beyond the intervening days.

§ 2

The day of departure came. A still misty morning resolved itself into brilliant sunshine and great heat. As the first train left the railway-siding near the Poperinghe Road, cheer upon cheer went up to the blue sky. It was the soldiers' farewell to " E-prez," as they called it. " To the south!" They knew what the future held in store. But what mattered it! Nothing mattered—to-day. To-day there was to be nothing but singing, shouting, and laughter. With every mile the dread Salient, the treacherous canal bank, the death-stricken city lay further and further behind. . . . The train rolled on. Its rhythm, its regular " clank-clank-clank " burnt into the heat. By ten o'clock a broiling sun poured its rays upon the young oak-woods beyond Proven, upon the flat fields and vegetable gardens and the fruit-laden orchards, upon the white highways whence clouds of dust arose. By road the relieving corps was moving up to Ypres. For many leagues—even as far as Wormhoudt—the railway line ran beside the road and that road carried unending columns of perspiring, khaki-clad troops, unending lines of horse transport and motor-lorries, unending columns of artillery—moving east. They had come from the Somme. They had come, they announced, for a rest!

Wormhoudt was left behind, and with it the eastward-bending army. There was a glimpse of three white roads converging on a wide, sun-baked square, alive with troops. Then the Hill of Cassel came into view, and northward a wide vista of the Pas de Calais. An undulating expanse of green fields and groups of trees and farms and cottages bounded sharply by a semicircular rim, and beyond this the blue ribbon of the Channel. At the edge of it, many miles away, a group of red-brick buildings surmounted by tall chimneys and a faint haze of smoke—Calais. Gravelines not far away, another little cluster of houses and chimneys on the verge of the sea.

A panorama, wonderful in its freedom and freshness, to those who through four months had seen nothing more spacious than Ypres viewed from the Salient on a clear day.

The detraining point had an unpronounceable name; that did not matter. It was a mere sun-baked, sleepy railway-yard without a square inch of shade. Here, for the first time—no hint of war. For the first time they seemed to leave the war behind, and as they marched out into the country—a merry, chaffing, laughing column—no stench of motor-lorries and petrol or sight of troops greeted them, but only the heavy silence of the woods and fields and villages, dreaming away their midday rest. A yellow cat strolled across the village street, dogs lay basking outside cheerful-looking *cafés*—peculiar-looking dogs, and sleepy. Barely could they raise the energy to wag a tail at the flies which everywhere buzzed and hummed, creating with the drowsy heat an indescribable languor and murmur of summer. The column halted in a shady oak-wood, and the men, recklessly happy, threw themselves down amid the long grass, convolvuli, and wild parsley. In this drowsy hum of summer, in the measured beat of the greenfinch's song and the "ting-ting-ting" of the yellow-hammer, in the wistful cry of the soaring kestrel, in the quiet, mysterious woods and the sun-dappled, mossy earth, in the poetry of the long white roads, in the glimpse of great distances fading to mist and sea, in the "chop, chop" of the wood-cutter and the deep contrasting silence of the country—was found a hidden balm for all these war-weary souls.

And so at the zenith of the afternoon, smoking, singing, and dust-covered, they marched into billets. It was such a village as may be found in Devonshire or Dorset. It was redolent of England with its thatched farmsteads and cottages supporting masses of creeper, honeysuckle, and clambering roses.

At their billets the three officers were met by an aged woman, in a shawl and sun-bonnet, who greeted them almost effusively at the door of her cottage.

She showed them two clean sweet-scented rooms opening out of the little parlour, their wide windows overlooking a vegetable and flower-garden with box-borders and a box-arbour in the corner. Beyond, the fields, and next to it other shady gardens, full of scents, hollyhocks, late roses and ripening fruit.

"This is luck, isn't it ? " remarked Eric. "I shall have a bath."

"Glorious, isn't it ? " echoed Cornwallis.

Adrian smiled.

After tea the three officers took books out into the box-arbour at the end of the garden and abandoned themselves to the stillness of the summer's evening. They dozed. The air was full of strange yet familiar sounds, the hum of insects, the twittering of wrens, warblers, finches ; the chattering of starlings, the " roo-coo-coo " of a wood-pigeon in elms near the church, the " purr-r-r " of stock-doves, and presently the tolling of a church bell.

Within the cottage the aged dame could be seen entertaining a friend. The two were chatting together while knitting, and through the snatches of conversation that occasionally came to their ears was conjured up for the three listeners a picture of the daily life of this obscure little backwater, so self-contained, so near to, yet untouched, unmoved by war. Lying about a meadow, separated from the garden by a tiny stream, they could see the men in worn and faded khaki, smoking, sleeping, talking. It was that hour so refreshing after the heat and burden of a summer's day when cattle meander down to the waterside to cool their blistered legs in the shallows, when the farm-hands come in from the harvest-field, when cart-horses clank into farmyards laden with children.

"Yes—this is a bit of all right ! " sighed Eric, lying back in a deck-chair with a pile of letters in his lap. "We've struck lucky—for once. Even old Adrian's gone to sleep over it."

"What's the matter with him, Eric ? He's changed a lot lately."

"Oh ! the war, I suppose—and other things. One wants to make life easy for him."

Eric took up a letter and began to read it presumably as a hint, thought Cornwallis, that he did not wish to discuss the matter further.

Presently his subaltern observed :

" The men look jolly over there."

" Yes, I like to see the poor devils enjoying themselves. They've had a coarse time lately."

" Funny creatures, aren't they ? " commented the other. " They're like a lot of children. I thought they were wonderful up in the Salient, though they did grumble a certain amount."

" Oh ! they're all right if they're treated properly. But, by the way, it's pay-day to-morrow, isn't it ? I suppose they'll all go round the *estaminets* and get drunk.

" Hark ! "

> " It's a long, long trail to Blight—y,
>   To the land of my dreams,
>   Where the nightingales are singing,
>   And a white moon beams ;
>   There's a long, long night of waiting
>   Until my dreams all come true,
>   'Till the day when I'll be going down
>   That long, long trail with you."

Seated in a wide circle a number of soldiers were singing this, their favourite sentimental ditty. Nearby other groups, some lying, some kneeling, were playing a mysterious game of cards.

" Five-and-a-half—seven—twelve — fifteen — twenty-eight ! Housy-housy ! " One man was calling out these numbers in a loud, monotonous sing-song.

It was the game known as " housy-housy " ; others in the field were playing crown-and-anchor.

Beside the stream were men washing, bathing and tending their feet. Some lay naked in the sun ; others, sitting under fruit-trees, were solemnly engaged in picking the lice from their bodies Others again were washing their garments, lying on their backs asleep, or talking and smoking.

The following day was spent in doing nothing. All dozed away the hot middle hours, and only in the cool of the evening walked out into the country, watched the peasants working in the fields—and even assisted them—admired the variegated cottage-gardens.

The battalion marched again at dawn—a misty dawn that presaged great heat. No one minded the early hour, for these moist blue mists which blotted out the countryside and cloaked mysteriously the woods and fields were cool and invigorating. All felt fit, there was the same laughing and singing as the battalion swung along the dusty road. They passed through villages—villages old-fashioned and sweet-scented like the one just left—whose farms and cottages and inhabitants yet slept. Only an occasional farm-boy, milk-pail in hand, came to a gate to see the long column go by. But as the morning advanced, shafts of sunlight began to pierce through the mists, people appeared at the gates of their cottages, at the cross-roads, and in groups and little family parties on their way to mass; which event was the first intimation the troops had that it was Sunday, for in the life of movement the days passed almost uncounted. Halts became more welcome as the noontide heat crept on; by the side of woods, shady and cool, on the edge of cornfields, in lush grass, cornflower-starred and scarlet-splashed with poppies, on village greens where geese and turkeys wandered and children gathered round. Out of the mists there peeped presently, now close at hand, the Hill of Cassel, with grey, old-world houses grouped on its summit. Thence might be seen on a clear day Ypres and the dreadful Pilckem Ridge on the one side; on the other, the sea about Nieuport almost to Ostend, and the ships in harbour at Dunkirk—away to the south, Armentières and Merville and the dim Forest of Nieppe, westward the quiet villages of the Pas de Calais as far as that town itself.

They halted for dinners at the foot of the hill close to the railway-station. After a couple of hours' rest, during which the majority slept, they moved again. Cassel shimmered in the heat-haze; the sun scorched down upon another bare station-yard. Two long trains stood in sidings, the engines with steam up; part of the brigade had already gone on ahead. Here stood a group of red-capped Staff Officers, there a couple of gendarmes in black, silver-braided uniforms, and a few French railway officials in sky-blue. Once the men were aboard, there was no waiting; the train started on its sixty-mile journey at a good speed.

And what a perspiring, jolting, stifling journey it was! It reminded Adrian of going home from school for the summer holidays. When the train stopped, as it occasionally did, no sound came but the song of the heat; then he listened for the familiar clatter of milk-cans, which seems a thing inseparable from hot days at wayside country stations.

The landscape, from being flat and ordinary at first, grew more and more Arcadian after they had passed through the tract of coal-mines and slag-heaps between Béthune and Loos. In the neighbourhood of St. Pol came hills crowned with green woods, valleys and deep combes tumbling into one another, full hedgerows and farmsteads and villages, grey or reddish lichen-grown church steeples peeping out from the dense foliage of trees.

The train ran through quickly, there were few stoppages, and in the late afternoon the detraining-point was reached at a small country town in Picardy. When they had detrained they found the field-kitchens drawn up in an open grassy space; under shady chestnuts nearby the quarter-master had arranged a repast consisting of boiled eggs, tinned salmon and salad, coffee and rolls *ad lib.*, jam and honey, omelettes and light beer. The gay spirit of the troops was shared by most of the officers. It was infectious. No sooner had arms been piled and the " dismiss " given, than jesting and " ragging " began among the subalterns sitting and lying under the chestnuts. The company-commanders smoked pipes and looked on :—Eric Sinclair, cool, amiably detached and immaculate as to uniform ; Alston with his large frame and features, self-contained, critical, a little inhuman perhaps—a little hard ; Vivian, with his engaging manner, his quick, subtle features ; Darell, tall and dark, with bold and flashing eyes that bespoke a warm-hearted impulsiveness, a spirited temper.

A short distance away under an especially large tree, Colonel Steele was enthroned, dividing his attention between a map and a large tea-basket which he shared with his second-in-command, Major Brough, whose well-fed appearance so far belied the meaning of the term " active service," and his adjutant Langley, in polo breeches and a khaki stock.

A row of stretchers on the railway station platform, bearing recently-wounded men, and occasional Red Cross motor ambulances arriving and departing, alone served to remind the new-comers of the grim business that was going forward some twenty-five kilometres away.

The typical tree-shaded, white-faced, provincial town lying in a basin among low hills, wore its Sunday air of relaxation and rest. The *bourgeois* were taking their evening stroll along the central boulevard, stopping and gazing with a mild interest at the resting troops. There were the precocious French youths, with their varicoloured bow-ties, their rakishly-perched soft hats, their canes in hand, strutting about in parties, ogling the hatless girls, laughing, sporting and showing off. Others stood about chatting or playing leap-frog outside their houses.

When, near to six o'clock, the battalion marched out in a cloud of dust with drums and fifes playing, the entire population gathered at the cross-roads, and the scene was one of animation, even of enthusiasm. A twenty-mile march lay ahead. And how far, how straight, how white the highway looked with its long gradations rising one beyond another until it faded at last into that golden land where the sun would presently set! Eric rode at the head of the company, Adrian and Arthur Cornwallis marched in rear.

"Well—I wonder how it will all end," Cornwallis remarked after they had tramped in silence for some while. He seemed to assume the utterance of a common thought.

Into the faces of these two something of the calm evening light had crept, the one expressing deep thought, the other a yearning half-suggested.

"I don't wonder—particularly," Adrian replied.

His tone had a positive quality that caused Cornwallis to look up from the road in surprise.

"How do you mean?"

The other did not at once reply.

"You're always making these cryptic remarks, Adrian. I wish you wouldn't."

Cornwallis had not in the foregoing months been able to make out what was passing in his brother-officer's mind. He had never accepted the theory of war-weariness. He knew there was something more to be accounted for, but just because he had been of Adrian and Rosemary's little coterie in London, he felt barred from inviting confidences which the former did not offer. Adrian had earned in the battalion the nick-name of "The Silent (K)night." But his present companion had given no hint to anyone but Eric that he suspected the cause of the silence; and the mystery remained.

This evening, however, Cornwallis noticed for the first time in his friend's eyes (for all their deep preoccupation) a look that was not altogether of unhappiness.

"Do explain yourself, Adrian!" he begged.

"Well—we're going over the top, aren't we?"

"You're not looking forward to it, though?"

"Oh!—I don't worry. One might as well go through with it now as any other time."

"I always thought you loathed the war."

"I do—in a way."

Cornwallis thought a moment. Presently he said:

" Adrian ! "

" Well ? "

" Are you out to get killed ? "

The question took Knoyle unawares; but the fact did not betray itself in his voice or manner.

" Why—on earth should I be ? "

" I don't know. Perhaps I oughtn't to ask. But—you're so queer and—secret. I wondered how other people felt about it."

" There comes a point when one doesn't care much either way."

" I wish I could get to that stage. Frankly, I want to live."

" I did, too."

" Honestly—do you think one an awful coward for that ? "

" There are no cowards in this war. There are people who fight, or try to, and—lookers-on."

" Adrian, if you went, I should feel—well, that everything had gone."

" I'm glad somebody feels like that." Humour, faintly ironical, flickered through his eyes.

" Don't be so dreadfully—fatalistic," Cornwallis said. "Can't you see how much there is to live for—still ? Evenings like this, for instance. . . . One thinks of the happiest—I mean the quietest—times of one's life. We live in Dorsetshire. Dorsetshire's rather like this. . . . Those bells pealing down in the valley make me think of the time between tea and evening church in summer when Beryl—that's my sister—and father and mother and I, always sit out with books under a big cedar opposite our hall door. The rooks make a tremendous noise there. It's like a big crowd of people all talking at once."

" I hate church bells, personally; they make me think of the family pew—and all that."

Why he made the rather brutal remark, Adrian could not

himself have said. Perhaps Cornwallis's discursive senti-
mentality irritated him. Yet wasn't he himself thinking of the
Three Hills—the Three Hills with the sunlight carmine and
deep on their steep sides, the wild song of the skylarks, the
golden mist lying upon the Vale, a long procession of rooks
strung out across the western glow, and the view looking down
on Stane Deverill.

Yet he found it impossible to express their common
mood in words. Something withheld response. Open his
heart—he could not.

" I don't understand you," Cornwallis continued, " but I
can see you're in some trouble and I wish I could help you."

" Whatever must be, must be—that's the truth of life.
And it's a long job learning it."

" It isn't death in the abstract one dreads—it's the before
death. It's—the sheer ugliness, the utter negation that kill—
the antithesis to—this." He pointed to the peaceful landscape,
speaking with much earnestness. " It's this—living in a sort
of Hell. I sometimes wonder whether we aren't going through
Hell now for our own sins or the sins of some previous existence.
I know I'm not the stuff soldiers are made of. I think I must
have been meant for an artist or something. I've always
wanted beauty—the quiet delicate sort of beauty. Land-
scapes and fine poetry and wonderful music, and—wonderful
people. I've always dreamed of something less crude and
more—rare than the material life we live. I suppose that's all
too—too nebulous. "

" No ; it's simply not true—on the average."

" I believe you've still got it, Adrian. Only something's
crushed it out of you—or deep, deep into you. . . . It's the
utter—grotesqueness of everything that appals one. You look
at this "—and he again indicated with his hand the sunset
colouring woods and fields—" and think of—Walker. Well,
Walker's women meant a lot to him. I can't forget Walker.
It's the contemplation of that I can't face—the physical

degradation of one's body. I suppose it's a silly idea ! But I seem somehow to have learnt to love my body for its own sake out here—to respect it. It was a nightmare to me to think of anything one has known so *personally*, mixed and mangled with that filthy soil like—like an old sandbag or something."

" Oh, well," said Adrian, for the first time serious ; " one must think of—the long sleep and the quiet."

" But there's so much still to be lived."

" Death can't be harder than life."

" The meaning and purpose of it all—that's what I want to know."

" Sometimes one thinks one sees light breaking," Adrian said, " and sometimes—it's all as black as pitch. And sometimes one thinks there *is* a meaning behind it. And sometimes . . . I don't know."

§ 3

They tramped on. All tramped on with measured tread that seemed to symbolise something more inevitable, less ephemeral than they.

Always the road stretched, poplar-lined and straight as a ruler, seemingly leagues ahead. Sometimes it was obscured by clouds of chalky dust, usually it simply disappeared over the rim of the horizon into that sunset land whose promise was not of earth.

The men began to sing their marching song about " The long, long trail " ; it sounded to Adrian like a dirge without sadness.

They were passing through a country far different from the flat, closely cultivated small-holdings of Belgium. Rolling hills, crowned with woodland and scored with high leafy hedgerows, stretched away into distances infinitely deep and blue. It was the season of the harvest. All about the tumbled valleys and hillsides, the stooks and sheaves lay awaiting the wagoner. The reaper had done his work ; rooks rose from the fields and wended their homeward way ; from grey village churches hidden in combes and clefts came the sound of bells. There could be found in this late summer scene no jarring note, but as the long column mounted the last rise the whole calm panorama lay outspread behind them, a study in blue and gold, untainted, unsullied by any hint of war. Blue sky, blue mists, blue distances, a greenish-blue tinge on the woods—and golden sunbeams sloping across the yellow stubble, kindling to copper-red the wheat and oats.

At the start the march had been noisy and boisterous, laughter and singing rippling along the ranks, but after the first halt every man settled down grimly to his work. It would take every man's utmost strength and determination to reach his journey's end. So, as the sun was setting and only four miles of the journey had been covered, no more shouting and laughter were heard, but the column tramped on in a silence that was almost uncanny. They passed through a large village with a long, wide, grass-bordered street of foolish-looking white-and-blue painted houses. The place was full of troops ; another brigade had marched in only a few hours earlier. Beyond the village a forest stretched, entirely covering the surrounding hills.

When they entered the forest the sun had barely set, but under the great oaks, whose turning foliage arched over the road, forming seemingly an endless tunnel, night reigned. It was quite dark there, and when after a mile or two they emerged, twilight had descended upon the larger world and they could barely distinguish the hillside opposite. Here the column halted ; the tired troops rested in the cool dusk, watching the last embers of a lingering sunset die out of the sky The ceaseless chirruping of grasshoppers and crickets, the occasional croaking of a bull-frog in some distant pool, and the oft-repeated " whoo-twhoo-whoo " of an owl coming from the depths of the woods made a sort of sleep-song. From a railway-cutting not far off one lone lamp blinked mysteriously, and the fitful whistle of an engine emphasised the remoteness and solitude of the place.

Now it was completely dark. A thousand summery scents rose from the earth, the sky was bejewelled with stars, and low down on the horizon a golden-coppery harvest-moon, not yet at the full, sailed into the heavens.

Adrian and Cornwallis half sat, half lay side by side, their backs resting against the gnarled trunk of a giant oak, all about them ferns, moss, moss-scented earth. Neither spoke. The night was indescribably contemplative, blending strangely and sympathetically with the thoughts they had so lately been exchanging.

Close at hand they could discern the dim figures of the soldiers lying around in all shapes, all attitudes, all positions. Some on the back, hands to thigh, heels together, gazing upward ; some on the side and some curled up as though in pleasant sleep ; some flat on face, arms and legs outspread ; some with head resting on arm or pack, one knee raised. . . . What were *their* thoughts, he wondered ? Was it with this—this profundity of beauty and solitude and rest in their hearts— that they would enter upon the bloody nightmare which lay before them ? What did the stars say, those stars so wise, so inscrutable that in his childhood he had thought of them as the watching eyes of God ? What did the leaves whisper to them— of night, of sleep, of silence, of infinity ? Not, he conceived, of foreboding or any " sadness of farewell," for it was in England that they had left their loves, their griefs, their hopes, their longings or regrets, and all those things that make up the final sum of existence and mortal time. No ! He conceived of them as thinking calmly and rationally of Death as of a thing ordained—even as he himself thought of it— knowing that it was ever near, knowing that for many the end of the road was their journey's end, not dreading or even allowing themselves to dread until the supreme moment came; better still, not thinking at all.

He, for his part, dwelt in an atmosphere of reflection: of thought about the days still to pass, of the nights still to come and go, to be numbered perhaps on the fingers, perhaps a while longer yet. But one thing he never doubted—the road's ending. He knew brooding curiosities. Where at last would this body rest, where this soul alight or flit in the eternity to come ? Strange the thought that days and nights such as these would succeed one another with succeeding summers, autumns, winters, that the seasons he had felt so intensely would pass serenely overhead, and that even this miasma which blanched Nature and sickened the world to-day—that, too, would pass. Eric, Cornwallis, at home in England, married perhaps, leading steadfast and ordered English lives ; those other lives he had left behind and which had been so closely linked with his— they, too, going forward, cycling, rotating like the days and the nights and the seasons ; and this—this feeling, exacting being called Himself with whom he had journeyed through three-and-twenty years—where ?

Was there pity in this mood ? But he knew no conscious pity—only a looking-forward.

And he wanted—a looking-glass. He wanted to study the features, the outward expression, of this entity whose inner-most thought from the dawn of consciousness to this hour he had so intensely experienced ; that he might note—before its little Act was ended—what light, what shadow, what permanent line or wrinkle, what serene or sullen shade, Fate had imprinted there.

For the first time in many weeks he thought definitively of Rosemary. Almost a year had passed since their last walk together, since their parting. And here he was again—at the leaf-fall.

He thought of her objectively, in the abstract—for the first time in his life as something outside himself, as something that had left him and would soon pass beyond his consciousness for ever; and was already, as regards himself, beyond pain. Her also he saw as the years went by—after, long after, he had passed beyond her ken—playing out her part in a self-created drama, making and moving life: ever drawing and enthralling, entangling and selecting and rejecting as her nature was; challenging fortune and playing with fire as was her delight; obeying impulses she barely understood, swaying a world she but dimly comprehended, looking out upon that world, half-pleased, half-mischievous, yet doubting sometimes and fearful, with the *naïveté* of Youth. He saw her never as the progenitor or the instigator, never as the plotter or the originator in the complicating affairs of men—never certainly as the conscious agent of malice or of wrong—but as the sport and the instrument of a Destiny incomparably stronger than herself, immeasurably beyond her control. And, thinking of her, it was inevitable that he should think of Gina Maryon, with whom her fate and his seemed knit to some obscure and malign end. He thought of Gina Maryon, in contrast to, and yet in collusion with Rosemary, as the vital and the inspiring thing, as the human sprite, as the fitful spark lighting fires which might never be put out. He saw Gina Maryon hovering eternally in the wings of that little drama in which she, too, played an allotted part: now darting upon the stage, interfering now and now disappearing, instigating, originating, pulling strings this way and that, always the sprightly yet ill-omened being that had played havoc with human action since time began.

In the background and yet a potent figure, he discerned Upton. He looked through a microscope and perceived this molecule so inadequate to, so incommensurate with and yet so vital to the beings in whose experience he had figured. The vitality of molecules, the potentiality of germs! Nor could he regard this—re-agent as other than a pawn, an objective of some curious feminine perversity by man little understood.

Faith and Eric alone stood for him as substantially true. All the rest was fluid, nothing defined and stationary, nothing merely existed or remained ; all, it might seem, in the present time, too near the primal forces, too perilously situated, too instinct with chaos and strife, to admit of that. Love, Nature, Death, Pleasure, Evil, Pain ! Of these was their lot cast. How nakedly already the war had revealed each one of them ! And if in the case of the two women he could conceive of one as consumed at last by the very forces which had ordained her, the other—was without end.

Eric and Faith alone remained.

§ 4

Before nine o'clock the march was resumed, but the men soon began to tire again, and towards the middle of the night they could scarcely stumble onward in their fours. After many months in the trenches they had marched thirty miles since dawn, and the effort was proving almost too great. But the only form of complaint heard was the sullen swearing and muttered abuse which broke out every time Colonel Steele and his adjutant cantered along the column with their unvarying shout of " Keep step, there ! March by the right ! Don't straggle ! Keep in your fours ! " and so forth. Then among themselves the men muttered, " Blast his soul ! Let 'im carry a rifle and forty-pound pack 'isself. 'E ain't no bloody good nor yet 'is bloody adjutant either. Wait till we go over the top—you won't see either of 'em for dust ! "

At intervals of a mile or so, a footsore or utterly exhausted soldier would sink down by the roadside, gasping " I can't get no further," and have to be carried the last lap on a transport wagon. Then Colonel Steele would shout angrily, " Now then, no more falling out. Come along men. You've got to stick it." However, the end of the march was near, and soon the head of the column, after passing through a village which seemed to climb steeply a hillside, turned into the blackness of a wood. Huts were found in which the men threw themselves down on bare boards without a word. Nearby, was a farmhouse with courtyard and barn. On the floor of the latter Eric, Adrian and Cornwallis stretched themselves without even waiting for a meal.

Already, before they slept the birds were awaking, and they could sense that clean fresh feeling in the air which comes just before dawn in summer. Already the cool grey light began to creep in through the open doors and windows of the barn.

Adrian dreamt. . . .

All seemed dark, silent, closed in, and utterly lonely. Nor was there sense of any neighbouring human presence. He wished to move but feared to, feeling hemmed about on every side. He wished to open his eyes, but the lids seemed weighted down—and there came no gleam of light. He wanted to cry out, but his voice was constrained and he felt a dead-weight from above. He noticed a musty smell. He could neither move nor see nor utter; he had the feeling of being a prisoner beyond human aid.

At first he experienced no sensitiveness, seemed to retain no nerves. But gradually he began to realise that while he lay still and helpless, there was all about him movement, creeping, crawling movement, everything creeping, crawling, like a thousand atoms; and that while his body did not move, it, too, was creeping, crawling, hiving like a swarm of bees—verminously. He now began to feel upon his skin tickling feet —feet light and cold and slow of movement, creeping, crawling —verminously.

Every effort he made to rise, to shout, to scream, to see—was frustrated. He could not. But all over his body the movement went on—across his face, his chest, his arm-pits, the soles of his feet and the back of his head--feet lightly, coldly tickling. He seemed to be alive with them—those tiny pin-point footsteps of the clammy damp which he now felt above, close in, and around.

He struck out.

Emptiness !

Nor spiritually was he now alone. Faces looked out of the blankness above him. Walker he saw as he last had seen him, before he disappeared for ever; Pemberton of old; Eric and Cornwallis he saw—those two true and trusty friends. And Arden (why Arden ?) And Rosemary was there, pale, ethereal, remote, not as he had ever seen her in life—but there. She even came close to him, nestled down beside him—airily kissed him. Yet strange (he thought) that as they lay together he could feel no warm breath of hers upon his cheek, only cold lifeless flesh.

Mute terror seized him. . . . What was the meaning of it ? And where was he ?

Rosemary ? The dark, the damp, the emptiness, the musty smell, the stony silence, the cold flesh, the absence of any human sense or touch, above all, the creeping, crawling, tickling feet. . . . What did it all mean ? What could it mean ?

Unable to bear it longer, he sprang up, perspiring with horror, clutching at himself, and shouting.

Bright sunlight fell upon the floor of the barn. On either side of him his two friends lay sleeping. Over their prostrate figures and across their faces black-beetles swarmed.

* * * * *

The farmhouse by noonday light proved to be a wild, ramshackle place, overrun with poultry, overgrown with weeds. Evidently it had not been tended for years. Not less queer and untidy and dishevelled-looking were the tenants, a couple of frowsy old women and slatternly girls, together with a smaller and numerous family. The men folk were away at the front, the women quarrelled with shrieks and abuse like London street-cats. But the setting of the place made up for its squalidity, a richly-wooded hilly country, and a village of thatched and creepered cottages standing in gardens that were aglow with stocks, sweet peas and rambler roses. The day turned out to be one of torrid heat, so that nobody wandered far. Everyone lay and dozed or read.

At dawn of the following morning the battalion marched again through clinging mists which by eight o'clock had melted into scorching sunshine. On every hand tossed the glory of the harvest—the corn cut and standing in sheaves on the hillsides which sloped steeply down to the valleys from wooded summits. Among the corn-stooks flitted flocks of finches, sparrows, and linnets; by the roadside, yellow-hammers and crickets vied with each other in beating out an endlessly monotonous heat-song. Overhead, a sky of unclouded blue; all the blue and gold and greenery of the year seemed concentrated in these August days.

Of course, the roads were ankle-deep in white dust; of course, the distances were often very long and straight, and there was not always shade at the halts. Already Ypres was forgotten while yet their goal still seemed far away and the war yet farther, so that shouting and singing ruled and all marched well to the cheerful strains of drum and fife. The villages, lying deep down in the troughs of the valleys, looked utterly asleep. The inevitable dog slept, head on paws, in the middle of the road, the inevitable cat basked on a sunny window-sill or wall; at their cottage doors, old women, with wrinkled yellow faces peering out of white linen sun-bonnets, sat sewing. Somewhere, as they passed, a blacksmith could be heard beating out the sultry minutes on his anvil. (If there was one sound that could call up to Adrian's mind Stane Deverill's many-tinted village street, it was that!) Few, however, troubled to come to the roadside to see the soldiers pass; so many thousands must have tramped that dusty way since the Battle of the Somme began.

And at the end of the march—Colonel Steele.

There he stood as they marched in, beside the officers' baggage which, having been sent on in advance, lay, like a mountain after a volcanic eruption by the roadside. Stout Major Brough, the second-in-command, who always seemed a bit short of a job and therefore looked for a chance of making trouble, was already poking his nose into it.

Everybody knew what to expect now—the word "kit-strafe" went round. Only the worst remained to be seen—on the already hottest day in the year, too! There were black looks and much under-breath swearing.

"Who does that extraordinary-looking article belong to?" The Commanding Officer pointed to an immense shapeless green bundle disfigured by string and straps.

"Cornwallis, sir." Captain and Adjutant Langley was lounging elegantly against the transport wagon.

"Cornwallis!"

"Sir!"

"What do you usually carry in your valise?"

"Nothing—at least—just the ordinary, sir."

"Open it."

The untidy bundle was dragged asunder and the unhappy Cornwallis' possessions exposed to view.

"What do you want with a drawing-room cushion, Cornwallis? Think you've come out to a picnic or what? Finished with that in England, y'know." (Titters from the young ensigns at the back.) "Photographs? Good heavens—how long have you had all these? Books! Poetry, if you please! The feller's a walking library! Put 'em all on the scrap-heap. I never saw such a chap. What d'you think you're doing here, my good boy—reading party or something?" (Renewed titters.) "A collapsible bath, a knitted scarf—it's summer, y'know—a patent washhandstand, a collapsible bed

. . . God bless my soul! Is there a war on, anybody? Make a scrap heap of the lot! We must make an example of this young gentleman, Brough!"

The varied collection of articles was thrown together like relics at a jumble sale.

"Please, sir, the scarf——"

It was the first time Cornwallis had ever attempted to remonstrate with his Commanding Officer. There was a note of agony in his voice now. Interest quickened among the bystanders.

"Well, what about the scarf? It's the least necessary of the lot."

"Please, sir—my sister——"

Everybody tittered. One had a right to, after all. "Art" —wasn't he a standing joke? "Art's" face wore a look of profound misery.

"I can't help that. You must read your orders. Next lot, Brough!"

Eric spoke.

"He wants to keep it, sir, because his sister made it for him. Do you really see much harm in that? It doesn't weigh more than a few ounces."

"That's not the point, Eric." But Colonel Steele's voice perceptibly modified. Eric had a quiet, undeniable manner for certain occasions. Colonel Steele knew it. "The point is it's an order. However—he's your boy. Do as you think best about the scarf. But the other things have *got to go*— d'you hear, Cornwallis?"

"Yes, sir."

"And as you apparently haven't read your orders or at any rate taken the trouble to obey them, you can take break- fast roll-call parade for the remainder of this week. I must make an example of somebody."

"I'll see him, sir," snapped Langley, clicking his heels.

"That'll do. I won't look at any more to-day. Come along, Brough!"

The unhappy culprit had crept away as unobtrusively as he was allowed to.

Entering the tent they were to share a few minutes later, Adrian found him sitting on his wire-bed, fumbling the offending scarf with his spectacles tilted at an unusual angle half-way down his nose. His first impulse was to laugh. There were tears in Cornwallis's eyes and a look of pain on his face. His senior's heart went out to one who could be so easily wounded, so bitterly made to suffer by what everybody else regarded as a huge joke.

"You mustn't mind, Arthur," he said. "Steele doesn't really mean it. It's his blundering, stupid, offensive way of doing things."

"Oh, it's not Steele I mind," Cornwallis protested. "It's —this little thing being made fun of in front of everybody. It's my books and photographs. Oh *God!* Adrian," he suddenly burst out with an awkward kind of gulp, "how shall I get through with the thing? How shall I ever get through it all?"

He sat with his untidy head between his hands and Adrian realised in a degree that he had never suspected the misery, the abhorrence that lay behind the youth's quiet and shrinking exterior—just what war meant to a nature like his. For Cornwallis had been an unobtrusive—except when his mistakes on parade were too glaring—and always unselfish shadow at the back of the battalion. "Poor old Art!" people said, recognising him as a "trier"—though a "hopeless" one; but how they must have hurt! Even Eric's attitude, though always patient and forbearing, was one of kindly ridicule. (How could it be otherwise towards a man who spent half his time reading poetry?) Adrian thought of the months at Laventie and at Ypres, of the uncounted "cursings" his friend had received from his

Commanding Officer, from Brough, from Langley—above all,
of the blood-red future as he knew it presented itself to this
sensitive mind.

They took a walk together in the evening through golden
fields in which peasants, chiefly women, were loading the
abundant corn.

§ 5

The camp was deep-hidden in one of those large oak-woods
which abound thereabouts. Situated on the top of a hill, it
was shady and cool, and, although there were wooden huts
sufficient to accommodate all, everybody preferred to sleep
out of doors during the brilliant weather. Not many hours
had been spent here before there came the first reminder
of war since leaving Ypres. A German aeroplane, white
and silvery in the sunshine, was observed travelling rapidly
and very high up, pursued across the blue expanse of sky
by three or four British planes. That night the thunder
of the guns seemed to come very close, and from the eastern
edge of the wood a great shimmering could be seen in the
southern sky.

In other respects, these last days, quietly spent amid the
rich peace of early autumn behind the front, were, for the
common soldiery, a time of enjoyment. All knew that
the storm was at hand and in their hearts pondered deeply
about the future. But none spoke of it, and none gave way to
forebodings which sometimes when the roll and thunder of
the guns made sleep almost impossible, and their flickering
lit up the whole night sky, came very near. No doubt there
were moments of shrinking, of reflection, of dread, especially
among the younger men. These, again, simply could not
visualise the proximity of fearful things. Away out there
beyond the eastern horizon the storm muttered ; but here were
peace, sunshine, rest.

The mellowed quality of that resplendent autumn entered men's souls. And the plains of Picardy are very fair at harvest time. There were parades, marches, practice-attacks, drill, physical drill, bayonet-fighting, field schemes in the early morning. It was like a horse being trained for a race or a boxer for a glove-fight, every exercise being carefully calculated and apportioned against the ultimate day of reckoning and of trial. But by noon all parades were finished, and the soldiers lay about in their shady wood through the hot afternoons, dozing or reading, while when evening came they took country walks, assisted the peasants in the harvest fields, or got up a game of football.

One day, Eric had the whole company photographed; and beneath the laughter and "ragging," everybody realised the significance of the occasion. Another day a party of Staff Officers came unexpectedly round the camp, resplendent in gold lace, red caps, and blue or red-and-white armlets. The guard turned out—one face seemed especially familiar. All stood to attention and saluted, the guard presenting arms.

It was the King. And across the immeasurable gulf of two years there sprang to Adrian's vision a burning afternoon of mid-June, a setting of dark green pinewoods and pale green turf, and the shouts and cries, the agglomerated roar of a race-course crowd. . . .

The mood of these latter days was not lost upon him. They were very near to Nature there among the oaks. And in the heat of the slumbering afternoons, with sunbeams dappling through nut-fronds upon the mossy floor, he would lie dozing on his wire bed, listening to the laughing cry and mysterious "tap-tap" of a green woodpecker at work, the shriek of a jay in alarm, or the rich deep "roo-coo-coo" of a wood-pigeon's evening notes. It was such an experience as comes back to men in after years when the crudity and tragedy of a thing are forgotten, as a sad and precious recollection.

Nor was there lost upon Adrian an echo of the previous autumn—an echo ghostly and terrible as a voice from the dead past, yet softened already by suffering and time, cherished in the solitude of his heart. Nor yet in his own regard alone was this season memorable. These days revealed to him a new meaning in existence, together with a kind of quiet and steadfast happiness without for one moment shaking his assured conviction of impending death. A new philosophy came to him, too, as he watched others drink their fill of joy and peace, living to the full their little hour.

By the side of these, indeed—the selfish storm of his earlier grief now past—he felt unworthy and ashamed.

But as the days slid by and the sombre muttering of the guns grew more threatening—increasing to paeons of thunder every morning just before dawn—all seemed drawn together in a truer and a deeper comradeship. Officers and men alike endeavoured to show by a greater kindliness, by an unobtrusive, almost diffident exchange of goodwill, the sense that animated each, the sense of being travellers along a common road towards a common goal.

Even Colonel Steele, Major Brough and Captain Langley—who constituted an exclusive society of their own known as "headquarters"—seemed not to be entirely unaware of this atmosphere. It is true, they drank more and more, sat up later and later, making the night ring with their conviviality—so that the men seeking sleep in their wooden huts called down every imprecation upon them—and indulged in ever greater orgies of obscenity in conversation and caricature. But the former perpetual "strafings" unaccountably ceased.

Adrian and Eric never spoke of Rosemary, and only once did Eric allude to the subject which Adrian knew lay nearest his heart. It was on the last of their rides to the beautiful forest and château of Lucheux. Cornwallis was not with them. Adrian had gone to a farmhouse to ask for a glass of milk or cider, while Eric watered the horses. When the former returned, he found his friend sitting beside the stream, looking down at something he held in his hand. Coming up behind he perceived that this was a cigarette-case, in which reposed a snapshot of Faith.

That concentrated attitude, that unexpected discovery, revealed Eric's inner life—thoughts which he was too simple to dissemble now, or to be in any way self-conscious about.

" Faith, you see ? "

Eric smiled.

After all, was it not with this same woman that both corresponded—daily in the case of the one, weekly in that of the other ? Faithful she was in a different way to each.

Adrian said :

" Yes. It's good. I got a letter from her yesterday. I gather—things are not easy."

He had gathered, in fact, that Lord Arden showed no disposition whatsoever to sanction the marriage of his daughter while the war lasted.

" I sometimes think . . . it may never come off."

Eric snapped the lid of his cigarette-case, and put it back in his pocket. After which he was again his bland, smiling, seldom-serious self.

§ 6

One sultry afternoon when everybody lay dozing within the grateful shade of the home wood—Cornwallis was correcting a poem he had written on a writing-pad—a battalion orderly went from company to company.

" The battalion will move at once."

All knew what it meant. Over, the day-dreams and the long pleasant rides, over, the cool, quiet dusks and fresh early mornings, over, the mellow beauty of the Picardy harvest. And the end of the long road at last.

There were no grumblings or cursings, no futile regrets.

Every man had had his fill of peace and sunshine—God had been good—and now every man felt fit to face whatever lay before him. So when the moment came, they loaded their packs, shouldered their rifles, and tramped away, laughing and singing, along the dusty highways of France into the autumn haze.

CHAPTER IX

A Battlefield

§ 1

THEY perished.

When the roll came to be called at a little village in the valley of the Ancre, barely one-fourth of those who had marched into action ninety-six hours before answered to it.

Colonel Steele fell gloriously. From a shell-hole in the midst of the battlefield, though mortally wounded, he directed the swaying fortunes of his battalion while consciousness remained, thus at the last earning the admiration of the officers and men who had hated him. His second-in-command, Major Brough, had fallen an unexpected victim to illness and, without taking part in the action, went home. The young adjutant, Langley, coming up with all speed from reserve was fatally struck down. Alston, grievously wounded, lay a prisoner in German hands. The two other company-commanders, Vivian and Darell, supported by the remnants of their men, were last seen fighting at the bayonet's point, a grey sea of Germans in full counter-attack closing round. The subalterns and ensigns fared no better on that great and terrible day. But Cornwallis went happily—oh! how happily—home to England with a bullet in arm and thigh.

Of the rank and file, the non-commissioned officers and private soldiers, the majority of those not accounted for were found to have attained their ultimate rest.

Out of the fight which for twenty-four hours swayed up and

down the green-brown, shell-scarred slopes of Ginchy, Morval
and Lesboeufs until at length the victory was won—out of the
fight came Captain Sinclair, smiling, dirty, tired, limping . . .
and alone.

§ 2

Night brooded over the battlefield. It was the hour for
the burial of the dead.

To Lieutenant Sir Adrian Knoyle—who, as it happened,
had been detailed to remain among the officers in reserve—
befell this duty.

A cold rain drove in gusts. A wet wind blew. Gloom
and darkness lay over all. Gloom and darkness reigned in his
heart. Bitterness strangled it.

They lay around—scores of them, a hundred, three—four
hundred. Impenetrable blackness hid them. But when the
star-lights went up they could be seen as men sleeping—vague
forms outlined upon the ridge of a trench, upon the lip of a
shell-hole.

All shapes, all attitudes, all positions. Some on the back,
hands to thigh, heels together, gazing upwards ; some on
the side and some curled up as though enjoying pleasant dreams ;
some flat on face, arms and legs outspread ; some with head
resting on arm or pack and one knee raised. Some whole ;
some twisted, bent up, in halves or shreds ; some with nails
dug deep into mud and weird contorted faces ; some rigid,
some stiffening by degrees, and some quite limp and loose.
Some in couples clasped like children who crouch together
from sudden fear ; some lying across one another—carelessly.
Some drunk with rum in death. . . . Germans, too, Germans
—very much like the rest. And once, once only, a grey and
a khaki figure locked on each other's bayonets.

He touched them at times—stumbled over them. Picking
his way among the shell-holes, he felt the soft, un-

natural flesh, the hair, rough, draggled and wet, without life, coagulated ; the body stiff, unyielding, unresponsive—empty.

Mingled with the soil, torn from their bodies—their letters, their pipes, their photographs of women, their tobacco-pouches, their lockets of women's hair, all the poor paltry things they valued once—tied up with the pay-book, hung around the neck, tied to the string of the metal disc.

The rain drove in gusts. How the wind keened! There was an occasional rifle-shot. Figures moved in the gloom.

" Who are you ? "

" Kamerad ! Burial-party ! "

They, too—creeping like jackals among the slain !

Earth upon earth. Dust back to dust. Into the shell-hole, fling them. Cover them up !

Darkness and gloom. Gloom and darkness in the heart. Bitterness strangling it.

Clink of the spades.

" Come on ! Heave in this one ! Heavy, ain't he ? . . . Cover him up ! "

§ 3

Over that dread scene, over that waste of shell-holes, of greenish water, of scarred and upchurned earth, broken trenches and mangled wire, all night long, it seemed to Adrian Knoyle, a vague familiar figure stood. Through the paling gloom and the swish of the rain, through the shrill of the wind and its driving gusts, through the livelong night, he saw it standing there—a sombre stooping form with hands folded and head bent as one pondering.

And when the star-lights went up, they revealed the white and mirrored room. And the woman of the dazzling tiara and the reddish-golden hair smiled. And the violins shivered out *Humoreske* while dancers spun and whirled.

END OF PART THE THIRD.

PART THE FOURTH,
DAWN

And the nations were angry, and thy wrath is come, and the time of the dead, that they should be judged, and that thou shouldest give reward unto thy servants the prophets, and to the saints, and them that fear thy name, small and great; and shouldest destroy them which destroy the earth.

REVELATION XI, 18.

CHAPTER I

Another Winter Passes

§ 1

THE part that it had so greatly played in the later stages of the Battle of the Somme, left the Division to which Adrian Knoyle and Eric Sinclair belonged little more than a skeleton, and for the time being a legend. Out of a fighting strength of six thousand bayonets, barely two thousand remained. Before October—so soon as was practicable indeed—it was withdrawn from the neighbourhood of the battlefield into one of those refitting and training areas which had been established west of Amiens, there to await reinforcements and equipment. Captain Sinclair remained in command of the relics of the battalion he had brought out of action, all survivors having commented upon his distinguished conduct in the engagement.

In due time the reinforcements arrived and it was practically a new battalion that early in the month of November moved up to trenches on the northern edge of the Somme battlefield, there, it was rumoured, to pass the winter. The Colonel was new, the officers were new—with the exceptions of Eric, Adrian and one or two others who had been left in reserve—the non-commissioned officers and men were new, and the spirit of the battalion was new.

The Commanding-Officer, Lieutenant-Colonel Forsyth, was preceded by a good reputation. He had been a company-commander in the battalion on its initial arrival in France and had been dangerously wounded at the First Battle of Ypres. He was a tall, quiet fair-haired and blue-eyed man of a professional military type. Adrian took an immediate liking to him. He had a deliberate efficient way with him, and a passion for fairness among officers and men alike. At the same time he quickly showed he would stand no laxity. He brought with him an adjutant called Tritton, who also acted as second-in-command. The three new company-commanders, Hamilton, Rice and Mead, were all young regular soldiers who had been wounded early in the war and had attained unexpectedly rapid promotion. Burns and Fotheringay were the new-comers to the Left Flank company.

There could be little complaint about the trenches which were permanently taken over in October. Here in the earliest Somme attacks the British had been beaten back with heavy loss; here, in consequence, were found old elaborate permanent field-fortifications with vast underground " dug-outs," deep trenches, immense fields of wire—part-German, part-English —and an easy approach by long communication-trenches to the front line. The mud, it is true, became increasingly cruel as winter advanced; but was not this the case everywhere? And when they came out of the trenches, it was to a village in a not unpleasant country they repaired, one at all events little scarred by war.

On the whole everybody was satisfied. Those who had taken an earlier part in the campaign compared the situation favourably with the discomforts of previous winters; those who had not were agreeably surprised. With the exception of occasional raids and a spasmodic artillery activity on both sides, the enemy remained quiet. It was as though after the terrible experiences of the summer and autumn, friend and enemy alike had resolved to settle down—in so far as the Higher Commands allowed—to " peace warfare."

§ 2

To Adrian, the tragedy of the Somme, or rather the long pilgrimage which preceded it brought a mental reaction in the direction of sanity : following upon the abyss of Ypres, these experiences had perhaps exhausted his capacity for emotional feeling and experience.

He was, however, left reaching out for anything which might re-establish moral and mental balance, which might pull or hold him together. Sanity, cogency, power of reasoned reflection had returned, but not feeling, and in the months that followed he lived through a monotone, merely reasoning, knowing, observing—a monotone from which three aspirations, significances, call them what you will, stood out like hills in the dead plain.

The dominating influence upon him at this period was Eric Sinclair.

In Knoyle there existed a strain of aspiration, an idealism a leaning and a longing toward some ultimate better thing which baffled his own introspection, and which Lady Knoyle alone, perhaps, had divined and understood. It was the thing his father had never understood. It was the thing Rosemary Meynell had never understood. It was the thing Eric conjectured only as something beyond his knowledge. It was the thing Gina Maryon might have understood had he allowed her to catch a glimpse of it. It was the thing which in rough contact with the world had remained suppressed and concealed, a locked secret, a treasure of the heart rather than of the mind.

And it was this quality, no doubt, this capacity for emotional experience which had reacted upon him so disastrously, which had plunged him so far downward after his love's betrayal. All this hidden force in him had been defeated, thrown back in confusion upon itself, for the time being annihilated. Never, perhaps, in the same degree, with the same original intensity could he experience again. But since consummation had been denied that other wooing to which he had turned in his extremity, was it surprising if this, the vitalest thing in him, arose triumphant ?

So it was to Eric that he now turned—anxiously—leaning upon him as against a pillar of steel, visualising in him something higher and stronger than himself.

Next to Eric, and next to him not in degree but in point of actuality, were the Three Hills; and bound up with these his mother. To that mother he had not been over-considerate; to Stane he had given little enough thought during the years of illusion. Yet these came recurringly to him in his need, as two constant reassuring facts. His mother's letters reached him twice weekly; letters full of sympathy and of encouragement, full, too, of a certain native charm that hovered between humour and tears. After all she knew him, though how little of confidence in the living thought had passed between them! Daily almost—and nightly—were with him rapt visions of Stane, an aching for that calm and remote spirit, that sanctity of association, that intimacy of feeling and earliest recollection, which linked him with the far-away spot. It was an altogether more than physical intimacy. The autumn road to the Somme had illuminated this train of thought. Sometimes the hills were his companions; sometimes the wind-swept silence of their summits, the cries of kestrel and plover, the autumn wild flowers, the mounds and barrows of the long-vanished race, the Roman dykes, and Early British encampments so immense in their obscurity; sometimes the sunset view of the vale and the looking-down upon his own creepered and lichened home—the creepers turning red and saffron upon the Portland stone—its cedared lawns, its sunlit terrace, its red-walled garden, its park and copses, its green rushy bed under the Three Hills; sometimes the thatched farms, the clover-studded fields where cattle grazed, the hedged lanes and villages half-buried in woodland and orchard. Dawn and dusk and the bright noonday, sunlight and shadow, autumn, winter, summer; and then the blossoming spring.

The third influence and the human embodiment of his renewed hold on things was Faith Daventry. Her letters came week by week, regularly, unfailingly. She was—Faith: somebody associated with Eric, the being whom Eric's lively and careless fancy had selected; the being whom Eric's fastidiousness and self-sufficient personality had chosen for its own; therefore to be cherished. Yet she was more than this to Adrian. How often—as he read her letters—he thought of the frank and steadfast look, friendly and sympathetic, of Arden days!

They contained news, too, these letters. They told of the labours of the hospital, of how the Voluntary Aid Workers persistently did those things which ought not to be done, and left undone those things which ought to have been done; of her own comic earlier mistakes as sub-commandant in writing out the reports; of everything, from the peculiarities of the patients, the trials of the cook (who could or did not cook) and the problems of the wardrobe and the linen cupboard, to the intricacies of the household books, and how she tired of the "whole business," yet still rather liked it. She told of her visits to London, where "a violent season is in progress"; of dances which did not attract her; of "numerous new attractive little minxes" who had appeared on the scene; how *chaperons* were dispensed with, indeed utterly despised; how the *régime* of "sandwiches to a gramophone" which set the ball rolling had quickly given place to considerable affairs in big houses, with all complete except champagne; how young ladies and gentlemen went out "joy-riding" in the small hours—"a thing they couldn't do in our day" (it had come to that with her!); and how fashionable London was getting a bit bored with the war, which, after all, had ceased to be either novel or exciting. She told of visits to Cyril Orde who was "just the same," but wheeled about in a chair, still tended by the faithful Miss Ingleby, and having periodical operations; and how he never would be much better or much worse. She mentioned what she chanced to have heard of the Freemans, and how Lady F. was more than ever

an " indefatigable war-worker," opening bazaars and patronising
the families of absent soldiers, while Sir Walter, it was rumoured,
had held a kind of pistol at the head of the Government,
signifying his right to a peerage if he couldn't retain a portfolio. Mr. Heathcote she mentioned, too ; Mr. Heathcote
who had got " war-work," but did it mostly at the Carlton
Club. Of her father she wrote—" that lion-hearted man "
—who was still striving, threatening, cajoling, beseeching all
ranks and grades from his own Commanding Officer to the
Army Council itself—" using his influence," as he expressed
it—to be sent to the Front ; and of how, knowing him as
she did, she felt he would probably succeed if the war went
on another twelvemonth—only, she hoped, not in a combatant
capacity : " for," said she, " he aspires to command a
battalion."

§ 3

In November, Eric went on a leave long overdue. He returned at the end of a fortnight with items of intelligence
of the first interest.

He had spent all but three days of his sojourn at Arden.
The matter of his marriage had been conclusively and
definitively fixed. It was to take place on his next leave—
whenever that might be. How had the miracle been worked ?
Faith herself by an act of determined independence had
worked it.

" I think she saw I was getting a bit fed up," said Eric. " I
think she's getting fed up with the uncertainty of it and the
incessant grind of that infernal hospital herself. Anyway one
day she said, all of a sudden, ' I want to be able to have a home
for you when you come back on leave. I don't care about
mixing you up with the medicines and the dressings and the
patients and all that. Come on, let's go and settle it now ! ' "

And they went—to Lord and Lady Arden in the smoking-

room. Faith smiled and Eric smiled and Lady Arden said
next to nothing; and his righteous lordship felt that the odds
of opinion were against him. Nor upon being pressed could
he quote any *particular* ground against the marriage: a score of
precedents could be cited by the young couple in favour of it.
He did not give way there and then, his dignity as a father at
all events required salving; he would "think the matter over
—and they must on no account build any hopes on that."

Well, future fathers-in-law had a habit of thinking matters
over!

The young couple, so far satisfied, proceeded to act with
sagacity. Again, it was Faith's suggestion. They went up to
London for the day; they went to see Cyril Orde. They
consulted him, as a friend of the family no less than as a man
of the world, upon the matter of how they should ensure
her father's consent or, failing it, how should next act. Cyril
said, "Do nothing!" And within a week his wisdom—and
their wisdom—were vindicated. Lord Arden went direct to
that same friend in whose judgment he placed confidence
and asked his opinion not only of his prospective son-in-law's
future but of the war future in general; how, in short, would
he recommend a father to act? Orde played up manfully.

"Let 'em marry. They know what they're doin', damn it.
They're not fools. You'll find precious few flies on either of
'em. Eric's got money and a career in front of him
if he comes through the war. Faith's got a head on her
shoulders. Let 'em go and do their worst!"

Lord Arden did not return to Arden. At heart he was a
coward in such matters. He allowed his lady to communicate
his august decision. Both the young people wrote him
affectionate letters of thanks. He replied to each with dignity.
The wedding, it was settled, should take place "some time in
the summer," Eric's next leave being the deciding factor.

It was from Faith through Eric that Adrian had tidings of
Rosemary, though, indeed, he did not seek the information.

The two old friends discussed the matter dispassionately, unemotionally, critically almost as those do who discuss the affairs of mutual friend. She "went about," it appeared, "everywhere"; danced, sold tickets for charity, acted for charity; was admired; was sought after; Harold Upton invariably with her; the whole of the Clan Maryon—hovering. People talked. Were the couple engaged, they begged to know. It had been going on a long time now; no lack of money; why wasn't it announced? And where did Sir Adrian Knoyle come in? Society's curiosity was piqued. The world interests itself in such matters. Well—it felt in decency it ought to be informed.

Adrian for his part refused analysis. He refused to consult his feelings in the matter. It all seemed outside and beyond him now, the mere abstract affair of someone he had once known, though deep down in his heart a voice tried to find utterance. If she so much as breathed, hinted, gave a sign—even now? The instant of that thought he could not stifle. At such times feeling threatened to swamp him, and in a sort of terror he would resurrect the spectre of one never-to-be-forgotten winter's eve.

Needless to say, there came no sign.

§ 4

As the months went by and the monotony of winter trench-life ate into his soul, a certain indifference came. Beaumont Hamel was on the whole comfortable, too comfortable perhaps; danger there was little and of work merely routine; the rear billets were good; reliefs frequent. Hours, many hours, were spent both in the trenches and out of them, doing nothing, smoking and drinking, playing cards, talking, trying to read, but chiefly thinking—thinking. . . .

One incident did occur to relieve the tedium of the winter. This was the award to Lieutenant Knoyle, of the Military Cross

" for gallantry and presence of mind on the night of June 25th,"
etc., etc. Adrian looked at his diary.

June 25. It was the night of Walker's death. . . .
" Gallantry and presence of mind," indeed !

He laughed whole-heartedly for the first time in many
months, then crumpled up the sheet of paper on which the
brief notice was typed and trod it under heel. Three weeks
later he was summoned to the orderly room to show cause
why he was not wearing the decoration which His Majesty
had been graciously pleased to confer upon him.

" I thought it was a joke," he replied with due regard for truth.
Everyone remarked upon his modesty.

§ 5

Early in December it was his turn for leave. He
spent the fortnight with Lady Knoyle at Ascot, reading and
playing golf. He did not want to see anybody or to re-visit
any remembered haunts. Yet on the instant of an unex-
plained impulse—it was a Sunday evening—he rang up
Grosvenor Mansions on the trunk-line.

A voice that still had power to quicken every pulse in him
answered.

" Hullo ! Who is it ? "
" Adrian Knoyle."

There was a second's pause. . . .

Blood rushed to his head.

Then the receiver at the other end slammed down.

§ 6

Upon his return to the front, week-end trips to the gay
city of Amiens, no great distance away, became common
throughout the winter, and these made for the distraction
everybody desired. Eric always insisted on his friend's

company. As senior subaltern, Adrian had paramount liberty. The two officers who had lately joined the company were entertaining companions, not less so, perhaps, because they could agree on no one subject and quarrelled without bitterness but without pause : Burns, a Colonial who wore two South African ribbons—he had already fought in German East—Fotheringay the dandified scion of an " effete aristocracy " who had yet to outlive the rather too evident polish of Sandhurst. The earlier contrast between Cornwallis and Walker could not have been sharper than that between these two.

Burns held forth at every opportunity, licence being extended to age and experience ; Fotheringay denied—with oaths. So it went on. In private they appreciated each other's point of view.

It was an epoch of violent dinner-parties and violent discussions. One occasion, in especial, Adrian remembered, partly owing to the fact of its being a Christmas dinner-party. The subject was the professional versus the citizen army, a favourite bone of contention.

" One can never think of the army again in a purely professional sense," the South African veteran announced. " The old idea of it as a highly specialised and technical thing— even in the case of branches like the artillery and engineers— has been washed out. The war itself has done that. As for the infantry—one has only to look at the case of a man like Alston or our noble friend over there with the beautiful ribbons."

He indicated Eric Sinclair, who since the Battle of the Somme wore the Distinguished Service Order in addition to his earlier decoration. Burns himself provided a singular contrast to his youthful company-commander and, indeed, to everybody else present ; his hair was turning grey, he had a rough and aggressive exterior, his moustache was grizzled, his face lined and wrinkled, his eyes deep-set under bushy eyebrows. Altogether he deserved the term " hard-bitten." He admitted to being forty-five, but was reputed to have passed the half-century. In him age and impetuosity so combined that he was a source of entertainment to all ranks—and of some admiration.

"Yes, we're both good examples of the unprofessional officer," said Eric.

"Take Alston, for instance," the elder man went on, "a barrister by profession. The only uniform he ever wore was a wig and gown. Never done a day's soldiering in his life. Joins the regiment, comes out here, and within six months has a company. And he was as good a company-commander as the battalion's ever had—wasn't he? Of course he's sacrificed his professional career."

"What about G.H.Q., Burns—they're all Sandhurst people," put in a high-pitched confident voice. It belonged to the fair-haired Fotheringay, sitting further along the dinner-table. His sleek appearance and fresh countenance suggested nineteen as his probable age.

"The Staff!" Burns sniffed with rather ostentatious contempt.

Two or three of the junior officers at the end of the table began singing a verse of a popular and ribald song which began:

"Then up spake the gallant Red-cap——,"

others joining in until the large wooden hut in which the officers were gathered echoed and re-echoed to the limits of its tin roof.

"Where are your red tabs, Fotheringay?" somebody shouted.

"Well, generals if you like," retorted the latter as soon as his voice could be heard.

"Oh!—oh!" howled the chorus. "Generals!" And they started another verse of their favourite ditty.

The whisky-bottle never ceased to circulate, and the fizzing sound of soda-water bottles being uncorked formed an impertinent commentary on the general conversation. The table glowed with candles stuck in bottles which focused the faces surrounding it in a sphere of light. Shadows filled the rest of the hut.

Burns, not to be denied, continued the conversation.

"My view is that this army's being run and this war will be won by common sense and common sense alone." ("Hear, hear!" interjected several voices mockingly. "Is that why you joined it?") "High technical training won't do it. Years of experience won't do it, because in a citizen army you haven't got experience. Most of the old stock infantry training tactics and the old shibboleths and the old commonplaces and conventions we lived by in South Africa were washed out within a month of Mons. The training of years went—I won't say for nought, but it had to be re-shaped and re-learnt in the light of experience. The machine-gun, for instance, heavy artillery and trench warfare, undid the old ideas; the application of the new arms had to be learnt as much by the old troops as by the new. Only war reveals these things as it reveals the quality of the men who apply them. Even South Africa showed that in a limited way."

"What about discipline?" put in Adrian, who was interested.

"Ah! Discipline for the men—common sense for the officers—*esprit de corps* for all. Discipline's the one thing that has never ceased to count, as we all know. Tactics may have changed, but the drill-book is more important than ever before. The best-disciplined troops have fought best in this war. But after all it's largely the discipline of loyalty. Well-led troops will always fight. Disciplined troops under an incompetent leader will fight no better than they must."

"The men like following a gentleman," contributed Fotheringay.

"Therefore there must always be an 'officer class.' But they will also, you may have noticed, follow a brave man whatever he is. That's just—English."

"Yes—and not *boche*, Burns," interposed Tritton, the new adjutant, rudely. He was a tall young man with a dissipated and rather vacant face.

There was laughter at the play on words, especially as it was a point scored against Burns who, among other controversial humours, sided with the Germans whenever possible.

"When all's said and done, though, the German soldier and the British soldier are pretty much alike. I know it's not the popular view. Don't howl me down."

Tritton said: "You've joined the wrong army, Burns."

Somebody else called out: "Yes, you lousy old Fritz! You have."

"I'm not," the grey-haired man replied. "I'm not pro-German. I hate him because we're fighting him. It's our job to kill him and beat him. But I am up against mere newspaper cant and jingoism. Frankly I respect the German as a soldier. He's done some bloody things. But history will show that we've all done bloody things. War's a bloody business—rather particularly this war."

"What tripe he talks!" commented Fotheringay, turning to Adrian, confident in the latter's agreement.

The senior subaltern raised his eyebrows.

"You think so?" He liked, but nevertheless felt a constant desire to snub this redundant young person, for whom the traditional standpoint so conspicuously sufficed. "Why?" he added.

"Well—obviously." Fotheringay turned to Tritton, upon whose support at any rate he could count. "Mad, isn't he, Tritton?"

"Mad isn't the word," replied the latter. "Drinks his bath water, I shouldn't wonder," he murmured to himself.

The conversation ended with the usual frivolities about women—and Fotheringay intoxicated.

"God bless 'em, the little angels!" the youth hiccoughed, clinging to his crony, one Gerald Sutton. "Oh, how I love

'em ! Just little Lily and a bottle of fizz at the Savoy Grill
—how happy one would be ! "

Laughter and applause followed this sentiment.

" Sinclair—Sin—Sinclair old boy," bawled the irresponsible
youth. " I—I love you. D'you know I feel rather tight ? "
(" You are," murmured his company-commander, lighting a
cigarette. He was accustomed to and rather bored by his
subaltern's vagaries.) " Stand by me ! Take me home !
Slosh that old blighter Burns, somebody ! Ah ! here's m'old
friend J—J—Jerry. Have another drink with me, Jerry !
Then we'll slosh old b—b—bloody Mr. Burns a couple.
Hooroosh ! "

He whooped and yelled—his friend in a like condition.
Burns smiled grimly.

" Oh ! Jerry old boy ! " the inebriated young gentleman
continued in piercing tones. " Oh ! Jerry, why aren't
we going to a dance to-night ? Why aren't we taking
Kitty and—and—the other one to the Grafton—Oh ! my
lor, how tight I am ! I'm blithero . . . not a respectable
dance I mean—not—not one like Mrs. Riv—what's her damned
name—gave. That one of Gina Maryon's, d'you remember ?
What were those cigarettes she gave us to try, old boy, d'you
remember ? And that funny muck. Lor ! You snuffed it
up your nose out of a little gold box. They were all trying it,
all snuffing it up their noses. . . . And that gal, Rosemary
What's-its-name. Lovely creature. And the Romanes ! And
Gina ! Oh, lor, what days—what days ! What—er—nights
of joy ! Old days—never come back ! Damn it ! . . .
There's that wicked old man, Burns, laughing at us ! Come
on, Jerry, slosh him a couple ! "

Lord F. reeled drunkenly towards the older man, who took
hold of him and laid him gently on the floor.

Eric said sharply : " Come on, off you go to bed ! " and with
Burns' assistance dragged his protesting subaltern outside.

Adrian followed, very white.

§ 7

So the dinner-parties behind the front sometimes ended. And it was in this Bacchic atmosphere—this atmosphere of loudness, of semi-intoxicated, half-humorous quarrelling, endless " ragging," gossip, Divisional " shop," and a large amount of rather reckless card-playing—that the winter passed. In the early spring of 1917 the German withdrawal from the Somme front began, and anticipating it by only a few days, the Division was withdrawn for a long period of training and rest near to Peronne. The country to which they came consisted of wide grassy uplands in whose hollows the villages lay, and it was peculiarly suited to those equestrian and other exercises in which the British officer has always excelled. There were horse-races ; there were field-sports ; there were hare-chases on horseback in which all the officers of the battalion took part, amid the loudest whooping and excitement ; there were judging-competitions and jumping. The men meanwhile made gardens, played football, and when the warmer weather came took to bathing in the nearby river.

Light fatigues lightly undertaken, such as the laying of railways and the digging of a rear defence-line, occupied the earlier part of this period of rest. Later, training earnestly began, drill was constant, and field-practices on a large scale took place two or three times a week. Everybody bemoaned these as an unheard-of labour, it being the regulation army habit to do so ; as a fact, the weather being fine and the work not uninteresting, they were rather enjoyed. Though a good deal of walking was entailed, together with occasional spurts of unwonted energy, there was also much lying about in the warm spring weather. Adrian, for his part, inclined to take the operations seriously. He foresaw the time approaching when he might expect to command a company—was, in fact, overdue to do so. Much as he might desire to remain Eric's lieutenant in the Left Flank Company, this other was a prospect

he could not afford to neglect. He was sensible of his short-
comings, having realised long since that he never could become
a soldier of quality as Eric was. What had been true of the
era before Neuve Chapelle remained true now. Eric in
battle or manœuvre did the right thing instinctively; for
himself, only by a more or less exhaustive process of thought
could he arrive at correct solutions. This difference between
them there would always be. If brilliance, he reflected,
could not be the lot of all, efficiency might yet be won by
labour and creditable pains.

Burns proved himself sound, solid, conscientious; the boy,
Fotheringay, for all his reckless, feckless and riotous behaviour—
smart. He knew his drill, he handled his men like a martinet,
he knew the technical things by the technical names, in the
field he was apt to accomplish sly and clever feats of his own
choosing. This was under the eye of a superior; behind the
superior's back, he played shove ha'penny with his platoon-
sergeant, or, placing a man on guard, went to sleep.

During all this period, rumours were afloat. " Spring
offensive " was in the air; " spring offensive " was the topic of
conversation when nothing else served. In April, the Battle
of Arras was fought a few miles to the northward, which failing,
no more appeared to be contemplated in that direction. " St.
Quentin " was then on everybody's lips—" to take over a new
bit of line." That, too, was discounted by events. Then
Bullecourt, La Bassée, Armentières, each was mentioned in turn,
the real solution—as generally happened in such cases—being
left out of account.

It was Ypres.

Yes! After all the tramping and all the fighting and all the
resting, and all the guessing and the hoping, it was back to
the Ypres Salient they eventually trekked. And a June day
of such heat, such dust, and such fair promise as had seen them
depart rejoicing ten months before, found them encamped
once more in the oak-woods north of the Poperinghe road.

CHAPTER II

Faith and Eric

§ 1

BIG Ben has just chimed a quarter before two of a warm afternoon in July, 1917.

And already St. Margaret's Church is more than half filled. This impression is perhaps unduly emphasised by the fact that the guests have spread themselves widely about the pews. Still, the more important ones have yet to arrive. These like to be—well, not late, but as nearly late as possible.

Enter Heathcote. He is at ease. He is suavely dressed. He smiles with the smile of white spats, a turquoise pin in a black stock, a well-groomed moustache, a carnation buttonhole. He trots a short distance up the aisle, bowing and smiling from the waist—whom shall he sit next ? Anybody "interesting ? What a nice wedding it will be ! Ah ! Mrs. Ralph Clinton—*such* an agreeable woman, and very much *affairée* with "everybody ! " Pleasantries, whispered comments, smiles. . . .

At the west entrance of the church, a slight commotion. Three-quarters of the assembled congregation looks behind it— the remaining quarter is looking at the three-quarters. The bride ? One is frankly disappointed : it is only an arrival. Mrs. Rivington (of Rivington) sails up the aisle, decorously and properly attended by her nieces, Miss Kenelm and Miss Lettice Kenelm. (Miss Lettice Kenelm, without the curate ?) Mrs. Rivington is, immense—and grand. Plumed and feathered uppermost, beneath her large, good-natured face and double chin she is caped, furred, frilled, and laced to an extent, one would think, incompatible with human nature. (But who is to analyse, let alone comprehend, the anatomy of Fashion ?) Passers-by had a look at her—and wondered. The common herd on either side of the red carpet had taken her without hesitation for a Duchess. Such quantity allied with quality—of raiment.

And Miss Kenelm and Miss Lettice Kenelm, too, for all the warmth of the midsummer day, are caped, furred, frilled, and laced—and also plumed and feathered—uppermost.

On their heels, the Countess of Cranford and Lady Rosemary Meynell followed by the clever young political private secretary (and searchlight operator) Harold Upton. Lady Cranford, handsome in black and pearls with elegant carriage, white hair, and jewel-like eyes, attracts attention. People are cowed by aloofness. When they see it, they cease to believe in—humanity. The tall and graceful daughter is in dark blue with a broad-brimmed hat. Lieutenant Upton, in the uniform of the Royal Naval Volunteer Reserve, looks the part he so capably plays—that of the sailor-poet.

Whispers, audible enough, greet this entry. " How well she looks ! " " He's very rich, isn't he ? " " Ain't they engaged ? " " Oh, yes—ages ago." " When's it coming off ? " " Helena Cranford disapproves of war-time marriages."

Then the Freemans. Lady Freeman, smart—Parisian, or should one say Palm Beach ? Before alighting from her car, she has arranged herself, acquired an expression of good-looking wickedness (while entering the porch), and feels self-confident in virtue of being so very down-to-date (as she trips up the aisle). It is a precious moment. She is followed by Mrs. Granville-Brown and by her husband, Sir Walter. They enter their seats and all bow to Lady Cranford, who looks.

Little Miss Ingleby darts in through a side-door like a

squirrel. With his arm in a sling, slightly pale, very diffident, and in uniform, Mr. Cornwallis shows her to a seat.

And now the great British Aristocracy appears in the respectively portly and reduced personages of the Earl and Countess of Doncaster, who march up the aisle occasionally nodding, occasionally bowing, not smiling, but frowning and scowling. That high domed brow, that steely jackdaw eye, that shrivelled biting presence! The important couple, grandparents of the bride, take their seats beside their daughter, Lady Arden, who embattled by children has been for some time sitting placidly in the front pew on the right-hand side.

And at this moment, the best man is wheeled into view— grim. It is Major Orde. "Not I!" he had said when pressed to act in the absence of Sir Adrian Knoyle. "It wouldn't be decent. Think what a scene in a wheeled-chair!" Nevertheless, he has been bested by his young friends' joint entreaties.

Yes—and here at the same moment—as is proper, for two o'clock strikes—here comes the bridegroom. Captain Sinclair looks very little changed ; who would think he'd been through so much ? Delicate of complexion, girlish, his little moustache carefully trimmed, he wears an affable smile which reflects pleasantly the hilt of his sword, his buttons, his accoutrements, his boots. If suggestively bored by the proceedings, he scarcely shows it. He plays his part with an air of quite insolent self-possession.

Lady Doncaster—elderly martinets will !—has had her way. In face of the combined protestations, the prolonged entreaties of Lord and Lady Arden, all the little Daventrys, and the young couple themselves, she has insisted on what she calls a "decent wedding." "No Wardour," she has averred when pleaded with for a quiet affair at Arden, "no Wardour has ever been married in that hole-and-corner way people have of doing things nowadays. Nor has a Daventry." And as for the war, what on earth had that to do with a wedding ?

The logic was not perhaps unanswerable, but it was inexorable.

And now there is a stir at the church door. *Is* the bride arriving ? The hum of conversation that has almost filled the church momentarily ceases—ceases because everyone has turned to look round. Those in front whose view is impeded by those behind, half-rise in their seats : one such is Lady Freeman, her ostrich feathers and slashed cloak being unmistakable. Some have to peep round pillars. Lady Doncaster and Lady Cranford alone look rigidly to the front. . . . And after all it is a false alarm. Yet not quite an anti-climax. The famous—or should it rather be notorious ?—some say one thing, some another—Gina Maryon and her friend, Mrs. Gerard Romane. Well, this couple are always—interesting. And they push their way in, kissing the pages and maids of honour, who, herded by their mammas, govern esses and nurses are grouped at the foot of the aisle in readiness for the bride's arrival—smiling, waving, shaking hands, carrying on animated, declamatory conversations with friends as they pass up the aisle—modernly attired in bits of chiffon vaguely attached to brilliant-hued ribbons, the one wearing a very large and the other an uncommonly small hat, both entirely unselfconscious.

Lady Freeman's eyes are raptly fixed on this—this so effective *entrée*. For it is effective. . . . What *is* there about this Gina Maryon ? . . . Lady Freeman comes to the conclusion it is " descent." After all—she reflects—the young woman, however perilously she may coquette at times with the music-hall stage or the *demi-monde*, is a true-born daughter of the noble and ancient house of Penrith. Which fact obliterates all venial sins. . . .

Smiling and not apologising, the two objects of her reflection push inconveniently past Lady Cranford into a seat next Rosemary Meynell.

The bride, too, is late. That is no ill omen, however, but

a prerogative of brides. And Lord Arden is always late. However, conversation goes on merrily, the ladies having all their work cut out to detail and piece together again each other's garments. The bridesmaids come off worst. Being small people, carrying bouquets larger than themselves and attired in frocks the most delicate and elusive, they are constrained to stand about at the bottom of the aisle, taxing their own and everybody else's patience, getting distressingly intermixed with those who pass backwards and forwards between the outer and the inner doors. It goes without saying that they demand to be taken home ; that the big bridesmaids do not know how to control the little ones or do not attempt to ; that, as near as possible, there is an *infra dig.* affair with the pages.

At length, the bride does arrive : treacherously, basely, unfairly, for the organ is playing a voluntary and the front people do not realise what has happened until the back people stand up and the vision in white has nearly reached the altar-steps. Yes—only the back people get a fair look. On the arm of Lord Arden she advances—slowly. Lord Arden in uniform, field-booted and spurred, looks hearty, with a complexion more than ever the colour of ripe mulberries. Of the bride little can be seen. She is no longer a woman : she is lace and veil and orange-blossom.

Then the service begins. In a sharp parade voice Eric Quentin on his part undertakes to love and to cherish, etc., etc., Faith Helena Mary ; and in a clear, firm voice Faith Helena Mary undertakes on her part to love, cherish, and obey Eric Quentin until death them do part.

All sing the time-honoured hymns : creditably on the whole, though (Rosemary Meynell whispers to Gina Maryon), with faint suggestions that a penny has been slipped into the slot for the occasion. The Vicar of Arden provides a short valedictory address on the eternal quality of marriage, strongly advising his two young friends to acquire as quickly as convenient such trifling virtues as they may not already possess.

An anthem is sung ; and a hymn. And then the full band of Captain Sinclair's regiment plays the " Wedding March " rousingly ; and down the chancel steps come the happy couple —Mrs. Eric Sinclair radiant through her veil, the bridegroom smiling a bland and suitable smile which—Mr. Arthur Cornwallis reflects—seems neither more nor less bland and suitable here than upon the battlefields of Ypres and of the Somme.

It cannot, of course, be helped. But once again everybody is unable to obtain a quite comfortably good view. Lady Freeman overcomes the difficulty first. Balancing herself against a pillar, she places an elegant foot upon the seat of her pew. Several ladies who are in a position to do so follow suit—not always with satisfactory results. A marchioness, it is observed, collapses beneath the weight of her wig, her ornaments, and her person. Precisely the same thing befalls Mrs. Rivington, who having insisted on being uphoisted by the united efforts of the Misses Kenelm, sinks back selfishly, thereby all but pulping the one and pulverising the other.

While the register is being signed, everybody talks. " How well the bride looked ! " " What a lovely gown ! " " What a nice-looking boy, that Eric Sinclair—and plenty of money ! "

Outside a raucous voice yells : " Storming of the Messines Ridge ! " Yet—well—really—how much more exciting a wedding than a war !

And so they go their several ways in motor-cars, carriages and taxicabs. There is to be no breakfast ; no confetti ; no facetiousness. Lord Arden and the bridegroom have stamped their feet on all three. Just a small family party. After which the newly-married couple disappear in the direction of Sheringham, where nice, kind (and useful) Mrs. Rivington has lent her villa.

§ 2

And although Society sees a great many things—especially at weddings—and delights to poke its nose into people's private lives and devour and batten upon, if given half a chance, their special little intimacies and their special little secrets, it does not see quite all of the game.

Neither Society—nor any one else in the wide world—has any part to play or any look-in at that moment when the train increases speed passing out of London, and in a reserved first-class compartment, a smart young man draws a fair young woman to himself; and the young woman whispers "At last!" with that look in her blue eyes which a nice young woman wears only once or twice in this mortal span.

CHAPTER III

Their Dream

§ 1

THREE years had passed. And once more the heat of a summer's night lay heavy upon London.

In the sombre gloom that now prevailed, the swaying of the midnight crowds through the once garishly-lighted thoroughfares around Leicester Square and Piccadilly Circus made an even more deeply-moving and mystical impression than of old. Across the starless night searchlights stretched spectral fingers. In these three years great emotions, stresses, dangers had fluttered the heart of the strange and wonderful city without for one moment alleviating its sorrows or obliterating its shames. Yet the inner consciousness had indubitably changed; among the hurrying crowds could be found scarcely an individual but bore some hidden scar or secret pain. Fear had stalked these streets. Dread knocked hourly upon the door of every house, grief waited upon all. But the world danced on, danced ever.

And upon a certain night in a square situated just off Piccadilly, a party was in progress. At first—from a sense of decorum or what-not—ladies and gentlemen had restrained themselves; then they had been unable to restrain themselves longer. And all at once in the London world there had burst out a passionate furore of—" boy and-girl dances."

To-night Miss Gina Maryon was holding such an affair in honour of Captain Sinclair and his bride. Their honeymoon over, Captain Sinclair was on the eve of returning to the front—which was convenient of him, since there was nothing Miss Maryon so particularly desired (at the moment) as an excuse for giving a " boy-and-girl " dance. (The expression was hers; it has, you will kindly note, a disengaging air of youthful spontaneity.) The trouble was to find an excuse. Captain and Mrs. Eric Sinclair provided one.

Though not long past midnight, the thing was going with a swing. The floor was a good one; the band half inebriated; everybody knew everybody else to the point of Christian names; and all the children—the prettiest children, the best-dressed children, the best behaved and most entertaining children—seemed perfectly happy. Not merely happy—excited, thrilled. Here was one of the last of a long series of " boy-and-girl " dances that had extended all through a London summer; and although there had sometimes been two or even three a night, the thing had not palled. Rather had the flame been fanned; and beneath the free-and-easy surface, the perfect flippancy, a discerning person might have discovered a note almost fierce, a kind of hunger, a kind of reckless craving and endeavour.

Under the electric light the eyes of the girls were daring with laughter—the girls in their variegated satin gowns, the colours strikingly slashed and intermingled; the eyes of their youthful partners less expressive but with the same gleam of uncontrollable excitement. In their dark blue uniforms with the broad scarlet stripe down the trousers, gold buttons, and stiff collar, the young officers of the Guards and Cavalry looked handsome. Others in evening dress were no doubt on leave from the front. Not many of the old Maryon " clan " were present; they did not patronise such youthful entertainments. In a variety of contortions, in a medley of twirls, twists, runs, turns, half-turns, dips, side-walks, rushes, and reverses, the twenty or thirty couples gyrated round the peculiar Maryon drawing-room. The musicians —black fellows and drunk—made all sounds but of harmony or music. They shouted, sang, stamped on the floor; played

madly, madly on their banjolines and castanets. They
thumped the drum, thumped each other, made sounds like
fog-horns, whistled—dramatically threw the sticks away and
stopped.

Everybody stopped.

Eric and Faith stopped. Like many others, they hoped the
dance would not end. Clapping their hands, everybody
called out for more. And the band began again.

§ 2

"Oh! my dears, isn't it hot. I'm exhausted!" Gina
Maryon descended upon a group that comprised Eric, Faith,
Upton, Rosemary Meynell, and Arthur Cornwallis, making a
gesture, as though to stand up was a feat almost beyond physical
capacity. "Rosebud, my darling, *what* a rather lovely frock!
Is it Manille? I thought so. . . . Drink, children! Drink!
Eat, drink, and be merry, lest to-morrow—ye die!"

They were standing beside the impromptu buffet that had
been set up uncomfortably in a recess of the hall.

Arthur Cornwallis politely filled everybody's glass.

"Your very good health!" he said, raising his to Eric and
Faith.

The glasses clinked all round.

"To the married couple! Long life and happiness!"

"What about the unmarried couple?" cried Gina. "I
drink to them!"

Everybody laughed.

"Don't anticipate events, it's unlucky." said Rosemary,
laughing too. The laugh was on her lips; there was none in her
eyes. Eric watched her.

"Why is it unlucky to anticipate?" he inquired. He was
not just then disposed to let the subject drop.

"I deny it's unlucky. Anticipation is the breath of life,"
answered Gina.

"But hardly fair to love," interjected Upton. "I thought you were one of those broad-minded people who believe that——"

"All's fair in love and war," put in Eric, addressing Upton directly. He detested this type of conversation, and was coldly furious at being thrown in the fellow's company; he was determined to be rude. Faith threw him a restraining glance.

"Don't be a fool, Harry," said Rosemary, adding, "But how nice to be all together again!"

"All?" murmured Eric, staring hard and straight at her. Perhaps it was the cruel streak in him.

Rosemary coloured and looked away quickly.

"We've had great fun this summer, though, spite of your wars and rumours of wars," Gina prattled. "Faith you *are* a mad creature to bury yourself in that hospital and appear at the end of everything—even amid a peal of wedding bells. You can't *think* what a lot you've missed."

"I had to help mother."

"Help mother! Mother's-help, you mean. It's inhuman. It's not possible. You're just not going back there, though." She turned to Eric. "The thing must be seen to, Eric. It must be taken in hand. She's wasting 'er bloomin' youth!"

"But, Gina, you forget I rather like it on the whole," Faith protested; "at least, I have so far. All the same, I'm looking round for a doll's house now, if anybody can produce one."

"You *must* take a house, Faith," Rosemary urged with what seemed to Eric a rather insincere enthusiasm. "And why not come into the Italian tableaux? We're just beginning rehearsals."

"Mrs. Sinclair would make a divine St. Ursula for the Carpaccio thing," suggested Upton. "Of course, she's a Madonna," he said in an undertone to Gina.

"I think not, thanks" replied Faith—for her, shortly.

"Aren't you afraid she might put her foot on—in it?" queried Eric. Faith cast at him another imploring glance.

" I'm sure Mr. Upton would design you a halo or a background with equal facility," he added, turning to his wife.   This referred to the young poet's newly-acquired talent for designing fancy dresses to which Gina Maryon had lately been drawing the company's attention.

Upton smiled defiantly.

" You'll help, anyway, won't you, Arthur ? " demanded Gina.

" Oh ! of course, I'd love to," replied Cornwallis from the background.   He was Gina's latest protégé.   Already she had roped him in to the Maryon circle, while into the constellation of " Rays " and " Stars " she had roped his poetry.   He had " plenty in him," she declared—only he wanted drawing out."

At this moment a tall, thin, gliding woman with the face of a ghost and large-pupilled dark eyes, strikingly but scantily attired in jewels and embroidery, sailed up.

" Gina," she remarked, " I want food."

" Venetia, my angel ! " the young lady of the house exclaimed in tones of treble amazement, pointing dramatically at three lonely sandwiches that sat on a plate in the middle of the completely denuded buffet.   " You don't expect to find food in this house !   Haven't you brought anything with you— in a paper bag ?   You might know by now there *never* is anything to eat at these gatherings.   But have these "—she proffered the sandwiches—" and welcome, as they say.   And if you want to damn anybody, damn the Food Controller."

" Damn the Food Controller, then ! " exclaimed Mrs. Romane passionately.   " But he can't prevent one drinking champagne.   Any oysters ? "

Music had now begun again, and the group broke up.

Mrs. Romane marshalled to her side a certain young soldier-politician whom she had " in tow."   Rosemary and Eric went off to dance together.   Faith and Cornwallis followed suit.   Gina, for her part, declared that she was far too hot and exhausted to dance.

"Come along, Harry!" she cried. "We'll go up to my *appartement* and have a talk. That's the only quiet place."

And upstairs they went, brushing past several sitting couples, up two flights of the crooked, unmannerly stairs of those lesser London houses.

It was a very small room, Gina's own; it looked like the inside of a biscuit-box, the walls and ceiling being silver-papered, without picture, ornament, or relief. Severity—simplicity, were the topical keynote of the Maryon "cult." It was, she explained to people, a reaction from a renaissance decorative style that had prevailed for nearly a year. The artistic life of the Clan Maryon, indeed, subsisted on reactions. So this room was just black and silver. An immense black divan with large round black cushions occupied the whole of one side. The carpet was black. There was a black lacquer cabinet at the farther end. On the black mantelpiece were three silver-wrought images—two Madonnas and a crucifix. The writing-table was black, relieved by a gleam of silver, and so were the chairs.

"You haven't seen it since it was done up, have you, my Harry?" said Gina sprawling on the capacious sofa. "Isn't it *rather* attractive?"

"You always had a feeling for atmosphere, Gina. Black has a wonderful sense effect   One could create here—wonderfully.   One could dream—and, what's more, one could think."

"Give me a cigarette," she said. "One of the new ones."

"You like them—the new ones? They're strong. All right for me, but look out they don't send you off. She had one the other evening—the little wretch, she insisted on it. It sent her straight off to sleep."

"Who—our Rosebud?"

"Yes. I'm sorry we gave her so much as a hint of it that night; she's—such an infant."

"Why, the Rosebud's not—smitten, is she?"

" She's always asking to see your birthday present." He laughed and produced from his waistcoat-pocket a small gold-enamelled snuff-box of the Louis Quatorze period. " It's ever since that night, you know. But I only give her the cigarettes."

Gina said, " Give it me ! " opened the box, took a pinch as one takes snuff, and handed it back. " You must get me some," she added. " I've nearly run out."

" Be careful, though, for God's sake, with—her. One doesn't want——"

" Talking ? I agree. She's very much of a child still, isn't she—an adorable child ? But I suppose you're—educating her ? "

" I spend most of the time looking at her. That head and neck—the profile—it's a dream."

" You're happy together, then ? Don't forget who you owe it all to ! "

" I owe it to—the one and only——"

He took one of her hands, and pressed it.

" And so it's all comfortably settled ? "

" Practically."

" Practically ? " There was a note of surprise, real or simulated, in her voice.

" Well—it's understood, I think——"

" But not absolutely ? "

" You see, she's such a child. She doesn't know her own mind. It would never do to force the pace——"

" What about Lady C. ? "

" She's all over it. She's all right."

" Wants your money, I suppose ? "

" Oh, well, Gina ! Hang it—really ! " The remark was obviously not a palatable one. " Don't put things quite so crudely."

The volatile creature took no notice.

" Still I don't get there. . . . She's fond of you ? "

" Of course. She's got a temper, though. I tell you, she's a little spitfire sometimes. It's part of her attraction, I suppose. But—in time—I think she'll understand me."

" What's the difficulty then ? "

" I don't think she knows herself. She can't make up her mind."

" But you are taking her in hand ? "

" I try to. You'd do it better, though. I must say she is rather perverse. One mentions art or music or poetry and she answers in terms of fox-hunting and salmon-fishing. One shows her a Matisse or a Vlaminck, and she says it looks like a picture-puzzle upside-down. Well——! " Upton spread the palms of his hands with a hopeless gesture. " However, I think in time she'll understand things."

" She liked ' Rays '—and ' Stars.' "

" Yes—and didn't understand a word of them."

" She's in love with you, though—with us—with all of us ? "

" She's in love with excitement."

He lit another cigarette, and then they sat very close together. The heavy scent that filled the room sank like a velvet pall about them. They revelled in such moments. He convulsively squeezed her arm.

" I adore this perfume," he said.

" I think I shall marry you after all."

" Nobody's ever understood me as you have, Gina. "

" And so you'll go and marry her and forget all about me? " She held him with her violet eyes.

" Never that," he declared. " I couldn't. You've taught me—a lifetime. But—why wouldn't you have me . . . then ? "

" Because I knew I had got you already," she answered promptly.

There was a pause during which they sat very close together. Gina said unexpectedly :

" What about the ' also ran ' ? "

" Knoyle ? "

" Yes."

Upton laughed.

" Washed out."

" Completely ? "

" Utterly."

" Never mentioned ? "

" Never mentioned. Why do you ask ? "

" You scored there ! "

" Yes." A self-satisfied smile crossed his unhealthy face, and the two lustreless eyes shone. " Yes—I think—I scored there."

" Quite sure ? "

" Well—— ! "

" You wouldn't have pulled it off without me, you know."

" Perhaps not——"

" It's really I who've scored."

" How ? "

" Never mind. 'A woman never forgets.' Is that Marie Corelli or Ethel M. Dell ? It's true."

" And never forgives ? "

" Oh, yes ! When the scores are level—with a balance on the right side ! "

" You defeat me, *ma chère* Gina."

" Oh, well ! It's my affair. And now. . . . I'm not sure whether I'm sorry."

" For him ? "

" N-n-n-o. I don't think—for him."

" He was mad about her."

" Funny boy. Queer mixture of weakness and strength, cleverness, quixotry, childishness. I've never quite got to the bottom of him."

" Oh ! He's—a fool."

" I wonder."

" He might have married her——"

" If he'd stayed at home."

Upton, nettled, rapped out :

" No—she simply didn't care enough for him to stick to him."

" I think—I rather admire him."

The young man's eyes shot malice. But he did not have time to reply. Gina purred :

" So you still like little me . . . a little bit ? "

She glanced up at him sideways like a bird. Her old love responded.

" More—a little more than that. After all—you're Gina."

He leant across and kissed her on the lips.

§ 3

The handle of the door turned and both started back. They acted perfectly, and when Rosemary and Eric entered were discussing the Italian tableaux.

Gina, as though breaking off the subject, said :

" End of a dance, Rosebud ? "

" No, we've just come to sit it out. I'm going soon, Harry."

" Let's have a dance, Gina."

" Yes, Eric dear. The one after next ? "

" Thank you."

" Come on, Harry ! We'll go down."

Rosemary and Eric took the previous couple's place on the black divan.

Another couple entered and took possession of two chairs at the farther end of the room. Eric said :

" What a weird room this is ! I haven't been up here before. Why does she fill it with this horrible scent ? "

" Don't you like it ? " Rosemary looked round indifferently. " She' says it makes one *feel*. It makes me—sleepy . . . I'm not sure I do like it, though."

For several minutes they did not speak. They were content to listen to the snatches of conversation that reached them from the other end of the room.

" You've heard about Dick and Sybil ? " She was what

is called *ingénue* in "simple white"; he a mere boy. "I think it's all fixed up. You know they disappeared for hours at Ranelagh and turned up looking frightfully self-conscious ? Of course, that put the lid on it."

She laughed—"girlishly."

"Everybody was *so* cross at being kept waiting. It's been the talk of London ever since."

The voices wandered off into something else. Rosemary and Eric smiled without speaking.

Rosemary said :

"That's exactly the way we used to talk three years ago, Eric—and you used to do tricks with matches and glasses of water and knives and forks and things. Remember ? "

"I suppose we—I mean I—did. I'm ashamed of myself ! "

"Oh, you were very infantile, Eric ! What a lot's happened since ! I wish it hadn't," she sighed. "I suppose it's the war. You've changed. I've changed."

Another fragment of talk came to their ears.

". . . Oh ! That affair ! Of course, you've been away. That came to an end ages ago. Violet broke it off. Oh ! no particular reason. You know what she is. Besides, it's the fashion. He's one of the dull, faithful sort. I suppose she just got bored with having him hanging about. . . . But come along ! I can't resist this divine tune."

The two on the sofa glanced at each other with that involuntary movement which often results from a simultaneous thought. Eric looked quickly away. He felt uncomfortable. It was difficult ground.

"Eric, old boy," said Rosemary suddenly. "I'm so awfully glad about you and Faith."

"Yes—we're lucky," he agreed.

"You deserve to be. You're a wonderful person. I've been wanting to see you—to talk to you."

His blue eyes opened wide.

"Charmingly said. But why ? "

" You're a wonderful friend."

" Well—one hopes so."

" That's where you are wonderful. I think you could carry the world on your shoulders—and all the little people in it."

" I'm not Hercules, my dear Rosemary—or was it Atlas ? "

" After all that's happened. . . ."

" Still—what ? " But he guessed.

" You know about us—Adrian and me ? You must "

" Oh ! . . . that." He shifted his feet uneasily.

" Eric, I couldn't speak to anybody but you about it. I know he tells you everything, and we've—we've known each other such ages, haven't we ? "

" Of course we have. I'm his friend and I'm yours."

" Well, I've never had a moment's peace since—since that dreadful time. All this rushing, racketing life—it's nothing to me, and yet—it's everything. It's necessary to me, I can't do without it. All these people—I don't know whether I really like them—or what. They're not the people I was brought up with. But I can't get away from them. They're necessary to me, too. I want to forget—forget—forget—I don't know what—just everything——"

" My dear Rosemary——" Eric felt he must gain time to deal with the situation. " It's over and done with now, any-way—isn't it ? Why worry ? "

" *Is* it over and done with ? " She spoke hurriedly, intensely, and with a strange sorrowful passion. " *Is* it ? That's what I want to know. Can things—of that sort—ever be over and done with between—two people—like him and me ? "

Eric began fingering his moustache. He was thoroughly perplexed, unprepared alike for an outburst or a confession. He did not know what to say or how to say it. He glanced at his companion uneasily and was disturbed by the change in her face and voice. Fresh, yes, and beautiful she still was, yet a change was unmistakably there. Gone the old simplicity, the old gaiety—yet not entirely gone. Gone the old challenging independence—yet, at moments there. He even thought he detected a trace of some cosmetic on cheeks and lips, a hint of something unnatural about the eyes. Knowledge and a suggestion of painful experience had taken the place of innocence in this girl's face.

"*Is* it over and done with?" she repeated. "I can't make up my mind till I *know* that. I cannot — and I will not. . . . But if anything should happen—to either of us, Eric—I should like him to know how I feel—that I do feel about it. If he knew . . . if he knew . . . he'd understand. He must have suffered, Eric. No one who cared for me as he did—— He did care desperately."

"He did." Eric was in no mood to spare her. She flinched at his crude brevity.

"Somehow"—a wistful, almost foreboding look crossed her face—"somehow we always just missed each other, he and I. I dunno—the world's such a queer place. People seem to be always—just missing—or just crossing. . . . I never got to the deepest depths in him. There's something dreamy and far-off about him sometimes, and he used to come out with things I didn't understand. I failed him there, too. . . . He never understood me either—quite. It's only in the last month or two I've begun to understand myself. The war's revealed such a lot—the real nature of people and things and —oneself. It's made one think—and it's made one dread to think. We're queer, of course—all the Meynells are. Well, you know the family history? . . . I s'pose I'm queer too."

"Oh, nonsense, my dear Rosemary, nonsense!"

"We just missed each other—somehow. But I want him to know that always, always he's something different and apart to me—from anybody else—even if he can't ever forgive me—ever."

"Of course, he'll forgive you—if he hasn't already."

"I'm not so sure. I'm not so sure he even ought to."

"I'll talk to him. I'll tell him all you've said."

"Thank you, Eric. I shall be happier."

Up the stairs and through the open door floated the strains of a valse, thinly rendered by a mandoline. And a girl's voice sang.

"That must be Gina," Eric suggested. "The band's gone to supper, I suppose."

They listened in silence—Rosemary intently.

"Oh, Eric!" she whispered presently, "that's the thing we danced to—he and I—at the Astoria years ago. And he asked the name of it—and now—I can't remember." Her fingers, clasping and unclasping, betrayed her agitation. "He said it haunted him. . . . To me, it's like an echo of his voice, but—I can't remember."

"Let's go and dance to it," said Eric briefly.

He did not look at her, did not need to. He had heard in her voice the knell of a great illusion; he apprehended her great mistake.

§ 4

They danced. All danced. But to the accompaniment of the girl's weak singing and the solitary mandoline, there seemed no joy of music in the room, only the pattering feet of ghosts or autumn leaves that swirl on any garden path.

When it was over there was clapping. Rosemary and Eric descended to the hall. Upton stood waiting.

"I've got a taxi," he said. "It's raining."

"Raining?" A sort of tired disillusionment spoke in the girl's voice, though she had recovered her self-possession. "Well, anyway, let's go. . . . I'm tired."

One of those rapid changes so characteristic of the English climate had taken place. And instead of the sultry summer night, a cold air came creeping into the house through the wide-open door, and they could hear the plash of the rain without.

Farewells were said. When they were in the taxicab and splashing homeward, Upton sat close to Rosemary, as earlier he had sat close to Gina, and took her hand.

"Give me a hug, my Rosebud," he purred. "You look beautiful beyond words to-night."

Her reply was almost impatient. "No, Harry. You can do something for me, though. I want to sleep. I want to dream. I want to be happy. . . . Give me some of that—delicious stuff that makes one forget."

"Was ums tired, then ? It isn't good for little girls, though."

"I don't mind. Only give me some."

"It's a bargain, then," he laughed.

"Oh ! very well," she answered wearily.

From his waistcoat pocket Upton produced the Louis Quatorze snuffbox.

"There. That's for a naughty girl."

She took a long, deep breath as Gina Maryon had done—but a longer and a deeper one—until he tried to snatch the box away.

"No, Harry ! Give it me ! Let me keep it," she pleaded. "I want it." There was a struggle. "Oh, do, please ! Make me a present of it ! "

"Well, then, you'll have to pay for it. . . . A kiss. Two kisses. . . . Half a dozen kisses. . . . As many as I want ! "

He laughed vibrantly, holding her hands, which still clasped the snuff-box.

"Oh ! no, Harry ! Just . . . give it me ! "

"But why should I, little tyrant ? It's not good for children—or angels."

"Well—out of friendship."

"Friendship has its obligations and—rewards ! "

"No, Harry—please ! . . ."

"One can't have anything for nothing in this world, my Rosebud. And that little box is worth a lot of money."

"I know. But give it me, Harry ! "

" On conditions."

" No, Harry—don't be horrid ! "

" On conditions."

The taxicab was slowing up.

" Here we are at Grosvenor Mansions."

" Oh, well . . . dash it ! "

Leaning out of the window, he ordered the cabman to drive to another address.

* * * * *

Within the House of Maryon the dance went on.

Black shadows were thrown upon white blinds, so that to one watching from without it might have seemed that spectre danced with spectre, shadow with shadow, ghost with ghost— all belonging to a world not of this world.

Like ghosts or spectres the dancers swirled, dipped, and ran—turned and turned as the music called to them. Once or twice they stopped, then went on again.

" Way down in Tennessee." " Down where that Swanee river flows "—the ragtime music lured them, mocked at them or beckoned. The black men sang—sang of the old days and the cotton fields and the slow, warm gloaming of their native South, their love and the rising moon. They shouted, called out, stamped on the floor, played madly, madly on their banjolines and castanets. They thumped the drum, thumped each other, made sounds like fog-horns, whistled, threw the sticks away—and stopped.

All stopped.

Two lovers, caught up in a dream, wrapt in their youth, immersed in one another. . .

Pale and sickly grew the lights ; pale and ashen-grey, the faces. . . . Drab daylight stumblin in.

CHAPTER IV

Their Awakening

In spite of the early hour—barely seven-thirty—Victoria Station wore an air of bustle and animation.

Rain was still falling. The roofs of the taxicabs glistened, and their wheels thrust through the mud with that hiss which is so characteristic of a wet morning in London. The drivers wore shiny capes, as did the policemen at the station entrance; all who alighted wore waterproofs or coats.

The station was lively with khaki; parties of men in heavy marching order, carrying rifles and small bags or packages, officers wearing bulky haversacks, no two alike, yet all partaking of a similar air of imminent departure; relations and friends, the predominant note among whom was black.

There was a great deal of noise—engines shrieking, steam escaping, whistles blowing, orders being shouted, newspaper-boys calling, bells clanging. " This way to Number One leave train ! " or " This way to the breakfast train ! " All these sounds were multiplied by the high vault of the station roof.

Through the crowds, without hurry, Captain and Mrs. Eric Sinclair made their way. The former, in uniform, carried a newspaper in his hand, wore a waterproof, and had a haversack slung on his shoulder. Trim, polished, and alert, he looked as though he had made a leisurely toilet after a long night's rest. Faith wore a tweed coat and skirt. They walked the length of the train until they reached the breakfast car, in which Captain Sinclair, who had previously reserved a seat, deposited the haversack, the waterproof, and the newspaper.

He then descended to the platform and stood beside his wife. A number of other officers stood around, conversing with friends who bore the unmistakable stamp of farewell upon their faces. But it was characteristic of these two, newly-made man and wife, that they betrayed no emotion —might, to all outward appearance, have been setting out to spend a week-end at Brighton. Beyond the broad semi-circle formed by the span of the station-roof, they looked out at the straight, slow rain and the murky London gloom, into which countless lines of shiny metal disappeared.

"Have you got the chocolate and sandwiches, Eric ? "

"Yes."

"And the flask ? "

"Yes."

"And the little locket ? "

"Of course." He patted his chest.

"By the time you come home I shan't have any hair left." Faith smiled.

Captain Sinclair lit a cigarette.

"Give my love to Adrian," his wife said.

"I will. And by the way—but I can't tell you here. I'll write. . . . Rosemary," he urged ; "be a pal to her. She wants one."

"Yes—if she'll let me."

There was a renewed bustle, redoubled shouting. A bell rang.

"Take your seats, please ! "

Captain Sinclair turned to his wife.

"It's good-bye, my dear."

"Yes, Eric." She spoke with a kind of meekness, as though there finally surrendering her life into his keeping.

"Take care of yourself. Don't work too hard."

"Eric ! "

In this word the world. . . .

He climbed into the car, others pressing after him.

A whistle blew, doors were slammed.

" Good-bye ! . . . Good-bye ! . . . Good-bye ! "

Two pairs of blue eyes met in a long last glance. Two hearts silently bled.

That was Reality.

The train glided slowly out of the station. The women hid their faces behind veils, handkerchiefs, hands. The rain fell. . . .

Outward bound, the men made a hearty show over breakfast.

CHAPTER V

Their Morrow

§ 1

THIRTY-SIX hours had passed.

The Third Battle of Ypres had broken out, more fierce, more relentless than any conflict since the Somme.

It was evening, and still raining.

Eric Sinclair's company, as part of the battalion in reserve, was lying in recently-captured German trenches along the eastern bank of the Yser Canal. Eric himself had just arrived and, with Adrian Knoyle, was about to take the company into action, Burns and Fotheringay being left out, the former in reserve, the latter laid low with trench-fever.

The company-commander was sitting under a dangerously tilted piece of zinc, addressing his non-commissioned officers, as was his habit before battle. All around lay broken rifles, pieces of equipment, shreds of clothing, bombs, grenades, food-tins, every sign, in fact, of a hurried evacuation on the part of the Germans. There was, indeed, hardly a square foot of ground that had not been churned up by a shell.

"We are going up," Eric said in concluding his little address, "to consolidate the objective captured to-day, that is, the line of the Steenbeek river. We may get shelled on the way. We shall have to be careful and quiet, and ready for anything. We shall have to dig like the devil. There'll probably be a counter-attack. At seven-fifty we move. Packs on!"

They tramped off by platoons. At the same time the rain ceased, and the late sun began to cast fretful beams across the vast battlefield. The evening was quiet. An occasional shell whined drearily overhead but seldom fell near. Small parties of men passed—men coming out of the battle, filthy, nerve-shaken, and scarcely able to drag their feet through the mud. Guides, orderlies, and pack-mules passed at first. Then, as they struck out across the grey waste, picking their way in single file, all sign or suggestion of life vanished. Socket-like shell-holes whose sunken eye-balls were discoloured glistening pools, gaped and grinned on either hand. They passed through a wood, the trees of which resembled skeletons, skeletons of giant men, maimed, killed, and rotted where they stood, stark upright except for those that had fallen, crushed down by superhuman force.

Soon the laden men called for a halt. "Halt and close up!" "Pass the word down when you're all closed up!" These were the oft-repeated cries.

Eric Sinclair marched with the leading platoon, Adrian with the hindermost. The latter was plunged in thought, immersed in the atmosphere of his surroundings. As though to reflect the complexion of these thoughts, his gaze presently lit upon the recumbent figure of a dead soldier lying in a shell-hole. It was a complete picture of human loneliness. The man had been forgotten, the burial parties had passed him by. He lay, as he had fallen, backwards, the golden light of a stormy sunset shining full upon his face—the arms thrown out—the legs slightly apart—the fighting order meticulously exact even to the respirator at the "alert" and the grenades sticking out of his pockets—the rifle lying a few feet away as it had dropped from his hand—the steel helmet on its crown as it had rolled from his head.

The rest trudged on phlegmatically, not even noticing so common an object, but Adrian's mind dwelt upon the figure, embodiment of his thoughts through so many months. At first he tried to call it back to being, to evolve its beginnings and its personality, to envisage the things that had once made it human, to rekindle, as it were, the cold ashes of its life. Was this a lively man perhaps, much given to laughter; was he a great talker or a wag, townsman or countryman—the latter, to judge by build and features; a peasant, perhaps, from some remote English village like his own, where the hills watch, steeped in the age-long passion of the soil? Had he those—a father or mother, sweetheart or wife—who through five-and-twenty years perchance had doted upon that once-mobile face, upon every hair of that bare, bedraggled head, upon that once-eager body now of the clay clay, so soon to return to the soil again? Held he but a few hours since in his living heart, the hopes, the lookings-backward, the solemn terror of ordinary men; and as the dark drew on and as the midnight before last crept towards dawn, had he said to some comrade, "Well, if I come through this——"

The darkening landscape presented itself to Adrian as some seared and dreadful human face wrought by its passions, horrors and sins to a last extremity.

With bowed heads and backs, he (and they all) trudged on like figures of the Christ in Ghirlandaio's Procession to Calvary, the rifle of each being his cross.

§ 2

They waded through semi-liquid mud. It grew dark. The guide was not confident of his way: who could be in that trackless waste? A caution was passed down to move quietly. Occasional shots were heard and once or twice a stray bullet droned overhead. A wild moon rose.

Quite suddenly—a ditch full of men. Whispering and strung-up now, they lay down on the top of the ground, fearing to be seen in the moonlight; those in the ditch clambered out. The enemy's outposts were reported to be not more than a hundred yards away. The situation was hurriedly explained to Captain Sinclair by an impatient, overwrought officer; then the relieved company filed out. The half-dug ditch being in three sections, there was not room for all. Some would have to stay outside till the digging began. It was difficult to discern anything at first. Only a row of splintered trees forty or fifty yards in front indicated the whereabouts of a small stream. A road glistening white descended the slope behind and cut the trench-line. At a German blockhouse of reinforced concrete some two hundred yards in rear the company-commander established his headquarters. It was a mere cell, stoutly constructed but facing the enemy; its narrow seat barely offered room for two.

Midnight approached. It was imperative before daylight, Eric said, to make trenches of the ditches, to deepen and connect them up, to find out the lie of the land, to get in touch with the companies on right and left, to find out just what lay in front. The Germans, doubtless not wishing their whereabouts to be discovered, remained silent; they even sent up no lights. Opposite the Left Flank company's sector was a bridgehead where it was decided to place an outpost.

Very soon the men were strung out in a long shadowy line. Their stooping, moiling figures could be seen working at the ditch. The clink of the spades became the dominant sound.

Adrian and Eric, taking an orderly, made a detailed examination of the line, trying to get their bearings, trying to make contact with other units. In this they failed, for the sector appeared to be an isolated one, its flanks in the air. They only found a black, motionless stream bordered by stunted willows, which grinned gnomishly. Once, creeping through wastes of shell-pitted, ashen grass, three Germans sprang up like startled hares on a downland pasture. A voice shouted, " Was ist dass ! " and a revolver shot was fired before they disappeared into the shadows. Eric's runner fell wounded.

It was near daylight when they reached their tiny blockhouse and told the men to leave off work.

§ 3

Overcome by weariness, after the routine reports had been sent off, the two friends fell into a deep sleep on the narrow seat of their little den. They awoke to the full light of day. The cool quiet of night had given place to a harsh glare, to the buzzing of bluebottles, to a noisome stench and heat. Nor was this stench the usual stench of that nether-world, but something more fœtid, clinging, something from which there was no escape. The guns were thundering. They seemed tuned to different pitches and different rates of firing—the rapid bark of the field-guns, the deep-toned echoing reports of the howitzers, followed by rapidly-succeeding concussions. So with the shells, which never ceased to whistle and race overhead. In their crude symphony they struck all keys, now whining and almost plaintive, now creaking and hollow in sound, now roaring like an express train. Those which burst close at hand were scarcely noticed amid the universal din. Only when an explosion occurred within forty or fifty yards there came a crash and the earth quaked beneath the unsupported concrete shelter, which itself trembled from top to bottom.

All through that day a sense of foreboding, of imminent personal catastrophe, never left Adrian. If anything it increased as the hours went by. There was the perpetual threat of a counter-attack, of course, but with Eric beside him he felt no apprehension on that score. Eric's presence alone gave an extraordinary sense of competence and security. He sat curled up in his corner, dozing or sleeping. There had as yet been no opportunity for conversation between them, the company-commander having returned from leave only an hour or two before they marched away. He was obviously very tired.

Yet as though in response to his friend's thoughts, Eric now woke up.

" What about some food ? "

A couple of sandbags contained all their comestibles and cooking utensils. One by one these were extracted. Water to make tea and boil the eggs ; how to heat it ? A patent spirit-cooker : how to light it ? And such an abominable conglomeration in a sandbag as never was known ! The salt and the sugar had merged in one ; the tea and the marmalade had joined forces ; the margarine had formed an illicit association with the candles ; the bread had assumed a delicate sulphur shade as the result of intercourse with Flanders mud. What squalor ! What distaste ! Sandbags, mud, paper, tins, and the remains of food ! Eric nursed the spirit-cooker on his lap ; Adrian tended it. The water would not boil but it simmered, yes, it simmered. Into it they plunged the eggs, then the tea.

" *What* a mix-up ! " said Eric with a laugh. " I must say I prefer it to Gina Maryon's supper, though."

" Bad, was it ? "

" There wasn't any."

" Oh ! well, life's all hogwash and this is a pig-sty," Adrian remarked gloomily. He never even pretended to see the funny side of squalor.

" Better hogwash than hunger. And very soon you'll be chanking your stars for the pig-sty. Cheer up, you confounded old pessimist ! "

No sooner had Eric said this than heavy shelling began. A couple of high-explosives hit the ground with a roar and a thud just outside the entrance to the blockhouse, without bursting. Smaller shells—the sort known in the Army as " pip-squeaks " and " whizz-bangs "—burst in quick succession close behind it. Shrapnel cracked repeatedly above the trenches in front where the men lay. German aeroplanes like huge hornets with red, black, and white bodies and fish-tails appeared flying low over the line, and, following upon the " tac-tac " of machine-guns, flights of bullets came "pinging" to earth. Eric put his head out and making a funnel with his hands, yelled in the direction of the trench line.

" Shoot, there! Shoot back at 'em! What in God's name are you doing? Lost your rifles, or what? "

He himself seized his orderly's rifle which happened to be leaning against the blockhouse-wall and started blazing at the nearest aeroplane until Adrian pulled him inside.

" Do you want to get sniped? " he demanded angrily, " because it bores me seeing you do that sort of thing."

Eric's impulsive exposures of himself always irritated him ; it was Eric's one weakness and, Adrian often thought, would lead to his destruction. Soon a rattle of musketry and the " rat-tat-tat-tat " of the Lewis guns proclaimed that the company-commander's exhortation had had the desired effect. The aeroplanes sheered off, and the British artillery, near and far, began to roar and roll until there was such a vast chorus as presaged unmistakably the beginning of a general engagement.

A large red face shading to purple now peered in at the narrow entry ; it was that of the Company Sergeant-Major.

"Them last shells fell very close, sir," he stuttered, a note of alarm in his voice ; " it looks like big show beginning."

" We're warned to expect a counter-attack, you know," Eric answered. " Get the S.O S. ready and keep a sharp look-out on the trench. Blow your whistle if you see anything. They won't attack before dusk. Say the Lord's Prayer and drink your rum ration! "

" Sir! "

The brilliant countenance turned away without a smile.

" Wait a minute—are you pretty well off in front there? "

" As well as anywhere, sir. I think you'd be safer there,

too. It's only the back-bursting shells can touch you. This place won't keep out a whizz-bang."

" Oh, well !—we've only one life to lose. We'll stay here for the present."

The face withdrew.

" Lord ! " yawned Eric, stretching himself, " I must get another forty winks. Then you can have a turn. Wake me if anything happens."

He curled up again and shut his eyes.

But a good deal of Eric's *sang-froid* on these occasions was simulated, as Adrian had long since discovered. And from the fact that his friend's eyes soon opened again, though he did not move, he knew that Eric had no intention of sleeping.

There was reason for anxiety. As a unit they were completely cut off. Behind, on either side, the bare open *glacis* of the Salient extending for three miles ; in front a massing enemy with only the narrow Steenbeek stream between. The field telephone was cut by shell-fire ; no runner was likely to survive the intervening curtain of shells.

" Keep well into your corner, Adrian ! "

The foundations of their concrete dwelling trembled as three big shells burst outside in quick succession. Reddish-brown iron splinters drove hissing-hot into the mud at their feet and pattered upon the concrete roof ; loose earth and stones came rattling down like hail.

Always the sun glared pitilessly upon that stricken spot. The guns never ceased to roar and boom, the buzz of the bluebottles at their scavenging made a mocking monotone. The two officers became more and more aware of the stench that grew with the noonday heat, deriving as it did from human bodies and poisoned earth, from clinging fumes of gas, from a mixture of mud, old sand-bags, stale food and stagnant water. Did they look out, they saw beside their shelter a greenish slimy pit from which a German boot and a German leg protruded—mute reminder of that which formed part of the sucking mud beneath. The pill-box must have been captured after a bloody fight; they became aware that its immediate neighbourhood was littered with the sodden dead. Here the lethal gas had reached them, hither maimed and failing the defenders had dragged themselves to die. Here at last the British infantry must have bayonetted or shot them down as, darting out, they threw up their hands and shouted for mercy.

Nor was it long before wounded men began to trickle back. Some irrational idea that they would be safer near their company-commander seemed to possess them. Arms shattered by shrapnel, wounded heads, fragments of flesh torn from legs and bodies—little of the legendary stoicism of the battlefield was here. They whimpered, groaned, and moaned while the stretcher-bearers dressed their wounds behind the blockhouse. They called for water and relief from their pain.

The two officers took it in turns to keep watch. As far as could be seen the battle was raging along the whole front. Grey smoke eddied across the landscape, white puffs of smoke flecked the blue sky. In the foreground, a shattered house or two of the village of Langemarck showed through flame-shot smoke. Now the English shells came racing, racing, roaring and hissing overhead as though fearful of not reaching their goal; now the German. The British field-guns began to fire short, killing and wounding their own men but there were no means of communication until dark. All calibres, all sizes, all keys of sound and rhythm. How they hurried, how grimly pursued one another! Great iron cases of explosive—twelve-inch calibre and larger—plunged into the ruins of Langemarck, throwing up at one time as many as a dozen brick-red or sulphur-yellow columns of dust, masonry, and earth fifty or sixty feet towards the sky.

Alone of any building the tower of the church defied smoke

and flame, friend and foe alike, silently lifting its scarred white finger in protest up to heaven.

§ 4

Thus the afternoon wore by. The two friends sat side by side in their blockhouse, occasionally looking out and, through field-glasses, watching the bombardment. They spoke little.

Towards evening a lull came, and they talked.

" I hate this uncertainty." Adrian lit a cigarette.

" I think it's bound to come at dusk or daybreak," said Eric. " I only wish we'd dug out the flanks and linked up last night. It's those two gaps I'm afraid of."

" We shall have to stop 'em in front, if we stop 'em at all."

" Well, that wiring Number Fourteen Platoon did is pretty good. That ought to make 'em think if they try to get through there."

" Yes, and they've got to cross the river."

They did not speak again for several minutes. Adrian was thinking.

" All this must be pretty damnable for you, old boy," he said at length. " Why didn't you get a stomach-ache and stay a bit longer ? A ' pill-box ' on the Steenbeek is not the best way of rounding off a honeymoon."

" Yes, it's a bit rough at first, this—after that. . . . But of course it couldn't last for ever."

Eric, too, lit a cigarette with some deliberation.

" You've told me nothing about the wedding yet," Adrian reminded him. " I suppose all the rank and fashion were there ? "

" Oh, yes," laughed Eric, " the ' best people ' ! "

" You spent the honeymoon at Sheringham ? "

" Yes, and gave Faith golf lessons. She ended by beating me."

" Gina Maryon gave a carouse of some sort in your honour, didn't she ? I wonder you submitted to that ! "

" I had to. The woman ordained. Faith obeyed. I was taken."

" Who was there ? The elect ? "

" No, chiefly Philistines, like ourselves. I think most of the ' chosen ' have gone back to Jerusalem or Salonika or somewhere out of the way."

" Was it amusing ? "

" Well—it was astounding. I hadn't been to any shows of that sort, you know, since the war. It fairly showed up, the —what d'you call it ?—the mentality of the Maryon crowd. One used to think of them as—well, ' scintillating ' a bit, at any rate, in the Arden days ; one was occasionally impressed by Gina's indiscretions. The other night they looked like rather overfed goldfish floating in a glass bowl. They've taken out copyright—in themselves. Gina is getting up tableaux by way of showing herself off, Upton is designing the backgrounds, and all the rest are lending a hand in the intervals of dancing and tennis. They live on a merry-go-round."

He paused and lit a cigarette.

" Frankly, I hate the whole unhealthy crowd. There's something about that house, about the girl herself, about that prodigious Venetia Romane, about all of them—I don't know —it's like sipping absinthe in a hot-house."

One name trembled on Adrian's lips. It was of no use pretending to himself or to Eric that it was utterly banished yet—or forgotten.

The same name trembled on Eric's lips. But were the surroundings and were the circumstances propitious for what he had to say ? Should he not rather wait until they came out of the line and went back ? . . .

Sinclair was debating this point in his own mind when a five-point-nine inch shell landed almost in the entrance to the blockhouse with such terrific force and so great a blow-back of air that both were hurled off their narrow seat, and the little cell became filled with gun-powdery fumes. The food, equipment, and all the squalid contents of the place were thrown together in even worse confusion than before. And when they helped each other up they saw that the whole of one end of the " pill-box " had sagged over with the subsidence of earth.

" Are you all right, Adrian ? . . . Come on, let's get out of this, or we shall have the whole damned thing on top of us."

They crawled with difficulty round to the back of the pill-box, were sniped at *en route*, and found the Company Sergeant-Major, two stretcher-bearers, an orderly, and a servant squatting in a shell-hole with the wall of the block-house as a bulwark against the blow-back of shells. A number of wounded lay near. The two officers remained there till dusk.

The bombardment intensified, and the roar of the guns from either side made connected speech out of the question. But as soon as the light had waned sufficiently to hide them from the keen eyes watching the exposed slope, they crept out into the open. The German shells had now begun to fall further back. The night sky was lit up with gun-flashes ; shells rolled through the air with a peculiar moan ; wafts of pineapple-gas came to them on a suffocating breeze. Eric gave the word to put on respirators.

With nightfall, his presentiment returned upon Adrian more strongly than ever.

A runner glided up—like a messenger from another world —with a note from Headquarters to the effect that a counter-attack on a big scale was to be expected, the Germans having been observed massing in the forest of Houthulst; and that in accordance with the defensive scheme, the line of the Steenbeek river was to be held at all costs.

§ 5

Like shadows themselves they crept through shadows down into the trench. They found the men standing to arms. The stretcher-bearers were lifting out the wounded. Three or four dead lay outside the trench.

There could be no rest. Exhausted as the men were from exposure to the full heat of the sun, parched from lack of water, and terribly tired—for the bombardment had precluded sleep and their limbs were cramped—they set to work with all the energy they could command. Somehow or another the shallow ditches had to be deepened and extended. French wire had to be run out; as on the previous night, a post was sent forward to guard the bridgehead.

They dug demoniacally. They dug with a sense of imminent peril, of complete isolation, of mutual inter-dependence. All, it was realised, depended upon good comradeship now, upon the faith of one man towards another, upon the staunchness of each to all, and of all to one—the company-commander. The bombardment gradually increased as the night wore on. Again the gas came down—mustard-scented this time, choking, warm. Their eyes began to smart; it was difficult to see. Ogres laboured in the gloom; satyrs with monstrous, swollen heads toiled with the spade; spectral shapes crept to and fro. The straining eyes of sentries kept unceasing watch through the blurred glasses of their gas-gear.

Midnight came. . . .

Adrian and Eric stood together above the line of diggers, watching the moonlit scene. All around the " banging " and " booming " of the batteries went on behind dancing pin-points of flame, whilst a couple of hundred yards away beyond the stream, beyond the naked stumps of trees, crash after crash amid showers of sparks showed where the British shells burst. Miles away towards Poperinghe bomb explosions reverberated amid a far-off humming of aeroplanes; the reflected glare of ammunition-dumps burning lit up the western sky.

As they watched, a covey of bullets suddenly whipped past their heads—one, two, three, four. The men digging paused and looked up; any new sound caused them to look up. Away to the right a splutter of rifle-fire broke out like sticks crackling on a newly-kindled fire. It spread along the further river-bank, little spurts of flame darting from the shadowy background of undergrowth. Ill-directed bullets sang high overhead. The shells began to race over in a now unbroken symphony. The voices of the guns gradually swelled into a vast reverberating chorus.

Eric turned to Adrian. "This sounds like the real thing, doesn't it?" He told the Sergeant-Major to get the men to their fire-positions.

Within seconds every man had thrown down his spade, seized his rifle, and was crouching up against the newly-made parapet. All along the line the rasp of fixing bayonets was heard, followed by the click of safety-catches being pushed forward. Bandoliers were emptied, each man laying a pile of cartridge-clips beside him on the parapet. The automatic gun-teams lay in a bunch up against their weapons, each No. 1 gunner fingering the trigger whilst the man next him a little in rear held a fresh magazine ready to jam on the post.

Excitement grew among the men. Exclamations broke out in the moments that followed such as, "Roll on, Fritz! You're going to get it hot this time," or "Give me plenty of room, Billy. I don't want to miss any," or "I'll give 'im something to take home with 'im."

Figures bent double scurried towards them through the moonlight.

"Don't fire! Don't fire! It's the post coming in from the bridgehead."

Eric intercepted them.

" Seen or heard anything ? "

" Yes, they're coming down through the fields in open order —hundreds of them. We could hear them talking." The young corporal in charge was almost incoherent with excitement. " Rejoin your platoons ! "

Eric maintained an air of detached interest in the proceedings and presently strolled off, saying that he proposed to take up his position on the road which divided the trench-sector in half and whence the whole field of action could be surveyed. Adrian jumped down into the trench among his men.

German machine-guns from half-a-dozen hitherto unsuspected points now began to reinforce the crackle of the rifles, the collective sound being a deep metallic bass. The bullets, though high, were evidently directed point-blank at the trench itself, the idea doubtless being to keep the defenders' heads down. Here and there a man sank back shot through head or chest. Coloured signal-rockets went up singly from behind the German lines. At a word from Eric the white spiral of the British S.O.S. shot up from the company-headquarters. A sound of faint shouting could be heard to their left. Now and then stray shells burst near.

No shot had yet been fired by the Left Flank Company. Through the tremendous din Eric's voice could be heard giving cautionary orders, as it had so often been heard on the field-range, and his slight figure could be seen by every man in the company silhouetted against the moon above them. " We're here, little Percy ! " " Good old Strawberries-and-Cream ! " " The old firm knows what it's abaht." Suchlike observations passed between one man and another.

Now came the sound of bombs being thrown a little way off, the gruff explosions puncturing the roar of musketry, machine-guns, and artillery.

" Hi ! Look ! They're coming ! To the left—by the

broken tree! See 'em move?—there! there! Why doesn't 'e let go? They'll be right on top of us in a minute!"

Eric's voice could still be heard.

"Steady! Wait for the word! Take aim when you fire! Don't waste your ammunition! Aim at the foot of the wire in front! Wait for the word, and then all together!"

Every man's cheek pressed against the stock of his rifle. Here and there bayonets gleamed in the moonlight. The shattering collaboration of machine-guns and artillery increased. Seconds passed. . . .

At last the word came.

"Now then! Rapid—*fire!* . . . Let go! Give it 'em!"

His words were crushed. A roar, like the hammering of a thousand rivets broke from the whole line at once.

Adrian's eyes had hitherto been fixed on Eric. Seizing a rifle, he now rushed to the parapet. He could see at first nothing more substantial than a few strands of French wire in front and twisted tree-stumps grinning out of the mist. Then tentative shapes disentangled themselves from moonbeams and shadows and strands of wire, upon which they seemed now to dance like puppets or tight-rope walkers, now to dart this way and that like blinded rabbits. From end to end of the line the rattle of the bolts being worked made a background of sound to the furious firing.

The whole period of action was probably less than a minute. The unreal acrobatic shapes vanished away among the moonbeams and shadows as intangibly as they had come. All knew that the attack had been repulsed.

Gradually the musketry slackened—ceased. A lull succeeded. The big guns fired spasmodically. The men began to talk, congratulate one another, speculate as to the number of Germans killed.

Adrian looked round for Eric. He was nowhere to be seen.

But his orderly came running down the trench, shouting
" Stretcher-bearer ! Stretcher-bearer ! The Captain's hit ! "

§ 6

Eric lay out on the road. As they lifted him down into
the trench he made no sound.

" Where are you hit, Eric ? " Adrian lived a lifetime of
apprehension in these moments.

No reply came. But after nearly a minute's silence a voice
so weak as to be hardly recognisable said :

" Is that you—Adrian ? . . . Have you stopped 'em ? " The
voice rose scarcely above a whisper. " Good."

" For heaven's sake where are you hit ? "

" The company . . . you're in charge of it. . . . The
money—you'll find it . . . in my valise."

" I know. Don't bother about that. Only, for God's sake,
where are you hit ? "

" In the chest, I think . . . two or three places. . . . I'm
finished, anyway. . . ." The voice sank to nothing.

They tried to raise him to a more comfortable position.

" I want—to say something——"

Another pause. Then :

" Morphia—give me morphia ! . . . and put an M on my
forehead."

No one present had morphia, a recent order having prohibited its use other than by medical officers.

They cut away the coat and shirt. In doing so a little locket
fell out ; the chain was broken. A tiny punctured wound was
found above the heart, another in the back. It became
evident that life was ebbing fast.

" The Captain's hit ! "

All down the line men could be heard passing the news.

" Little Percy's copped it at last ! "

They tried to give him brandy, but he was unable to swallow.

Only at intervals he repeated " Morphia ! Give me morphia . . . and put an M on my forehead."

Then he began to swear, methodically to himself as he sometimes did when things went wrong. The moments that followed revealed to Adrian the infinite preciousness of life's feeblest spark.

At last Eric articulated his name in the voice of one speaking from a long distance.

" Adrian ! "

" I'm here. I'm close to you." He took his friend's hand.

" I want . . ." The voice carried no farther.

They raised him onto a stretcher.

" Rose—Rosemary. I . . . damn it. . . ."

Pain strangled him. Then once more, " Morphia ! Give me morphia ! . . . and put an M on my forehead."

The boom of a solitary gun was succeeded by silence.

A shadow passed from the moon and the misty light revealed that Eric Sinclair's turn had come.

CHAPTER VI

Intimation

WAR is not merciful. It recks neither of place nor circumstance nor time. It recks nought of the love of the human body, of the love of women, of the claims of human pity, of the warmth that life once held and that death alone can destroy and that no earthly power can give back. It does not laugh, it does not weep, it cannot make beautiful or make good ; neither can it destroy the immortal soul.

There is a plot of ground set in the northernmost corner of the Belgian plain, within sight and sound of the great Poperinghe-Dunkerque road, where many British soldiers lie. No tree stands near ; no grass or flowers are at hand. It is four-square, bounded by wire and iron stakes with a ditch beyond. It is reached by a straight and narrow by-road on either side of which are small and symmetrically cultivated fields and bare, sunbaked areas of ground where wooden hospitals stand, or used to stand. The remains of horse-lines and camps are visible. One or two bright red houses may be seen amid hopfields. All day long and through the night the clatter of motor-traffic once was heard upon the neighbouring paved highway.

It is an area of bare yellowish soil and of yellowish wooden crosses set in rows, all being alike except that some partake of a paler and some of a darker hue. Upon each is inscribed a name, the legend " Killed in action," a date, and the letters " R.I.P."

To this place were borne the mortal remains of Eric Quentin Sinclair, upon a stretcher covered with a Union Jack ; and there laid to rest. On that August day the rolling of drums blended with the shrill crying of fifes in the Dead March in "Saul." There followed with slow step and in long train his brother-officers and the rank-and-file who had served beside or under him.

It was a fresh, sunny afternoon—one of those afternoons charged with a premature breath of autumn when billowy white clouds blow across a sky ethereally blue before a south-west wind ; a day full of life and hope, the which, indeed, gay sunshine alone has power to impart to that featureless landscape.

The solid ranks of khaki formed a square around the newly-dug grave. A little in front stood the chaplain. All heads were bared. Almost at Adrian's feet—for instinctively those around had given prior place to him, as it were to the chief mourner there—rested the stretcher, with its Union Jack covering the still form of his friend, the outlines of whose body were nevertheless entirely visible. The young man's inner grief found no outward expression. His predominant feeling, indeed, was of wonderment and awe in the presence of that so-great mystery. The coverlet merely added to his sense of it. He could not see the face he had known better than his own, any more than he could hear the voice that had been with him so few hours before. Those two familiar companions were for ever stilled. For ever ! They were blotted out ; would no more be. Herein lay the awe and the mystery. It was inconceivable ; it was true.

Prayer, for his own part, he neither uttered nor required nor yet understood. It was foreign, hopelessly foreign, to the memory of Eric, who, indeed, had never mentioned God—but irreverently. That was a fact, not excusable, perhaps, not right, nor creditable in him. But there it was. Eric had lived to all outward seeming without spiritual inspiration or intimation ; had experienced sensually, materially, and even cynically ; had died with a string of blasphemies on his lips.

Adrian felt that he could not for his part approach the Almighty in his friend's behalf now. Were there not others to pray for this soul's peace ?

The service lasted but a few minutes. They sang the hymn " For all the saints who from their labours rest." A fine hymn yet—how strangely, ironically inapposite ! What would Eric himself have said could he have known ! . . . The Last Post sounded. And after the Union Jack-shrouded body had been lowered out of sight, each officer in turn marched up to the grave and saluted his comrade's memory. They, then, talking quietly, walked back along the road to the camp.

Adrian lingered behind. He wanted to be alone, entirely alone, with this lifeless husk that had been so intimate a part of his life, before the cold earth should for ever come between them. They were at any rate alone together here. And though the windy sunshine and the gay, swift-moving clouds might seem to mock his grief, that grief was precious to him in this hour. His sense of isolation even was precious to him— such a sense as once only he had known before. He could not but couple Eric's memory with that of another who, too, for him was dead. Both gone—these two who more than any mortal beings had counted in his life ; these two who alike had shared his bravest and his saddest moments, whose separate intimacies, each a sacred thing, could never be shared and never could be recalled. His mind paused there, and even in this hour of bitter desolation a figure stood at his right hand.

It was Faith. . . .

Quite distinctly she stood beside him—she, the solitary link with the past, whose knowledge of the departed was not less true and deep nor less enduring than his own. She stood beside him in his thought, she who had represented all of Eric's young emotional life ; and knowing her, he realised that in this thing that was so utterly common to them both she would feel as he felt, she would think as he thought, and that their tribute would be a united one to the life both had equally shared.

With this thought he turned away presently, leaving the little cemetery to its habitual society of grave diggers, and sparrows. He would often return; or perhaps he would never return. God knew, and perhaps God after all understood.

CHAPTER VII

Time and Tide Roll on

§ 1

WHEN the first shock of Eric's death was overpast, and when again the weeks and months began to roll by in colourless monotony, Adrian Knoyle found that life held new purposes for him. For one thing, he became heir naturally to the company which had been Eric's. To uphold that Left Flank, not only in the tradition of Eric, but in face of the common duty and necessity of the time, was his first consideration. Officers of experience were scarce. More and more depended on the company-commanders. Colonel Forsyth never tired of impressing this upon them. Adrian Knoyle's life became valuable to others—and once again, therefore, to himself.

In the next place, there was his duty towards Faith. That was a duty sacred to himself, and for Eric's sake sacred ; it drew them steadily, spiritually nearer together. He had, of course, written the bride-widow an account of Eric's last hours, enclosing the hair-locket and its broken chain. He received in reply lines which concluded as follows :

' . . . Thank you for the locket. I cannot write much now, because in a sense I cannot realise it. I only know that something has gone utterly out of me—for ever in this life. I think of you always, Adrian. We two who are left must go on through these times together. Somehow we must find or fight a way out. . . . Live, my dear, *live* for his sake and for mine. . . .'

She added that she knew work, work, work was her one chance of salvation, and that so soon as the Arden hospital could spare her she intended to go to France and take up "serious" nursing.

This letter brought comfort; it brought him a sense of companionship in the aridity of his vast loneliness. He felt, as she clearly did, that so far as this thing was concerned, they two stood together apart and aloof from the rest of Eric's world. If it might be, he must *live*. And if his immediate sense of personal isolation increased and if it were remarked by his brother-officers that he every day became more silent, more morose even, on the other hand he once again felt a grip on existence, became conscious of a mission, a resolution. He re-found—his soul.

Perhaps the supreme moment of desolation had been when, arriving back from the trenches at dawn, Eric's servant, who had not heard the news, had sought him out. "The Captain's things are all ready, sir. Is he in yet?" And entering the tent, Adrian had found Eric's sleeping-bag laid out as usual beside his own, the corner of the blanket turned back on a wooden box, beside the bed Eric's peculiar array of brushes, hair-washes, eau-de-Cologne, and toilet equipment: a photograph of Faith. For three days afterwards, these had been his companions, a constant reminder of what once was and would never be again—until he had summoned sufficient resolution to pack them away out of sight.

§ 2

They got along very well together in the Left Flank Company on the whole. And this despite the fact that Burns and Fotheringay rarely ceased to quarrel. So pronounced, so chronic, and so relentless was their antagonism that without it the life of the battalion would have lost much harmless entertainment. Each played joyfully upon what he imagined to be the other's weak points. For if the elder man was strong in self-control and a sort of gruff determination, he was plodding, lacking in sense of humour, slow and ponderously conscientious in his military duties. And if Fotheringay, when necessity arose, proved himself an efficient and even brilliant platoon-leader—of which fact he never himself lost sight—at other times he was lazy and undependable.

"You are an extraordinary cove, Burns," the young gentleman would begin in the mess whenever he had nothing better to do. "Tell me, have you ever been drunk?"

"Don't ask silly questions, my little man!"

"Tell us the story of your life, Methusaleh."

"If you talked to me like that in the country I come from, I'd lay you across my knee and spank you—not so as to hurt you, of course."

"Would you, you horrible old man! I dare say you'd try. Well, I don't come from the country you come from—and I'm not going there. Just tell us how many times you've been married?"

"Didn't they ever swish you at Eton? Thought it too rough, I suppose?"

"Mind your own business. . . . Or divorced?"

"Can't you talk sense occasionally?"

"Not to you. You're so funny."

"You—little swine!"

At this point Burns would half rise from his seat as though to seize the other, whereupon Fotheringay would leap up nimbly and hold a chair between them.

Often there was horseplay.

"Now he's getting annoyed. Dear old Burns! Don't get rattled. Keep your hair on! Have a cigarette. . . . Don't come near me, though, you old brute."

Convention! Convention! Convention! This was Burns's pet cockshy. Forsyth, the Commanding Officer, was conventional; Sutton, the junior ensign, was conventional;

Tritton, the adjutant, was conventional. He spared only Adrian, to whom something less (or more) than convention was allowed.

"You're becoming enlightened, Adrian," he would say. "You're beginning to see the narrowness, the ludicrousness, the cut-to-pattern outlook, the falsity of standards of your 'Army tradition.' One day, please God, you'll be emancipated. By the end of the war we may all be emancipated—even that kid over there. I see signs of it. If the war's done any good, so far, it's been a revelation of the truth of things. Eh? It's washed out a lot of your conventions and pretensions. It's made men, not gentlemen, and they're what count nowadays—always, in fact. I learnt twenty years ago when I first went to South Africa to judge a man as a man. You still ask whether such and such a person is 'quite a gentleman.' Oh! it's—pitiful! Who cares a twopenny damn where Bertie buys his boots or Cuthbert has his hair cut or whether Archie aspirates his h's, when half the world's tottering and the only thing that'll save it is CHARACTER. Why should I conform to a standard set up by whipper-snappers like Fotheringay and Sutton?"

At this (if overheard) there would come shrieks of "Oh! Oh! Shut up! Tell him off! Lay him out!" from the other end of the mess hut, where Fotheringay, Sutton, and other boon companions were sniggering together. Tritton —who never seemed to have much to do—would sit, hands in pockets, smiling with bovine tolerance.

"There's the old man—off again! He and Adrian have started a new jaw about something. Why don't they give him a gramophone to talk into? The worst of it is Adrian takes him seriously."

The latter, indeed, had suggested that although War was a leveller, in a business like the Army everybody had to conform to some standard.

"I object to being robbed of my individuality," was Burns's reply. "It's about the only thing I haven't given up to come over here. Now they want to crush it out of me and make me at my age a specialised Sandhurst product, like those two lads. That's where Steele failed, didn't he ? He never recognised his officers and men as individuals, as camouflaged civilians trying to do their bit ; he never got rid of the old peace-time pre-war idea that all subalterns are naughty boys, more or less, and have to be treated accordingly. Well, he never got the best out of his men ; they hated though they feared him. I've always heard that about Steele."

And he went on to say that the Army was an admirable institution for teaching people how to do nothing.

Adrian sympathised with Burns without caring to say so outright and without sharing Burns's violence. The latter was after all a philosopher with the courage of his convictions ; a curious mixture, he had read deeply, if pedantically—Lecky, Herbert Spencer and, for some obscure reason, Machiavelli. And while he, Adrian, was unable to discard at once all the anæmic prejudices of his upbringing and earlier environment, it was with hostility, with resentment even, that he looked back upon his mental attitude in 1914—its shallowness, its inanities, its conceits, and its shams. He wearied not a little at times of the effervescing self-satisfaction of Fotheringay and Sutton, chiefly because it represented a dead self resurrected. Burns himself, after all, grizzled, grey-haired, with a life-time of work behind him, a neglected farmstead in the Orange Free State, and on every count a perfectly good ticket of exemption from military service—Burns was the flat denial of that bygone illusory existence.

It was during the period of rest which they spent within the shadow of the Hill of Cassel, after the Corps had been withdrawn from the battlefield of Ypres, that these con-troversies took place. The battalion here reposed for a brief period in a peaceful oasis amid the harsh desert of the war. Around and about them Time and Tide rolled on. It was in the middle of October that they returned to the cows,

the green fields, the farmsteads, the slow-moving pastoral life
of the Flemish plain. A month went by, and something
stirred, some secret word went forth, and they were marching
steadily, chiefly by night, due South. From late November
to the second week of December in this year the first Battle of
Cambrai raged. To the British Division fighting for possession of the village of Fontaine-nôtre-Dame, which lies
five miles north of the town, they lay in reserve. Then,
early on a still, misty morning in the vicinity of Havrin-
court—the crisis of the battle having seemingly passed—
they were awakened by the thunder of a great bombardment,
stood to their arms without breakfast, and a couple of hours
later met scattered bodies of infantry, many of them unarmed,
tumbling back in full retreat, proclaiming indeed that all was
lost. It was Adrian's first experience of the British in defeat,
and the spectacle was an unhappy one. Rushed forward,
they took part in the desperate counter-attack on Gonnelieu,
recaptured the ridge, were pushed back again in a whirl of
bitterest fighting. Fotheringay, whose enthusiasm for the
fray had been unbounded, was wounded by a fragment of shell,
and went to England accompanied by the strangest possible
recommendation for the Military Cross While conscious,
he never ceased to jest and swear. Burns and Adrian survived.

This was the latter's first ordeal as a company-commander.
Steadfastly, though indeed laboriously, he set himself to lead
his company without discredit. Eric—and it may be Faith—
stood behind him through the perilous days and the frost-
bitten nights of the climatically-hardest fortnight he
had so far known. On the whole, he did not fail. If he
faltered in decision or execution, the thought came to him
of the unperturbed, the smiling, the brilliant figure of his
dead friend ; if he felt nervous or hesitated—and this happened
more than once—the thought came again, and with it something of his dead friend's faintly contemptuous attitude
towards irresolution. Then Faith watching—she who

depended on him. The supreme individual test, it is true, did not come; it was the Left Flank company's turn for battalion reserve. With methodical painstaking care he made his dispositions; but in the heat of the engagement events decided. His resource, his initiative were not conspicuously called upon; the intuition which he lacked was not required of him. He held his men in hand, and avoided entanglements; he kept his head; he led correctly by the map. As for death, he felt a simple indifference.

"What a queer chap he is!" somebody remarked of the Left Flank commander when, after the fortnight's fighting, a group of officers sat round a brazier in the grim old prison of Arras.

"Oh, he's a bit off!" said Sutton, Fotheringay's friend, toasting his feet at the brazier. "He really is."

"No, he's suffering from too much war, as you may be, young feller, if you last long enough," Burns retorted warmly. "That's what's the matter with him. I wonder he sticks it."

"He doesn't seem to care a tinker's cuss for God or man—I'll give him that. But I wish he wouldn't be so damned officious. He came poking round when we were supporting your rotten company at Gonnelieu and told me off as. if I was a—a——"

"A new-born babe!" Burns suggested.

"As if I'd just come out, simply because I ventured to close my eyes for a second-and-a-half when everything was quiet. Yes—blast him! I know what I'm doing when I'm in the line."

"That's enough, Sutton," remarked the adjutant sharply. Things had grown very free and easy in the battalion nowadays compared to its earlier discipline. And Colonel Forsyth had given Tritton a hint to this effect.

"All of which you richly deserve," added Burns. "Supposing the Germans had broken through just then? He's seen a good deal more of the bloody game than you have. Don't forget it!"

"All right! All right! Keep your hair on, old hotstuff! I like the chap all right." ("Very good of you, Jerry," commented Tritton.) "Nobody's saying anything against him. But he does overdo it. You must admit that, Tritton!"

"What does the Commanding Officer think of him, Tritton?" inquired Hamilton, of the Right Flank.

"Oh, I don't know, he says 'He'll do, though not brilliant.'"

"He's quite a good sort when you know him," an officer called Rice put in.

"You must admit he is a rum 'un, though," Sutton persisted. "Foth. always thought so. So did everybody. I'm glad I'm not in Left Flank."

"Who's 'everybody,' anyway?"

"I think Eric's death half did for Adrian," said Burns. "But before that I noticed something funny and—difficult about him. You could see he was not happy. He gets along all right but he seems to do everything in a kind of dream. He's under constraint. His real self, you feel, is somewhere else."

"I heard he got turned down by some girl," contributed Sutton. "Anything in it?"

Everybody became doubly interested at this disclosure, but nothing more was forthcoming.

Cornwallis, who could have supplied the required information, remained silent.

Tritton, drawing at his pipe, said reflectively, "Women are the devil."

§ 3

Arthur Cornwallis had lately arrived with a draft. All in the battalion who had previously known him expressed surprise at his return, it being generally felt that one so little suited to warfare would not again be sent out. His *métier* was so obviously elsewhere. As a matter of course he rejoined the Left Flank company. And in the many conversations they had together, Adrian divined the young man's purpose, which was to "make good." He sympathised with this desire while, for practical reasons, regretting it.

Cornwallis's arrival, however, bespoke matters of more personal moment for Adrian. Among the stray items of intelligence from London he brought that of Rosemary Meynell's engagement to Harold Upton.

Nor was it without a sharp, an unexpectedly sharp, struggle that Adrian brought himself to face this fact. His mind, it is true, during eighteen months had been accustoming itself—more or less consciously—to no other expectation; the thing was, of course, inevitable. Yet here he was, face to face with it; and the process by which he finally closed the door on this intense episode in his life—for it came to that— was bitter.

The fact is, there was no knowing what might have happened if, even then, some sign, some intimation, some hint of regret or remorse had come.

Nothing of the sort did come. And for two or three days after the receipt of Cornwallis's news Adrian was a prey to reflections at once morbid, poignant and persistent. Vivid moments flooded back upon him. Old days and hours crept back into his knowledge like ghosts. They were seen in a cold, wearing, regretful light. Had he but acted differently two-and-a-half years earlier! Had his chivalry been less pedantic, his sense of duty less impetuously conceived! . . . He even accused himself of a loose sympathy with, or careless psychological study of, that being whose future had been so entirely his future and whose existence had so nearly become his own. Why had he not more thoroughly understood her ? How not foreseen ? Why had he not apprehended the needs of a nature so spirited, so eager, so glad and necessitous of life ?

Well—it was past. And gradually the future and his new grip on the future—through Eric's memory, through Faith, through his immediate preoccupations—gained the upper hand

and he was able to slam a door finally on that past, to relegate what had been to the place where it properly belonged, to set his shoulder to the wheel once more. In so doing—and this was not the least devastating moment of his personal tragedy—he burnt a faded photograph and the words of a song.

Cornwallis, it was evident, had not passed through the intervening fifteen months in England unscathed. Some of his *naïveté* had been lost, though none of his simplicity. He wrote more poetry than before—and read less. As in earlier days he defied the batteries of his fellow-subalterns by nightly kneeling down to his prayers—and finally vanquished them by his unaffected manner of doing so. He, too—it was possible to conjecture—had experienced. The truth was quite soon and ingenuously forthcoming. He came back obsessed with the " Clan Maryon," its art, its ideas, its wit and " wonderfulness," its " Rays " and " Stars " and other evidences of constellatory brilliance—above all, dazzled by the genie herself. For days and nights he would talk to Adrian of nothing and nobody but Gina Maryon, reviving conversations, recalling personal contacts—most indiscreetly. But when weeks sped by without any sign, word, or communication from the source of his inspiration, his tone changed.

Well, Adrian reflected, Arthur had to buy his experience as everyone else did! It was such an old, dull, shop-soiled story to Adrian ; to Arthur, such a new and wonderful and absorbing adventure.

" But why doesn't she answer my letters ? " the latter would despondently inquire. " I can't make it out. We parted on the best of terms. Do you think I can have offended her somehow ? But I—I knew her so *well*, Adrian. We were so—so *happy* together. . . . And yet she can't send me one little line."

Adrian could not quite bring himself to tell his friend in so many words that Gina had probably forgotten his existence. Nor would kindness permit him to add that Arthur's scalp lay in a heap with upwards of half-a-hundred others in a dusty cupboard somewhere at the back of Gina's memory.

§ 4

They spent the winter, 1917–18, between Arras and the trenches east of it. It was a monotonous brooding winter, which on the whole enhanced Adrian's mood of looking-backward, of lingering regret, of suspended animation. The old city itself breathed of these things. For Adrian, a faded letter found in the drawer of his billet expressed them.

" Ayez courage ! " it ran ; " les Allemands n'arriveront pas jusqu'à vous. Nous avons besoin de toute notre foi dans ces heures-ci."...

The date of the letter was August 25th, 1914.

Adrian and Cornwallis never tired of walking about the streets and squares of this town that seemed so full of a curious half-abandoned charm, a reflective dignity and sorrow which set it apart, as did its Franco-Spanish architecture, from other French provincial towns they had visited. Together they rejoiced in the beauty of its Grande Place, where pillars support colonnades and old over-leaning houses, as in some Dutch town ; its high, blank walls and narrow alleyways, like streets of Italy or Spain, its bridges and publicgardens and hidden-away gardens ; its cobbled quay. They sought out uncommon corners and stored up wintry impressions of the place—sunsets from the ramparts or the racecourse, interspersed with beautiful ecclesiastical monuments in the Spanish style ; hidden in an obscure part of the old cavalry barracks, a deserted chapel without doors or windows, into which snow and autumn leaves had drifted, and where in a perpetually-falling twilight a brass memorial told of Napoleon's engineers who fell at Waterloo. Strange, too, Arras under the snow—a city of the Neva, grey and white, grey and white ! The civilisation of the inner city seemed to strive with the ruins of the outer, with the vast, half-ruined cathedral and with the quite ruined railway station. And always there lay upon the place a foreboding, a prescience of Fate. For although the shopkeepers had taken down their shutters and the inhabitants emerged from their cellars, shells and bombs occasionally fell in the heart of the town; and although for months at a time an almost normal civilian life went forward, it was felt that the coming spring would bring such a struggle as the world had even then not known.

But that was not the only side of life in Arras. There continued in contrast to it a certain gay, convivial activity. There were clubs. There were concert-parties and good meals and much singing and much drinking; there were bands and the cinematograph; and a theatre upheld in its own estimation by worn and faded plush, by tawdry gilt, and bizarre decorations. Genée—a man!—danced there. Harry Lauder's double laughed and sang. Pantomime and *revue* succeeded one another. Something stole back into men's faces—some quality of joy in things illusion resurrected. Or perhaps only an echo of things gone and half-forgotten.

One day Clemenceau appeared—from nowhere. A little old farmer-like man, in gaiters, stepped out of a pale blue motor-car followed by three brilliant French officers in horizon-blue, scarlet, and gold; a Highland guard presented arms; a hastily-collected band crashed out the "Marseillaise." The little old fellow trotted round the guard-of-honour, raised his hat, and passed into the city by the St. Pol Gate.

From that, all that, by a narrow-gauge line of railway following the shallow valley of the Scarpe, or by the smooth, silent river in barges, or even by road, they passed five or six times a month to the trenches about Roeux. That was a ghostly journey—through the straight, upright, greyish-white poles of the shell-shattered woodland, through the reedy marshes of the river-bottom and the wide lagoons where duck and water-fowl called mournfully and shells would some-

times send the water hissing upward. Long passages led
to the trenches. In the vast caves of Roeux lit by electric
light and in the secure underground chambers, a sepulchral
stifled life went on. Without, the landscape was one of
melancholy and distance. Greyish-brown hills overgrown
with coarse grass and vegetation offered no relief to the eye.
There was indeterminate mud : mud so besetting that after
the January rains English and Germans alike emerged from
their trenches and lived above ground, making no secret of
their habits or of their presence.

And with the approach of spring the moment approached
of that German offensive which had been so long expected,
so often discounted. Every minute of this period could be
felt. The hours grew longer and more exacting, the
suspense ever more trying and intense. Days of wearisome
preparation were followed by nights when the sleep of
those off-duty was broken an hour before dawn by the call
to "stand-to." Yet, save in this brief period before
daybreak the guns were preternaturally quiet. Silence,
waiting and watching, lay upon the land.

For days, for weeks, the attack did not break. Warning after
warning came from the General Staff. "The utmost vigi-
lance must be exercised at all times in the front line." "The
enemy is expected to attack at any moment." How the men
shivered and swore as, huddled up in their greatcoats, they
stamped upon the fire-steps and beat their mittened hands
together in the saffron light of each frosty sunrise ! At last
they began to ridicule the idea of the coming onslaught,
setting the warnings down as part of a "scare," as so much
else in the war had deserved to be set down. But the company-
commanders knew better—and knew no rest. To them had
been disclosed as early as the second week in March the plan
of the German attack so far as this was known :—the frontage
of it, the weight of it, its objectives, even the date of it. The
last, it is true, proved one day out but, for the rest, Adrian

and his brother-officers afterwards marvelled at the competence in this instance of the British Intelligence Service.

The Division at the expiry of its normal three months' " tour " went out of line. At this very moment, the attack broke, and among other important points on the British front, the hill of Monchy fell. To the defence of this important tactical area the battalion was rushed, and for three days and nights they lay across the Arras-Cambrai road, listening to the crackle of rifle-fire out in front, to the ill-directed German shells which screamed rearwards. Once, and only once, they secured a fair target of Germans in the open ; upon that every available weapon was turned. It was a glorious opportunity. At the very height of the slaughter, Adrian heard a voice at his elbow.

" Adrian ! Adrian ! Why won't this rifle go off ? I press the trigger and it doesn't fire ! "

Beside him was Cornwallis, his face flushed with agitation. He also perceived that his rifle was at half-cock.

" Push your safety-catch forward, you damned fool ! " he shouted.

" Oh !—why, of course ! "

And that was Cornwallis's first attempt to " make good."

A week later they marched back to rest. And although a few miles to the southward the grey German tide, rolling forward to its high-water mark on the long-silent Somme battlefield, threatened hourly the partition of the Allied armies, at Arras (north of the Monchy hill) the line held. By the middle of April the supreme peril seemed to be past. Temporarily the guns died down, only to blaze out as fiercely in the north. What a month ! What a struggle !

Through the latter part of April and early May, Adrian Knoyle and his comrades lay in the flat lands about Avesnes-le-Comte. This is a pastoral and pleasant, though featureless country. Here spring found them—in the château of Grand

Rullecourt. Such a spring seemed to Adrian—little accustomed to unscathed country—to leap out of the womb of time. Rooks were nesting in the great trees, and in the neglected château garden anemones, bluebells, speedwell, daisies, violets, daffodils tenderly raised their heads. Fruit-blossom snowed up the orchards. Out in the fields whole families of peasants worked the livelong day, while pale green shafts of corn mounted beneath a sunshine that grew ever warmer, kindlier, and sweeter scented. Bees began to hum in great limes near the house. How the larks sang!

One day, Adrian received a letter from Lady Knoyle announcing that the lease of Stane was due to terminate at the end of that present year, 1918. And she hoped he would decide—yes, she hoped he would decide—to settle down there after the war. . . . After the war! A world without war—was it conceivable? Yet, in a way it was like his mother to contemplate such a future!

He began to think again very often of the Three Hills.

§ 5

May in trenches south of Arras found the trio, Knoyle, Burns, and Cornwallis, still together. But the tension of the battle-line was not relaxed. It never had relaxed since the morning of March 21st. One great German attack succeeded another after a brief, breathless pause; and none could say where the next would fall. The Arras front seemed hourly threatened, once the more northerly attacks had been beaten back. Finally, towards the end of May (and to the surprise of those who held the centre) the main weight of the onslaught fell upon the French armies between Soissons and Rheims.

The tension then, if anything, increased. Everyone bent a little under it. Through the foregoing months of conflict and of movement, through the long days of suspense before the bursting of the storm—when alone his impelling sense of necessity preserved a mental equipoise—a change had already been at work in Adrian.

If Lady Knoyle's letters offered counsel and stimulus, Faith's—for she continued to write week by week—caused him to set his teeth and fight grimly on. For all these, however, and for all his grimness of determination, the war had begun to wreak its vengeance, to take its toll, in spite of himself. Burns had been right. Adrian experienced a physical reaction so acute, a sense of weariness so devastating, so overwhelming, that the mere hanging-on from day to day seemed a burden almost too great to be borne. Danger, indeed, left him indifferent even as the future did. Not so the burden of the always-impending conflict, the noise, the violence, the unsightliness, the prolonged discomfort and lack of sleep ; not so the ever-present strain of responsibility. After all, the man's existence for over two years had been little better than a living death. And life calls to life. . . . He grew physically tired and weak : irritable with a nervousness that he could not control. His philosophy of indifference, so carefully nurtured, so long maintained, seemed to forsake him. He began to dread, to hate each return to the front line, to feel nausea almost insupportable at the thought of the grind, the imprisonment, the ennui, the squalor of trench life.

Some noticed this change in him suddenly : this irritability, this moodiness, followed by periods of comparative gaiety. Others had long watched it developing.

Among the latter was Colonel Forsyth, who, like all good commanding officers, had a habit of studying his juniors severally—his company-commanders in particular. He was familiar enough already with the symptoms that now began to appear in Captain Knoyle. English leave had long since been stopped, but when early in June a vacancy for Paris leave came through, that officer was not consulted, his name having been already submitted and approved.

CHAPTER VIII

Adrian and Faith

§ 1

ABBEVILLE station lay grilling in the glare of June. Adrian felt bewildered by the noise, clamour, and vociferous energy, the hooting of sirens, the blowing of horns, the backing in and out of long supply and troop trains, the shouting and calling out of railway officials, Railway Transport officers, and the *Mission Militaire* the wild bustling and wrestling with luggage. It was a great railway-junction.

Cosmopolitan and variegated as the crowd was, khaki remained the dominant note—the khaki of the heavy and stolid English, the square, thick-set English with their unromantic, imperturbable calm ; of the Americans, lithe and slim, rather like keen commercial travellers, with nasal voices, odd cynical faces, and an air of being perpetually amused ; of the Belgians, bearded, new-looking, too new-looking (the English said), with their yellow boots and belts. French officers in horizon-blue darted like brilliant kingfishers through the crowd. There were many French infantrymen-of-the-line going on leave or returning. On the platform opposite stood a group of Portuguese in grey uniforms with sallow and ochre complexions. Swarthy Australians and Canadians, of independent bearing and muscular build, lounged, smoking, against pillars or railings. A couple of Japanese officers, attached to the General Staff, stood by themselves. Behind all these, the worried-looking, close-packed throng—demure V.A.D. workers in dark blue, grip in hand ; gaunt, angular military nurses in grey hats and grey, scarlet-bordered cloaks ;

and then a mass of untidy civilians, herding like cattle with their luggage, seeking only to escape from the heavily-bombed and already half-ruined town.

Then the Paris express clanked in. All made a wild rush for places, shouting, gesticulating, using freely fists and arms, sticks and umbrellas, dragging and pushing luggage or each other as best they might. Adrian, burdened only with a haversack, elbowed his way in a leisurely manner towards the rear of the train. In the midst of the commotion he heard his name called.

" Adrian! Adrian! Hi! Here!"

The voice, a woman's, was oddly familiar, yet for several seconds he could not discover the source or direction of it.

" *Adrian!* "

He glanced eagerly up and down the train. . . .

Then he saw Faith Sinclair waving at an open carriage door.

§ 2

" Faith!"

He forced a way to her.

" But this is too wonderful!" she cried. Their hands clasped. " You're going to Paris?"

" Rather."

" Jump in, then!"

She was in a uniform—grey, with a veil closely framing her face, a red cross on the front of it. Her fair hair strayed elusively from under the hood. Her fresh complexion struck him as unmistakably and delightfully English; so did her pleasant features and her serene blue eyes. Faith Sinclair was not beautiful; he never had thought that; but she was miraculously cool and fair and good to look upon after that perspiring, distracted mob on the station-platform. Yet— he was aware at once of a change in her: something in the

And presently :

" You were a small boy then. Now you're—a grown-up old man."

They laughed at that.

" Yes, and a sadder and a wiser——" he began ; " but I won't say the obvious."

" I wonder what kind angel has brought us together. . . . It's like an omen, isn't it ? "

The *Bon Dieu* has smiled on us for once. We are good children."

The train stopped at Le Trèport, with its grey houses and its great hospital-hotel perched high up on the sea-cliff. There they caught a glimpse of the sea. Animation prevailed. English nurses and V.A.D.'s alighted, others, attached to the various services, were assembled on the station-platform. Then the train, returning on its track, moved Pariswards again.

Adrian suggested they should go along to the restaurant-car for *déjeuner*. They sat opposite a small French soldier who was reading *La Revue de Paris*. Faith nudged Adrian and smiled.

" Imagine an English Tommy reading the *Nineteenth Century !* " He smiled too.

They spoke of indifferent matters during the meal, of the thousand-and-one incidents and impressions which had agitated the surface of the three years' interval, Faith laughing and talking gaily.

A chain and locket that seemed familiar hung in the folds of her nurse's attire. And when they were back once more in their carriage he drew attention to it.

" I see you've got that," he said.

" Of course, Adrian."

Her face was most nearly beautiful when sorrowful. Or was it not then quite and even very beautiful ? It grew sad now. It grew upon his consciousness ; his eyes kept coming back to her face.

They were passing through a monotonous country whose broad, marshy valleys, traversed by streams, were bounded by low and often wooded hills. The meadows were brilliant with cowslips, buttercups, and marigolds; on the folding woodlands was a still springtime green. The corn ripened almost visibly; magpies of a brilliantly contrasting black-and-white sheen constantly flitted from tree to railway embankment and back again.

"I can never thank you enough for all you did," Faith said. "But I know you don't want thanks."

"Want thanks? My dear, what *have* I done? What could I do, or rather, what else could I do? Don't let's be—conventional."

"I felt—you were feeling, and that's meant very much to me."

"It's been a hard time—for us both, Faith."

"Adrian . . . it's as if one's *living heart* had been dragged out."

A long-suppressed grief seemed to force itself out in these words.

Silence supervened, silence except for the unvarying throb-throb and clank-clank of the train.

After several minutes she spoke again:

"Nobody will ever know—nobody *can* ever know—what he—what those few weeks meant to us both."

"He was so reserved about the things he really felt that even I hardly knew what he was thinking," Adrian replied. "He only mentioned that once."

"What did he say?"

"We were sitting in that horrible blockhouse, being shelled. He said, 'It's a bit rough at first, this—after that. But, of course, it couldn't last for ever.'"

". . . . my poor, poor old boy!"

She gazed out of window at the afternoon sunshine upon the smiling country, twisting a handkerchief between her fingers.

Presently she said :

"Adrian, I'm thankful, oh! so thankful that *you* were with him then. When you are with me I shall always feel that —he is near . . . us both."

After that they spoke no more for a long time.

§ 3

"Of course, you know, it's the end of a chapter for me." Her voice was calm, almost matter-of-fact again. "It's the end of—something more, too. Nothing so tremendous, so overwhelming can ever happen to me again. There was a time at Arden and after when—I was not sure. Then the war . . . seemed to bring him out. It revealed him in a new light to me—himself. I never really knew till those three little weeks of ours—what sort of man he was. Of course, poor darling, he wasn't perfect, but—there was something great about him even "—she hesitated a moment, a look of great tenderness crossing her face—"even in his sins."

"He was a soldier before everything out here. He did not show the—personal side of him. All his active life and thought were given to our Company. But I know he did think a great deal about you and—the future."

"Tell me this, Adrian. Why is it always his sort—the finest, the bravest, the best that go ? And people—rotters like—like that man Upton—are left ? "

The mention of that name, he was curious to find, left him cold.

"I suppose it's part of the price we have to pay. There are so many things one cannot explain. Why, for instance, should Eric be taken with everything worth having in life before him and—a derelict like me left ? "

She studied her friend's face long and carefully. "Why do you speak of yourself like that, my dear ? "

"You mention Upton—why not me ? " He spoke without

emotion. "Upton and I have things in common. . . . I, too, have often wondered at the profligacy of it all. I don't understand—anything."

She did not answer at once.

"I see, Adrian," she said meditatively. "I know. Still, you're past that now? Unhappiness makes one egotistical, or I should not have said that. You've had your bad time. You've—had your heart wrenched out too."

"Oh, well, it's done with now. That man's name was gall and wormwood to me once. Now—I think . . . I don't care a damn."

"But she?"

"Rosemary? It's strange we should speak of—all that. The last person I mentioned her name to was Eric."

"And therefore you can always speak of it to me, Adrian. Don't I know her as well as you did yourself? And didn't he know her, too? Why, he used to write to me every day about you both! He felt it nearly as much as you did. He was fond of Rosie—until then. But he never forgave her in his heart. He begged me to be a pal to her, and I've tried to be. Heaven knows she needs one."

"Needs one? She's all right, though, isn't she?"

He found himself speaking of his old love without a twinge of emotion or of pain.

"I don't really know . . . what she is," Faith replied slowly. "We're no longer friends, except in name. We never see each other. She never comes near me. She refused to be a bridesmaid at our wedding. I've asked her to come and see me again and again. She's always had some excuse. Except once. . . . She was the very first person to come round after I heard about Eric. Curious, wasn't it? Entirely of her own accord, and—she was—well, what only Rosie can be when she chooses. . . . I could see she was really and truly moved about it, too. I think she must have been very fond of him, in her own way. We talked as we had not talked since that week-end at the outbreak of war. We talked of everything—what we used to call ' heart-to-hearters ' in the old days—everything except herself. When I asked how life was treating her she shut up like a knife.

" Haven't you seen her since ? "

" She never came again. I asked her, but she did not come. At first she made excuses—transparent ones. Finally I wrote and told her always to think of me as her true friend and to feel that I was there if ever she wanted me. She never even answered. The fact is she knows, and has known from the first—because I told her, stupidly perhaps—that I hate the life she leads and I hate the people she lives with. I'd give anything to get her away from them—*anything*. But she's self-willed and she's intensely, irrationally proud."

" She's afraid of you, I suppose ? "

" She resents advice or even the semblance of it. She thinks I'm going to interfere or lecture her or something, I suppose. As if I should be such a fool—now. The time for that's long past. . . . She's got to make—or mar—her own life, and learn her own lessons. And she will learn them—in time."

" Is she still fond of Upton ? "

" I think she's infatuated with them all. But if she isn't, wild horses wouldn't make her admit it. No, she's got to go her own way now to the end—whatever it may be."

" Do you see much of Gina ? "

" I don't want to. I hear quite enough."

" What—scandal ? "

" Rumours. People talk. I don't believe all one hears. It's too dreadful even to think about. But there must be something in it. . . . I keep out of her way. I don't want to meet her—not because of that, though. Because I think she's largely responsible—she and Helena Cranford—for this engagement and—the whole thing ; I never can forgive either of them."

"Doesn't Lady C. know all about the Maryon crowd ? She must, surely."

"I think she's criminal, Adrian. She practically washes her hands of her own daughter. If you speak to her about it, she simply says she 'doesn't understand the girl of the period.' Really, I suppose, though one doesn't like to say it, she's thinking of his—that man's—money."

Faith was silent a moment. Then :

"And it's more than that—it's more than that I blame Helena Cranford for, Adrian. It's . . . the whole arrangement of things—the whole system she stands for. Where do facts come in ? Where do common-sense and knowledge of human nature come in ? Helena Cranford has the reputation of being broad-minded and intelligent. But how has she brought up this girl—how have any of us been brought up ? Like our grandmothers were—by rule of thumb. We're told that the only things that matter are to dance well, ride and play tennis well, be well dressed, be amusing to young men, and look pretty. Then the war comes along, and the whole system breaks down, and where are we—products ? High and dry, with nothing to fall back on, no guiding hand, or principle. And a girl like Rosemary drifts, and her mother— because the old landmarks are gone—looks the other way, or rather goes her own way in the society that interests her, and says she doesn't understand the 'girl of the period.' . . . And the marriages ! Oughtn't there to be a censorship or something ? *What* is Cranford—*where* is he ? So effete, as far as I can gather, or so dissipated that he has to be shut up. A complete wash-out. And such people—because they've got coronets and 'places '—a few thousand a year—are allowed to have children who, nine times out of ten, inherit their own tendencies. And those children are allowed to marry—creatures like Upton because *they've* got a few thousand a year."

Her bosom rose and fell and a flush warmed her cheeks.

" When are they going to be married ? "

" Soon, I believe —any day, in fact."

Faith clenched her handkerchief convulsively, and in a sudden access of feeling exclaimed :

" Oh, my dear, it's a tragedy ! . . . Rosie—our little Rosie and—that poisonous man. . . . But there are tragedies everywhere—the world over."

Her voice broke, but she would not relinquish her self-control.

§ 4

Evening had come, and the sunset flooded their carriage while the train jolted and rumbled onward towards Paris.

They were come to the rolling, wooded country about Creil ; little more than an hour would bring them to the threatened city. Adrian found it hard to reconcile the golden peace of the passing country with the restless surge of their two hearts, puny as that was beside the sum-total of the vast tragedy that lay beyond.

He was moved—moved deeply by this phantom-shape of Eric's happiness, moved by Faith's words about Rosemary, moved by his own long-smouldering pain, moved by a profound tenderness for this good woman whom Fate had cheated of her happiness.

As the train rolled on and they sat in sympathetic silence, he knew that their common thought had gone back to Eric. These words in a low tone presently broke from her :

" He passed through agony and is now happy. He is purified. I know he is always near me. I know we shall meet in some future place."

And then, as one quoting from memory :

" ' The souls of the faithful who have died in the service of their country rest for ever in the lap of God.' . . . So it doesn't matter if he wasn't very good and moral and—and all that, does it, Adrian ? "

He inclined his head.

Another long silence followed. Adrian had an idea that she was praying, and did not feel embarrassed.

She presently looked up.

" Adrian—do you believe in anything ? "

He hesitated. " Well, yes—I suppose so. Yes—I think I do."

" Conventionally—as an institution ? Because you were brought up to—like being a Conservative in politics ? "

" Well—yes, perhaps."

" That doesn't count. That's not believing. That's taking things for granted."

" What do you mean, then ? What ought one to believe in ? "

" In a supreme guiding principle. In some beneficent purpose at the back of all this—this insensate destruction and conflict and universal death ; at the back, too, of all evil and passion and suffering."

" But what sort of purpose ? "

She thought a moment.

" I don't know—now."

" But yet you believe in it ? "

" I do—absolutely. It's the only thing that's kept me going ; it's the only sheet-anchor for a man or a woman in these times."

" Show me the way to—daylight, and I'll believe too."

" Faith. Faith in a Supreme Being, and in a Hereafter. Dear old Eric never had it, but he had faith in himself, and that carried him through. The war revealed his soul. . . . But I mean faith, too, in the end of the struggle. These you must have. Wash out everything you've ever learnt, everything you've ever been taught. Start the world anew. Keep your mind on the simple and elemental things—and truth. It's hard sometimes, I know, but there's something wonderful at the end of it."

She spoke with great earnestness.

" I've come to that in these months.   Or rather it's come to me—come to me just since Eric died.   It's brought hope and sometimes rest and often a wonderful sense of—communion with him, though he's beyond sight or sound or touch."

Adrian turned to her a thoughtful face.

" I wish I could feel like that, Faith.   But I can't.   Until to-day I don't think I've seen daylight, not a glimmer, for —for two-and-a-half years."

" But Eric—— ? "

" He saved my life once ; he gave me what I didn't want. He was all in the world a friend could be ; but he could not bring back what had simply gone out of me."

They were silent a moment.   Then she said :

" I would like to try and do that."

" Faith, we are both of us—rather—thwarted, disillusioned people——"

" But that is everywhere in the world.   How many people there must be like ourselves !   Thwarted, disillusioned, worn-out—that's the very process of the war itself.   But the war will end.   I think of this time as of one of those wild and stormy nights one sometimes gets in an English spring when the wind howls and the rain beats against the windows till near daybreak.   And then, like a miracle, light comes and reveals a calm sunny spring morning. . . .   Adrian, we must struggle out towards that dawn.   I believe I can show you the way.   Shall we—do that together ? "

She held out her hand with the old frank smile.   He took it eagerly—kept it in his.

" We mustn't *let* life be a tragedy," she continued.   " Eric laughed at life—and death.   Eric wouldn't have stood it for a moment.   Doesn't it strike you there's still so much to— enjoy ; there's so much beauty and light and love in the world still !   This nightmare will pass, Adrian. . . .   What a wonderful evening sky ! "

All the west was rose-colour, deepening by almost imperceptible gradations to the indigo shades of night. About the zenith were strata of pale gold, amethyst-green and deep turquoise-blue. A phantom moon sailed into the sky. The evening star glimmered like a jewel.

The train slowed down and pulled up with a jerk. There were shouts and a horn blown. It was Beauvoir.

§ 5

So they came to the last short stage before Paris.

Darkness began rapidly to close in. The evening mist partially veiled the thickly-wooded country about Chantilly. Lights as yet undimmed began to twinkle in the windows of villas and country-houses and clustered in small towns. According to regulation, the carriage-blinds had to be pulled down.

A pleasant breeze blew in at the window. Adrian came across and sat beside his old friend.

There was something in her face—grave as it was with the permanence of experience—there was something in her voice, in her—as it seemed to him—intensified personality, that drew him out of himself. How was it he had never plumbed the depths in her before ? A new phase of sympathy had sprung up between them in these half-dozen hours, a mutual comprehension and understanding, different in quality and basis from their old friendly relationship. And the dim light of the shaded lamp seemed to him to lend a new quality, perhaps a new dignity, to her face. He saw that, but he saw also the woman's mature character revealed ; her strength and equanimity, her courage that was greater than his, her woman's spirit triumphing over the selfishness of sorrow. . . .

Dimly he began to glimpse that dawn of which she had spoken.

During the remainder of the journey they talked only of

the future, and they talked with quiet hope and confidence.

"You must write to me every week," she said. "Don't forget!"

"Of course not. But couldn't we meet? You'll be able to come into Paris?"

"Yes, but I don't think I shall. And besides—you've a duty to other people. Lady Knoyle is eating her heart out for you. Don't you ever give a thought to England?"

"Oh, well! Perhaps—now and then. Let's see—yes, it's a good year-and-a-half since I set foot on a London pavement. It doesn't seem like that."

"No, I think it will be better," she said, "if we don't meet again until we've each fought our fight and the victory is won."

He did not fully comprehend her meaning then; he answered:

"This winter Stane will be ours to live in. In the spring mother will go to live there. Summer is wonderfully beautiful on the Three Hills—most of the wild flowers are out, the thyme scents everything, and the days are long. I shall spend my leave there. You must come to us then."

Muffled lights whirled by. The train rattled on, swaying to this side and that. They were soon to part—she to go to her future home at Neuilly, he to the mysterious heart of Paris. Beyond that . . . who could say? Yet there was no pain for either of them in the thought. Both intuitively felt that they were destined to meet again. There was only the regret of two fellow-travellers parting at a journey's end.

The train glided slowly, heavily, into the Gare du Nord. They had little luggage, and going into the street outside the station Adrian (with bribery) secured a taxicab.

A pressure of the hands told of all they felt. And she was gone before he realised it. . . .

He elbowed his way through the crowds to the offices of the Railway Transport Officer, where he had instructions to report. Soldiers, officials, and refugees from the newly-invaded districts pushed and jostled him on every side; impetuous Frenchmen thrust past him, bawling excitedly; groups of old women and children sat marooned amid their baggage in his path; nuns in silent resignation, were perched on little packages, clasping old-fashioned umbrellas; middle-aged women and youths rushed between soldiers and officials, begging (usually in vain) for information or advice.

In a brilliantly-lighted *crèche* opening off the station platform Adrian caught a glimpse of American nurses tending waifed babies that had been cast thus early upon a topsy-turvy world.

His sense of personal tragedy vanished before this vast, impending, impersonal calamity. . . .

A newspaper-seller cried repeatedly, in a voice which seemed to pierce all other sounds that the German Army had crossed the Marne and was once more at the gates of Paris.

CHAPTER IX

A Vision of Paris

§ 1

THE morning sunshine came pouring into Adrian Knoyle's bedroom at the Hotel Paris-Astoria. It banished the sense of impending calamity which had been his final impression of the previous night. Life called to him. A sense of lightness, freedom, came to him such as he had not known since 1914.

He felt equal to enjoyment—adventure—gaiety even.

He saw through wide-open windows the white trellis-covered walls of the hotel-courtyard and the garden of exotic plants where a fountain played. He caught a glimpse of a glass verandah, a gravel walk, one or two beds of flowers and groups of palms and orange trees in circular wooden boxes; his eye lit upon little green tables set about in shady places and upon a leisurely waiter flicking these tables with a napkin. He heard a twittering of sparrows, a musical plash of water from the fountain, and watched for some time with pleasure the dancing pattern of light and shade that Venetian blinds made upon the walls of his room.

He thought, too, of Faith and their overnight journey; all that seemed far-off and unreal. He did not dwell upon it—did not connect his present resilience with it. They brought him coffee and rolls and cherry syrup in bed. That was better, he reflected, than chicory compound in a tin mug! He was loth to get up, but—Paris called. A hot bath was not permitted on week-days, but a cold one would serve. He dressed in a leisurely manner and went out into the streets.

The streets sparkled. Everything twinkled, laughed, and danced this June morning. The world sang. This city of spires and towers, of great hotels, museums, and magnificent monuments, of boulevards, squares, wide streets, parks, vast white buildings—to an eye so long accustomed to the barren monotony of war's devastation, they were an entrancement.

He knew Paris passably. And it was not long before he perceived that beneath a surface dazzling and seductive, something lacked, something of the essential Paris. As he passed out through the hall of his hotel he observed that it was empty save for a gorgeous *concierge*, a polite, mysterious gentleman in a tail-coat, a hovering waiter or two, and a couple of American officers. The same note of emptiness, of something vital missing in the powerful dynamo, impressed itself upon him in the streets, for all their alert movement, varied animation and colour, ubiquitous motor traffic, and shops fully and brilliantly displayed.

Those streets—they were a fascination to him. When he grew tired of walking he sat down outside a café in the Avenue de l'Opéra and was content to watch the stream of traffic and foot-passengers flow by. Something of the old restless fever of 1914, the old intensity, the old craving for animation, music, light, amusement, stirred in him again ; something of that " inspiration " of youth which he thought had gone out of him two years before. . . . And this was such an— experience ! With a certain quiet satisfaction his mind dwelt on the overnight conversation with Faith, and he wondered more than once what—at no great distance away—Faith might be doing now.

He next repaired to a world-famous bar and imbibed two champagne-cocktails. Near to the luncheon-hour he found himself in the Bois, where it was cool. He passed the time of day with an old man in a seedy frock-coat and felt hat who was sitting on a seat reading the *Echo*.

" Eh, bien ! Ah ! "—he spat—" the Boches ! They're at Meaux, I see—only fifty kilometres away."

The old gentleman addressed a series of incomprehensible observations to the world at large.

" Next week they'll be here."

Adrian, as it happened, had succeeded in forgetting the war. Now this accursed old man came to disturb his illusion. But—he would soon forget again.

The old man continued to converse—apparently with himself—but presently addressed Adrian in particular.

" Did m'sieu hear the shells this morning ? They say a couple fell near the Sacré Cœur and killed a woman. Eh, bien ! —ah ! eh !—we have not long to live . . . it's a lovely morning." He spat—finally.

Assenting to this last incontrovertible observation, Adrian fled into *les Ambassadeurs.* A row of motor-cars stood outside. Within, all was as he had last seen it. The restaurant indeed was nearly full. Only where Englishmen had reigned supreme, there dallied now a majority of uniformed Americans and a few French aviation officers. He noted the usual fat, untidy-looking Frenchmen, napkin under chin—artists or literary men, *bon viveurs*—accompanied by women friends. There were ladies sitting in couples and mixed parties making merry over iced champagne-cup, mayonnaise and strawberries.

Adrian sat down at one of the tables under the outer awning in a cool and delicate gloom. He ordered his luncheon with care as befitted the occasion : melon, *œufs à la portugaise*, asparagus, strawberries, and a bottle of Bollinger in cup. Conversation floated out into clotted sunlight and leafy shade ; beyond the awning there was a vista of the leafy Bois and its gardens, flower-beds and deep pools of grassy shadow. Not far off a mowing-machine was at work, its purring note attuned by memory to the height of summer.

Nor was it long before he became aware of sparkling glances

from starry eyes. Some flashed sidelong at him, some peered
from under vast hats, some surreptitiously beckoned.

In a reasonably short space of time he found himself basking
in the frank smile of a small person in a black frock, pearls,
and a natty little student's cap of velvet, who with a friend
sat at the next table but one. There was no disputing her
plumpness ; but she had a pair of bewitching black eyes, a
heavenly complexion and a quite evident capacity for mischief.
It was a gay and a friendly and a quite ingenuous smile that
dimpled her cheeks, whose " warm " tint might have deceived
the male eye at no great distance. A small black-shod and
ribbon-laced foot peeped from under the white tablecloth
that draped to the ground. Her companion a tall fair young
woman, attired in pink and mauve, also threw him encouraging
glances, while retaining in her large peculiar eyes an
expression of languor and discontent.

Adrian responded to the joint invitation. He smiled back,
smiled repeatedly and emphatically ; they were all smiles,
all three of them. Determined not to spend this day alone
—this memorable day upon which life had laid claim to him
again—when the moment for coffee came he strolled across
to their table.

" Bon jour, m'selles ! "

" Bon jour, m'sieu ! "

" Est-ce-que je suis permis de me s'asseoir près de vous,
m'selles ? "

" Avec plaisir. Comment ça va ? You look—lonely there."

She spoke English then ! What a relief ! His knowledge
of French was that of an educated Englishman.

" Vous parlez Anglais très bien, m'selle. . . . What will
you have ? Liqueur ? Coffee ? "

" Tu nous paies un verre chacun ? Une Bénédictine pour
moi, s'il te plaît, et une pour toi aussi, Lola ? Hein ? Dis donc
tu es gentil, mon p'tit anglais ; mais tu ne parles pas français,
non ? "

" Un petit peu."

" Oh-h-h," chided the smaller of the two with a crescendo drawl. " C'est bien dommage ! " Then briskly : " We talk Engleesh. I wish to make better my Engleesh."

" And I my French. You speak English also ? " He turned to the taller of the two ladies, who had so far only smiled in a fixed sort of way. There was a nameless and, on the whole, a repulsive attraction about this second woman. Tall and thin, with a dead-white face, a vivid patch of colour on each cheek, and a setting of pale hair which seemed to contain more of dross than of gold, she looked like a withered lily— or some ghost of a former self. And her eyes, with their oddly distended pupils—they seemed to follow one uncannily.

An elusive yet powerful scent, puzzling in its familiarity, hovered about the couple.

The livelier girl intervened in response to his last question.

" No. Mlle. Lola does not speak Engleesh at all ; don't bother ! "

" Un peu, Ninette ! Un peu ! I speak a leetle."

" Not—how you say ?—so as you notice it."

Adrian and Ninette laughed. Lola did not.

" I speak the américain—très bien," she said in an injured tone, an unpleasant expression taking the place of the mirthless smile.

Ninette took no notice.

" You are on permis, leetle boy ? I know your r-reg-i-ment —your badge—surely—— ? "

" Very probably."

" You know—er—let-me-see—the small one—so fair, so funny—let-me-see—Gaie—Follay ? "

" Fotheringay ? Ah ! yes, rather ! "

" Ah ! ce-ci, Forrangaie. Oh ! "—again came the crescendo drawl—" but he is so droll, so amusing . . . and his friend, leetle Gerree, you know him ? "

" They're both in my regiment."

"Lola, tu connais ces deux petits fous anglais, n'est-ce-pas ? "

"Peut-être. Je ne sais pas. Ça ne fait rien. Au revoir ! I go."

And with a nod and with her fixed air of languid indifference, Lola rose and walked out.

"Ah ! Lola ! poor Lola," her friend exclaimed, looking after her. "She has her troubles. She has what-you-call a—past."

"Is that all ? "

"In New York, in Paris. She has lived fast. She had a friend—you know ?—a rich—*very* rich fellow—américain."

"Is that the only tragedy ? '

"No. She is getting old."

"We all are. She should not sit beside you ! "

"Seelly boy ! "

"Well, we all get old, don't we ? Is that why she looks like the ' ghost of innocence ' ? "

"Mais, non ! I do not understand."

"What's wrong with her, then ? I'm interested."

"She—I whisper—she . . . drugs."

"Good Lord ! Poor thing ! She's not the first, though. And the American ? "

"He has—how you call it ?—' gone west'. "

"And left her—with the past ? "

They laughed. Adrian called for liqueurs.

"But you thought her pretty ? " Ninette demanded.

"Comparisons are not fair."

"Her complexion ? "

"Charming, but I prefer——"

"Her hair ? "

"One cannot beat Nature." He glanced pointedly but insincerely at Ninette's coiffure. The latter remarked tersely :

" They do not belong. C'est triste. Poor Lola ! But you must not say anything against her," she added reproachfully "She is—how you say ?—my—my—*ve-ry* dear friend

" But, now she has left us—— ? "

They smiled at one another puffing at their cigarettes with emphatic amiability—an amiability that outran their powers of expression.

" How do you call yourself, mon cher ? Tom—Dick—'arry ? "

" Adrian. Just that."

" Ah ! C'est-ça. A-d-r-i-a-n. That is nize ! Say—where go we now, Adrien ? "

" Anywhere you like."

" We drive ? You come in my auto—yes ? "

" Delighted."

" Come then—mon ami."

Leaving the Bois, they drove to shops. They drove to many shops. Adrian bought her a present. Ninette was gay and companionable and chattered without ceasing. The " auto " was a good one and the chauffeur wore a livery. Couples like themselves flashed past on the Champs Élysées, in open automobiles. The pavements were crowded. No flaw could be detected in the rippling surface of that smooth-flowing life.

They finished up at d'Armenonville, which was deserted save for a couple of ultra up-to-date *demi-mondaines* drinking coffee with two bejewelled young Jews. They sat at a green table under a striped umbrella for a long time, which seemed a short one, and sipped non-intoxicating iced drinks through straws and kicked each other foolishly under the table. They laughed and chattered—all about nothing. Then heat over-came them, and they leaned back in easy chairs listening to the hushed song of chaffinches and linnets, and through wreaths of cigarette-smoke watching the flycatchers dart back and forth from their perch on the opposite railing.

" What a perfectly objectless day ! " he reflected with much satisfaction. Ninette was its *motif*.

The Bois slept. Old men slept on seats, head on breast,

newspaper lying unheeded on the ground. Nursery-maids slept on the grass beside their perambulators, oblivious of faintly-protesting babies. Middle-aged ladies and beggars slept in cool places under trees. Slum children lay about in heaps. Even the waiters slept—while waiting.

Adrian thought indistinctly once or twice of the railway-station as he had seen it on the previous night. That was reality, this—the world of make-believe. There one bit the hard core of things—there, and in the churches perhaps, and in the heart of the middle-class homes. How much, he wondered, did the girl beside him know of—all that? And what did it matter, anyway? . . .

When they left d'Armenonville and returned to the streets, a certain staleness, a certain dusty emptiness and dreariness seemed to have descended upon Paris. At tea-time Rumpel-mayer's, where the couple drank chocolate, was utterly deserted. In the Rue Royale, the Faubourg St. Honoré, the Avenue de l'Opéra, a few little milliners, a few officials and business people might be seen hurrying homewards. A pause seemed to supervene between the heyday of afternoon and that other mysterious spell which transfigures Paris after dark.

They thereupon repaired to Ciro's, where at all events illusion might be sustained. And in the suffused glow of a great white room flooded by electric lights concealed in cornices, they trifled with cocktails, with coffee—with each other.

Maurice, coal-black, grinning, paternal, with a fatalistic air gravely exaggerated, brought queer conserves on an Oriental tray.

" He'll do that," Adrian said to his friend (who did not understand) studying the immobile face, " unchanging and still grinning to the end of time—if not beyond."

§ 2

So the hour of the pleasure-seekers arrived. And the pleasure-seekers were crowding in, as they did every evening, to the restaurants and cafés. The Café de Joie was nearly full, its white and mirrored interior brilliantly lighted, its yellow satin settees round the walls crowded, as also were the tables in the centre. People kept coming in, an endless stream, and pushing along to the end. Waiters darted and ran, acrobatically, dramatically, unnecessarily, superloaded with plates and viands. It was a typical war-time crowd—chiefly uniforms, all the women in hats, no evening dress anywhere. From it arose a confused murmur in which the knives, the forks, and the plates conducted their own orchestration as against the chattering voices, the treble laughs of the women, the sharp cries of dissent or interrogation, the eating, drinking, and amusing, the breathless intensely business of humanity.

A florid, red-faced, fair-haired man in a short evening coat and black tie—with the air of an English bookmaker—conducted them to a table near the door. A man of influence, this, sought after, rather particularly disposed towards British officers. He smiled approvingly down at Ninette, who made a whimsical grimace ; he beamed upon her companion, seeing visions of intoxication and extortion.

" Look !—with an américain." Ninette, seizing his hand, pointed.

It was Lola.

There she sat in pink and mauve, with her dead-white complexion and its two patches of colour, and her strange eyes fixed on everything and yet nothing, smiling her mechanical smile. And again he had the feeling of being confronted by a ghost, a haggard and evil ghost—of some former self.

It was not *the* American ! Ninette reassured him as to that. The entire world of Ninette and Lola was there— Renée, Georgette, Gaby—each pointed out in turn—all a little drunk, gesticulating at one another, and laughing piercingly.

Well—the couple waxed merry under the influence of champagne. They sat close together, their feet touching under the table. They held hands. How endlessly diverting Ninette was with her quick-change face and quaint figure, her endless *répertoire* of drollery and mimic! And—yes! it was even possible she had a heart—or was it the champagne? . . . Nineteen and a finished Parisienne! She had accomplishments. She was never still. She blew straws at old men, whistled between her teeth; puffed out her cheeks and made queer clicking noises with her tongue; parted her lips and rolled her eyes until, slightly alarmed, he came to the conclusion they had gone to the back of her head; adopted a rubber face and screwed it into inhuman shapes; did astonishing things with her tricky cap that tied itself with velvet under her pert chin. Now and then an envenomed look came into her eyes when she pointed at someone of the sisterhood.

"Poor Renée!" It was always "poor" Renée. "How tired she looks! (I know that American too!) She has not even troubled to look nice this evening. That girl will not last long. . . . Ah! Denise, regardez!—there's a bad one! It was she . . ." (Whispers, looking daggers at the enemy.) "Yes, and she was forbidden Maxim's. Damn! She points at me! She laughs. I snap my fingers at her. I . . . (She extends five beringed fingers from the tip of her nose.) "Any more insults, and I send for Georges. Georges likes me. He will have her turned out."

She constantly pinches Adrian's arm. And every now and again she whispers.

"Ma tear leetle boy! You like me—yes? You like Ninette? I am pretty—yes? You love me a leetle bit? . . . Alors! Allons!"

And through the mist of the scent and the cigar-smoke and the champagne, her dark eyes glow at him like lamps in a still, warm garden.

§ 3

The scene changes.

Sitting close together, they look down from a height. To Adrian all is trance-like, unreal, suffused with a kind of headstrong, wine-given romance.

He sees the interior of a large round building packed from floor to ceiling; many nationalities crowded into the auditorium and the boxes, all the *crème* of vice and the fine art of sin to be found in the world compressed between those circular plush and gilded walls and that high dome, all the dancing bubbles of life, all the drunken frolics of fancy boiling together in that astounding cauldron of a music-hall. The atmosphere is pungent with cigars, stale scent, and overcrowded humanity. Alternate spasms of violent mirth and equally violent emotion ripple over the crowd like wind on a wheatfield. A dazzling stage crowded with human figures, elaborate scenery in garish colours, a lantern shooting at the stage violent beams. On either side of it, a stout, tall female posed in pink silk tights, wearing an imbecile smile. Women, all women, on the stage, in all colours, many patterns, wheeling, weaving figures :

> "Like strange mechanical grotesques
> Making fantastic arabesques."

—interweaving, ogling, grinning, smirking, mincing and marking time in a whirl of painted faces.

Then music. Music of sheer frivolity, of utter folly. Wild, disconnected music. On the stage, the girls prance, going through the motions of the "Gaby Glide," or the "Ragtime Wedding March," throwing out snatches of the English music-hall song, "For you're here and I'm here, so what do we care ?" . . . This idiotic ragtime jangle—whence its power to make life seem good, hopeful, liveable, inspiring ? Adrian seizes and he presses Ninette's most willing hand. . . .

Hush! A pause. A stillness. The stage changes—it is an Apache scene—a Grand Guignol setting. A frail and distant voice:

> " C'est la valse brune
>   Des chevaliers de la lune,
>   Que la lumière importune,
>   Et qui recherchent un coin noir."

Adrian starts and shivers like one awaking at daybreak from a hectic dream.

§ 4

The curtain falls. It is the entr'acte. Mechanically Adrian permits Ninette to link her arm in his, and with the rest of the throng they promenade around the vast *foyer*. She laughs and chatters, but he has no attention for her now. He is lost in his thoughts, but those thoughts are not of her. He only wants to be rid of her. . . .

Alone of all Paris through four dynamic years the Temple of the Daughters of Joy has not changed. All the world of Renée and of Lola are there (in boxes), all the world of Gaby, Yvonne, and Ninette (in boxes), and the world beneath theirs and the under-world again. It seems to Adrian that for the first time he sees the soul of Pleasure—face to face.

It distresses him. It frightens him. He longs to get away —longs for darkness and quiet and air and space—for hills and the sea.

He touches Ninette's arm.

" I'm going," he says. " You will stay ? "

" Mais non ! Mais non ! Mon cher ! " she protests emphatically. " Cer-tain-ly not. You go—I go too." She seizes and she squeezes his arm.

They pass down the length of the *foyer*. Crowds of every nationality wander aimlessly around and around. All the twisted saturnine faces; all the flabby, gross, and sensual faces; all conceivable expressions of vice and malice, of cruelty and evil; all features seared by passion, painted, rouged, wrought by the devil; all meanness, furtiveness, sordid craving, and grasping lust are written there. Never a woman's passing face—and there are hundreds—never a pair of woman's eyes but on them are stamped this nameless sign, plainer, fouler than the mark of Cain. How expressive of evil, more expressive than a man's by far, a woman's face! Paint, powder, and rouge, these cannot hide it—nor Youth nor Age.

And over all, among the palms, among the little tables, in the pale blue half-light, in the yearning, quasi-romantic music of the band—they are playing a pathetically banal London air, " Hullo, my dearie ! "—at the back of it all, a vast weariness. He looks into sad eyes—for among the Daughters of Joy there is no mirth—and sees there only the weariness of self-willed children who have played too long and too well.

Snatches of conversation come from the crowd. As they pass out a voice with a New York accent says :

" Well, chérie, what'd you do if the Boche came day after to-morrow ? "

A girl's voice :

" Oh, what do I care ? Let 'em come ! "

Outside—black night. In the heart of Paris the Eiffel Tower soars up to the sky. From it may be seen the flickering or guns, the rising and falling of star-lights where, towards Compiègne, the German armies lie.

§ 5

The auto has long ago been dismissed, and the couple walk. After dark the Boulevard Montmartre is peopled with ghosts. They strut singly and in twos, they strut noisily with men, they slide by in the shadows peering up at the passer, they loiter under street lamps and stroll aimlessly in front, they flit round street-corners and dart out of the dim recesses of shop-doors. And if they see a man alone they creep up beside him, whisper to him, pluck him by the elbow, even call out to him at a distance of several yards. To one from the trenches it is a strange experience, this great formless, nameless company of spirits—pursuing, importuning—here, there, everywhere—so many and so hungry.

Presently the couple stop a rickety *fiacre* and rattle slowly down the Rue de Castiglione, under the great archway of the Tuileries, through the courtyard, over the Pont des Beaux Arts, and so across the Seine. Along the Boulevard Saint Germain, past the listening statue of Voltaire. Silent and dark the river, overpowering the mass of the Louvre on the side they have left. Then through a labyrinth of old and narrow streets, tortuous lanes between high walls, vast buildings, courts and alley-ways, many churches. It is impossible to recognise anything. . . . Whither are they going ? Neither knows—or cares. Adrian only knows that the night is warm and close, that his brain throbs furiously, that two faces confront him fitfully, interchangeably, per-plexingly like faces seen in delirium ; Ninette only that she has her Englishman—still.

She nestles against him, her head rests upon his shoulder, her arm entwines itself around his neck ; in the fitful lamplight her eyes try to reach his. Yet he is oblivious of her. He hates her. He wishes only to be alone. . . .

And they are lost ? No, the driver knows—that old man who must have driven a lifetime through these streets. Ah ! they're in the Quartier Latin ! For here is the Sorbonne and here, after many windings, the rounded dome of the Panthéon seen dimly against a gun-lit sky.

"Mon chéri ! Mon chéri ! Kees me ! Love me !—a leetle."

The chimes of Nôtre Dame silver to the city's sleep.

Yes—midnight and the world forgetting ! A frightened

moon gazing down, and loneliness and the screaming of cats
A nameless figure flits by hugging the wall like one ashamed.
Here and there a light burns in some student's window, some
student poring over his books or keeping late company in
his attic.

> " C'est la valse brune
> Des chevaliers de la lune,
> Que la lumière importune,
> Et qui recherchent—"

The very cobble stones repeat it, the very night
echoes it—and so do the dim old streets. It revolves in the
turmoil of his brain, mingles with faces and the fumes of
champagne. . . .

The city dreams and dreaming seems to wait—this Paris
that is like some wayward, imperial woman in her mystery, her
deception, and her passion ; her pride and beauty and her joy
of life ; her comedies and tears, her magnificence and wickedness ; her tremendous past, her future—? Her laughter at the
destinies of men. . . .

" Let us go home, my Adrien ! You are sleepy—and I
too."

Ninette's voice is caressing, soft as the purring of a little
cat.

But he recoils—yes, repels her roughly. He is suddenly
furious with himself, averse from her. He wishes to be rid
of her—at all costs, to be alone. He shouts to the cabman :

" To the Hotel Paris-Astoria—quickly ! "

He scarcely hears, and does not heed, Ninette's weak
cry :

" Oh no ! But no, Adrien ! You are not going to leave
me, you are not going to leave me, mon petit, petit anglais——"

That broken snatch of a song ! Buried, best-forgotten
memories touched back to life ! All the obliterated past,
the imperfect present ; all the confused crowding faces of

these tempestuous years; all the old faded atmosphere of —a girl at a piano.

Yet strangely it is not the memory of *that* face which accuses him, which haunts him as they rumble back over the way they have come, which lingers with him through the remaining night.

Ninette whimpers but he does not notice. He is cruel to her when she tries to take his hand. He thrusts money into it and does not know he has done so. And Ninette still whimpers.

And gun-flashes light up the night sky. . . .

And out of his uneasy vision of Paris, revelation comes.

CHAPTER X

Rencontre

§ 1

UPON a bitter evening of early October Adrian Knoyle's battalion set out upon its march along one of those roads which, having traversed the Somme battlefield, strike across the much-fought-over tract of country between Bapaume and Cambrai. There was little to cheer the heart. The kits were late in being hoisted onto the transport wagons ; the quartermaster was correspondingly annoyed. Tritton, the adjutant, was in a bad humour ; a scratch-up meal before the start had to be eaten under circumstances of chilly confusion which if possible enhanced its nastiness ; most of the cups, plates, knives and forks had been already packed up, these misfortunes being apparently inseparable from a move at such short notice. Nevertheless the troops marched gaily, glad to be up and doing after four months in the trenches, reinforced by rumours that the British Army had " broken through " (blessed phrase !) at last, that the Germans were "on the run," and that the cavalry had entered Cambrai several hours previously.

During the four months that had passed since Adrian's visit to Paris, the fortunes of the Allied Armies had veered, bringing a corresponding reaction in the spirits of the combatants. Victory appeared to be almost in sight. Instead of a desperate defence before Amiens and the gates of Paris, the Allied Armies were now attacking along the greater part of the front and it was the turn of the Germans to fight rear-guard actions. The French had captured Soissons, the heights of the Aisne were in danger. Even the line of the Meuse was threatened. Further north, the British in a series of mass attacks had pierced the outer works of those vast field-fortifications known as the Siegfried line.

In the foregoing operations Adrian's Division had so far taken no part. Its share in the earlier of the year's fighting had been a heavy one. Until the very eve of the general attack in the latter part of August, it had remained in occupation of the quiet trench-sector south of Arras which had been taken over early in May. Just before the advance, however, it was relieved by another Division and moved so short a distance south as brought it back to the very edge of the great burial-ground of the Somme with its poignant memories of two years before.

So the tramp eastward began and once more Adrian Knoyle and Arthur Cornwallis found themselves marching side by side through gathering darkness at the head of the Left Flank Company, while Burns, sturdy and combative, brought up the rear.

" Well—for it again, Adrian ! " remarked Cornwallis almost jocosely.

" Yes, but this time I think we're going through."

The buoyancy of the marching-step and of the lively drums-and-fifes echoed the optimism of these words. The familiar strains of " The long, long trail " eddied down the column.

Arthur, who was quick to study his friend, had noticed in him a new optimism since his return from Paris, and like a barometer responded to it. For that matter, it was the note of the whole army. He had further remarked a new look in Adrian's face, so long unresponsive to good fortune or ill —a happier look. And the well-meaning fellow rejoiced accordingly.

Adrian explained.

" I gather it's largely a question of whether we get Cambrai and the high ground west of it. If we do, we shall start open fighting—cavalry and all that. We ought to push 'em back to the Rhine, or at any rate the Meuse. But from what Forsyth says, we're being held up somewhere—by some high wooded ground as far as I can make out from the map, which commands all the plain to the east. He seemed to think it would be our job to tackle that. It always takes us to do the dirty work."

"If we do get them back to the Rhine, they'll want to make peace, won't they ? "

"I should think so."

Cornwallis reflected.

"Adrian, how soon after peace has been declared do you think we should get home ? "

"Ask me another. You're out of step, my boy. And your haversack's all over the place. Why in Heaven's name *will* you use bits of string ? "

Cornwallis had lost none of his dreaminess, his " hopeless " habits. Nor had his soldierly qualities improved. Tritton declared they never would because he hadn't got any. On parade he was everyone's despair. On the other hand, as Sutton facetiously put it, he " never ceased doing good " in his platoon, was perpetually inquiring of his men whether they had mittens and books to read, and how often they heard from home. Burns was caustic at the expense of his efficiency. And yet everybody liked Cornwallis, including the men who laughed at him. At trench-mortars—to which he had been delicately transferred at Colonel Forsyth's instigation—he proved no more adept than at drill ; in fact, the trench-mortar commander described his handling of these weapons as a menace to the whole Brigade. He thereupon returned to duty, crestfallen, apologetic, but more willing than ever. He continued to peer patiently and amiably at the world through spectacles ; he continued to write poetry—and print it ; and at intervals spoke sorrowfully of Miss Gina Maryon who had never vouchsafed him one single line. He moreover continued to say his prayers in the most unsuitable situations. In the current jargon, he remained a "trier," through and despite all.

After two hours' marching with only one brief stop, they halted for some time under a little ridge that formed one side of a hollow in which a number of artillery-horses were picketed. The sun had gone down in a loom of red and grey, in a strange, distorted fantasy of ochre, wind-blown clouds shot with dying autumnal scarlet. Early the night became splashed and spangled with the gleam of camp-fires, and around these fires and braziers groups of men could be seen warming their hands or boiling water for tea in their mess-tins. Loud was the laughter and the singing of songs, uproarious at times the exchange of compliments from one fireside to another. A stranger might have imagined that of all these noisy fellows none had a care in the world—certainly not that they stood on the threshold of eternity.

Knoyle was, as he had ever been, almost morbidly sensitive to the *macabre* quality of these nights on the eve of battle. Sleep he could not, and, feeling a strong disinclination to lie down, he climbed the low ridge that protected their bivouac. The spectacle which presented itself was one of those that haunt men through their lives. There was something supernatural in it and—sempiternal. Along the horizon flickered the lightning of countless guns; here and there, though still far away, rose Vérey lights, red and green, yellow and white, and golden shower-rockets and other powerful rockets that seemed to cast their glimmer even back there. The dark mass of the country lay brooding between. It was like a vast open amphitheatre enclosing within its walls of sky all the storm and passion, the illusion and terror, the mystery and obscurity of human life. Watching from this high spot was like a man at his birth whose unseeing eye looks out into the future with its glimmerings of hope and fate, its little lonely lights and prodigious unprobed shadows. Only in this scene there lurked a sombre note, something wild and melancholy, something closer akin to the end of things than to their beginning.

Yet he did not now, as so often before, feel any despairing loneliness of his thoughts. He never was alone now. Often Eric accompanied him on the long marches—often Faith.

He only wondered, as men do at such times, what this new—and last ?—crisis of his destiny might bring forth. . . . Looking up, he saw the starlight serenely smiling the starlight that never changed, that was on the whole kind.

§ 2

Soon the men were awakened and they resumed the march forward. So dark was it that only occasional belts of barbed-wire or German stakes could be discerned, and opening from the roadside banks, deep trenches that seemed to face westward. On one side squatted an abandoned tank. A little farther on three dead horses lay in the roadway. For the rest, there was nothing definite to show that they were passing through country which had been in German hands only twenty-four hours before. Once the column halted to let a battery fire immediately across its front, once in the street of a big village whose shattered silence was uncanny. Then they were out in the open country again, with the Vérey lights marking a wide semicircle and the north-east wind singing its wintry song in the telegraph wires. The chatter of machine-guns came nearer, but it was spasmodic, and the night remained unexpectedly quiet. The moon that should have illumined the scene was hidden by piled-up clouds. Shells began to burst a few hundred yards ahead, and presently a large one exploded close to the junction of a grass track with the high road as they were passing. A few men " ducked." Cornwallis gave a convulsive leap, recovered himself, and exclaimed :

" Oh !—dash it ! I was thinking of something else."

Somebody behind laughed.

Then the leading fours struck the *pavé* of the Cambrai highway. Last autumnal leaves on sentinel poplars shook and hissed in the wind. In front, a vague shape loomed up—that of a great wood surmounting and clothing the sides of a conical-shaped hill. An artillery-limber clattered along the road. They came to the remains of what had once been a wayside inn ; behind it pack-ponies and medical troops were sheltering : a number of wounded lay in the lee of a wall. They halted. The glass had been blown out of the windows, but in one of the rooms some men had lighted a fire of dry leaves and sticks that had drifted in and lay heaped up. Tempted by the cheerful-looking blaze, Adrian entered. A man sat nodding on a wooden box before the fire. In a corner a prostrate figure lay on a stretcher, partially covered by a soldier's greatcoat.

It was the latter drew his attention ; it worried him ; it fascinated him. The fire played about it so affectionately. It lay so still.

" What's it like up there ? " Adrian addressed the figure by the fire, jerking his head in the direction of the wood.

The man proved to be a quartermaster.

" Oh ! great snakes ! it's been a filthy job. Our casualties 'ave been somethin' crool. Well, thank 'eavings we come out of it to-night. I'm waiting for them now. . . . 'Ave a cig. ? Give us a light, will yer ? . . . Tar."

" What's that there ? " Adrian indicated the form on the stretcher.

" That ? That's our Commanding Officer. . . . Dead. 'E got a bullet through 'is chest this morning just after they went over."

The wind howled outside, blew gustily in, and swept the coverlet aside from the face, making the fire burn all the brighter.

It was a jovial-looking corpse. The face was that of an oldish man with a heavy fair moustache. The antics of the flames, coupled with some smears of congealed blood, gave it the appearance of being in the act of a ghastly laugh. The head lolling rakishly on one side added to this suggestion of grotesque mirth. There was indeed something so peculiar about the whole attitude and expression that Adrian went over to look closer.

Glazed blue eyes caught a merry glint.

Adrian stepped back.

" Good God ! . . . It's old Arden ! "

" Eh ? What ! Somebody you know ? " the quarter-master mumbled drowsily.

" Why, it's—it's Arden ! "

The other looked up.

" That's right. 'is lordship was our Colonel. Met him before, then ? "

" I—knew him well."

" You knew a good man, then—one of the best. Brave ! 'E's earned the V.C., that old chap, half-a-dozen times over since 'e's been with us. But everybody knew 'e'd stop one. Too impetuous, yer know, too 'asty. 'E never oughter been up where 'e was—insisted on going, y'know—*would* go. That was the Colonel all over. An elderly man, too ; turned fifty, I believe. 'E 'adn't been with us long. . . . Well—we shall never see the likes of 'im again. 'E was all right."

" Where are you taking him ? "

" We're going to give 'im a decent funeral somewhere 'way back when the boys come out. . . . 'Elp yerself to a drink before yer move on, won't cher ? "

" Lead on ! Lead on ! Keep closed up in rear ! "

Burns was bellowing outside ; the men were beginning to shuffle forward. Adrian turned to take a last look at Arden before joining them.

Yes, there was no mistaking the attitude, the—hilarity.

"Glad the old colonel's 'ad a pal to look at him before 'e goes under the daisies. Good-night!" The quartermaster settled down again to his interrupted doze.

Adrian's mind was far away. It was a hot August afternoon. Arden was standing at his baronial front-door, laughing; his head was thrown back and slightly on one side, and he was shouting to Gina, Eric, and himself "not to get mixed up in the war."

Death, after all, was the supreme caricature!

§ 3

Yet as they wound up a sunken lane into the heart of the great wood it was not with Arden that his thoughts busied themselves, though he did mutter to himself, "Poor old Arden! Poor old Arden!" in a mechanical way. The fact was he had grown too accustomed to death, and in a sense too contemptuous of it, to receive any very acute shock even from so unexpected a *rencontre*.

His thoughts instead flew half across France—to Faith. Well, the dawn had not crimsoned the sky for her yet! If he could but be beside her, near her in this second visitation! If only he could break the news to her, make his sympathy known to her! It struck him as supremely natural, as indeed inevitable, that she should turn to him. To whom else should she turn?

CHAPTER XI

The Last Fight

§ 1

THERE were no shell-holes, no visible desolation or destruction in the wood. It bore little resemblance, as far as could be seen, to Delville or St. Pierre Vaast or Sanctuary Wood. The leaves were still on the trees, though autumn had begun her ravages.

An occasional discarded khaki jacket, grey German overcoat, rifle or relic of equipment alone showed that the fighting had passed that way. The wood seemed immense. After twenty minutes' marching, a cross-road that must have been near the centre of it was reached. Wheeling to the left, they turned into a long, straight ride that seemed to rise steeply at the farther end. (Adrian remembered such rides in the home coverts at Stane, where young pheasants flocked out at sundown in response to the keeper's whistle, as he scattered handfuls of corn; there, too, at night a lamp dangled from a stick to scare away foxes.) The rifle and machine-gun fire, which for long had been desultory, now suddenly became fierce. Lights began to go up all round; bullets hit the trees with a " smack," sizzed, twanged, and zipped overhead. It was not long before the usual message came: " Pass down the word for the stretcher-bearers "; two or three men in rear had been hit. From mouth to mouth meanwhile was passed the order, " Keep well into the side." Here and there the body of a cavalryman lay half in, half out of the ditch. From the high part of the wood in front came the furious crackle of musketry, drowned at times by the slow, methodical " rat-tat-tat " of the machine-guns and the faster rattle of the light automatics. Some muttered " Wind up ! " others " Counter-attack ! "

Then something curious occurred. Down the centre of the ride, and quickly in the midst of the advancing troops, hurried a small body of men. They were bawling excitedly. Their faces as they approached showed chalky-white in the darkness ; they seemed incoherent, distraught. At their head strode a toweringly tall soldier, capless, and shouting :

" Retire ! Retire ! They've broken through. They're coming down through the wood. Get back ! Get back ! "

The tall man appeared to be an officer. He chattered wildly, disconnectedly, yet with a method of sense like a drunken man ; tried to pull himself together, then wandered off again.

" The bay'net ! " he kept repeating. " The bay'net ! That's the only thing. Show 'em the bay'net, get at 'em with the bay'net, and they'll run. . . ." He made curious, erratic movements with his hands.

It was a moment that called for quick decision—such a moment as Adrian had long anticipated. How should he act ? Colonel Forsyth and his adjutant with the remainder of the battalion had gone round a different way. Should he proceed on his own initiative ? . . . Inspiration born of long experience came to his assistance. He knew roughly from his map the configuration of the wood and that a few hundred yards farther on two rides crossed one another at right angles. The advancing enemy must be taken in flank, if at all, and the best way to accomplish this, it seemed, would be to post a Lewis gun at the cross-rides and catch the Germans as they swept across the lateral ride. It appeared, indeed, the only chance of saving the rest of the battalion, with which he was unable to communicate, from being cut off.

But whom should he trust with this all-important mission ? Burns, of course, was absolutely safe. But he wanted Burns if it came to a hand-to-hand fight. Cornwallis—— ? His heart had many a time secretly bled for Cornwallis. . . . Arthur should have his chance.

He passed along word for him and explained the situation.

When I blow my whistle, loose off every belt you've got until I blow again. Then cease fire and wait for them to come back across the ride. It's straight ahead to the cross-rides. You can't lose your way. Go right ahead, and good luck ! "

"Very well, Adrian." There was a frenzied eagerness in the other's voice, and he disappeared with his gun-team in the darkness.

Burns with two more Lewis guns was covering the upward sweep of the ride. The rest of the company fixed bayonets and quietly lined the roadside banks.

They waited. . . . There is at any time something weird and ghostly about a large wood at night. Darkness fills the spaces between the trees ; the trees lean together and whisper and take on strange shapes ; in the dim recesses, vistas and secret places that the eye cannot probe, the mind pictures imaginary terrors and unsubstantial dreads. The woodland seems peopled with a shadowy company of forms and sounds.

Hark ! The crackle of twigs, the breaking of branches. Here and there an excited shout and the shadowy form of a scout flitting back. Adrian drew his revolver. Every moment he expected to see a grey mob swarm out between the tree-trunks. Three shots from a sniper cracked out a short distance in front. It was a prearranged signal. He judged the critical moment to have come.

His whistle sounded.

One, two, three seconds passed. . . . An increasingly loud rustling of leaves and crackling of branches came to their straining ears. . . . Further seconds passed—a full minute. Still no sound of a Lewis gun's whirlwind clatter. The situation became perilous. The suspense was shuddering ;

at any moment they might find themselves surrounded. Had Cornwallis failed him ? For the first time in his life he cursed the ill-starred youth from the bottom of his heart. He blamed himself, too. Imbecile ! Idiot that he was ! Why had he, a company-commander, been fool enough to trust such a long-since-broken reed ? But it would be the fool's last chance. He should never be forgiven if, indeed, they emerged alive. He would have to be got rid of.

There could be no doubt the Germans were close upon them. Even now it might be too late to hold them back. The crackling and snapping of twigs sounded immediately in front. The sense of unseen people moving became almost intolerable. The order to fire trembled on his lips. . . .

Suddenly the scene he had visualised became a living fact. The grey trees became grey Germans, out of the dripping brambles crept ogre-like figures in steel helmets, carrying rifles and bayonets at the "ready." There were one or two stifled exclamations in German. Adrian barely had time to notice that the dim figures of the enemy glanced furtively this way and that as though uncertain of their direction before he yelled the word "Charge ! " His men rose and stumbled forward, shouting. A loud shout came from Burns on the left. Two revolver-shots rapped out, then several rifles. There were half-strangled oaths and exclamations, there was hard, fierce breathing, once there was a squeal like a pig being killed, and—once or twice—the rasp of bayonets. A whirlwind scattering of leaves followed one or two sharp commands in German. Then a prolonged pattering of feet that gradually grew fainter.

Adrian yelled, "Rapid—fire ! " The intense gloom was stabbed by pin-points of fire. The wood echoed and re-echoed with volley after volley ; bullets whirred, thwacked, and ricochetted from the tree-trunks ; for some minutes the noise was deafening. . . .

They saw no more of the enemy that night—or of Cornwallis.

When Adrian and an orderly crept up to the cross-rides no trace of him or his Lewis gun could be found.

§ 2

Half-an-hour later Adrian gave the order to " lead on," and they stumbled in single file along a narrow path, the trees and undergrowth pressing close in on either hand, the constant drip-drip from the frosty boughs being the only nearby sound. The darkness was such that a man could not see his hand before his face, nor, however close, his neighbour's back. Not a word was uttered. The path wound now steeply between high banks, now tortuously, avoiding the trunks of fallen trees, now over stony and now over marshy ground. The Germans, they knew, must still be close, though none could say where. Occasionally a Vérey light lit up the moist, shiny tree-trunks and the network of brambles ; once, when all stopped, the pale glimmer disclosed a group of men in steel helmets, standing close together in a tense listening attitude some fifty yards away.

Eventually the head of the extended file reached the farthest extremity of the wood, the latter stretching back along the twisting path almost to the point where that path joined the main ride. By this time everybody was tiring. No one knew what to expect or what to do next, until a runner arrived from Colonel Forsyth with instructions to dig in before daybreak. Contact was obtained with outposts of Highlanders and dismounted cavalry, who had already beaten off two counter-attacks that day. The Germans, they reported, were established in the north-east corner, but in what strength could not be determined. Daybreak being no more than a couple of hours distant, there was no time to lose. The men, tired as they were, got out their entrenching tools and began digging, each a hole for himself. There was no grumbling. They were even too tired to swear. The non-commissioned officers, it is true, were inclined to be captious, the men being perhaps stupid from lack of sleep. Yet all worked on patiently, and after a time their hard breathing and the grate of entrenching spades against roots or stones were the only sounds heard. . . .

Gradually, almost imperceptibly, a grey-blue, misty light began to filter in among the trees. Adrian watched with a kind of fascinated curiosity the dawn stealing through the woodland, now so natural-looking and quiet—where, nevertheless, a few yards away death lay in wait. Presently, as sure as the sun rose, the wooded hill would echo and re-echo with the sinister messages of rifle and machine-gun.

Many a time in his boyhood he had crept out into the great woods that clothed the cup-like arena at the foot of the Three Hills, where lay his home, and watched the light steal in among the tree-trunks, heard the birds awakening, and seen the first sunbeams gild the high, green summits of the downs.

Now the light spread and grew so that he listened for the birds to awaken; but it was as though Nature had fled the place, leaving Man to fight out his bitter quarrel alone. No chatter of magpie or jay, no woodpecker's laugh, no crooning of wood-pigeon or wistful cry of the soaring kestrel, or sparrow-hawk's plaintive whistle, no squirrel's chuckle as he played with beech-nuts or acorns. The shy little community that inhabits every French woodland had vanished. Only the drip-drip-drip of the frosted trees went on, and the daylight became real and hard and cold.

§ 3

There was in the very centre and highest part of the wood a large open clearing, in which stood three ramshackle huts that had obviously been used by the Germans, partly as a wood-store, partly as a tool-shed, and partly as quarters for those whose business it had been to fell and cut up the trees. One of these huts, the largest, had also evidently been used as a kind of office. It was littered with papers, with advertisements, with portions of German equipment, with oddments, such as an old-fashioned gramophone, a pipe-rack, a kettle and the like. On the floor were several recent copies of the *Berliner Tageblatt*, together with a pile of carefully-ruled, neatly-kept pay-sheets and accounts. There were also a table, a couple of chairs, and five or six wire-netting beds.

Here, shortly after noon of this same day, gathered all the officers of the battalion. A conference had just been held at battalion headquarters—a small shooting pavilion nearby. Orders had come " from above " that the Germans were to be driven out of the wood immediately and " at all costs."

Colonel Forsyth, looking tired and worried, briefly explained his plan. There was to be a short machine-gun barrage, he said, no artillery preparation. The two flank companies, commanded respectively by Gerald Sutton and Adrian Knoyle, were to lead the attack, supported by the two remaining companies, and were to capture the enemy's machine-gun emplacements (with which the wood was believed to be lightly held) at the point of the bayonet. Zero hour was two o'clock.

" Speed is the essential thing," was the note upon which the Colonel impressively concluded his *précis* of the situation. " Once you start, go for all you're worth and get in with the bayonet. . . . I needn't lay stress on the importance of what we're going to do. On our success depends the immediate advance of the Allied armies, for until this high ground overlooking the Cambrai plain is captured there can be no general forward movement, and consequently no victory on a large scale. I have given my word to the Corps Commander that we'll succeed where the other battalions have failed, if it's humanly possible. I know I can rely on you all to do your best."

Colonel Forsyth was esteemed in his battalion, and his words carried inspiration.

At this moment a diversion occurred.

A forlorn, pale, and weary-looking figure limped into the hut. It was Cornwallis.

Silence fell upon the group of officers.

"Where have you been, Cornwallis?" Colonel Forsyth inquired kindly, but without quite concealing a sorely-tried patience.

"I—I went out in front with the Lewis gun, sir. I—got lost."

The Colonel looked at him, tugging at his moustache.

"Well, you're not fit to go into this show. You're about done up already. You'd better get back to headquarters."

For a fraction of a second Cornwallis's eyes met Adrian's. The youth winced and looked away hurriedly.

"I—I'm quite all right, sir," he stammered. "I—I would rather go with the company, please, sir."

Faintly-amused glances passed between his brother-officers. There were audible whispers of "Poor old Art!"

Cornwallis shrank back into a corner of the hut.

A bottle of whisky had been mysteriously produced, and before separating upon what everybody now recognised as a desperate, if not doomed, adventure, there were "drinks all round." Tritton waxed tepidly facetious and announced that after the "show" was over he intended putting everybody in orders for breakfast roll-call parade until it was found who had smuggled that bottle up. Somebody retorted—amid rather forced laughter—that, on the contrary, this individual ought to be awarded the Victoria Cross. For the rest, business-like gravity predominated in every face except that of the boy, Sutton, whose cherubic countenance was smilingly happy. For—his senior officer, Hamilton, having been wounded during the night—he had been promoted to lead his company. Nor could he forbear to exchange a final pleasantry with his old adversary, Burns, as they drank together.

"Well, old hotstuff!" He dug the elder man in the ribs.

"It's all very well for G.H.Q. to say these things have got to be done," began Burns. "Now, in my opinion, it's not so simple. If I had the——"

"Oh! well, you haven't, you silly old man! What's more, you ought to think yourself damned lucky to get a chance of sticking a Boche before you go underground. . . . Take care of yourself, though, Methusaleh, old boy—don't run any unnecessary risks!"

He impetuously pressed the old fellow's hand. A softened look rarely seen there crossed the grizzled face.

Colonel Forsyth took his stand by the door, watch in hand. The whisky-bottle was passed round. Everybody drank except Cornwallis. Nobody happened to notice him in his corner or the look of almost defiant resolution that he had forced into his face.

The minutes ticked by. . . .

Adrian, whose heart beat rapidly beneath a calm exterior, loaded his revolver and adjusted his equipment. Burns did likewise. Upon all faces was the strained look of men who try to face lightly a desperate situation. Tritton raised his flask.

"To our next merry meeting!"

Colonel Forsyth snapped down the lid of his watch. "Time's up, I think," he said quietly.

§ 4

They filed out into the pale uncertain sunshine of a typical autumnal afternoon. The blue sky was flecked with dark and gleaming clouds that, driven before a biting north-east wind, foreboded snow. A bank of leaden grey grew out of the west; they shivered as they met the icy blast. Oaks and saplings were creaking, whining, and whispering together as they had probably done here for generations. It was one of those days when Nature is at her cruellest, when she seems to mock us poor mortals—to mock, deceive, and scourge.

The business of the afternoon was explained to the men by their platoon-commanders; all were calm, patient, and prepared in spirit. Quietly and quickly, each platoon crept down into the sunken road and climbed up the opposite bank, which was to be the jumping-off place.

Close at hand under that bank lay six tall Pomeranian Grenadiers in grotesque attitudes of death. Evidently they had been shot down together. The six waxen faces expressed many and strange things, adding to the puzzle which the dead cannot help the living to solve. Upon one was writ surprise, upon another dread, upon a third peace, upon a fourth sleep, upon a fifth terror, upon a sixth—emptiness.

Then the sunlight faded out. A storm of sleet swept up the sunken road, the little white particles danced and tossed as they were driven before the wind. The trees rocked and moaned; the black leaves, that had lain so still, now stirred and spun and whirled.

The greyness of everything sent a chill to the heart. At a muttered word of command the men, grave and quiet, fixed bayonets and crept a little closer up to the lip of the bank. Already the machine-guns were talking, and there came an answering fire from a German gun in front.

Captain Knoyle blew his whistle. . . . The first wave of the company under Burns went over the bank slightly in advance and to the right (according to plan), vanishing in the undergrowth and high brambles. Then Cornwallis, white to the lips, jumped up and led the way. He thrust through the bushes ahead of his men swiftly, steadfastly, looking neither to right nor left, but with features firm-set, like a man running to win a race. It was as though he feared his resolution might fail him at the last. . . . And the men—who had hesitated at first—followed. Dodging and running to this side and that, Cornwallis kept well ahead of everybody. Adrian, in the centre, tried to maintain direction. A machine-gun fired uninterruptedly immediately in front.

Away to the left another had opened—the place was alive with them. Rifle-fire, too, had begun. Somewhere ahead, the Germans could be heard shouting for their supports. All together, and well in line, the three platoons came to an open space, a kind of glade. With a vague feeling of surprise Adrian noticed a short distance to his right a group of khaki figures lying prostrate in a pool of sunlight on a mossy floor —one in front lying on its back, then two or three, then others. His eye focussed instantly on a grey, lined face, on grey wisps of hair blown about by the wind. It was Burns.

The platoon must have been wiped out. . . .

Well ahead of their men, Adrian and Cornwallis rushed on across the open space in front, the former realising in a flash that they were right on top of a machine-gun—that it could not be more than fifteen yards away. It opened point-blank at them. " Get down ! Get down ! " Those in rear threw themselves flat. A rush of bullets knocked up earth about their feet and furrowed up the ground and ricochetted against the trees.

Adrian suddenly knew nothing.

* * * * * *

When he recovered consciousness it was to sickness and, across the forehead, blinding pain. He could see light only through a red mist. Something seemed to have gone from his head or his brain—some integral part of it ; his temples, his face, his neck were soaking wet. When he lifted his hand to his head he found that the shape and texture of his forehead had mysteriously altered ; instead of being hard and round, it was spongy and flat. He smelt blood, saw blood on his hands—tried to raise his head, and could not.

An agonised voice whispered in his ear : " I'm here, Adrian. Lie still ! Lie still ! "

He could think of nothing, for nothing was clear to him.

Then wave after wave of shattering sound seemed to break across his consciousness—and he remembered. It was agony to move his head, but, turning it a little, he saw Cornwallis lying flat beside him.

"Keep still, Adrian! For the love of God, keep still! They're only a few yards away."

He could feel Cornwallis's body against his own, and it was trembling like a live wire.

He saw not only Cornwallis now, but knife-like sunbeams playing upon the russet tints of the little glade in which they lay. They were close up against a single young oak-tree, upon which bullets thwacked every time the machine-gun swept round. It seemed that he must have been unconscious for hours ; yet he could only have been stunned. He gradually realised that they lay between opposing forces. A number of their own men were firing from a shallow dip twenty yards in rear as they advanced. Riflemen and Lewis gunners—eight or nine in all—were coming on in little rushes, the latter out in the open now, giving steady covering fire, as they had been instructed to do by himself times out of number on the field-range. Of this particular field-practice, indeed, following Eric's tradition, Adrian had made a speciality. Had not the Left Flank team won the inter-company Lewis gun competition ? And now, helpless though he was, he watched, with a strange thrill of pride, his No. 1 gunners crawl forward, rest their guns, draw back the cocking-handle, adjust the magazine on the post, aim steadily, and fire burst after burst.

The gunners were doomed—he knew it. And first this man fell backwards squirming and groaning, then another rolled quietly over and lay across his gun. Still, the riflemen —only a handful of them now—came on behind, blazing away clip after clip while their company-commander lay and groaned and watched. Each man in turn was hit as he crossed the bullet-swept area—they tumbled over, squirming like shot rabbits. One man struck in the ankle spun rapidly round and round, shouting with pain till, blindly trying to crawl back to cover, he was shot again. Two men had fallen across each other—one dead, the other mortally wounded. Every few minutes the latter would make fruitless efforts to rise and crawl. For these two the worst was reserved. Through the air sailed a little silent spot of light. Adrian recognised it as a phosphorous bomb; he held his breath. Descending upon the topmost of the two prostrate figures, it slowly flared up. At once the dead man was burning; the other, his clothes alight, dragged himself painfully a few yards, then lay still, face downwards.

The two officers pressing up against the tree-trunk were now isolated. Heavy firing to right and left proclaimed that the attack had spread—that the whole front was now engaged. Whenever the machine-gun swept round Adrian could hear Cornwallis mutter to himself, "My God! Oh, my God!" and he dug his nails into the ground. To try and cross that sunlit space to a shallow dip among some brambles which offered the nearest cover seemed certain death. Again and again at point-blank range the machine-gun swept round. Each felt that it was only a question of moments before the end came. Still, the slim oak tree and a motionless horizontal with the ground protected them. Cross-bullets from another machine-gun now began to go high overhead. It was evident that the wood, far from being lightly held, was defended in great strength. Minutes dragged by like hours, and what period of time they lay there neither could have told. Only the wood seemed gradually to grow darker. There were intervals, too, longer and longer intervals, between each shattering burst of the machine-gun.

Adrian, bleeding and growing weaker, whispered to Cornwallis during one of these interludes:

"Get back, Arthur—now—while you can! Don't bother about me."

" No. We'll go together."

" Run for it—run. " Adrian could say no more.

After a further quarter-of-an-hour's silence Cornwallis' face, bespectacled and timid, peered into his.

" They're quiet now, Adrian. I think we'd better try and get away."

The wounded man was dragged. It was agony. Everything spun round and round in an opaque red mist. He could hear Cornwallis, panting and straining, exerting all his inadequate strength to propel them both across the open space. He lay a helpless bundle across his friend's back, his legs trailing behind.

Cornwallis crawled, pushing himself forward with his elbows. Their movement must have looked like that of some great tortoise. Twenty-five yards to cover—twenty-five yards of grass and sunlight. Even now they might not be observed, the young oak-tree might mask the enemy's vision. Already they were half-way. . . . Then the machine-gun opened. Bullets skimmed their backs, kicked up grass and soil, spattered earth around them. Cornwallis redoubled his efforts, panting and groaning in a frenzy of exertion. A fringe of brambles showed how near to safety they were. A few yards more and it would be within arm's reach. Now they were on the very lip of the shallow depression, with its carpet of dark, discoloured leaves. They only had to roll into it.

Saved ! . . .

In that instant, Cornwallis uttered a short, sharp cry. A prolonged vibration quivered through his frame. He gave a little whimper, rolled forward—and lay still.

Adrian must have lost consciousness again then, for when he awoke twilight was falling. A weight lay across him —at first he thought it was a heavy bough. Then he saw Cornwallis's dead face lying among the leaves beside his own.

§ 5

The frost came down. The velvety sky began to twinkle with stars. Some distance away he could hear sounds of digging. Close at hand the Germans were creeping about in the undergrowth; and now a bomb would be thrown and now star-lights, going up all round, illuminated the glistening trunks of the trees. Then firing set in wildly along the whole line, accompanied by the familiar snap of the rifle-bolts, and the rattle of Lewis guns and machine-guns. After a while these died away into comparative silence. Once all the German batteries opened like a roll of thunder, and for half-an-hour the sky was alight and a-quiver; then gas-shells came groaning, grunting overhead.

Adrian grew cold. The blood about his head coagulated, stiffened. He dragged himself from beneath the body of his friend. They thus lay side by side as they had lain in bivouac and billet.

He apprehended the oncoming of death—" arms wide to embrace, sleep strong to enfold, a friend there, faithful and true."

Yet how he longed to live!

A long time passed. Once when a star-shell went up he saw Cornwallis lying beside him, and was shocked by the caricature Death had made of his poor, weak face. His spectacles, broken, were tilted at a peculiar angle on his nose, his untidy hair tumbled about his forehead; these, together with some brown smears about the corners of his mouth, gave him the appearance of a badly " made-up " comedian. If Arden in death had seemed to laugh, Cornwallis was laughable. And that, after all, he had been—in life.

About the middle of the night wild cries came out of the sky. " Honk! Honk! Honk! "—and there was a sound as of a mighty rushing wind. He knew that sound. It was the flight of the wild geese down from the autumnal North. It was as if the souls of the faithful were fleeing, distracted, from a fallen world.

A phase of mental drowsiness succeeded; he pondered quietly over many things. Dreams and fancies, dreams and fancies stole upon his mind—those merciful dreams which clothe reality in happiness and peace. . . . Why and whence and whither—who should say? And where was the place of beauty in this self-destructive creation? The wood—it must have been fair enough in spring-time, and summer. Even now it held the pleasant contours, the russet and mahogany colouring, the warm red-and-black tints of the falling year. But its little community of birds and beasts, its immemorial silence, its dim and secret places, its wind-rocked solitude that had remained unbroken for generations: when this horror was over-past and themselves forgotten, would those calm and beautiful things return again?

That was his happier thought. And out of the tangle of his doubts and questionings and vague uncertainties understanding came at length. . . . Cornwallis, who was weak and a failure, who had endeavoured and wrestled with himself, who had suffered—he at the last had triumphed; those Lewis gunners, those sleepers yonder who knew nought of God, who never thought of themselves, who never approached in imagination their own sublimity—out of the humble simplicity of their lives had been achieved the greatest of all things.

So he knew—though it were his last conscious thought— that there moved in the world something greater than fear or grief or mental agony or earthly pain—some human force, undeniable, that triumphed over these and surpassed civilisation and vanquished the powers of the Prince of Darkness himself.

A sound of shouting broke in upon these dreams.
Voices came as a far-off murmur to his ears. . . .

" Lead on ! Lead on ! Advance ! " The voice, he thought, was Sutton's.

A bugle sounded.

" Where are they ? "

" Gone. Cambrai's taken. They're falling back all along the line."

" Advance ! Advance ! "

A faint light grew in the east, paling the tree-trunks. Adrian's eyes closed. His hand, reaching out, clasped that of Cornwallis.

END OF PART THE FOURTH.

PART THE FIFTH:
PEACE

And I saw a new heaven and a new earth: for the first heaven and the first earth were passed away; and there was no more sea.

And I John saw the holy city, new Jerusalem, coming down from God out of heaven, prepared as a bride adorned for her husband.

And I heard a great voice out of heaven saying, Behold, the tabernacle of God is with men, and he will dwell with them, and they shall be his people, and God himself shall be with them, and be their God.

And God shall wipe away all tears from their eyes; and there shall be no more death, neither sorrow, nor crying, neither shall there be any more pain; for the former things are passed away.

REVELATION XXI, 1-4

CHAPTER I

Converging Courses

§ 1

AN October afternoon in London.

Soft, pearl-grey light filling a room high up at the top of a great house in Mayfair. Two beds in the room, one occupied. Silence in the room. . . .

Adrian Knoyle had been lying in a state of coma for nearly a week. His head was bandaged; he might as well have been blind. For days in semi-consciousness, he had been wondering and asking what had happened and where he was—there seemed to be a conspiracy not to tell him. Only from time to time an authoritative woman's voice said:

"Keep still! keep still! keep still! Don't move. Don't touch those bandages, or I shall be very cross."

He had tried to lift them. He wanted to see the light.

There was something wrong with his head; he could not say what. It did not exactly hurt; but there was a worrying, unnatural pressure, a strange feeling across the brows. He had phases of dull pain and of sickness. Once he had heard a man's voice—a cheerful, irritating voice—say:

"By Jove, this chap's had a wonderful escape; it must have just glanced across the forehead—so. Severe concussion, no cranial damage . . . nothing cerebral . . . he'll do all right."

Adrian took interest in such remarks merely in so far as they might have referred to somebody else.

It was as though he had been asleep a long time and had

hardly yet awakened. He knew now that he was in London, in hospital; but recollection carried him no further than a wood, a sunlit open space, and a racketing fury of sound. He recalled the attack and the sensations just before the attack. After that nothing but the comic look on Cornwallis's dead face. . . .

He did not want to think. When recollection crowded back upon him he had no wish to disentangle it. He wanted only to lie still, to listen to the far-off London sounds, to luxuriate in the sense of being where he was, and to picture in his mind the life of the familiar town. He had not indeed at first realised that he was in hospital, but had an idea that he was at home in Eaton Square. Yet he was not particularly curious on the subject at all; he could not be troubled to think.

The door of the room softly opened and he could hear whisperings.

" Will it really be all right ? "

" Just five minutes. No more, please."

" I only want to peep at him. I'll be ever so quiet."

The door closed. Footsteps came tip-toe towards his bed. Was it the nurse—or who ?

He became aware of someone looking down at him. He only wished to continue his dreaming; he resented being disturbed—unless it was his mother.

Quick, short breaths. Whoever it was bent down. Light pleasant breaths, upon his face and neck. A cool hand touched his. Two or three minutes passed. . . .

It was a woman, of course. But it was not his mother, who could not have approached swiftly like that. He was interested at last. Who could it be ?

Risking his nurse's wrath he deliberately raised his bandages and opened his eyes. Two blue eyes met his. A quiet solicitous gaze met his. . . . There was no mistaking it.

She put a finger to her lips. Her face was framed in black

and a black veil had been lifted from it. Her wavy fair hair showed at the sides above pearl ear-rings.

" Hush ! We mustn't talk."

Was there any need to talk ?

She gazed down at him thoughtfully and rather maternally, as women do when tending someone.

" I got a week's leave because of father's death. I heard you were here. So I came."

She smiled, but there was a deep seriousness in her eyes.

" I'll tell you all about it——"

" Hush ! Not now. Another time."

The five minutes were nearly up. Yet human destiny is not decided by numbers of minutes or of hours or of words spoken.

Question and answer passed between them, though no word was uttered.

Only the beautiful soft pearl-grey London light flooded the room. . . .

After a while she bent down and kissed him.

* * * * *

On this same October afternoon a girl sat in the drawing-room of a flat in that same quarter of London. Here, too, the soft blue light came flooding in. The girl sat alone, perched on the fender-stool. An open newspaper lay beside her. She gazed into the fire, the fine, slender lines of her figure accentuated by this half-turned position.

Her face was very pale and its expression not happy.

She sighed once or twice, as though a weight of anxiety lay upon her, and then, taking up the newspaper, read aloud :

" Captain Sir Adrian Knoyle, Bart., has been admitted to the Curzon House Officers' Hospital, Curzon Street, Mayfair, suffering from a bullet wound in the head. His condition is not dangerous."

Rosemary Meynell resumed her fire-gazing.

"He's in London . . . he'll recover . . . and we shall meet."

She spoke these words slowly aloud, as though trying to establish their full significance.

"Something must be done—the sooner the better. At any rate, *my* mind's made up. I *know* . . . oh! absolutely beyond a doubt—that's the great thing. It's only a question of whether . . . funny, though, how one's mind makes itself up all in a minute! It's a great thing that. . . . Be firm with yourself, little Rosemary! Don't be an ass! Pull yourself together. Have it out right away—and finish it dead—for ever."

"Finish it dead—for ever," she repeated. "If one only could. . . . Oh! to get away from it all! But we will. We'll go right away to Stavordale—just mamma and I. I'll hunt all the winter, and then in the spring . . . come back and start afresh."

She rose and went over to a looking-glass that hung on the wall.

"Will he recognise me? Have I changed a lot?—I must have. Is there any speaking difference in me, though? *Does* —that sort of thing—change one externally? Gina says not. . . . My God, but I am white this afternoon. If it was anybody but that—"—a look of contempt crossed her features— "I'd touch up a bit."

An electric bell rang.

"There it is! Now for it. Adrian, be with me! Wait a minute, though! . . . yes, I think I must. . . . It gives one such strength, such confidence. But—never again!"

She moved quickly across the room to a small drawer in a bureau, unlocked it, and took out a gold-enamelled Louis Quatorze snuff-box. Opening it, she inhaled a deep breath, as one takes snuff, and replaced the box in the drawer. She then resumed her sitting posture in front of the fire.

§ 2

Upton entered, smiling.

" Well, my angel "—he went up to her with an air of proprietary affection and patted her on the head—" and what's the little one been doing this dull afternoon—eh ? "

He bent down as though to kiss her.

" No, Harry. Don't be foolish, please ! Go and sit down quietly, like a sensible person."

" All right, Rosebud," he said, taking the arm-chair beside her. " I've come for a serious talk with you, anyway. . . . She's a spoilt little angel, though, isn't she ? "

Rosemary compressed her lips ominously. This was the kind of raillery that had always grated upon her.

" Who is ? " she inquired.

" The little Rosebud, of course. Who else ? "

" Oh ! . . . And where do you appear from this afternoon ? "

" Why—I'm just back from Paris, of course. I told you I was going on Sunday."

There was a shade of irritation—of wounded egotism—in his voice.

" Oh, yes ! So you did. I forgot."

He was not taken aback by this tepid reception, because he had become increasingly accustomed to these moods during the last few months. He put them down to the " Meynell temperament " ; she generally " came round " in the long run.

" They're tremendously elated in Paris over the advance," he continued. " Waving of flags and cheers for the Allies on every possible occasion. They talk of an armistice within a fortnight. Wilson is believed to have drawn up the terms of one already—or, failing that, a capitulation by the end of the month and a dictated peace in Berlin. So we shall soon be having Victory Balls, and what-not. . . . By the way, you're coming to Gina's roulette evening to-night, aren't you? I'll call for you——"

" No, I'm not. I'm busy."

" Busy? What's my Diana got to do to keep her at home? Duty to mother, or—letters to write? "

" Mamma's out to-night. Yes—letters to write."

" Oh, nonsense, Rosebud! Cut it out! I insist on your coming. It's going to be fun. ' Little horses ' and my loot from Paris—the divinest *violette* liqueur, my child, and some new cigarettes you're sure to like and—various condiments and experiments which you'll appreciate. It'll go on till any old hour. Just the sort of party *intime* you do like. Oh! but of course you must come ! "

" I think not—thanks."

Upton studied his finger-nails, smiling confidentially to himself.

" You two—had a little tiff, eh ? "

" What two ? "

" Why, you and Gina."

" A quarrel, do you mean? No, I haven't seen her for over a week. "

He evidently did not believe her; he continued to smile to himself in a self-satisfied manner. " H'm—troublesome this afternoon," he reflected. " Better be careful."

" Well, I hope you'll change your mind, Rosebud. You must come to Venetia's birthday supper, and afterwards a little dance at the Savoy on Wednesday night, though. She's got a private room, and Bertramo to play. The French Modernists—"

" I shall be up at Stavordale."

He stared at her.

" Up at Stavordale? What's this? " He whistled. " Change of plans? . . . Ma getting restless? "

" No. We just decided we should like to open it again— that's all."

She spoke with chilling composure, though her heart throbbed painfully.

" Is it worth while, though, dear—just for a week or two ? "

" It isn't just for a week or two. I propose to get the horses up and hunt all through the winter."

" Rosebud ! "

There was real concern in his voice now. There was even alarm.

" Yes—what's the matter ? " She looked at him, raising her eyebrows.

" Why have you suddenly sprung this upon me, Rosemary ? What new game's this you're playing ? "

" Sprung upon you ? Game ? I—I don't quite understand. Mamma and I were discussing what we would do this winter— we decided on that."

Upton rose and leant against the mantelpiece, looking down at her.

" And what about me ? " he said in a challenging tone.

" You ? I dunno . . . I suppose you'll have to be at your Office a good deal, won't you ? "

Upton took an aimless turn across the room and back again. Then he stopped in front of her. There was an unpleasant glint in the large, " interesting " eyes.

" We must come to an understanding over this, Rosemary."

" An understanding ? Why ? We're going up to Stavordale. I can't imagine anything more simple."

Her bland innocence seemed to him impenetrable.

" You know why, Rosemary. You know perfectly well what I mean. What is this game you're playing ? I'm getting a bit sick of this—these tempers and—and prevarications. Are you trying to make a fool of me or—or what ? "

" Not in the least. Why should I ? "

The answer was obviously and literally true. It stung him.

"Look here! What do you think I've come to see you for this afternoon?"

"Haven't the least idea. To pass the time of day—or to make love to me, perhaps? You certainly won't do that."

"Oh! so that's the game, is it! As a matter of fact, you know perfectly well what I've come for, and you know perfectly well what I'm driving at. You're one of these 'nappy' women, are you? I might have known it—after Adrian Knoyle." He drawled out the name with an emphatic sneer.

"If you want to mention people's names, don't talk so loud, please. The servants are in the next room."

"So that's where I stand, is it? Not even consulted when you decide to go away for months at a time! I don't mind telling you, your moods and tempers have become absolutely impossible these last weeks."

She did not reply, but picked up the newspaper at her feet and glanced at it.

When Upton spoke again his tone had changed. He was no fool. And having regained control of his temper, he perceived that no purpose was to be served by trying to domineer over a young woman of the stamp of Rosemary Meynell—that such a course would merely harden any resolution she had formed against him. He sat down again, and his manner became conciliatory.

"Well—it's no use quarrelling. We know each other too well. All I want is your happiness, as you know. You must admit you've sprung this 'Stavordale project on me pretty suddenly, though. How am I to get on without you? How am I to get at you up there—and what can one do up there, anyway? I hate plans on principle. But the time's come, dear girl, when we must fix up something definite—well—in fact—a date. Be business-like now—for once! . . . When's it to be?"

She turned upon him a look of cold dislike.

"When's what to be?"

" Our wedding."

" *Never.*"

Saying the word, she looked him full in the face with an expression of emphatic hostility; then looked away again.

Upton winced. He smiled thinly and stretched out a hand as though to take hers which hung by her side. She immediately removed it.

"Dear girl," he purred, "Think! You cannot—cannot mean that. Think—think what you're saying."

His complete ineffectiveness in face of the *fait accompli* irritated her more than anything he had yet said.

" I mean what I say," she replied. " And for the love of Heaven don't call me ' dear girl '! It's an expression I detest."

Upton's normally pallid complexion assumed a livid tint. The unpleasant look came back into his eyes.

" You mean . . . you wish to break off our engagement ? "

" Yes."

" May I ask why ? "

" Certainly. It never was an engagement. You persuaded me against my will. I didn't understand—then. You only wanted to marry me because you thought it would give you a leg-up socially. I've no other reason to give except that I never wanted to marry you, and don't intend to."

She rose and stood before the fireplace as though to intimate that she considered the interview at an end.

Upton rose too.

" Oh! ah—*indeed!* This is interesting—very. The worst of it is, it'll prevent my being of any practical assistance to the—er—unfortunate house of Meynell."

She took no notice.

" I not only want to break off what you're pleased to call our ' engagement,' " she said, " I want to break off every connection with you and all of you. I simply want to get away from you all. That's my only wish."

Upton, coldly furious, leant against the mantelpiece, with one foot on the fender.

"This is very sudden," he sneered. "Don't you—rather forget one or two things?"

She made no answer, but stood looking straight before her, fingering her pearls.

"Eh? What about that?" he continued. "We may be— a bit Bohemian—we don't pretend to be anything else. But our way of life has its amusements, its enjoyable moments. They seem to get rather a grip on some people. . . . Have a cigarette—'one of the nice ones,' as a certain little girl once used to say!"

Rosemary Meynell went across to the bureau, unlocked the small drawer as before, and took from it the Louis Quatorze snuff-box. This she handed to Upton.

"Thank you," he said with a disagreeable smile; "but these little things aren't given up quite so easily as all that, you know. However, if you want any more . . . pleased to oblige at any time!"

Silence followed, during which the girl gazed steadily in front of her with an expression of fine contempt. The meanness of the man's soul had never revealed itself as now!

Upton began to hum the words of a popular *revue* air, tapping in time to it with his foot.

> "If you were the only girl in the world
>   And I . . ."

"Well, the rest doesn't matter," he broke off. "You're not, you see."

He watched her closely to note the effect of his words, the vindictive smile still on his face. So far as any change in her expression went, he might not have been in the room.

"Eh, bien! So you've made up your mind, then, Rosebud? You've decided not to throw in your lot with your lovesick

Harry? So be it—I must be off to dress for Gina's party. We shall miss our Rosebud. We shall meet again, though—often. Don't forget your—your ever obliging friend and instructor. He won't forget you."

His expression, as he turned towards the door, was one of concentrated malice.

" Good-bye, little Rosebud ! " he called as he went out.

She made no answer.

When he had half-closed the door, he came back.

" A keepsake," he laughed. " Catch ! "

He tossed across the Louis Quatorze snuff-box. It fell on the rug at her feet.

The door slammed.

§ 3

The girl sank down on a cushion by the fender-stool.

She stared into the fire for a long time. Then :

" What a brute ! " she murmured. " What a brute ! How I could ever have—— ! "

A sob shook her.

" How idiotic, how abominable I've been ! . . . If I'd only listened ! If I'd only stuck to old Faith ! If I only wasn't such a fool—such a fool—such a *crashing* fool !"

Her friend was the soft pearl-grey London light which, stealing into the room, kindled the gold in her hair.

" But he will be the same—he will be the same," she moaned. " At Stavordale I shall get well. I will fight myself. I shall be away from everything and everybody. And in the spring I shall come back . . . clean and happy. Then we will meet. Yes ! Faith will bring us together. And I will go to him in sackcloth and ashes like the woman in the Bible, and he will take me back to him ! "

Her sobbing grew less.

" And then—in the spring . . . we will start afresh."

CHAPTER II

Reunion

§ I

EARLY in the month of November of that year, nineteen-hundred-and-eighteen, the principal thoroughfares of London responded once again to the roar of frantically-cheering crowds. At eleven o'clock in the morning on the eleventh day of the month an Armistice was signed between the contending nations. And with a single impulse all London abandoned itself to an orgy of emotion.

When night fell the wingéd archer in the heart of Piccadilly Circus smiled his faint elusive smile upon crowds that sang and shouted and waved hats and went mad around his base. Revelation of Light had come to a multitude which had passed through the Valley of the Shadow of Death! Men embraced; soldiers were hoisted on people's shoulders; the street-crowds pressed into the service of their enthusiasm all who passed, irrespective of age or class or sex. London was once more lit up. Never had the powerful arc-lamps shed their glare upon a wilder gaiety. And wherever the crowds opened out or did not surge too thick and close, couples danced like coster-mongers on a Bank Holiday; and wherever a passage was cleared through the press gambolled processions of young men and maidens waving flags, singing, laughing, and shouting hysterically. The traffic stopped. Such scenes, people recalled, had not been known since the night of August the Fourth, nineteen-hundred-and-fourteen.

And night after night these revels went on, the lighting of the lamps being the signal for Carnival to start afresh.

So came the night of the Grand Victory Ball.

The preceding act to this memorable event was a succession of banquets and dinner-parties given in various restaurants and important houses of the capital. And it happened that a little after eight o'clock a young man made his way through the crowds towards the soaring white mass of the Hotel Astoria. After four-and-a-half years—every comparison came back to that—the building was once more a blaze of light. Once again a long line of motor-cars disclosed successive pairs of lamps stretching down Piccadilly towards Hyde Park Corner. Each as it drove up discharged its four, five, or six occupants into a lane of spectators, and, amid the exhortations of enormous uniformed porters and policemen, passed on.

The young man entered by the circular moving doorway, and handed over his military cap and greatcoat to a lacquey, with whom he seemed to renew quite cordially a hat-and-stick acquaintance. He wore a dark blue uniform with gold buttons and a scarlet stripe down the trousers, Army regulations not permitting to officers the wearing of fancy dress.

Adrian Knoyle was pale, and stooped somewhat. A strip of plaster across his forehead indicated the nature of his recent injury.

Mme. Rodriguez seemed to have invited half London to her dinner-party. Such was her custom; she could not afford to do things by halves. Of a number of dinner-parties foregathering, hers was the largest. Perhaps the most striking preliminary impression of the scene in general was the number of British and foreign officers present in uniforms of varied colours and aspects. All the rest were in fancy dress, the company including many of those the most distinguished in Society, in the Army and Navy, in politics, diplomacy, and affairs, in sport, art, and in the drama and literature of their day.

The picture indeed was positively dazzling to a new-comer—so full of colour, of animation, of refined light, of reflection and scintillation, of gleaming jewels, of flowers banked up and bursting through moss in golden baskets, of high and stately palms, orange-trees, tall marble pillars draped with the flags of the Allies—and then a vista of long corridors, mirrored and multiplied, opening upon the soft, warm glow of the restaurant.

Adrian Knoyle hesitated to join the imposing throng. The jewels and variegated garments of the women dazed him; their mystery and formality dazed him. The scent of the flowers dazed him, the lights shimmering and reflected, the hum and buzz of conversation, the sudden poignant speaking beauty of the thing.

He put his hand to his forehead, a feeling of faintness came over him—now come, now gone—and he was for retreating through glass doors. At this moment he heard his name called, hands seized him by each arm, and he looked round to find—Fotheringay and Sutton!

Two small, natty figures in a uniform like his own, two laughing, pink-and-white faces.

"Well, Adrian, old boy, so you've turned up! Enterprising fellow! The whole world's here. Come and sit down—come and see everybody!"

His polite duty supervened. Mme. Rodriguez, handsome and hung and strung with pearls, wearing a great broad-brimmed hat as though she had sprung from a Rubens picture, stood upon the top step of the daïs flanked by her daughter.

His name was announced.

"How do you do?"

"How do you do?"

He shook fingers with the mother, then with the daughter, the latter adding a timid and amiable smile. Neither had much idea who he was. It was as though he had awakened in the summer of 1914. Mme. Rodriguez glanced at a list.

"Will you take Miss Lettice Kenelm in to dinner, please?"

He bowed. Inferentially he bowed to Miss Lettice Kenelm, whose name came to him as from another world. Once again he felt sorry for Miss (or was it Mlle. ?—he could not remember) Rodriguez, who was so " eligible." There she stood, a Seville dancing-girl—it was almost indecent. Four-and-a-half years —the best of intentions—and nothing come of it. Did not her mamma assure people—as one who nourishes a grudge against Fate—that she had had everything money could provide ? . . . No wonder the girl looked ashamed.

He thereupon fell into the arms of Mrs. Rivington (of Rivington), who stood nearby, a Miss Kenelm on either side. Yes—she almost embraced him. Each of the nieces smiled, holding out a moist hand. Each looked sweet as nothing in particular. Mrs. Rivington was a Queen—of sorts.

" Like the old days, Adrian, my dear," she crooned over him in a kind of sing-song (but she had never called him by his christian name in those days) ; " quite like the old days. Only so many dear faces gone. And everybody so hard up. You remember Hilda and Lettice ? And I hope you're better, you poor soldier." She lowered her voice. " I'm running this entirely for her." She nodded at the Lady from Rubens, who was still busy shaking hands. " I've asked every mortal soul. And everybody's coming. I guarantee the champagne ; it's pre-war. So go and enjoy yourself and—by the way—bring up any nice young men you know and introduce them to the girls."

He next ran into his friend, Mrs. Clinton. She was in a grand evening gown that looked like an advertisement of Queen Victoria. " Reconstruction," she called it.

" And," she added, " that's only too true ! "

Adrian laughed.

" You're not looking well," Mrs. Clinton announced ; " you're not taking enough care of the old head. Your mother —where is she now ? "

" She's rather an invalid, I'm afraid. At the present

moment she's down at Stane, getting it ready to inhabit. The let's up, and we're going to spend the summer there."

Then Fotheringay and Sutton, who had been hovering near, pounced upon him again and carried him off to a corner where Cyril Orde sat between sticks.

"Congratulate him," they whispered, "he's been and gone and got married. Awful, wasn't it, about poor old Burns—and Arthur, too!"

All this was said in one breath, Adrian being given no time to reply.

Orde's tired smile greeted him. He was in uniform and a wheeled-chair.

"It's very nice to see you back!" he said, holding out his hand. "How's the head? A bullet across the forehead, was it?—h'm! sounds nasty. Surely a bit premature this, though? . . . Married? Yes, I'm married, old boy. I think you know my wife?"

Miss Ingleby that was stepped forward, smiling. Adrian had not noticed her. (One never did unless one looked twice.) Her fancy dress was the uniform of a Red Cross nurse. He murmured appropriately.

"Yes—Cyril and I were married on Armistice Day," she piped, like a robin on a frosty morning. "We're *so* happy looking round for a house in the country."

So little Miss Ingleby had found her vocation after all!

"Heard anythin' of Faith?" Orde inquired. "I had a line from Mary Arden the other day sayin' she was about. I hoped she'd come and see me."

"She's gone back to Neuilly to nurse, and probably won't be home till the spring. You're coming on to the ball, aren't you, Cyril?"

"If I can get there, old boy, if I can get there. I like lookin' on at the passin' show, y'know—wonderin' whether there's been a war or whether it's all a rumour!"

At this point Lady Freeman rushed up.

"How d'e do, Sir Adrian? Pleased to see you back. I heard you'd been *so* badly wounded. Oh! it's the head. What a shame! Nothing permanent, I hope. The last time we saw you was at Ash-hanger, I think?"

"Yes—in 1915."

In the confronting mirror Adrian caught Cyril Orde's eye.

"Seen anything of Rosemary Meynell? I hear she's *quite* one of Miss Maryon's friends now." There was a hint of malice in this, he thought. Nor did she wait for an answer to her question. "Now tell me, Sir Adrian—*what* am I?"

It was a crisis of his life.

"Ah—er!" was all he could say.

"My costume, I mean?"

Her garments presented a series of zig-zags and geometrical diagrams in black-and-white surmounted by a sort of flame-coloured toque. It was appalling. And what *could* it be?

"Charming! Most becoming! But what is it?"

"'To-morrow.' Doris, whom you see over there,"—he espied Mrs. Granville-Brown—"is 'Victory.' I'm *so* glad you like me. Some people think it a little too—Futuristic, y'know."

"Pessimistic, perhaps. It looks as though you expected an early renewal of hostilities!"

It was such a bad joke that they both laughed.

"Oh, no! you nasty man, how could you——! But have you seen Lord Freeman?"

"*Lord* Free——?" He was given away.

"Oh yes! Didn't you know? Last New Year. . . . But I'm sure he'd like to shake hands with you. You were always quite a favourite with him. Ah! and here he comes!"

She was "all there"; she was chatty. Something deep down inside him murdered her, but he only saw the great man, advancing like an expensive doctor, attired (after the manner of the younger Pitt) in a mulberry-coloured frock-coat and white knee-breeches. Conjointly, the Freemans personified—Success. The War, they assured you, had been a success. Had it not provided Sir Walter Freeman with opportunities ? Lord Freeman had accepted those opportunities. Great men always do.

" Well, well, young man, pleased to see you. Glad to see you ! Still quartered in London—still leading the gay life ! It has its attractions even for a worn-out, worked-out old machine—ha ! ha ! (Been at the front, has he ? Well ! well ! poor chaps, they've all been there.) It's going to be a most enjoyable night, I think. We haven't seen such gaieties since—I'm afraid to say when. So much the better. ' All's well that ends well,' as they say. Ha ! ha ! "

The couple passed on in a blaze of prosperity and self-satisfaction.

Lady Cranford now arrived in poudre and crimson satin—some suggested Madame de Maintenon, others Catherine of Russia—attended by Mr. Ralph Heathcote attired as the illustrious Lord Chesterfield. The high lady greeted Adrian with a bow ; it was a bowing evening. On these occasions (someone remarked) she put the world in its place.

Mr. Heathcote, for his part, became so engaged in bowing *and* shaking hands as to be ineptly mislaid.

" Ah ! Adrian Knoyle ! " he exclaimed, *en passant*. " Hardly recognised you at first. Heard you were so badly wounded. Leg, was it ? Ah ! head—yes. But quite right again ? Capital ! That's the thing."

The young man had said no word. It was evidently a ritual, suitable to each and every such occasion—and punctually produced. The elderly gentleman darted off at a tangent.

" Ah ! the Duchess. Dear me ! Quite lost, beautifully dressed, and nowhere to sit. I must really go over and say how-de-do." And struggling slightly with his Court-sword but recovering himself (as a gentleman should), Mr. Heathcote trotted across to a bewigged, becalmed, bedizened figure.

There was one thing to be said about Mr. Heathcote—he was the same. Men had come and men had gone; Mr. Heathcote went on for ever. . . . The war had strolled by him in Piccadilly.

§ 2

The Rodriguez dinner-party, unwieldy though it appeared to be, was now all but complete. Yet, "We're still somebody short," Madame R. was heard to remark. And she glanced anxiously towards the revolving doorway with that politely abstracted expression so characteristic of worried hostesses. As for the daughter, she looked as though the guilt ought to be traced to her.

Meanwhile people were not a little intrigued by the gradual assemblage of another dinner-party on the opposite side of the palm-court, this being the " Clan Maryon " in full force. One advantage of the Hotel Astoria, it may have been noticed, is that you can watch other people's movements and comportment in its innumerable mirrors without rudely or crudely appearing so to do—though this advantage may be said to cut both ways. Each of the members of this noted or notorious circle, as he or she arrived, passed through a running fire of (mainly hostile) comment—which was indeed no more or less than notoriety required. There was, for instance, a murmur of disapproval when Mrs. Gerard Romane arrived, on the arm (so to say) of her cavalier—the young soldier-politician. Sylphlike and gliding, she represented " The Arts of Peace " in trousers and a naked back.

The genie herself was naturally the centre of the Maryon gathering. It was her party. She was Columbine, and Columbine's skirt barely approaches her knees. Beside her, and assisting to receive the guests, stood Harold Upton ; he represented (some said) a rather Mephistophelian Harlequin. . . . And the news had already spread. It only had to pass from one side of the *foyer* to the other, and such items of intelligence have been known to cross mountain-ranges and even continents in an incredibly short space of time. The fact was, Miss Maryon had "done it"—at last. The fifty-first proposal had been accepted. Gina was no longer Maryon—she was Upton. The event had taken place at a Registry Office that very morning.

Everybody was talking about it. Some had seen a paragraph in the evening papers. Some had heard it in a club. In a Registry Office? Really! . . . But where else would you expect?

Adrian had already remarked the proximity of Gina to Upton with feelings of perplexity; it was not what he had been led to expect. Once in the distance he had caught the young woman's eye, had thought he detected in it a subtle mockery. Upton avoided his gaze. Over and over again he heard Gina's high-pitched laugh. . . .

§ 3

Mrs. Clinton, on a sofa beside Lady Cranford, was talking in low tones.

"I thought your girl was engaged to that young man, Helena?"

"Which young man?" her ladyship replied; "there's been more than one, you know."

"This young Upton who's married the Maryon girl. It seems to have been a very odd business altogether."

"Oh! don't ask me, my dear. A gal's mother is the last person on earth to ask whom her daughter is engaged to. Goodness knows, I've tried to bring her up to decency and duty; it's not my fault that she prefers a dull *demi-monde*. It's the war of course. . . . these children have gone mad."

"Don't you think it's just a 'phase,' Helena, dearest?" suggested Mrs. Clinton vaguely. "But where is Rosemary to-night? Isn't she coming?"

"Nothing would induce her to." Lady Cranford became earnest. "There's something wrong with the gal. She worries me. Whether it's to do with this young man—or another—I don't know. Most of your 'gals of the period' don't know their own minds. Three weeks ago she suddenly took it into her head she wanted to go to Stavordale, get her horses up, and hunt all the winter. We opened the house; it was dreadfully expensive. She seemed in a perpetual state of nerves the whole time. I left her there yesterday in floods of tears, declaring she would rather die than come down for this ball, though Caroline Rivington invited her weeks ago. I thought it would do her good—take her out of herself. The Meynells *are* so morbid. But no! Nothing would induce her to."

"I shouldn't worry, my dear. As I say, it's a sort of stage they all pass through. It will right itself."

"One hopes so, but——"

There was a stir among those near the entrance. Lady Cranford's voice suddenly froze.

"Blanche! . . . oh! good gracious!"

For the first time in her life, the aristocratic lady's self-possession deserted her. She stood up with an expression of horror.

§ 4

Rosemary Meynell—alone—came up the marble steps.

There was a flagging of conversation amounting almost to complete silence, broken only by one or two suppressed exclamations of surprise. All eyes were turned in the direction of the solitary advancing figure. The girl, however, appeared not to notice the quizzing and curious glances, but to move in a dream, through a world exalted above the present

At the head of the steps she paused and hesitated—as though in doubt whether she belonged to the Rodriguez gathering nearest her, or to the smaller Maryon group opposite. She turned to the former.

Recalling the incident afterwards, people professed to see something pathetic and indeed poignantly significant in this unexpected apparition. But at the time it was the young lady's appearance and unusual garb that excited comment, forming as they did so pronounced a contrast to the elaborate gowns, gleaming jewels and brilliant uniforms of the majority. She was dressed in some coarse brown stuff, such as monks or women doing penance, are seen wearing in pictures of the Middle Ages. The garment fell in straight folds, with a knotted cord round the waist. Her hair, golden as September sunshine, was drawn back without ornament, without ribbon, without colour. Everybody hazarded a guess as to what or whom she designed to represent. Yet everybody agreed that hers was the most striking and effective costume there. So simple, so plain—and yet so original! And it suited her to perfection. When someone suggested " Martyred Belgium " the idea was at once taken up. Why, of course! Really—very artistic. But surely rather extraordinary Helena Cranford not bringing her daughter with her! Then people's memories got to work; had she not been engaged to Upton, Lord Freeman's political private secretary? Mightn't the sombre dress be somehow connected with that matter? And everybody took up that idea. It was interesting; it was picturesque. Months afterwards people were still canvassing the point: had Rosemary Meynell's severe garb of that memorable night other than an accidental or fanciful significance?

And Lady Cranford's daughter had never looked more beautiful. Yet was there something strange about her too— the eyes set in an unusual pallor, the brilliant spot of colour on each cheek. Her figure, height and erect carriage, however, could never be forgotten by those who saw her then, nor the fine swan-like poise of her neck.

Adrian Knoyle, strangely moved, watched her go up to

Mme. Rodriguez; knew she was apologising for being late; knew she said she had " only got down from Stavordale that evening." Then she went across to Lady Cranford, who stood like Nemesis. . . .

After the briefest minute's converse, during which the words "telegram" and "taken leave of your senses" were distinguishable to some who stood near, she turned to Fotheringay, Sutton, and a group of young persons, with whom she exchanged greetings. Her spirits were evidently high; she was animated; the quickened colour bespoke something hectic. Yet all the while she wore an abstracted look, glancing this way and that and appearing oblivious on the whole of the world about her, as though searching for something—or somebody.

§ 5

It was then their eyes met.

They met across the dazzling centre of that London stage upon which, had it not been for a world's upturning, their lives (as countless other lives before theirs) would doubtless have played out the normal comedy of make-belief.

The physical alteration in her vaguely shocked him. Beautiful as she was, Change held sway; yet could not be defined. Was it the look in the eyes—the pallor—the dress?

A tinkling laugh broke in upon that second's intimacy. Columbine's violet eyes were watching them, and in the opposite mirror Adrian saw her turn to Harlequin, whisper, a smile curling the scarlet of her lips and passing to his. . . .

Thenceforward the old lovers were oblivious of all but each other. Their gaze seldom wandered from each other. The long dinner passed in a haze of illusion. The guests sat at a number of tables, each loaded with Malmaison carnations and beribboned with the colours of the Allies. The two sat at different tables, but could see one another in circumjacent mirrors. She was seated between Fotheringay and Sutton; he had Miss Lettice Kenelm on one side and Mrs. Clinton on the other. A ceaseless hum of conversation went on beside and around and between them, but, had they been questioned on the instant, neither could have given any account of it. He answered questions mechanically; she with levity. Mrs. Clinton thought him odd, abstracted, and most difficult to talk to; Miss Kenelm gave up the job. Both made up their minds charitably that he had not recovered from his head-wound—perhaps never would. Mr. Heathcote perpetrated a bland pun about the Armistice being better than the Army, and was correspondingly piqued at receiving no response. As for Fotheringay, Rosemary Meynell had never seemed to him so attractive, so enchanting.

And ever and again Columbine's tinkling laugh rose high above the level murmur of conversation, as the mocking treble rises and falls in the dominant theme of a symphony.

Somewhere outside a violin orchestra murmured softly. Champagne flowed freely and Adrian drank freely; Rosemary too. As the evening passed the warm colour rose in her cheeks, the spark kindled in her strange eyes until she became again—or seemed to become—the Rosemary of his earliest recollections and of his dreams. And if her gestures grew more and more feverish and elated, and if the old laugh expelled a haunting suggestion from her face, her glance rarely wandered far or long, but came back to meet his across the chasm of years. It was as though Time alone parted them. . . . Yet he was never without a growing sense of something impending, something which—in the nature of mortal things—had always seemed inevitable to them both.

CHAPTER III

The Grand Victory Ball

§ 1

THE whole Rodriguez party now rose from its various tables, the ladies passing out of the restaurant first, the gentlemen staying behind to finish their liqueurs and cigarettes. Adrian's glance followed Rosemary, who passed, talking animatedly to a woman he did not know; and instead of the frank recognition he had expected, she lowered her eyes with an evasive look that might have implied self-consciousness or—he wondered. When the men in their turn left the restaurant, Columbine's laugh was the last sound he heard. . . .

Then they were gliding down Piccadilly and across Hyde Park Corner. Open Knightsbridge lay before them, its lights flitting by like mischievous, twinkling eyes. He was restored by the sharp air and rapid motion to a sense of physical actuality; yet with this his apprehension of crisis increased.

There was no doubt now—and he realised it—that he was under the spell of—it might be the night, it might be this strange illusion of a pre-war existence which he had thought dead, but which appeared to be externally unchanged—certainly of this wayward creature, girl or woman, who had so unexpectedly come back into his life.

Though it was not yet eleven o'clock, the numerous entrances to the great Hall were already crowded; and it was with difficulty that the party found its way along stone passages to the Rodriguez box which, in fact, consisted of several boxes thrown into one on the ground tier. Astonishing and magnificent was the scene which confronted them. It was as though some magic window opened in material earth, ushering from the hard and the real into realms of the unreal, the mystical, the make-believe; as though some glorious, glittering cavern exposed its secret life to human gaze; as though a curtain lifted upon some grand, portentous drama of the legendary past.

So the spectacle impressed Adrian Knoyle. A dazzling rush of colour greeted them—of sound, too, for now the music of military bands resounded through the hall. Everywhere displayed were the flags and banners of the Allied nations—billowing across the roof, covering all spaces around the walls, between and beside the boxes, over the entrances and exits. There was tier upon tier of boxes, festooned and draped with flags and masses of trailing flowers, aglint with silver and glass on tables supper-laid. Above each entrance hung a golden laurel-wreath surrounding an illuminated disc bearing the name of one of the Allies: France, Belgium, Serbia, Italy, Japan, China, Portugal, Roumania, the United States, Canada, Australia, South Africa, New Zealand, India—these being the rendezvous, the meeting-places of the dancers; so that one might say to another: "Meet me at Italy, or China, or India," or "Let's have the one after next at Serbia." The general background of the boxes was red-and-gold, but all were variegated by elaborate adornment, mirrored reflections, and by the dresses of those within.

In one quarter of the hall, that beneath the great organ and immediately opposite the box in which Adrian and his friends sat, was a large platform banked up by and embowered in groves of flowers. Above these, a mass of scarlet-and-gold held the eye where all else revolved and moved. This was the bands of the Guards, whose music of waltz and one-step swam up to the roof. Far up in the topmost galleries crowds of contrastingly sober hue gazed mutely down.

A vast open space was the floor, but never a foot to spare among the dancers. The dancers! All costumes of all periods of all countries. Crusaders—Crusaders in mail and casque, long sword, shield marked with the red cross, dancing with old-fashioned English country-girls in big straw hats, tied under chin; the spotted pierrot clasping the Quakeress, the Arab chief gyrating with the lady in the crinoline. Here were Court jesters dancing with Bacchantes, Chinamen waltzing with shepherdesses, the Comic Ass with the Elephant and the Kangaroo. Prince Charming and Polichinelle mingled with Indian Princesses, Pearl Girls with costermongers, "Ninette" with "Rin-tin-tin," Punches with Judys absurdly masked. There were Spanish Toreadors, and gorgeous outlandish uniforms and pink hunting coats and gay satiny reproductions of fashions of old French Courts and old French characters. Guillaume, the peasant, was there, no less than his friend the *gamin*, the student from the Quartier Latin no less than Madame la Pompadour. Among all these came and went foreign uniforms, from the sky-blue of French officers, the grey of Italy, and the mauve-blue of Roumania to American khaki-yellow and the red-striped dark blue of British officers.

Since leaving the Astoria, Adrian had not seen Rosemary. Now a throng of people filled the joined boxes, for Mme. Rodriguez had invited many besides those who had been present at the dinner-party. And although Adrian's eyes sought one face only and one figure, and although his mind was dominated by one personality—these were not to be found. She must be dancing! He made his way to the front of the box, and searching among the swirling colours and faces, the rainbow dresses, realised that the quest was hopeless.

He turned to Miss Hilda Kenelm beside him who was becoming slowly congealed against the wall by a stout gentleman's back. He felt something ought to be done.

" I'm not allowed to dance, but shall we take a walk round ? " The young lady flushed.

" Thanks. I was dancing with Lord Fotheringay, but——"

"He's not turned up?" Adrian laughed. "He never does."

They made their way as politely as might be towards the door where, however, the crush was greatest.

"It seems—hopeless," the young man said, with a grimace. They were promptly expelled into the corridor.

"Ah! There he is!" cried Miss Kenelm, who had been adjured by her aunt to make herself especially agreeable to young Lord F.

The latter was forcing his way towards them. Then Adrian saw Rosemary. . . .

The two couples came face to face. Fotheringay laughed.

"Look here, Adrian," he protested, "you've got my partner! Let's exchange! Here's Lady Rosemary dying to dance with you, and you haven't had the decency to ask her——"

The exchange was automatically effected by the onward pressure of the crowd.

§ 2

Neither Adrian nor Rosemary spoke as they forced their way along the stone corridor, in face of the crowd—for a dance was just ended. When they reached the gangway leading to the dancing floor they had to stand against the wall. There was nowhere to sit.

A momentary awkwardness supervened. Neither quite knew how to break the ice—of two-and-a-half years. At last he said in a constrained voice :

"I like your dress, Rosemary. But—what does it mean?"

"Myself, Adrian . . . for once."

A peculiar smile crossed her features, and more consciously than he had done before, he noticed the changed look in her eyes, the suppressed ecstasy of her expression. He felt moreover, with a curious certainty that he had seen the look before—in a dream, perhaps, or was it on some other face?

Near them stood a very tall young man dressed as a black-and-white pierrot, and a very small young woman dressed as a red-and-white pierrette. Adrian noticed that under the folds of their loose dresses the young man's hand repeatedly stole out and pressed the young woman's. Once he heard the latter whisper:

"Isn't it wonderful—a dream—isn't it a glorious, wonderful night!"

Then the bands struck up. And at the first bars the tall pierrot seized his little friend round the waist, whirling her off her feet and crying:

"Come on!—dance! dance!" And with a loud laugh, "The war's over—nothing matters. Isn't it all—*humoreske* . . . ?"

Without a word Adrian turned to his partner.

§ 3

From that moment all but themselves was blotted out. They were caught up in the swirl of the dancers. They were lost in self-created mazes, immersed in self-imposed intricacies; they spun around and around as only these two had ever done. Was he uncertain a little in the first two or three turns—he who had been cautioned by doctors and by nurses on no account to dance? He trod on her foot once—they laughed—and in the reverse swung her wide against another couple so that they nearly lost their balance. It was the moment to apologise, to stammer something. He did neither. Gradually consciousness of her—fierce, indefinable, vibrant—came to him, coursed through him in resurgent waves of intense feeling. He felt her hand upon his shoulder like a caress. Her every movement followed his with the accuracy, with the felicity of old. He felt her breath upon his cheek.

Once she pressed his hand ever so lightly; he returned the pressure. With that they fell into their Time-appointed places, and were at one with each other across and despite everything. And were lost in each other.

Faces passed; faces they knew and faces they did not know. Once they nearly collided with Columbine and Harlequin, who called out. And Rosemary uttered the low laugh that he remembered. And looking into each other's eyes—they understood.

The cadence deepened. The electric lights dimmed. All around grew dark, grew dark; only a greyish white beam shot down from the roof, lighting up now this face, now that, then leaving blank darkness. And in that whirl of ghosts were merged the living faces, the colours, the jewels, the laughing light of dancing eyes, the pulsing beat of youth quivering upon longing lips, the brilliant masquerade of the Harlequins, the Columbines, and the marionettes, the Crusaders, the spotted pierrots, the Napoleonic officers, the fox-hunters, the Arab women, the crinolines, the duellists, the Mandarins, the Parisian students and the Cowboys, the Ushers, the Quakeresses and Court Jesters, the Dominoes, the coloured cloaks of the Spanish Toreadors. The joy of the dance whirled all about and about while Dvorak's magic whispered "Time and Fate," of something gay or mocking—Death?

They were lost. And if she clung to him closer, closer, as though fearful—for her? for himself?—he on his part beheld phantoms of the past take human shape, one hot upon another, silently, insidiously—take shape out of that mad swirl. Now they merged in one another, a dim, opaque mass, and now broke apart with separate corporeal existence. And some were grey and some were gay and some gibbered or grinned, and some, ashen-white, were streaked or smeared and from some great drops fell, whether of tears or blood. And some wore the death-shroud, and some in uniforms drab and old fled swiftly by, and some were mud bespattered,

with matted hair and pain-shot eyes. And some held fear
in their eyes, and some horror, and some seemed caught up
in the passion of last moments, sightless, stricken; and some
even as they moved wore the gentle look of everlasting peace.
But all were there. . . .

Eric was there. And now he was as he had been at the end,
whispering, "Morphia! Morphia!—put an 'M' on my
forehead." And now he waved to them—they could even
hear his laugh—and now was lost among shadows.

One by one they stepped forth from the throng; his
old love clung to him as though in that embrace they must
dance onward to eternity. Once glancing down he thought
he saw the look with which she had come to him in his nightmare of the crawling beetles on the Somme; but still she
was his—she at least remained after this maniacal thing called
War had passed. Her body was there; flesh and blood, yes,
warm, life-giving, living. . . . Voices called. The flashlight
threw a pale glare on the scene. And now it was
Walker's face he saw, ashen, terror-stricken and—yes,
surely!—it was Walker's voice he heard: "I'm wounded!
I'm wounded! I'm choking! I'm dying! Will nobody
come— ? "

The phosphorescent glare had faded out and all he saw
now was the pale shimmer upon the quiet dead of Ginchy
and Lesbœufs. Faces of these—then others—rose one upon
another in the spectral swirl; now of Burns upon whom
sunlight fell, who babbled still somewhere of the Army's
conventions and his "rights," now of Cornwallis, whose
spectacles awry made comedy of his pitiful face. Now it was the
Lewis gunners lying stiff and stark amid the brambles and the
sunlight and the rich autumn foliage of the Picardy wood, and
now the lonely soldier in his shell-hole, transfigured by sunset's
glow on the field of Ypres. And now it was Arden with lolling
head and humorous droop at the corners of lips made merry
by firelight; and now Pemberton, just simple and dull, gazing

out upon the blue wavelets of the Channel while his soul passed hence. These, too, joined in the dance.

It was as though all had risen at the call of their comrades to celebrate with them the victory and the triumph. It was as though the souls of the slain formed up on parade, rank after rank, file beside file, awaiting their final dismissal. . . . Far above, it seemed to Adrian, a figure gazed down as though pondering—the figure of an aged, broken man with hands folded and head bent and eyes that would never smile or look up again.

•   *   *   •   •

The dance was still at its height, when he felt his partner lean heavily upon him. He looked down and saw complete pallor, where the two scarlet spots had been on her cheeks.

She whispered that she was feeling faint, and he half-led, half-compelled her out into the stone passages, up, far up the stone stairs. Did demons possess them ? Were phantoms pursuing them ? And what impulse was it that urged them up flight after flight of those stony steps ?

She clung to his arm. They brushed past revellers, paying no heed to the cries, the jests, the calls that greeted and pursued them. Out of breath, they climbed on, till they came to the highest bleak landing, with a door at the end, opening which they found themselves in a disused box. From this vantage-point the ball looked like a pirouette of gay toys. A couple of old cane chairs, a dilapidated arm-chair, with other dust-covered lumber, lay about. The only light came from the upward reflection of the myriad lamps below.

They here stopped—faced each other. She reeled a little. He caught her in his arms, and for uncounted moments they stood swaying together. . . .

A thin violet beam sweeping round caught them in its rays.

"Oh! my dear, my dear!" he whispered. "It's all

right. We are together at last . . . we belong to each other
. . . nothing—*nothing*—can part us now."

Honour, faith, his plighted troth scarce two months old ;
duty, the trust of a friend, life-loyalty—all, all were cast
aside.

§ 4

Below, the music of the bands had ceased. The great arena
was being cleared for the Procession of Victory

He laid her gently in the arm-chair, and for the first time
realised that the whole expression of her face had altered ;
that she looked inexpressibly tired. Her hands were cold ;
tremors passed through her. Alarm seized him. He began
to chafe her hands, to caress her flushed temples, her hair.

" Rosie, speak—say something ! You're tired ! You're ill !
Only for God's sake speak, move ! "

Beside himself, he rushed to the door of the box, thinking to
fetch water ; then heard her voice, and was back at her side.

She spoke with an effort, as though by strong exercise of will
alone, saving herself from swooning.

" Don't leave me, Adrian ! I shall be all right presently.
It's—that—wonderful music—and—our great happiness. . . ."

" Let me take you home . . . you cannot, you must not,
stay here."

" No . . . let us stay . . . and I will rest."

His anxiety easily relieved, he took her hand, sitting on
the arm of the chair.

Silence fell between them. Then—" We've found—
ourselves to-night, haven't we, Adrian ? " She leant forward,
a note of intense, of almost fierce eagerness in her voice. " I
mean . . . you forgive me . . . ? "

" Forgive ? What—who am I to forgive ? "

" All—*everything*. Oh ! Heaven help me ! You know,
you know what I've been—you know what I was . . ."

A discord of pain—of pain or wild regret—broke out of her, threatened to sweep her out of herself.

" You know what we were to each other ! These years—— Oh ! Adrian ! What wrong—what horror ! "

She rose to her feet uncertainly and stood before him in her sackcloth, with hands clasped and eyes large and suffering. The attitude moved him strangely, reminding him of that far-off evening when she had sung her French song at Arden —when she had stood at the piano in the first flush and freedom of her awakened youth. All the fine lines of her figure, all her old ethereal grace were there still. But her face—that was changed as the face of the world itself.

She bowed her head. " I have been wicked, Adrian—I have been cruel to you—I have spurned your great love for me. I have done worse—worse than you can know. I have paid "— anguish came into her voice—" I have paid—I pay—oh ! terribly, terribly !

" But I did not come here to lament." Her voice rose and the words poured out as though she was fearful something might intervene to stem the torrent of them. " I came—to confess to you, to implore your forgiveness, to—to say that I . . . belong to you still if—if you will have me."

She sank down on the bare floor. Her hair, loosening, felt like silk to his touch. He tried to raise her, but she cried :

" No ! No ! Leave me—till I've finished ! " She clung to his knees. " I came to-night to find you, to tell you that—I am not the Rosemary you knew—at Arden. That I am changed, that I am utterly different, that I never can be again the Rosemary you knew, that—oh ! God, how am I to say it ?—that I know all about the world—that I am wrong— utterly wrong——"

He bent down. He caressed her hair, framing her face in his two hands, and raising it up to him.

She, however, thrust back his hands, crying out : " No, you must not touch me—you must not be kind to me. I am not clean! I am not fit for you to touch—till you've heard everything I have to say—and have forgiven me!"

"Rosie, my darling, I do—I do forgive you."

"Oh, Adrian!" . . . .

She broke down, sobbing. The reaction from that first passionate remorse to their resurrected love was for her terrible. Had he turned from her, had he rebuked her, had he reproached her by so much as an inflexion of the voice, it might have been easier.

He would have let her sob her heart out. But the compassionate, tender yet firm tones of his voice dominated that uncontrollable outburst—mastered it.

"My Rosemary," he said, haunted perhaps by some dim recollecton of her words or of the place where she had first spoken them. "My Rosemary, of course you know about the world. . . . You were very young—in those old days. You were a child. You did not know your own mind. You did not know what you wanted—or what other people wanted. You did not know men—or women. You did not know what life demanded—or what it held in store. You were a child. . . . Perhaps you are still a child."

"But you must realise—I must somehow make you realise—" she urged passionately, "that I am different—different from the Rosemary you knew. I went with all those people. I became like the rest of them—worse than foolish, yes, wicked and bad, and then . . . oh, *God!* how I began to loathe myself, to loathe them, to loathe it all! I wanted to escape. I couldn't. It had got me, it had chained me and trapped me as people say those things do (but I never believed it) and—I couldn't escape. . . . It was just about then, I think, that I met Eric. I asked him to help me—I gave him a message for you. But you took no notice—or he didn't give the message."

"He didn't give the message."

"You—he forgot?"

" He was killed within thirty-six hours of his return."

A light of understanding broke in her face. " I never thought of that."

" And the message—what was it ? "

" It was to say—that I had learnt my lesson."

" So you came to-night ? "

" I came to-night to give you that message myself. I long ago lost hope of hearing from you. And in a weak moment, I— I made a—sort of—promise to—somebody else. Directly I knew you were back I realised that promise was—impossible."

He could have laughed at the naïveté with which she spoke the words had the moment been other than it was.

" You had to learn, I knew you would have to learn. Your time came, and the storm swept you down, like—do you remember ?—that beautiful fallen pine we rested on——"

She started up, a wild look in her eyes.

" But it was dead, Adrian," she cried, " it was rotting— rotten ! "

He hastened to change the simile, seeing that he had touched her old remorse.

" There were other pines rising where that one had stood. They were fresh still and young and beautiful—as you are."

" No," she protested weakly, hiding her face in her hands. " No. I am not like that any more. . . . You do not understand."

A mastering pity for her surged up in his heart—and all his resurrected love. How well he knew ! How well he understood ! Had he not foreseen—years before—this schooling, this buying of experience, this coming of knowledge, to a nature too impatient, too headstrong to accept it as a gift ? . . . And now she lay at his feet.

How should he " forgive " her ? How prove to her that as between themselves " forgiveness " did not exist—that the wrong done to himself was no wrong but a step on the road of her experience—that nothing, *nothing* stood between them and—fulfilment.

Nothing ? Did no voice whisper to him then ? . . .

If it did, he stifled it. He raised her, held her to him, rested her head on his shoulder, caressed her forehead, her hands.

That moment, too, passed. When he again laid her in the arm-chair, she rested, quiet and, as it seemed, happy, with lips a little apart, her pale hair straying loose about the back of the chair.

For some time neither spoke or moved. He sat beside her, her hand in his. Her last words—" I am not like that any more—you do not understand "—still echoed in his ears, and, despite his denials, his firm reasoning, his excuses in her behalf, like a boring insect, began to gnaw a little wedge into his mind. Her eyes, veiled by their lashes, were no longer potent to awaken his pity, nor did he fail to remark a blueness of the lips, a leaden pallor.

And even as he watched, something came between them. Her lips changed. Her lips became flaccid, thin, vindictive. Her mouth changed, falling to a looseness at the corners that gave to it the attributes of a mirthless sneer. Her fine nostrils coarsened, her complexion became waxen, her eyes seemed to stare through their lids malignantly, the spun gold of her hair became as straw or dross. Some grotesque intuition laid bare in this face the ghost of all evil and of all shame. Some grotesque intimation whispered a name. . . . It was Lola.

Quick as the word took shape he started back. A mottled greyness overspread his cheeks. His features worked uncontrollably. Twice, with a dry mouth and a supplicating terror in his eyes, he whispered, " Rosemary ! " But, receiving no response and unable himself to remain still, he rose and walked unsteadily to the front of the box.

His ears echoed with a horrible laughter, and he could not keep it out.

As he stood looking down the reflected light from below

cast a baleful glimmer upon his features, accentuating their outlines, emphasising their hollows. The gold buttons of his uniform refracted malicious pin-points like impish eyes, and against the dark background of the box its scarlet facings made the only relieving suggestion.

In the centre of the hall beneath, a solid lane of people had been formed reaching to the daïs at the farther end, where the massed bands showed as a brilliant cascade of colour. Through this lane to the majestic strains of " See the Conquering Hero Comes " the procession of Victory was passing, led by Britannia wearing a golden helm and sheathed in red, white, and blue, to be succeeded in turn by all the Allies. The music of organ and of bands pealed and rose and thundered as the procession advanced.

He saw and heard it all mechanically. His mind registered nothing of it. There was no reality. The only realities for him were Rosemary and—that other. The only meaning of it for him lay in her words lately reiterated, so earnestly spoken :

" I am not like that any more—you do not understand. . . ."

The change in her face, her eyes, her whole expression— these assumed a terrible significance at last.

A figure stood at his right hand, quietly confronting the horror of his thoughts. It was a figure that of all others he could not fail to recognise—the face, too frank and open, the eyes clear, blue as the sky. It neither accused nor remonstrated ; it was simply there.

" Adrian ! "

She called to him, and he turned. She still lay back, with marble-cold white features and marble cold white throat and neck, and straying hair, as he had left her. On her lips— those lips he had known so well !—was an unnatural blueness. Yet her expression seemed to him to have attained again that of the earlier time—to be so eloquent of innocence, of purity, of unsullied youth, that he almost doubted the justice of his thoughts.

"I am happy, Adrian," she whispered, "oh! happier far than I could deserve or expect to be because—we are together and because we belong to one another—for ever."

She looked up at him, smiling—stretched out her hand. In the dim light she could not see his face—or what was written in it.

"My darling Adrian," she murmured, "my worthy, worthy man. It has been a long, long—terrible—time. But it's summer for us again, isn't it, and the river's flowing, and—I am your Rosemary still, aren't I—though a wicked and foolish one."

He neither took her hand nor moved, but continued to look down at her with an expression half-stern, half-pitying.

"Rosemary," he said presently in a hard, level voice, "I've been—thinking. Perhaps I did not understand you at first. But we must understand each other now, once and for all. It may be painful—for us both. But—we must have no—illusions—either of us."

At the changed tone of his first words her hands had gripped the arms of the chair.

"Adrian!" she now cried, the note of agony once more in her voice. "Adrian! you don't know—you don't realise——"

"I do realise. What you said just now has made me think. . . . I don't want to go into the details of your life while I've been away—or your relationship with—anybody; that's your affair, not mine. But——"

"*It's the truth*," she burst out; "it's the truth. I told you because it's the truth, because I wanted to confess—everything, *everything*. I've wronged you, I've been wicked—you don't know all even now!"

"Stop!" he said roughly. "I don't want to know. . . ."

She lay, trembling and quivering in silence; he stood, looking down at her, wrestling with his anger and his misery.

"Then you don't, you cannot—forgive me—?" she articulated in a strained whisper.

He pressed his hands to his eyes as though to blot out the knowledge he would have given worlds to escape.

"You must go——" he began, but did not finish the sentence. In uttering the words he remembered:—the smiling couple, the object of congratulations, the topic of conversation at the Astoria a few hours before.

When he spoke again it was in an odd throttled voice.

"It is not a question of—forgiveness, Rosemary. I—here—in this hour—have done a wrong as great . . . have wronged your best and truest friend."

They stared at one another.

"Adrian, I—I don't understand."

"I'm engaged to marry Faith."

She cowered back.

"What—what do you mean?"

"It's the truth," he said, echoing her own words.

He left her side. He went over to the broken cane chair and sat turned from her, staring at the floor, striving to collect his thoughts, to decide what ought to be done. She began to sob wearily, helplessly, like a child that is lost. He took no notice, being only aware that in the space of a few minutes the complexion of all things, animate and inanimate, had impalpably changed. The little box looked like a prison cell; its faded hangings like those of a coffin. How tawdry, how empty, how sordid this Victory Ball now seemed! . . . Above all, how should he put an end to the scene?

A long time passed. Cries of merriment and laughter floated up from the dancing-floor.

Her sobbing ceased. Half-an-hour—perhaps more—passed before he went over to where she lay.

"If you are unwell, Rosemary," he said in a voice as gentle as he could make it, "you had better let me take you home. I can see you are. Stay here, and I'll borrow one of the cars and——"

"No! Don't leave me! I think — I shall be all right soon. Stay here, and let me finish. . . . Adrian "— she spoke in a whisper so low as to be scarcely audible— "Adrian, I've been thinking of—that afternoon on the Chilterns—long, long ago—and that I had a premonition then . . . and—now it's coming true."

"A premonition ?—of what ? "

"It's nothing sudden . . . it's been coming on for a long, long time. And after all—it's for the best."

Recalling dimly their conversation in the light of her present appearance, his vague earlier fears returned.

"Will you do one thing for me ? Take this and keep it . . . get rid of it, destroy it . . . but as you loved me once, never, never speak of it to anybody, or let anybody see it."

Her left hand, which had all the while remained clenched, grasping, as he thought, a handkerchief, exposed to view a beautifully-enamelled Louis Quatorze snuff-box. He recognised it immediately as the one he had seen years before on Gina Maryon's dressing-table at Arden.

"What is it ? What's in it ? "

"Keep it. Hide it. Destroy it. Don't show it to anybody. Don't let it out of your sight for my sake. Promise me that ! "

In her emotion she had risen almost to a sitting posture.

"But what is it ? What is this stuff ? What is this sickly scent ? "

"Don't ask me—oh! don't ask me, please ! Be merciful, my darling. I thought there was no harm at first, then—it got hold of me—it's the only thing that's kept me going these last days and nights and hours."

She looked up at him beseechingly but seeing the haunted expression that had come into his eyes, recoiled.

"To-night—I went too far. I had to. I wanted so to be gay to-night, to forget, above all to bring back that afternoon at Arden—in the punt. Now I know that cannot be . . . so will you promise me—just this one thing?"

"I do, I do promise. . . . But, oh, my God! Rosemary, what have you done?"

A nameless, speechless dread began to take shape in his mind.

"Thank you, Adrian. Now we understand each other—and I can sleep in peace! And nobody need ever know but you—at the worst they can put it down to the Meynell 'queerness'—or heart failure. The world need never know. . . ."

Something in the words or the way she spoke them caused him to peer closer at her in the half-light. He saw that in her face which he had seen on too many a human face before to make any mistake.

He leapt up, rushed to the door, and ran down many flights of stone steps.

Columbine and Harlequin, it chanced, were sitting upon these steps, so far absorbed in their eternal flirtation that when he rushed upon them crying, "Fetch a doctor, fetch a doctor! There's somebody ill up there in a box!" Columbine broke into her treble laugh, thinking it to be a capital joke. But, seeing his full face, papery-white and twisted with anguish, they were scared and dumb, and fled down the stairs, barely conscious of their quest.

Adrian, for his part, bounded up again, realising that several minutes might have to pass before a doctor could be brought.

He found her as he had left her, quietly and regularly breathing but with the bluish tinge more pronounced upon her lips, and her delicate features set as in marble.

He knelt beside her, took her cold hands in his. She

raised her eyelids that had been half closed ; the old childlike smile played about her lips.

"Will you forgive me—now ? " she whispered. " For it cannot matter—can it ?—any more."

He bent towards her, drew her limp arms around him.

"To rest in your arms, Adrian, to have you near me, to have your forgiveness, to know that you care for me still—that is the only heaven I want. "

"My darling, my beloved——! "

"Adrian, I'm glad—about you and Faith. . . . She will make you happier than I ever could have—though I, too, loved you in my heart. Only I did not know . . . that the world is such a terrible place."

She paused and sighed deeply, as though struggling against an unconquerable weariness.

"But what does it all mean, and *why* is the world so terrible, so—so wrong ? I used to think it wonderful once, perfect, glorious, and that Evil belonged to some other world, not ours, and that while one was young there could be no sadness in one's life, only laughter, and—the joy of things. . . ."

"Somehow—we got across one another——"

" Oh ! if only—if only—you had never left me," she pleaded.

"That was the war."

"The war ! Yes—*everything* was the war. . . . And now —I want so terribly to live everything over again—differently —if only in my mind. . . ."

Music came up from below—sad, warning, yet charged as it seemed with a curious pity.

"Humoreske ! " she cried, starting up with a great effort and listening raptly. "How that thing makes one suffer ! How it makes one love, despair, hope, joy—*yearn* for something beyond oneself, for something one cannot find or grasp or realise. . . ."

"It's the mockery of our lives," he made answer.

But she grew calmer, for they knew they understood one another, and his arm was about her.

For several minutes neither spoke. They were so perfectly at one that the very separateness of human existence seemed hidden from them, and in those fleeting moments they became an entity inspired by conviction of eternity.

At length she whispered :

"Adrian . . . I've never been taught to pray."

He drew her to him convulsively.

"Will God understand me—will He forgive me ? . . . Or—shall I be punished ? "

"Don't speak like that ! " he implored. "You are young ; you will live your life to the full. We shall both some day look back upon this night as—upon something that has not happened."

"No, that can't be. If I lived now I could not be happy. So it's for the best. . . . But stay with me, stay with me—for I am afraid ! "

"Afraid ? Afraid of what, beloved ? "

They were the words he had used on their last day together in the beech-wood ; but he did not think of that now.

"Of the loneliness and the darkness and—the emptiness. And of being separated from you, and of never seeing you or touching you or hearing your voice ever—any more."

He caressed her hand in a sort of controlled agony.

"Listen ! That valse ! I wanted to live to-night, Adrian. Oh ! but I wanted to live. I wanted to dance with you once more, to love and laugh and be gay. I wanted to forget all that's been, to remake my life. But happiness goes with goodness, and youth with happiness. . . ."

She closed her eyes and lay still.

"They will put me in a deep grave," she murmured as though to herself. "They will throw earth on me. Rats will come, and worms . . . and then . . . I shall be nothing. . . ."

A shudder passed through her. After a lapse of minutes

Adrian Knoyle's voice came hoarsely, brokenly as from a sepulchre.

"Our Father . . . which art in heaven . . . Hallowed be thy name. Thy kingdom come. . . . Thy will be done . . ."

The valse had ceased, and to their ears from the crowded world below came sounds of singing and wild cheering above the crash of the military bands. At the first bars of the English national hymn she murmured faintly :

"Adrian, do you remember—years ago, and how . . . we heard that ? "

They listened in silence.

"And, Adrian . . . I would like to think—to know—that some day we may all be together again—you and Faith and Eric and I—in some place like Arden."

No sound came from him. She whispered :

"Kiss me . . . as you used to . . . on my lips."

* * * * *

They burst in a few minutes later and found the couple as in a tableau : she lying back with lips parted, calm and beautiful, he motionless, kneeling in an attitude of prayer or of despair, his head buried in his hands, his hands resting on her breast.

CHAPTER IV

The Three Hills

THE Five Years had passed. . . .

And in the evening of a June day a man and a woman might have been seen climbing the steep face of a hill remotely situated in a western district of England. Their progress was slow, and it appeared as though one were helping the other, the helper being the woman. It was the early season of the down flowers, and the two would frequently bend low to gather these—the beautiful blue, bell-like campanula, the crane's bill and squinancywort, the delicate purple scabious and creamy butterfly-orchis. Sometimes, they would stop to examine the countless small fossil-shells and flints that bore so strange a resemblance to living objects, the eye of a bird, the head of a squirrel or mouse—bore testimony, too, to the prehistoric reign of the sea.

Their advance brought them to a flat shelf, by origin an ancient wolf-platform scooped out of the open hillside; and here they rested awhile. They were on the left or westernmost escarpment of a vast amphitheatre formed by three high and rounded hills. One of these might be distinguished for miles around by a tuft of stunted fir-trees growing upon its summit; upon the face of another was a white horse cut out of the chalk. The view, looking south and west, embraced a wide and fertile vale, the prevailing tint being a pale green. Against the low opposite ramparts of the Plain, a line of poplars rose like a rank of soldiers. The smooth outline was broken at intervals by beech-clumps and the sides scored here and there by steep, white tracks. There was corn on the Plain, but there was none in the Vale; here elm-studded hedgerows separated the little grass fields. Red and white of cattle in places dappled the green. There were villages and at least one market-town, but these only disclosed themselves where a glimpse of dull red brick broke the prevailing tone, or greenish-yellow thatch blended with elms, or the grey summit of some Norman church tower appeared at the height of rooks' nests. There were streams, but these, born in the remoter valleys of the downs, on reaching the Vale speedily dwindled to the proportions of a pebbly trickle, finally losing themselves amid alder-growth, watercress, and weeds. There were occasional large woods, and as a traveller approached the downs, wild little lanes, clotted and tangled and made almost impassable by clematis, honeysuckle, and dog-rose.

Hardly defiled by the railway, seldom touched by foot of tourist—for it offered no renowned " beauty-spot " or far-famed architectural attraction—the Vale thus outspread seemed to be the home of delicate light, cloud-shadow, and wayward contrast in contour and colouring; to cherish within itself an intense, a rapt seclusion.

The hills, too, had their charm—but it was a different one. In place of the rabbit, the hare; in place of the linnet, the wheatear; in place of the owl, the hawk. If the Vale was a sanctuary in which to linger through the haze of noon, the down was an altar from which to contemplate the splendour of sunset or sunrise and to meditate upon the beauties of God's world.

Here, indeed, Life seemed to take on a grander and more generous shape—Nature came into her own—Man, with all his struggles and aspirations, sank to a proper level of in- significance. The air was more potent than spring water. It was possible to walk all day long across the upland meeting a human being but a shepherd. The air uplifted the heart —cleansed and revivified. . . .

The man and woman had climbed half-way up the hillside when they paused.

Immediately beneath, as a pebble might be dropped into the flat, semicircular arena formed by the Three Hills, stood a fair-sized manor-house of grey Portland stone, with a weathered and lichened roof of chocolate-red. Nearby, a hamlet of thatched cottages showed among elms. Along the whole of one side of the house ran a balustraded terrace flanked by walled fruit and vegetable gardens, these facing towards the west. On the terrace was seated a white-haired woman in an invalid-chair.

"Your mother looks very happy there, Adrian. I hope she will always be with us."

Faith turned to her husband. The setting sun lit up both their faces, in which could be traced a curious resemblance one to the other, not in the features so much as in an expression of the eyes. Lines, a scar on the forehead, and an evident recent illness caused the man's face to look old before its time. The woman's had that mellow kind of beauty which comes in the nature of a legacy, after the bloom of girlhood.

"Yes," he said, "you and she—and Eric—have kept me alive in these years. I mean the soul of me—for war, you know, kills the soul as surely as it kills the body. And I thought that had died in me once. . . ." He fell silent, drinking in the beauty around them. "A wife, one's mother, a friend—what more could any man ask of a world that can be so cruel ? "

"But in the end one's life is oneself," she replied.

They turned again towards the steep.

Further climbing brought them to the summit of a smooth, artificial mound or circular earthwork, where they found themselves on the highest point of the Three Hills—the highest point, indeed, for miles around. The only sounds to reach them were the evening hymn of the skylarks and the bells of some sheep which were cropping among furze-bushes a short distance away. Evidences of a vast Early British settlement surrounded them, there being everywhere visible in the downland turf large cup-shaped depressions, platforms and pits, curious hillocks and low, circular mounds. The very earthwork on which they sat had formed the main bulwark of the Citadel, and upon its lip could still be discerned a faint shadowy line in the turf worn by the pacing footsteps of sentinels in the long-ago.

A delicate carmine light had begun to warm the downland's swelling breast. . . .

The two drew very near together.

He, pointing, said : " Look ! The sun is going down over Mendip."

" Yes—and to-morrow it rises upon a new world."

For some minutes neither spoke. Then,

" This place is wonderfully solemn and beautiful," she said. " I shall often come up here and look down at our home and listen to the wind sighing through those old fir-trees. Whenever I hear that I think of the voices of people one has known and who have gone from us."

His response was to take her hand.

" I feel they are very near to us now, Adrian. . . ."

" Eric is always near. But she—? "

" She suffered and is happy. I feel—I *know*—that she, too, is at peace."

" I think it must be so," he said quietly. " She paid—in full. . . . But the terrible thing about Death,"—a grave concern came into his voice—" is that one *cannot* know. One can only wonder and—and—try to believe."

He paused, then continued :

" And I need forgiveness, too, God knows, for I went back to her at the last—and forgot you."

His vaguely troubled eyes looked down into the steadfast candour of her face.

" You are hers still as I am Eric's," she said ; " the war itself could not alter that . . . and Time and Death cannot."

Both remained deep in thought, while the scent of the wild thyme crept all about them, and evening folded together hill and sky.

Once he looked at his watch, and said, "It's nearly time. . . ."

But it was not until night had fallen quite, that a dull red glow began to smoulder among the surrounding hills. On Mendip and on Quantock to the west, on Hackpen and Inkpen to the north and east, southward above the sheep-walks of the Great Plain, the beacons gleamed like living coals.

The Three Hills, too, caught the spreading light, so that the figures of the man and woman were flung into relief.

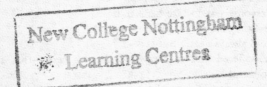